THE THIRD TRIUMVIRATE

WILLIAM F. JOHNSON
ALICE JOHNSON

Inks and Bindings
888-290-5218
www.inksandbindings.com
orders@inksandbindings.com

Contents

Chapter One: Chameleon 5

Chapter Two: Election 15

Chapter Three: Confession..23

Chapter Four: Surveillance 33

Chapter Five: Pedestal 41

Chapter Six: Interview 47

Chapter Seven: Seizure 55

Chapter Eight: Encounter..69

Chapter Nine: Initiation 81

Chapter Ten: Lesson..97

Chapter Eleven: NACAM..107

Chapter Twelve: Escape..119

Chapter Thirteen: Arrival 123

Chapter Fourteen: Confession..129

Chapter Fifteen: Sebastian 143

Chapter Sixteen: Double Cross..155

Chapter Seventeen: PANCAM..167

Chapter Eighteen: Gauntlet..173

Chapter Nineteen: Interruption 207

Chapter Twenty: Exclusive 213

Chapter Twenty-One: Remorse..227

Chapter Twenty-Two: Encounter 237

Chapter Tweny-Three: Caracas..241

Chapter Twenty-Four: Reunion 253

Chapter Twenty-Five: Discourse 257

Chapter Twenty-Six: Hijack..271
Chapter Twenty-Seven: Return..................................277
Chapter Twenty-Eight: Surprise................................281
Chapter Twenty-Nine: Reunion 287
Chapter Thirty: Debate..293
Chapter Thirty-One: Abigail 307
Chapter Thirty-Two: Counterplot 319
Chapter Thirty-Three: Incursion 323
Chapter Thirty-Four: Evasion 329
Chapter Thirty-Five: Exposure 333
Chapter Thirty-Six: Enlightenment...........................339
Chapter Thirty-Seven: Confederacy 345
Chapter Thirty-Eight: Dismemberment 349
Chapter Thirty-Nine: Siege 355
Chapter Forty: Reckoning..363
Chapter Forty-One: Anticipation 371

CHAPTER ONE

Chameleon

Three delta-winged hang gliders descended at staggered times toward Virginia Beach. Below a one-hundred-foot sand cliff, Chameleon was the first rubber-clad pilot to land. Wearing an equipment pack, she scanned the ascent with Spectrum Goggles and detected no one. She fired a pneumatic grapple hook trailing a coiling rope around two scrub pines along the rim of the cliff. Hand-over-hand, Chameleon's demure five-foot-eight-inch frame inched over the top. The backside of Mike Parker's mansion now loomed sixty yards ahead.

Beneath the cowl of her suit, Chameleon's earphones detected distant laughter. Then crisp, rhythmic footsteps began to overwhelm it as a face-masked sentry emerged from around a corner at ground level. Kneeling behind a pine, Chameleon aimed her pneumatic rifle.

Ambling to the cliffside, the target removed his facemask and sucked in frigid, salt air from the January night. Chameleon fired. A hollow dart impaled his neck with nerve toxin, which killed her target before he hit the ground. She tossed his body over the sandy precipice before climbing up to the housetop in seconds. The roof-line was a forest of skylights, chimneys, ventilation pipes, solar power panels, satellite dishes, and tile roofing—resembling the headstones of an unkempt cemetery. Chameleon padded over the roof scape like a cat.

Sheba landed her glider along the fog-shrouded shore of Misty Lake one hundred yards west of the Parker Mansion. Adjusting her equipment, she reconnoitered before approaching an immense, eight-foot-high juniper hedge maze. Hedge spines proved no match for her black rubber suit as she pressed her five-foot-ten-inch frame along a predetermined path through the thorny labyrinth. Sheba made it halfway before an armed sentry sprang out from around a blind turn.

Closing within eight feet, the guard ordered, "Hold it! Lace your fingers on top of your head and walk slowly in front of me!" Sheba obliged, held steady for a moment, then ran and twirled while kicking both sentry and weapon to the ground. Leveraging her sleek, muscular body, she locked bone-crushing knees under her target's chin, snapping both his neck and jaws like dried cornstalks. After stuffing the twitching corpse into the concealing juniper, she neared the maze opening before fading into a black embrace of thorns herself. She aimed her air rifle toward a lumbering, bipedal shadow now spanning the entrance.

The shadow spoke, "Number Nine, this is Number Seven. Report."

Silence.

"Number Nine! Blast it, Steve, quit screwing around and report your status!"

Dead air.

"That's strike two, pal. Keep this up and I'll report you to Senior Agent Richmond, who will report you to Commissioner Quimby; Quimby will pass it on to the old man and you know what *that* means! You'll end up on a blind date with *Sebastian*! Now cut the clowning and reply."

Silence persisted.

Number Seven walked into the maze ten yards before Sheba squeezed her trigger; her pneumatic rifle failed. Hurtling a poisoned knife from her shoulder sheath, the blade penetrated Number Seven's larynx before he slumped dead onto frozen ground. Sheba ditched her faulty rifle into the thorns before sprinting out of the maze and across a dark and open lawn. Reaching one side of the house, she swung her grapple hook and scaled the shadowy wall toward an unlit bedroom; pushing the window ajar, she crept over the sash. A concealed cross bolt fired from the closet and cleanly stabbed through Sheba before penetrating a lone outdoor pine tree.

Senior Agent Moses Richmond jumped up at the sound of his booby trap alarm and rushed into the rigged bedroom. The grinning, muscular black man removed the invader's cowl and goggles. Sheba's wide, frozen eyes were locked in death.

Now hyper-alert, Moses remembered his original reluctance to provide armed security at Mike's Virginia Shoreline Estate when Garth had persuaded him less than a week ago. The open beach access, pine forests, hedge maze, and massive flower gardens afforded at least a hundred places for intruders to hide. He knew that guarding Presidential Candidate Garth Brady and Vice Presidential Candidate Mike Parker tonight for their election party was too goddamn risky. But it was too late to back out now.

After radioing two subordinate agents to remove Sheba's body, Richmond returned to his second story command post, activated the base station, and contacted his perimeter sentries. "All exterior units stay frosty. I've downed an intruder trying to enter through the rigged second story bedroom on the west side. She should never have gotten this far! Report status, Number Seven."

Silence.

"Come in, Number Nine."

Muffled static.

"Blast it! Come in, Number Eleven!"

"Here, sir. I'm at the south perimeter and within eyeshot of Numbers Five and Six."

"Take your sniper rifle to the top a northern perimeter pine tree. Make sure you're overlooking both Misty Lake and the mansion's north face. Contact me when you're set."

"At once, sir!"

"Numbers Five and Six."

"Yes, sir?"

"Deploy along the hedge maze perimeter. I want you to set up crossfire positions along the west side. Do not move around once you're set, but keep your weapons trained on the house. I will prevent any guests from blundering outside. And kill anybody coming out of the maze! Everyone else will patrol the other three perimeters according to the original plan, but stay in pairs!"

Richmond's group acknowledged.

The third delta pilot, Nimrod, landed at the edge of a pine forest on the estate's northwest quadrant. He hiked a quarter mile to the main garden in back of the mansion. Crouching among the leafless, skeletal remains of dormant flowers, he tightened his equipment pack and goggled the mansion's north and west faces. Many ground floor windows betrayed light beams from dining rooms, parlors, adjacent terraces, and kitchen catering facilities in honor of Election Eve. Yet only a few lights were shining out from the second story. Nimrod scampered for twenty yards before sentries two and three flanked him.

"Hold it, sucker," threatened Number Two, "or I'll blow those lungs out your back!" The five-foot-six-inch, rubber-clad captive turned and planted both feet wide and firm. Number Two added, "Just relax, Gertrude, and we won't make Haggis out of your bowels. Okay, Bob. Frisk this bozo for weapons and peel his hood. Let's see what our guest looks like without the cowl and goggles."

Number Three got within a yard of Nimrod before the pilot kneed him to the ground. Extending his right leg, Nimrod's toe sheath sent a knife catapulting through Number Two's right eye, protruding the blade tip out the back of his skull. The dying guard jerked his trigger, tearing a muzzled bullet crease across Nimrod's right shoulder. Number Three was still down as the intruder pivoted and thrusted a right shin onto his target's throat while snapping both windpipe and vertebrae.

Pausing for a few seconds, Nimrod rolled off into a crouching position. Creeping like a gecko over broken glass, he disappeared into the boughs of a tall cedar tree near the mansion's northern wall. Anchoring a steel cable around the trunk, he then fired a pneumatic projectile into the doorjamb of a second story terrace. Taking out the slack, he glided along by cable roller toward the terrace.

Number Eleven took a brief glimpse before firing at the moving target, missing his first shot before the second passed cleanly through the target's right side. Nimrod managed to keep his grip before landing painfully onto the terrace floor.

Number Eleven signaled, "Commander Richmond, an intruder's on the north face of the mansion and behind the brick wall of a second-story terrace directly over the kitchen."

"Keep him pinned down. If he tries to leave, kill him. We'll bag him if he comes inside."

"Yes, sir."

Nimrod sprang onto the terrace railing before leaping ten feet out. His latex gloves gripped the railing of another terrace before he climbed over with his bleeding side steaming into the winter night.

Number Eleven resumed, "Commander, the intruder has jumped to the next terrace east of his original position. He's moving too fast for me to take down. He's already on the roof and disappearing behind a satellite dish."

"Acknowledged. Stay where you are! All six northern perimeter units will secure the rooftop in pairs. If you locate our guest, burn him down. If he gets inside, I'll handle him."

Nimrod dropped a rope into the recreation room fireplace chimney and strained every muscle while creeping down the soot-covered air-shaft a few inches at a time.

Richmond's interior unit finished checking every skylight large enough for human intrusion, but none had been disturbed. Taking a portable, two-way radio and starting in the kitchen, Moses inspected each fireplace, one-by-one, while avoiding the massive living room where Mike Parker and his guests watched the televised election returns.

A roof sentry signaled, "Commander, we've found a rope wrapped around the large chimney that descends into the main floor recreation room."

"Outstanding! Remain there in case he tries to retreat. With luck, we'll have him trapped like a rat in a tar barrel!" Richmond immediately led his in-house forces into the darkened playroom, deploying each agent to concealed stations while training his pistol toward the fireplace flue from behind the sofa.

Then Nimrod's movements were heard. Moses steadied his aim while watching an upside down, black rubber cowl with Spectrum Goggles slowly emerge below the chimney shaft. His muzzled shot pierced Nimrod's left eye, blowing the back of his skull onto sooty bricks. The invader slumped dead onto cold pine logs. The three sentries picked up Nimrod's body and walked down an outer deck stairway before depositing their load onto the dark lawn. Moses turned on his flashlight and pulled back the blood-smeared cowl, uncovering the bullet-shattered face of a stranger.

Richmond transmitted, "All units, I've bagged the north wall intruder. He's dead like a boot-heeled cockroach. Until further notice, Number Eleven will remain at his post. All rooftop agents will return to perimeter duty. Southern sentries will continue patrolling in pairs. All squads will avoid the Westside. Both maze guards will maintain their crossfire stations. That is all."

Every unit confirmed the orders.

Chameleon remained motionless inside her inactive, four-by-eight-by-three-foot solar panel while straddling the equipment pack between her feet. Earphones caught all the sentry cross talk. Enemies passed by her position at least a dozen times while failing to open the panel door she had secured from the inside.

Waiting five minutes after she heard Richmond order the guards off the rooftop, Chameleon emerged from her makeshift casket. Strapping on her pack, she proceeded to the dark skylight above Mike Parker's master bathroom. Cutting a hole in the glass, she lowered a golf ball-sized surveillance camera by an elastic cord; the spectrum lens within revealed complete vacancy. Retracting the camera and spraying solvent to dissolve the padlock securing the hinged skylight, Chameleon discarded her pack and anchored a grapple hook before descending to the floor.

Opening the medicine cabinet, she exchanged identical-looking canisters of shaving cream before climbing hand-over-hand back up to the roof. Regaining her pack, she closed the skylight and padded back toward the eastern wall.

When Chameleon reached the cliffside, her Spectrum Goggles illuminated two concealed sentries crouching along both sides of the only beach stairs descending to the surf. She slithered through scrub pines for over one hundred feet, loaded her rifle tube, and dropped both agents dead in their tracks.

Moments later, Chameleon plowed southward across the nocturnal Atlantic beach. Removing a five-pound air tank, facemask, and four barbed spears from her bag, she attached the aqualung to the mask, reloaded her pneumatic rifle like a spear gun, and waded into the waist-high surf before diving beneath it. Her rendezvous submarine would remain three miles off shore until dawn.

An hour after all roof top sentries had returned to perimeter duty, Richmond's adrenaline spiked again as an interior sentry radioed, "Commander, this is Number Fourteen."

"Go ahead, Chuck."

"Number Twelve and I have been double checking all interior rooftop openings for the last thirty minutes. We found a circular hole in the glass above Parker's master bedroom skylight, but nobody's in his suite now."

"I'll be there in one minute." Marching into the library for a ladder, Moses quickly set up a stepladder in the bedroom to examine the violated skylight. Number Fourteen sat on the tub, craned his neck upward, and asked, "Anything interesting, chief?"

"The padlock's been dissolved. Any melt spots down on the floor?"

"Not that I can see, but there must have been some residue hitting the floor."

Moses grinned. "Not if the intruder used a polymerized solvent, Chuck."

"What's that?"

"One that dissolves so completely that both substance and solvent evaporates while the active ingredients neutralize after use."

Chuck laughed. "You're pulling my leg!"

"It's real, Chuck. But that gives me a hunch about our intruder's identity."

"You told me you never saw our two party crashers before."

"Neither our cross bolt babe or her Santa Claus comrade hit this skylight. There was a third trespasser and it's obvious that she's long gone."

"*She*? How do you know that?"

"If she's planted a unique time bomb around here, I'll know her for sure. I assumed our invaders were after Garth Brady, but maybe they were after Mike Parker instead."

Chuck asked, "What *kind* of time bomb, chief?"

Richmond climbed down and examined the medicine cabinet. He stared at the shaving cream canister for several moments without handling it. He ordered abruptly, "Chuck, pick up two gas masks from the base station. Meet me at the cliffside lawn and double time it!"

Number Fourteen departed without another word as Moses lifted the canister off the shelf, walked downstairs through the nearest side exit, and padded across the frozen grass to the edge of the cliff. Chuck soon joined him while carrying two masks. Both men sealed their masks before Richmond spoke loudly into the wind, "I suspect this shaving cream may be a nerve gas canister."

"Are you shitting me?"

The senior agent pointed the nozzle past the cliffside while replying, "If I'm right, when I press this finger valve, only gas will discharge, looking snowy white in this frigid air." Richmond's smile dropped as the gas discharged and depleted within ten seconds.

"Who planted that bomb, chief"

Moses tossed the canister onto the lawn, pulled his muzzled pistol from his shoulder holster, and blasted it apart with a single shot.

Chuck repeated, "Do you know who it is?"

The commander barked while gathering up the debris, "I don't think we'll encounter any more uninvited guests! Besides, it's almost one A.M.! The election returns should be tabulated!"

CHAPTER TWO

Election

Mike Parker reclined on a blue velvet sofa, cradling his wife's head in his lap. Margaret sprawled full length on the sofa while awaiting the election outcome. Mike playfully pinched her. She sat up blushing, to the delight of their guests.

A voice emanated from a centerpiece, holographic television in their living room repeating its previous message, "We announce again that Senator Garth Brady of Virginia has just been confirmed the first President of the North American Triumvirate. He has soundly defeated former United States President Warren Miller. Our heartiest congratulations to President Garth Brady and Vice President Michael Parker."

Mike switched off his *HoloTel* by remote.

Margaret squealed, "Congratulations, darling!" and promptly kissed him hard on the mouth.

Garth couldn't resist. "Hey! I thought that *I* was elected President! What about *my* kiss?"

Margaret came up for air. "Sorry, Mr. President, I'll have to veto your request."

Mike added, "This victory's sweet. The only way it could be better would be to kick out all these cameras!"

Brady countered, "Would you prefer that Warren Miller was taking the bows instead of us? By the way, thanks for the use of your home, partner."

"You're welcome. Besides, your apartment's not big enough to contain this media circus!"

The President grinned, stood up from a red leather chair, and stepped to the center of the room. The preset television cameras activated as Garth announced, "Fellow citizens of the Third Triumvirate, the election trail for the past nine months has been demanding. My staff and I have spoken in every major metropolis, from Anchorage to Panama City.

"Now that our North American Triumvirate's a reality, we've added the expediency of a triple-pronged, provincial government to simplify essential services to our continent's inhabitants. Three provinces also mean three regional capitols: Anchorage, Alaska District, seats the Northern Province; Panama City, Panama District, crowns the Southern Province; and Washington D.C., Maryland District, now doubles for both our Central Provincial and North American Capitol.

"Our newfound unity's forged from the combined strength of five former political regions: Canada, the United States, Mexico, Central America, and the Caribbean Rim Island Nations. It required two brutal years of political negotiations to spawn this single government into a reality.

"As the world's Third Triumvirate, North America can now join the brotherhood of the First Triumvirate of Atlanterra and the Second Triumvirate of Indoasia on global terms. Through this miracle of technology, every qualified citizen has cast their encrypted vote, via televisions, telephones, Internet and our personal *Media Palm* pocket computers to spawn a truly popular vote."

Garth motioned Mike Parker to come and stand beside him; the six-foot-two-inch-tall, blond-haired, clean-shaved man wearing a dark brown suit, white shirt, and silvery gray tie joined his president.

Then the President declared, "Here is your new North American Vice President; his name is Mike Parker." Brady and Parker waved briefly to the cameras before Garth shook Mike's hand vigorously before motioning him back to his seat; Parker quickly obliged.

Then Garth continued, "Since I am empowered to directly appoint my executive cabinet ministers without any confirmation process, I will introduce them now…"

Brady motioned his ministers to form a single line beside him as he introduced them from left to right. The first one was a six-foot-four-inch-tall, bronze-skinned man with raven black, shoulder-length hair wearing a tan, three-piece suit over a muscular physique.

Garth announced, "This is Jocquin Martinez, my Minister of Trade. He's a native-born Mexican of proud Aztec heritage. Jocquin's also our governing Praetor for the Southern Province."

The second was a slender, blond-haired, blue-eyed man in his fifties who stood eight inches shorter than the Aztec. He wore a woolen, navy blue suit, silver tie, and black oxford shoes.

"This is Andre Roget from Quebec; he's my Minister of Travel. Andre will oversee all public and private North American transit regulations."

Minister Three was a bald, brown-eyed, black man in his sixties leaning on an ivory cane.

"This is Tyrone Williams, a former member of the Maryland State Supreme Court. His thirty years of experience makes him ideal to be my Minister of Justice. He's now the senior judge in all our land."

Minister Four was a Coppertone, black-haired young man displaying a single braid halfway down his back. His contrasting cream-colored suit paled against a blood-red tie and dark gray shoes.

"This is John Blackfeather. At twenty-eight, he's the youngest member of my cabinet. John has masters degrees in geology, climatology, and environmental studies. He's also a Native Kwakiutl Tribesman and my Minister of Environment."

Minister Five was a five-foot-eight-inch-tall woman displaying a dark tan complexion, chocolate brown eyes, and jet-black hair. Her military dress uniform could not conceal the sleek, voluptuous curves beneath. Her demeanor remained rock steady as if encased in emergency glass.

"This is Major Carmen Valdez-Franklin, our Minister of

Enforcement. Seasoned by combat in her native Cuba, her expertise in weaponry, mechanics, survival, and hand-to-hand combat makes her my personal choice for the highest ranking soldier in North America.

"Militarily, she'll be my second-in-command. Carmen and her husband, Captain Richard Franklin of the prototype submarine *Toroid*, are both soldiers no enemy would enjoy facing."

Minister Six was the last as Brady resumed, "And this is Irene Tupik. Many of you will recognize the former State Treasurer and Governor of Alaska, who encouraged the United States Congress to rescind its policy of using fiat money"—Every lens zoomed in on a blond-and-silver-haired, seductively trim, fifty-five-year-old woman smiling broadly—"returning America back to the gold standard, which issued in a new era of economic prosperity never seen during the twentieth century. Who else would make a better Minister of Finance? Irene's also the governing Praetor of the Northern Province."

The cameras followed and zoomed in as the President shook each minister's hand before they took their seats.

Then Garth concluded, "The Executive Cabinet, Vice President, and I now constitute the current bulk of your triumviral government. All district tribune assembly positions will be elected in ten months giving every potential candidate time to prepare. Thank you for your support and good night from Virginia Beach."

As the cameras moved from the room, all the photographers and journalist moved forward.

Garth scanned the room before saying, "I want to thank all of you for helping me get this triumvirate off the ground. Mike and I handled the speeches, but the rest of you supplied us with enough political ammunition to defeat our obsolete adversaries. Their doomsday propaganda wasn't easy to take. I still feel sorry for people, particularly in the former United States, who screamed that our new triumvirate would destroy individual freedom on the North American continent. I don't understand how expanding democracy into a collective, continental bloc could erode the established liberties of the Common Man."

Parker interjected, "Don't try to understand hysteria, Garth."

The President suddenly declared, "Now, ladies and gentlemen of the press, I believe you've sufficient information. Please leave this party now."

It took ten minutes for Parker's servants to usher the media out the front door.

Brady sighed slowly while displaying a Cheshire cat grin. "Now, let's party."

Irene replied, "Giving media hounds the boot wasn't exactly protocol, Garth."

"Right now, I couldn't care less. Besides, since when did you start worrying about protocol? You're about as politically correct as an Idaho survivalist."

Tupik smirked, "Although I don't use guns myself, I still lament their departure from individual Americans. Now that guns are a crime for the North American citizen, only criminals will carry them"—she briefly eyed the major—"except for our government's beloved enforcement arm."

Minister Franklin didn't bat an eyelash.

Tyrone's wife Bertha changed the subject. "So, Carmen, how long have you been married?"

"A little over six months. I met Richard when I was Cuban Ambassador to the Universal Regions Council. We were married one year later on June 25."

"You're a genuine June bride! But it must be difficult being married to a submarine commander who's away so much!"

"He was scheduled to come home today; he may be home right now. But that's all right. Absence only makes our reunions that much sweeter."

Bertha added, "Good for you! It's refreshing to see young people show a healthy respect for marital commitments, especially *these* days. Tyrone and I've been married for over thirty years. Garth also mentioned that you're a combat soldier. How did you end up being the last URC Cuban Ambassador before our triumvirate annexed it?"

"I fought for the Cuban Republican Revolution. Before that, I was a college graduate in marine biology and worked as a salvage diver in Santiago de Cuba. Then my uncle recruited me into the Universal Regions Council Peacekeeping Forces as a diver; I progressed from there."

Jocquin asked, "The Cuban Republican Revolution lasted only three months. Did you see much action?"

"I saw action every day. That may not sound like much time to get seasoned, but I also spent five years with the Peacekeeping Forces operating all over the Caribbean Rim. During that time, I mastered all the military training they could teach me: communications, hand-to-hand combat, weapons, artillery, and explosives, to name a few."

Roget blurted after tipping some champagne, "How did you transform from soldier to ambassador?"

"I became ambassador after my country achieved democracy. Because of my former URC experience, my people insisted on me representing them; I couldn't refuse."

Bertha inquired, "How did a submarine captain meet you at the URC?"

"During a Universal Regions Council forum, Richard, Garth and other officials were issuing grievances to both the Tribune Assembly and Universal Tribunal on an ecological crisis that still hasn't been resolved."

John Blackfeather interrupted, "What was that, Major?"

"Everybody, please call me Carmen. Anyway, the crisis involved three sunken military submarines on the bottom of the North Atlantic Ocean; all of them had been corroding in salt water for decades. The issue was potential marine life poisoning. Richard and Garth's delegation was imploring the URC to reclaim and dispose of those rusted hulks in an effort to remove them from the ocean before they contaminated the sea with highly volatile material."

Irene adds, "That sounds reasonable. What happened?"

"The URC's still discussing the situation eighteen months later. At any rate, that's how I met Richard. He and Garth have been friends and activists for years. When Garth approached me about joining his cabinet, my husband heartily endorsed the idea. He told me that I would go stir crazy without a challenge. He's probably right."

Andre drained his glass, yawned, and said, "Well, it's nearly two A.M. Since we're all meeting for breakfast, I'll have to say goodnight."

Margaret asked, "Andre, are you sure that you can find your way?"

"Certainly," answered Roget, finally standing up after three attempts. "I know this house qualifies as a mansion; however, I think that I can find my way just fine. Like everyone else, I was escorted to my room when I arrived. Goodnight."

"Goodnight," Mrs. Parker replied while motioning her head butler Geoffrey to insure Roget entered the right bedroom suite.

Jocquin chuckled. "Andre sure likes his champagne."

Brady replied, "I can't blame him; I've had three glasses myself."

Irene quipped, "Right now our Minister of Travel would be a deadly menace behind the wheel."

"That's one reason why the Parkers so graciously provided us with rooms for the night, which includes breakfast in the morning. But I know you, Jocquin. Comments about Andre's tippling are camouflage for something else. We're all on the same team here; what's on your mind?"

"Are the rumors about South America applying for triumviral status true?"

Garth sat his glass down on an end table. "Where did you hear that?"

"No matter. But now as Praetor of the Southern Province, I feel that I should be kept up to date on matters involving any neighbors south of our central province."

"I haven't heard anything about a Fourth Triumvirate. Now if you'll excuse me, I think I'll turn in as well. Goodnight."

The President's absence had everyone else in bed by 2:30 A.M.

Five minutes later, four servants were cleaning the living room and preparing for breakfast.

The now dormant HoloTel continued transmitting images and sounds within range of its internal camera.

The Parkers' living room surveillance relayed to a monitoring station where an operative recorded his routine oral report. "HoloTel 178,354,450 Summary. Date: January 2, 2040. Time: 2:35 A.M. Eastern Standard. Place: Mike Parker's Virginia living Room. President Brady's victory celebration's over; all guests have retired for the night.

"Report as follows: Irene Tupik launched scathing comments about triumviral citizens' lack of firearms. I recommend her file be upgraded to Top Roulette Priority. Andre Roget was intoxicated again. Major Carmen Valdez-Franklin revealed information regarding Atlantic submarine salvage. Jocquin Martinez knew that South America has applied for triumviral annexation. I recommend upgrading his file to Top Roulette Priority.

"President Brady dismissed all press members immediately after his speech, which was not authorized by any Cupola Flag Officers. I humbly suggest that Chairman DeSalle meet with President Brady as soon as conveniently possible.

"Scansat Nine will maintain HoloTel surveillances in the master bedroom, living room, indoor pool area, dining room, guest rooms, and servant's quarters, and locking the nearest Scansat onto Parker's outdoor property and Virginia Beach access as briefed. End of report."

CHAPTER THREE

Confession

The prototype was vibrating.

Eric Wilford didn't smell burning graphite, so no moving parts were involved. It had to be the magnetic flux out of balance. He killed the power to his Bipolar Drive. The magnetic fields within dissipated while every moving part continued on momentum. The automobile, housing the new engine, remained parked inside the inventor's private workshop.

For most of his thirty-eight years, Eric remained faithful to his love affair with motion. He'd received his first inventive patent two years ago, but he couldn't understand why North American Motors refused to market the invention they had paid him fifty million dollars for.

The Perpetual Vapor Carburetor had been his first triumph; no liquid gasoline entered its throat. Using a photovoltaic system to perpetually power the heating chamber, whether the engine was idle or running, this prototype combusted fuel vapors alone. The result was an eight-cylinder engine with a fuel rating averaging three hundred miles per gallon. Eric loved the fifty million. But what the hell good is his PVC System if no one used it?

Now he stared at his latest brainchild. Yes, the magnetic flux must be out of balance. Possibly the intake and outflow of electromagnetic fields might be clashing. The Bipolar Drive prototype operated on the same energy fields shaping all tangible objects in the world: the plants, animals, minerals, and even the myriad of chemical compounds that make up all physical reality. People couldn't see, hear, or feel them, but electromagnetic fields surrounded them nonetheless. Now Eric was trying to harness that power to his automobile, but so far he was failing.

His watch read 12:45 A.M. before the inventor locked up and walked to his back porch. Glancing through back door glass, he saw his father making a giant bowl of buttered popcorn. Eric yanked open the door.

Alvin Wilford whirled around; his startled fear melted, now seeing Eric amble toward him. "Sonofabitch, boy! You scared the shit out of me!"

"Sorry, Pappy. I don't remember you being this jumpy before the gun abolition. Those bureaucrats really screwed the pooch on that one, didn't they?"

"Bet your sweet ass! Crooks everywhere applauded that legislation! The Founding Fathers must be shivering in their graves, especially Washington! I'll bet he's convinced that America's been skull-fucked out of existence! Those global elite assholes really got into the public's minds and set up housekeeping!"

"That popcorn smells good. You've got lecithin mixed in with the butter and salt?"

"Damn right, boy! That's what gives my corn snap!"

Eric walked into the bathroom while Alvin plopped into a living room rocking chair.

The old man yelled toward the open bathroom, "Did you get the bugs out of that magnet yet?"

"No! There's some kind of polarity imbalance; they won't synchronize! My engine dies after reaching a certain power level, as if it overloads!"

"*Polarity? Synchronize?* It beats me how the hell magnets could ever replace gasoline! But you're the genius; you proved that already! It's just a damn shame no one's using your carburetor! Hurry up! It's almost one A.M. and that newscaster's coming on the tube! I think the Hawaiian totals are in."

Eric toweled his face and sat on a couch near Alvin's chair. He grabbed some popcorn.

Alvin rocked as the talking head announced from the heart of their console television, "The final tabulation's official. Garth Brady's become the First President of North America, defeating defunct U.S. President Warren Miller by a 38-percent margin. Congratulations to President Brady and his running mate, Vice President Michael Parker."

Pappy shook his head.

Eric was delighted; he'd voted for Garth Brady.

Alvin finished a couple of mouthfuls before switching off the TV via remote.

Eric blurted, "Aren't you going to watch the rest like we always do? President Brady's victory party speech, Warren Miller's concession, and what not?"

His father bemoaned, "We're fucked."

"What are you talking about? Doesn't having all of North America united make us equal citizens under the law? Doesn't adding over three hundred million people to our work force and markets help all of us?"

"Don't you get what's happening?"

"I know losing gun rights hurt individuals, but our other liberties are still intact."

"Ape shit, boy! We've been swallowed by a new triumvirate that didn't even choke sliding us down!"

Eric raised one eyebrow. "But the blueprint for this triumvirate was the United States Constitution! Our people wouldn't have voted for triumviral annexation without being guaranteed their rights! Even the new Central Provincial and Third Triumviral Capitols will remain in Washington, D.C."

"That was just bait so our people would bite the triumviral hook!" Eric grabbed another handful, "You're not making sense, Pappy."

"Eric, do you remember why I got so pissed off when we lost our gun rights?"

"Yeah. It was because you knew the new law only disarmed obedient citizens. You were right. It was stupid for people to believe that disarming ourselves would make us all safer."

Alvin replied, "This Third Triumvirate won't be any better."

"What makes you say that?"

"We North Americans aren't safe because we can't control our destiny. As triumviral citizens, we've been annexed into the Universal Regions Council. Being under the URC boot reduces all of us to slave status."

"But we have human and civil rights, Pappy!"

Alvin sighed before retorting, "We no longer have sovereign human rights, such as life, liberty, and property, to invoke in any court for our protection because the sovereign countries that recognized those rights no longer exist. All of us are now property of a new corporate triumviral state, which affords or revokes whatever privileges we qualify for under their goddamned regulations!"

"What kind of privileges?"

"Oh, our driver's, business, and marriage licenses; our birth certificates, legal tender, checks, mortgages, and electronic transfers; even our homes and property are regulated by the whims of the State."

"But I have the title to my home and property free and clear, Pappy. I paid good money for it all!"

"You really think you're a property owner and the captain of your own destiny?"

Eric scowled. "Goddamn right!"

Alvin smiled sadly, "Then stop paying tribute to municipal, county, district, and now the triumviral government in the form of income and property taxes and see what happens."

"But that's impractical! I'll end up in jail and the government would confiscate everything I own!"

"You mean everything *they* own."

Eric responded, "Christ, Pappy! Is there anything the State can't force from us?"

"If there is, I've never heard of it."

"North America hasn't even got started yet! How can you be sure that it'll operate the same way our old governments did?"

Alvin put his bowl on the coffee table before answering, "I don't know for sure. But human nature always desires to play God. Look at how the United Nations Charter superseded the sovereignty of all its member nations way back in 1945. That was the taproot for the Universal Regions Council, which absorbed the U.N. ten years ago.

"You never told me that before, Pappy."

"I just learned it listening to a morning news program called *The SOL Network*. With only three radio stations and an obscure Internet website, it's hardly a network, but with God's help, I pray it will grow."

"SOL? What does that stand for?"

"*Sons of Light*, boy! Peter Wicks, the network's spokesman, calls the name a play on words. There's a triple meaning: The first one refers to enlightened believers of the New Testament, particularly referring to John 12:35-36. Peter Wicks stipulated he has no religious affiliations; he simply likes the message of those two verses.

"The second aligns with the New Age Movement, which refers to people who seek enlightenment through their own experience instead of the Creator. They insist the Almighty is an impersonal force of nature. A lot of environmentalists subscribe to that philosophy. That's why they're always shoving media buzzwords like *Spaceship Earth*, *Mother Earth,* and *Global Community* down everybody's throat!

"The third meaning's the technical name of our sun, which is *Sol*. Peter likes to think that his broadcasts shed some light on what this *New World Order* or *Open Border Society* is really out to accomplish."

Eric coughed mildly. "He's a conspiracy theorist? Pappy, are you nuts? I'd never believe some radio voice or Internet blogger could ever turn your head!"

The old man suddenly welled up tears.

"Pappy?"

Alvin lamented while wiping both eyes, "It's my generation's fault and all those others since the American Civil War!"

"What the hell do you mean?"

"I'm talking about letting someone else keep track of our country when we still had one. I've spent my life raising a family, working for myself, loving my wife, and voting whenever the time came."

"What's wrong with that? You've always been a good and decent citizen. You've raised a damn fine family and were always faithful to Momma."

Alvin blurted, "I did what was required! Now I realize what I didn't do!"

"Christ, Pappy! You fought in the Middle East when you were eighteen! What more could you do?"

Alvin wiped eyes with his shirtsleeve. "All my life I questioned my country's policies, but I never got involved by sharing my ideas. Besides my family and a few close friends, no one ever heard my political opinions. That's what I regret. Now, it's too late." The old man leaned back in his chair. "Peter Wicks is right. Evil only conquers when good people don't unite against it."

"But you've always said that nobody can fight City Hall!"

"I was wrong, son."

"How?"

"A person can fight with an idea. But the majority of my peers didn't believe that any more than I back then. We were too busy running the treadmill of our own lives to realize that we'd ignorantly flushed the best things about our country down the toilet of history."

Eric fidgeted, "How did our people flush America?"

Alvin hunched forward. "The majority of Americans were convinced that their network news media was honest. We especially believed that *Freedom of the Press* was as healthy as ever. That wasn't true. The mainstream news media has been controlled by corporate investors since the dawn of radio. And when people get their knowledge, ideas, and opinions from a one-sided source, they never get the full story on any situation. We trusted their news media. But the lust for wealth and power can betray reporters just as well as any political mouthpiece feigning constitutional rights.

"Technically, our constitution's been a dead letter since the southern states walked out of Congress in 1861. That event made void the lawful quorum majority of sovereign states, whose authority ratified the U.S. Constitution into law. The facts were there, but none of us bothered to read them."

Eric asked, "You're mouthing Peter Wicks' words, aren't you, Pappy?"

"More or less, boy, but that doesn't mean they're not true. This man's personally challenged me not to take his word. He encourages listeners to check out the claims he's making against any documented authority we can find. That's what I've been doing for a while now in my limited capacity."

"I was wondering why you started reading history books instead of your favorite westerns and mysteries. Have you found out anything else?"

Alvin nodded. "Do you remember what your teachers said about how and why the American Civil War started?"

"I was taught it was fought over slavery."

"So was I. But the Civil War was really fought over sovereign states rights."

Eric grabbed more popcorn. "Then what about slavery?"

"That's what the North used to whip its citizens into a froth above the Mason Dixon Line. It's true that there were black slaves in the south, but they were in the north too. There were also indentured servants from every race and culture. Slavery was wrong, but the Civil War was fought because the federal government wanted to usurp the sovereign states having the right to make their own laws and ratify their own alliances. They also wanted to make every man, woman, and child a corporate citizen of the corporate U.S. Federal Government, that way all sovereign state Americans could be extradited by the Feds for whatever purpose they wished.

"The southern states rightfully opposed anything that didn't recognize their authority as individual states, even if that power was the United States government. I envy those Confederates for their bravery. They died for what they believed. The truth is the Federal U.S. Government had no lawful authority to abolish state sovereignty. That was an established political right that all American Colonies enjoyed since our Articles of Confederation."

"I never heard any of *that* before!" interjected Eric.

Alvin continued, "The Federal Government wanted jurisdiction over every American citizen, period. When they defeated the confederacy, the U.S. Constitution annexed the fourteenth amendment that gave the U.S. government power over *all* its corporate citizens for plunder and punishment. George Washington, Thomas Jefferson, and Patrick Henry must be screaming in their graves; the nation they fought for doesn't exist anymore! The U.S. government had become a greater tyrant than King George III ever was!"

Eric exclaimed, "I'll be damned! *That's* something the schools don't teach!"

"Public schools are federal, state, and municipally funded. They're not going to bite the hand that feeds them, even if they knew about this. But so much time has passed since the Civil War, I doubt 100,000 Americans know what I just told you. But it's never been a secret; it's just not been widely reported."

"I'm beginning to understand, Pappy. I'd never attempted to read between the lines of what the mass media ever spewed out. I always assumed that opposing points of view always rise to the surface."

Alvin raised both his hands. "They can't get the exposure, Eric. There have always been a minority of courageous journalists who spoke their mind against the encroachment of tyranny. But they didn't have the funds to reinforce their opinions against whatever totalitarian juggernaut's seeking power over our people. I believe Peter Wicks is such a journalist, but he's getting almost no support. You didn't even know that he existed and you listen to talk radio all day long in your workshop! "

"What time's he on, Pappy?"

"His obscure website is always available, of course, but he gets little support from that. But his live radio talk show is on from nine A.M. to one P.M. He replays excerpt recordings from previous shows from two to four P.M. Then from four to ten P.M., Wicks links his broadcasts with *ProvNet*, which commands the largest talk radio audience in the United Sta—I mean the Central Province. I suspect that's how he pays for most of his airtime.

"From ten P.M. to two A.M., Wicks rebroadcasts his previous live show the afternoon before. Peter also issues a fresh news broadcast for five minutes at the top of every hour. Then at 2:05 A.M. our time, the SOL Network shuts down from the radio."

Eric glanced at his watch. "Looks like we're just in time for Wicks' final news broadcast for the night. How about it?"

"Crank him on, boy!"

Eric picked up the remote control, turned the stereo radio on, and grabbed another handful from the bowl.

A broadcast voice announced, "Even ex-incumbent President Warren Miller bowed to the choice of North America tonight. Speaking from his home in San Juan, Puerto Rico District, Miller proclaimed, 'To the North American people from the Arctic Circle to the Panama Canal, I take this opportunity to congratulate Garth, Mike, and their new executive cabinet on this historic occasion. Although we were competitors, I can assure the President that I'm as dedicated to the Third Triumvirate as he. If I can serve the common welfare in any capacity, President Brady need only ask.'"

The broadcaster continued, "Warren Miller had no comment on what he currently intended to do. But since he has no restrictions to running for a Tribune Assembly Consul seat next November, perhaps we'll hear from him again. In the meantime, President Brady and his cabinet ministers will hold the reins of our government. And I've no doubt with the blessing of the Universal Regions Council.

"This reporter will be curious to see how our new Minister of Enforcement and Minister of Justice will measure up to the tasks of maintaining law and order in the Third Triumvirate. Isn't it a comfort to know that all of our largest Central Provincial Cities still house active Paramilitary Units, even if they're no longer confiscating citizens' firearms? But I'll wager those troops expand to the Northern and Southern Provinces very soon! After all, Triumviral Law mandates firearm confiscation across our entire continent!

"However, as fewer and fewer representatives control the lives of more and more people, this reporter would like to conclude with a sobering thought. Never forget that when political and religious leaders promote the New World Order, their collective goal is to dismember the Old World Order! Let's make sure that we don't throw the baby of liberty out with the bath water of national sovereignty!

"Tomorrow, I'll interview Dr. Rudolf Zadock, Chairman of *The Global Reaction Alliance*. This scientific coalition claims global warming's a cleverly orchestrated hoax supported by false data from politically correct computer modelers. Goodnight, citizens. Signing off. WXWNSOL."

Alvin inquired, "*What* executive cabinet and *what* ministers?"

Eric replied, "They must have been announced on TV after we turned it off, Pappy."

"I suppose so. Anyway, what do you think?"

"Wicks has sure given me food for thought! I'll be in my shop tomorrow morning by nine A.M.! That scientist may answer some questions I've been wondering about!"

Alvin yawned, "How about recording it for me? After tonight, there's no way that I'll be awake to hear him."

"Sure, Pappy. I'm hitting the sack. Thanks for the heads up. I'll see you tomorrow."

"You're welcome, son. Maybe it's not too late for human liberty after all!"

CHAPTER FOUR

Surveillance

Mike Parker awoke before his wife. At seven A.M. he slid out of bed and shuffled into a walk-in closet. After climbing into a gray sweat suit, he carried his running shoes back to the bedside. Margaret opened one eye, watching her husband tying up both laces.

Mike stood up while she whispered, "Do you really think you need a run after I worked you over, darling?"

Parker twirled around and suddenly buried his face between her breasts. Then he playfully pulled back, answering, "Princess, you're never a workout! You're always a dessert!" He slowly advanced again.

Margaret sat up and giggled before pushing him back. "Oh, go do your exercises! You must think that I'm still thirty!"

"You're forty and I'm two years older, but I'm the one who's out of bed, Princess. Tell Geoffrey I'll be in for breakfast about nine." Mike quickly kissed his wife and jogged out of their master bedroom.

Margaret slowly stretched like a royal Egyptian cat. She paused to survey the room before bounding out of bed. In seconds, she was relishing the private torrent of her bathroom shower. The hot steam camouflaged the skylight above her head.

Parker stopped after descending the main stairway.

President Brady was waiting for him while wearing clean yellow sweats and pristine running shoes. "I knew you'd be down eventually," commented Garth. "Come on, Mike, let's plow some beach sand!"

"You're on, chum, but are we going alone? Your safety's now a matter of triumviral priority. My estate's probably been crawling with camouflaged soldiers all night long."

"Are you going to hold me under the Atlantic surf until I stop bubbling?"

"That's not very damn funny, Garth!"

"I was only pulling your chain! We won't be alone, but my bodyguards are stealth itself!"

Predawn purple transformed into narrow streaks of reddish orange as both executives jogged down the wooden stairway connecting Parker's spacious cliffside estate to the open beach. Their course ran south along the shoreline edge taking advantage of firm, wet sand.

Mike scanned for intruders for the first half-mile.

Brady answered his partner's unspoken question in a labored breath, "Don't worry about my men. Are you still upset about my silly drowning joke? If I didn't trust you, I wouldn't be here."

Parker puffed white vapor in the morning cold. "I still don't see anyone!"

"That's the idea. How far are we running?"

"About three miles roundtrip, but I can modify my game plan to accommodate a slow-ass runner like you."

Garth commented, "By the time we return, I'll have a big enough appetite to sample everything in sight of our morning buffet."

"I told my staff to outdo themselves because they were feeding our triumviral government."

Garth chuckled before gulping air. "That might spoil our ministers. Whenever we meet outside the capitol, they'll all insist we rendezvous at Mike Parker's Virginia Shoreline Estate!"

"What's on your mind, Mr. President?"

"How'd you know I wanted a private talk?"

"You're too sociable to leave the others for this beach run."

"But no one else was up yet, Mike."

"Yeah, but you couldn't know that ahead of time. You were waiting for me in your unused sweats."

Garth panted heavier. "They don't feel unused now; the back of this shirt's welding to my icy spine. I compliment you on your deduction; you read my mind like a road sign!"

"Is it something serious?"

Garth continued, "Our ministers lost most of their inhibitions before bedtime last night. Some of them were pretty damn drunk before we broke up. I wanted to know if you had any regrets about inviting them. We did pound your home pretty hard last night."

Mike dry swallowed in the sea breeze. "No regrets. Roget got smashed worse than anyone else but didn't cause any trouble. But Geoffrey had to prevent him from entering Minister Franklin's bedroom by mistake."

"Mistake, my ass! The only lecherous gesture he didn't give Carmen was to stick his tongue out! But I'm glad Andre didn't find her bedroom! Carmen's good-natured, but she'd have twisted him into a pretzel before rupturing his pickled prick and balls for a week with a combat kick!"

"Even drunk, that French Canadian knows beauty when he sees it!"

Brady chuckled. "You think Carmen's beautiful, Mike?"

"Christ, Garth! I'm just married, not dead!"

Brady confided, "Be damn thankful we have such a woman. Carmen's the most expertly trained soldier I've ever seen. Her husband's almost a carbon copy, but even Richard admits she'd take him out hand-to-hand! I wonder if the Franklins' marital quarrels ever include lethal weapons."

"I sure as hell wouldn't want to find out, Mr. President!"

"By the way, how'd you know I'd run this morning? I had guests."

"Margaret said nothing short of death would keep you from running your beloved sand whenever you're home. Apparently, you and Virginia Beach are an item."

Mike blew hard. "You're amazing! I don't think I'll ever keep any secrets from you or your spies."

"Christ, Mike! You don't think Margaret's one of my spies, do you?"

Parker abruptly stopped running. Brady did the same. The Vice President glared. Garth stared back with growing apprehension.

Then Mike brandished a sinister grin before whispering, "Gotcha."

Brady fell laughing onto the wet sand, unable to rise. Parker helped hoist the President to his feet.

Brady wiped windblown tears away before managing to say, "Now we're even! For a moment, you had me worried!" He regained composure. "But now my sorry ass's wet and the wind's picking up. You mind if we head back?"

"Okay by me. We'd better hoof it before you get pneumonia!"

"That won't be necessary. Gentlemen?"

Mike whirled around to see a trio of men wearing windbreakers and standing ten feet away. The wind buffeted their open jackets exposing holstered, automatic handguns below the left shoulders of all three. Parker's blood chilled while noticing triple sets of parallel tracks behind them eventually disappearing behind a drift of clay and silt one hundred yards away. He backed up with a stare.

"It's okay, Mike," yelled Garth over a gust of wind. "These are some of the invisible men that I told you about. You're back was to them, but I saw them approach."

A single gunman uttered, "Sorry to have startled you, Mr. Vice President. We didn't intend that. We ran over when we observed President Brady fall in the water. We wanted to offer him the option of a ride."

The President nodded.

Every agent sprinted before disappearing around the drift before a distant engine suddenly roared. Then streams of silt and clay erupted into the air while an enormous, armored, six-wheel drive vehicle plowed over and crushed marsh grass, driftwood, and seashells toward both executives. Then a pneumatic side-door opened along the vehicle's right side as the all-terrain *Juggernaut* stopped. The armed trio rejoined both stationary runners.

Mike frowned. "Garth, are you sure that we should go with these clowns?"

"Let's accept the hospitality of my guardian angels."

"Are you damn sure these are your angels?"

"Who else would be shadowing us this morning?"

"You don't recognize these thugs, Mr. President?"

"No. I have over one hundred agents in my Executive Protectorate. So far, I've only met twenty. I think that's pretty good considering that I've been president for about seven hours."

Without hesitation, the agents revealed their collective identifications. Mike scrutinized all three before cautiously handing them back.

Garth laughed. "Come on, Mike! My ass's getting numb."

Everyone boarded before the armored behemoth backtracked across the VIP's running trail.

Garth nudged Mike. "What's the matter? You look like you've seen a ghost."

"I'm still watching three of them."

"My agents really freaked you out, didn't they?"

"When did you acquire these bloodhounds? It sure as hell wasn't this morning!"

"I've had Executive Protectorate Agents around me since we began the campaign. Former President Miller insisted on it as a gesture of good will. Now, his whole force's assigned to me. Chill out!"

Mike replied, "I'm sorry, Garth. I guess its hitting home that I'll be under surveillance 24/7 for the next eight years. Your agents must be damn good; I never noticed any of them through our whole political campaign. I knew about our CIA boys, but this is different."

"It's just an added triumviral safeguard. But you needn't worry about them. I'm the one who lives in a bubble."

"You mean I don't have to constantly be looking under rocks?"

"Hell no! That would drive you and Margaret nuts! You have Executive Protectorate access whenever you want it, but their primary function's to cover my ass. Relax, Mike, you'll only get sealed in the bubble with me when we're together like now."

Parker sighed hard before declaring, "Thank Christ! Margaret might've divorced me just to get away from prying eyes! Here's where we get off."

The President tapped his driver; the Juggernaut stopped.

Mike jumped to the sand before noticing that Brady remained inside. He yelled back, "Aren't you coming?"

"I'll be up in a few minutes. I need to brief my traveling companions!"

Mike shrugged before running toward his cliff stairs; long strides quickly put him out of Garth's eyeshot.

President Brady snapped at the driver, "Jesus Christ, Chuck! You guys almost scared my right hand man shitless!"

"We scared him, but you lied through your teeth. What was that bullshit about him not being under surveillance? We've been scoping Parker's ass and his juicy wife for the last year! Boy, that middle-aged babe can get it on! And what was that horse shit about you never seeing us before?"

Garth folded both arms in front of his chest, "Chuck, being my cousin doesn't give you the right to be disrespectful! If any Cupola Flag Officer heard you talk like that, they might ferment wine from your liver."

Chuck Brady stammered, "I apologize, Mr. President, it won't happen again! Please don't inform our chairman or I'll end up on a blind date with Sebastian!"

"I'll let it go this time. Besides, I'm confident your superiors will give you the proper instruction." Brady looked at his other two bodyguards. "Won't they?"

"Certainly," assured Moses Richmond, sitting back in a dimly lit rear seat.

His blond-haired, gold-toothed partner thumbed up while sitting up front beside the nervous driver.

Garth resumed, "That's fine, boys. By the way, that was a superior job of surveillance on the beach. Did you use local Scansats, thermographs, metal detectors, and submersibles to track us?"

The blond man repeated, "Certainly, sir."

"But why did you gentlemen appear out of nowhere? I didn't use my Scansat transponder. Did it activate on its own in my pocket?"

Moses replied, "No, Mr. President. We were obeying a direct order from Commissioner Quimby himself. A Scansat was recording your beach run from orbit." President Brady frowned. "In any case, sir, URC authority exceeds yours."

Garth answered, "I suppose if the Universal Regions Council ordered you to murder both Mike and me, rape his wife, eat their servants, and ransom their children back to Grandma, one body part at a time, you would've obeyed?"

Hans Gidolf swiped at his blond hair, glanced at Chuck, and blurted "Without hesitation, President Brady, even if we didn't have any ketchup to go with their fermented livers."

Garth lamented, "It's a shame that men must be monitored for protection from themselves, but human nature warrants mandatory surveillance, doesn't it?"

Richmond grinned before saying, "Absolutely, Mr. President."

Brady smiled weakly and leaped out of the Juggernaut. He cupped both hands before yelling, "Mose, you were right about this morning being a test, but I'm sure it was more for me than you. I hope Commissioner Quimby was pleased with the result."

The black commander replied, "Men must relinquish personal liberty for the collective peace of Spaceship Earth, sir!"

The Juggernaut closed its door and lumbered southward through shallow salt water before suddenly accelerating to 60 mph.

Brady vainly scanned the clear sky for any glimpse of a local Scansat, which was one of a thousand regional spies potentially locking on his position from a forty-mile-high, geosynchronous sub orbit. Local Scansats were a nuisance, but Central Scansats were a terror. Each solar-powered relay station could intercept and jam any communication transmission in the world within its range. Garth's blood chilled despite his exertions while running up the stairway. Central Scansats belong to his Crimson Cupola Fraternity, which traced a royal lineage back to the Pax Romana. And the fact that the Cupola's New Genesis Polar Base constantly monitored them with armed hypercraft didn't relax him either.

CHAPTER FIVE

Pedestal

Twenty minutes after leaving Brady, Mike cleaned up and headed down the oak hallway to rejoin his guests. Kitchen aromas from succulent foods permeated his nose with every step. Parker entered his living room and spotted Margaret and Carmen together on a couch while Tyrone and Bertha reclined on another sofa with Curtis and Irene sitting on a far loveseat. But Jocquin, Andre, John, and Garth were nowhere in sight.

The Minister of Finance spoke. Mike's curiosity peaked as he pulled up a wooden chair directly behind the Williams. Irene continued, "I begin to laugh whenever I'm told that developing the Amazon River Region will cause a climatic catastrophe from a lack of tropical rain forest. Some claim such deforestation will deplete the oxygen levels in our atmosphere because plants absorb carbon dioxide and give oxygen in return.

"Fewer plants supposedly means less oxygen and more carbon dioxide retained in our atmosphere. Supposedly added levels of carbon dioxide contribute to an abnormal global warming. But one smoke screen at a time. Does anyone happen to know how much of the earth's surface is covered by water?"

Parker blurted, "Seventy percent."

Margaret exclaimed, "Mike! Darling, there you are! What are you doing sitting on that silly wooden stool? Get over here and occupy the master's chair!"

"Princess, if I'm the master, why are you giving me orders?"

The group laughed as Mike got up, kissed his wife, and slid back into red leather. He apologized, "Forgive me for interrupting, Irene."

"That's no problem, Mike. Your answer was correct anyway. Since 70 percent of the earth's surface is submerged, doesn't it seem unlikely that cutting down plant life on a small fraction of the remaining land mass would injure our atmosphere in a substantial way?"

Bertha responded, "When you put it that way, it doesn't seem likely, does it?"

"Even if every square inch of dry land was infested with rich botanical growth, it couldn't come close to producing the total amount of oxygen the earth circulates in its atmosphere."

Margaret inquired, "Then where does the oxygen come from?"

"Why, Margaret, plants really do contribute the lion's share of our oxygen supply."

"What? You just said that they didn't. I don't understand."

Irene winked. "Forgive me for using you as a guinea pig, my dear. I was demonstrating what kind of confusion can be spawned by employing a half-truth. To explain, I must inform you that plants do contribute greatly to our oxygen supply, but the bulk of it doesn't come from terrestrial flora, which are the ones that radicals mourn over whenever developers clear their land. Our main source of oxygen's generated from a twin dynamic system spawned from our oceans. First, there's the myriad of tiny algae or non-flowering plants, in both salt and fresh water, which are the single highest biological sources of oxygen in the world. And the oceans themselves initiate the processes of evaporation, condensation, and precipitation to recycle our atmosphere.

"Both of these processes were in full operation before the first blade of grass ever sprouted. Otherwise, there wouldn't have been any grass to begin with. The relatively small amount of oxygen that terrestrial plants produce is dwarfed when compared with the processes at work from our seas. But that little item of information never reaches the public ear. It doesn't serve a politically correct cause. It wouldn't terrify the general public into making concessions. Radicals aren't really interested in the environment, Margaret; they're only interested in wealth and power.

"As to the question of plants altering climate, my opponents can't evade the fact that it's solar radiation on both landmasses and our oceans that regulate the global climate. High-and low-pressure systems are caused by cold and warm air masses in motion. Cold air descends and warm air rises. This fact of physics drives our weather and not the lack of a rain forest. The climate had to come first for that forest to grow."

Carmen was intrigued. "Irene, what you said about the rain forest makes sense, but is it good to slaughter unique plants and wildlife in South America just to have farm land? I understand the cleared land only grows crops for a season or two. Then South American farmers have to clear more to keep up production."

Tupik replied, "I don't really believe it's essentially a good thing to defoliate the South American Rain Forest. I don't relish the idea of eradicating whole species from the earth either. What I object to are the half-truths and blatant lies some radicals generate to achieve their own ends, whether those goals are respectable or not. I don't believe the end justifies the means.

"If radical environmentalists can twist facts to support their wide-eyed assumptions in this case, how can we blindly trust the reports and recommendations they make pertaining to other subjects? I'm alarmed to find that so many people blindly believe environmentalist politics without researching it for themselves. It disturbs me to the point where I always speak my piece whenever I get the chance; my poor Curtis can vouch for that."

Mr. Tupik added, "My darling, I agree with everything you said. It's just that I have heard it some many times I can't hang on your every word anymore."

The group laughed as Irene blew Curtis a kiss.

"At any rate," she continued, "I don't believe everything I read.

One must always consider the source. All people are capable of lying, even me."

Geoffrey, the head butler, suddenly padded into the room.

Margaret took her cue while announcing, "Breakfast is served, everyone. Eat all you like; Mike and I want you to feel at home." She led their guests toward the dining room.

Lagging behind, Mike asked, "Geoffrey, why aren't you headed for the dining room to help?"

"Mistress Margaret gave me instructions to allow her the pleasure of serving your guests. I have three auxiliary staff members standing by to assist."

"Outstanding as usual. By the way, have you seen the President lately?"

"I believe all four bachelors were in the gymnasium, sir."

"Thanks. I think I'll crash their exercise party."

The butler pointed toward the dining room, "It looks as if they are now crashing breakfast instead."

Mike rushed to join four casually clad men now heading toward the aromas. There was no conversation as everyone began their regal breakfast. Brady grew dismayed while Martinez, Roget, and Blackfeather were eating with proper etiquette, but with incredible speed. Then Blackfeather was first to go for seconds.

Garth commented, "Well, John, it seems geologists have a greater appetite than average people."

Blackfeather replied briefly, "Everything's too delicious to ignore."

The President resumed, "Mike, I noticed quite a little powwow in the living room earlier. What was our Minister of Finance's latest enlightenment?" Brady's brow darkened when Parker didn't reply.

Then Irene spoke, "It's my fault some of our associates are nervous. I was trying, in my own blustering way, to make their acquaintance. So I used them as a collective sounding board for one of my pet peeves. Guess which one, Mr. President."

Brady sighed relief, "Oh! That's the trouble! My staff was resembling a group of silent mutineers! Let me see. I'll bet you gave them the rain forest treatment. Am I right?"

Mrs. Tupik winked affectionately.

Mike interjected, "Damn! That's a relief, Garth! You already knew about Irene's rain forest position? I had misgivings about her qualifications!"

Irene dropped her fork in disbelief.

Parker uttered quickly, "Forgive me, Irene. That was an abominable choice of words. We all know your elite background in finance. I was thinking only that your personal position on the environment might cause a conflict for Garth's agenda."

She shrugged before continuing to eat.

Brady regained the floor. "Mike, you're one of the most honest people I know. That's one of the reasons I selected you as my running mate. But Irene and I know each other's position regarding the Brazilian rain forest. We strongly disagree. But why should I fill my cabinet positions with cringing subordinates if I ever needed constructive feedback on a crisis? None of us could agree on every subject, but I sure as hell wouldn't allow that to cost me the services of one of the truly great financial minds living."

Irene quickly stood up. "Garth and I disagree on many subjects. But none of you need feel our relationship would force you to take sides in any way. I simply know what I believe and why I believe it. But like many others, this subject's far from resolved."

Garth added, "Now that we have overcome our first misunderstanding, I pronounce this breakfast a success. Thank you to our gracious hosts. And thank you, Irene, for knocking me off everyone's collective pedestal. Now we're a team!

CHAPTER SIX

Interview

Eric woke up a half an hour before the SOL Network morning broadcast. He started the coffee and whipped up some French toast batter. Within ten minutes, he was eating four pieces dripping with butter and raw honey while sipping from a hot cup. He listened in the dining room with a small portable radio before suddenly remembering he needed to record the interview for Pappy. Racing into the living room, he loaded a blank CD before remotely activating his sound system. The SOL signal boomed just as Eric plopped onto the couch.

An electronic voice announced, "It's nine in the east, Patriots; the SOL Network's on the air. This is Peter Wicks speaking. I have a special guest this morning. Dr. Rudolf Zadock is chairman of the Global Reaction Alliance, headquartered in Denver, Colorado District. This group consists of climatologists, meteorologists, and other highly technical people. Dr. Zadock's views are not necessarily mine, but it's my job to provide you with useful information and not to do you're thinking for you! Good morning, Dr. Zadock. You're smiling at me; any particular reason?"

"I have two reasons. One, you're giving me the chance to speak this morning, and two, I agree with you about enlightening people with information instead of indoctrinating them through corporate media propaganda."

"Careful, Doctor, *enlighten* has so many meanings these days that a person doesn't know where someone's coming from whenever they use it."

"I'm using it to convey the idea of imparting knowledge. I'm a scientist and not a mystic; is that position clear enough?"

Wicks assured, "Very clear, Doctor. You have the floor."

"I represent a group of reputable scientists struggling to present objective proof that the URC's deliberately frightening industrial societies over a nonexistent dread. That dread's Abnormal Global Warming."

"That statement is a little vague. Please translate it into simple English, Doctor."

"There are no average temperature readings anywhere in the world to prove that the earth's warming abnormally."

Peter blurted, "How can that be? I've examined temperature records of major cities for several years. Places like Seattle, Los Angeles, Chicago, New York City, and Washington, D.C. all show a gradual rise during the last sixty years. The most recent report declares our new triumviral climate's increased three degrees within a single year."

Zadock quizzed, "Were those the latest statistics presented by the Triumviral Department of Intermodalism?"

"Correct, the TDI broadcasted their findings at eight last night over all three provinces."

"If the TDI's methods of analysis are the same as in the past, these new findings are negligible. Was there a complete list of recording locations in those findings?"

"The report sounded thorough when I listened. Temperature recordings were sampled for urban zones from New York to Los Angeles; other calculations included every provincial mountain range, the Hawaiian Islands, the desert southwest, the Alaskan panhandle, and the Great Lakes. Several measurements were also tabulated for the Atlantic, Pacific, Gulf of Mexico, and the Caribbean coasts as well."

Zadock continued, "Did any of those temperature recordings

appear abnormally high?"

"Absolutely, Doctor, some of our northern latitude cities seemed to rival metropolises in Arizona, California, Nevada, and New Mexico Districts. The levels were all attributed to excessive carbon dioxide in our atmosphere."

"Excluding cities like Las Vegas, Albuquerque, and Phoenix, which are actual deserts, do you *really* believe areas like Seattle, Minneapolis, New York, and Boston are becoming abnormally warm through any natural phenomenon?"

Wicks declared, "Why yes. Those readings were officially endorsed by the TDI."

"Those TDI lists are inaccurate, Peter."

"But the TDI didn't make up those recordings; they correlated with lists that municipal officials have produced for their corresponding cities. I spent part of last night confirming those statistics."

"That's just the point, Peter. When one wants to objectively measure the average temperatures of our earth over time, large cities cannot be involved in that study."

"Why? Cities are part of the earth's surface too. In fact, according to the TDI, they're the chief problem spots around the world. Their concentrated emissions from motor vehicles and urban manufacturing are prime contributors to increased carbon dioxide gas."

Doctor Zadock drew a long breath before answering. "Peter, if triumviral scientists really wanted to know the average temperatures of all regions around the world, they would deliberately avoid adding urban measurements to their research."

"And just why is that, Dr. Zadock?

"Urban areas are artificially overheated by solar radiation during the summer months, Peter. Cities are constructed of glass, steel, concrete, and asphalt. You've heard the expression about frying eggs on a sidewalk, haven't you?"

"Oh, I get you! You're talking about the excess heat that cities concentrate and radiate during the day because of all their glass, steel, concrete, and asphalt surfaces!"

"Correct. None of the natural surfaces around the world concentrate solar heat up to the levels our man-made surfaces do. Therefore, if climatologists include the overinflated temperatures of large cities in their natural atmospheric analysis, their conclusions would be tainted with artificially high readings."

Peter interjected, "Then their conclusions wouldn't accurately represent any climactic temperature averages for the earth."

"They certainly wouldn't represent any natural or accurate climactic averages, Peter. But accuracy isn't their goal anyway."

"But don't you believe that TDI environmentalists, who are a subsidiary of the newly mandated Triumviral Environmental Guardians or TEG, want to study and understand Abnormal Global Warming?"

"They understand it already; they created it out of nothing. They spoke it into being like the God of the Hebrews."

"Just because the TDI and TEG added urban temperatures to their data?"

Zadock resumed, "Precisely. No objective experimenter can assume anything to get accurate results. The physical universe's made of absolutes; scientists must be as objective as possible in order to discover truth. If scientists have a personal agenda, then they resort to half-truths and fright tactics to achieve their goals. Scientists possess the same human weaknesses as the common man. Just because someone has a Ph.D., that doesn't mean everything they say should be assumed as truth."

"Does that include the Global Reaction Alliance?"

"That includes everyone, but especially men of science. Our job is to uncover reality of the physical world. Since that world's objective, we must remain so ourselves. If earth's really warming abnormally, then objective science will bear that out. If not, then all the rhetoric and cleverly calculated computer models in the world won't change the facts no matter how badly a particular interest group wants it to."

"Doctor, that's the most diplomatic way of calling someone a liar that I've ever heard. Do you really believe many of your scientific opponents are intentional liars?"

"No doubt whatsoever, Peter. I had doubts when we first conceived the Global Reaction Alliance, or GRA, ten years ago. Since that time, I've consulted too many experts and have had far too many deliberate obstacles placed in my group's path to believe otherwise. I'm convinced that these Greenhouse Effectives are piloting some hidden agenda away from the general public."

"Doctor, how do I know you're not grinding a personal ax?"

"You don't, but physical reality cannot honestly be ignored. If I were lying, the last thing I'd want was public exposure in an open debate. Liars snare themselves in open discussions; their half-truths can't hold up when both sides of an issue are laid bare."

"Have you confronted your opponents about this global warming issue in public view?"

"The GRA has attempted that for a decade. Our antagonists refuse to debate with us; they won't even allow my group sufficient exposure to broadcast our findings. If Greenhouse Effectives believe they are right, why won't they participate in a public forum and allow our citizens to reach their own conclusions?"

"I can't argue with that, Doc. If you're on my show, it's plain the fat cats don't want anything to do with your group. I don't get high ratings, but my listeners are intelligent enough to reach their own conclusions."

"That's why I'm here, Peter. Besides, long term, abnormal global warming's physically impossible on earth."

"Can you back up that statement, Doctor?"

"Certainly, Peter. When Greenhouse Effectives postulate the earth's globally warming, they're telling a half-truth. Sunlight penetrates earth's atmosphere and strikes its surface, but the infrared heat built up cannot escape back into space at the same rate as the initial sunlight. The reason's because atmospheric Greenhouse Gases trap much of the heat and hold it like a blanket.

"Now, it's a scientific fact that 97 percent of all atmospheric greenhouse gas is simple water vapor. Carbon dioxide and the other remaining greenhouse gases make up only 3 percent. It's also true that water vapor's dense enough to reflect sunlight back into space before it can strike the earth's surface; therefore, long term, abnormal global warming remains impossible on the earth.

"Carbon dioxide and other greenhouse gases do trap solar heat on our surface. Now the Greenhouse Effectives claim excess solar heat abnormally warms the globe, but they fail to say that such heat would also increase earth's evaporation rate. Since over 70 percent of the earth's surface is submerged in water, excess evaporation would produce increased masses of water vapor that would reflect still more solar radiation into space, which over time would cool Earth's surface instead of heating it up.

"Any abnormal global warming during this process would be brief; it could only exist long enough to enshroud the planet with freakish fog banks, which would reflect the majority of solar radiation back into space before it ever warmed the earth's surface. Now, which theory about abnormal global warming's the correct one, Peter: theirs or ours?"

"Do you know, Doctor?"

Dr. Zadock paused and said, "Both the properties of carbon dioxide and water vapor are established facts. It has also been proven that excess carbon dioxide would be beneficial instead of a threat to life. Biosphere and botanical experiments on plant life have proven repeatedly that higher carbon dioxide gas levels accelerate plant growth and production provided sufficient sunlight reaches them for photosynthesis."

"But, Doctor, would enough sunlight get through the extra cloud layers of water vapor to keep the plants alive?"

"Certainly. Photosynthesis is never totally inactive unless plants are in complete darkness."

"But wouldn't these extra clouds block enough sunlight to harm plant life?"

"No, the earth possesses dynamic systems of high and low air pressure that constantly react and move from one global region to another; that process is called wind."

"Have you taken your findings to the Universal Regions Council for consideration?"

"We've attempted it several times, but we can't get a hearing."

Wicks asked, "Is there any more information about the global warming fraud you would like to share with SOL listeners?"

"Have I convinced you about our findings?"

"Only to a point. Your scientific evidence does make sense in the way you presented it, but I reserve judgment until I hear an open discussion between The GRA and some Greenhouse Effectives."

"All that any truth seeker wants is the chance to present their evidence. May I make a personal plug for the GRA in closing?"

"By all means, Doctor."

"Thank you, Peter. I appeal to your listeners to write to the new minister of the environment, John Blackfeather. Encourage him to establish an open, televised, North American forum debating the subject of abnormal global warming. It's possible he may have enough political clout to achieve it."

"Doctor Rudolf Zadock, thank you for speaking to us."

"Thanks for having me, Peter. Contact me anytime you want a voice on this subject. If I'm at all free, I'll be glad to come back, especially if you can get a Greenhouse Effective on at the same time. I promise not to bring tar and feathers, just data."

"Getting one of them on here would really be a miracle, Doctor. Good-bye. Well, my friends, the previous interview was stimulating to say the least. I don't know if I believe what Dr. Zadock has just told me, but he's certainly given me food for thought. I like that term 'Greenhouse Effective'; I think I'll employ that term into a buzzword of my own. If any listeners wish to contact the GRA for further information, simply write to the Global Reaction Alliance, P.O. Box TR467, Denver, Colorado District. You can also contact them at graecofraud.com…"

Eric left the recorder running for Pappy's sake. He walked into the kitchen, pulled the plugs connecting the coffeepot and French toast griddle, placed the remaining batter in the refrigerator, and walked out the back door, turning the porch light on behind him.

Alvin woke up at nine A.M., stiffly propped to a sitting position before standing up, and hobbled toward his open bedroom window. He saw his son walking down the drive and yelled, "Hey, boy!"

Eric turned around and waved.

Alvin asked, "Did you get any breakfast?"

"Yes! There's some French Toast batter in the fridge!"

"Did you record this morning's interview?"

"The CD is still running in the living room; that first guest was pretty interesting! I don't know when I'll be back in the house! We'll discuss the show when I come back, okay?"

"Good enough, son, see you later! Give those stubborn magnets hell!"

Eric entered his laboratory in a matter of seconds. He concentrated on his rotor shaft before discovering one positive pole was out of alignment. After correcting it, he activated the tabletop generator to jump-start his prototype. The Bipolar Drive rapidly accelerated to full capacity in three seconds without any vibration. Eric's invention was now drawing energy from electromagnetic fields for motive power. This source was inexhaustible. The superconductivity ceramics attracted and contained magnetic fields for fuel while simultaneously preventing leakage. His prototype was mildly humming at the whisper level of a hummingbird wing.

CHAPTER SEVEN

Seizure

Spencer Mitchell stood at one end of an elaborate, rectangular, cherry wood table at the center of a boardroom for the Triumviral Department of Intermodalism. Twelve well-dressed executives stared at him from leather seats forming a parallel gauntlet of six members alongside both table lengths. They didn't react to Mitchell; that privilege was reserved for Chairman Stromberg, who was occupying a seat at the opposite end.

Anyone could tell at a glance that Maximillian Stromberg was an athlete. His lean, muscular physique seemed chiseled beneath a custom-fitting three-piece suit. His indulgences in triathlons proved remarkable for a fifty-year-old man. His only vice was a passion for puffing cheap cigars. Max grinned through a clenched stogie before asking his right hand man, "Why the long face, Spencer? As of last night's election, our departmental authority spans North America! And thanks to TransTrak, the TDI will shortly be the motorist toll keeper for the Third Triumvirate!"

Mitchell slid into his chair retorting, "You don't have to explain that suborbital spy to me, Max. I helped you milk every lobbyist and politician we could get our hooks into. TransTrak is not only mandatory equipment for every vehicle in the Central Province; it will soon regulate the entire North American continent."

"Then what's eating you? TransTrak may have taken nearly twenty years and cost trillions to build, but that money was collected from a whole generation of eager beavers so caught up with their own pursuits that they never missed it anyway! Now that President Brady and his executive cabinet are the ruling class, our team will soon start procuring TransTrak fees from Canada, Mexico, Central America, and all those jeweled Caribbean Islands!"

Mitchell countered, "I thought TransTrak already had surveillance capability for all the areas of our Third Triumvirate?"

Stromberg puffed a smoke ring, "The parent system's on line. But we're going to require at least $700 billion to get TransTrak as functional in the Northern and Southern Provinces as it is here. But that's beside the point. You declared this emergency meeting, so let's have it!"

Mitchell's mind flashed back to TransTrak's humble beginnings: The surveillance system was spawned back in 2023, when the TDI was a minor branch of the United States Department of Transportation. TransTrak was the brainchild of federal engineers who wanted to cut America's urban traffic delays to a minimum. The culmination of motor vehicles, suborbital platforms, and onboard dash computers resulted in full tracking capability on a national scale. TransTrak had finally become operational two years ago within the former United States of America before the triumviral presidential election. Now, the TDI aspired to absolute authority over all North American motorists very soon.

"SPENCER!"

Mitchell's attention jolted to the present. He blinked at the smoke in his eyes.

The chairman snarled, "You're the one who requested this goddamn meeting! You're the one who claimed an emergency! Now you're the one who's daydreaming? It's eight A.M. and some of us have been here since seven. You're the one who's an hour late. Now spit out what you've got to say!"

"My staff's just tabulated the latest average temperatures for all fifty-one former United States during the previous year; our findings are alarming."

Max suddenly whispered, "Is it really that bad, Mr. Vice Chairman?"

"Yes it is. By the way, how does it feel to have a new boss? Andre Roget was appointed Minister of Travel last night; I wonder when he'll show up here to inspect us?"

Stromberg puffed before blustering, "What difference does that make? Bureaucracies always operate the same way; we just have more districts to regulate. Now, back to your report. How much time do we have?"

"I don't know. The average temperature of the Central Province has risen three degrees in a single year; global warming seems to be accelerating. I don't know if reducing carbon dioxide will matter now. After all, we're only one triumvirate. The carbon fallout pumped into our atmosphere was a collective effort; a single region can't alter it alone. We need to call an emergency session of the Universal Regions Council."

One of the subordinates shouted, "I don't believe you, Mitchell! There are at least a dozen climate experts who would disagree with your findings!"

Spencer answered, "Well, Sam, you get those experts to test the average temperatures and have them examine the same areas that my staff did; thermometers don't lie. Your experts have access to the same temperature records that municipal officials produce for their respective cities and districts. They are accurate everywhere from Alaska to the Virgin Islands. Averages have climbed three degrees in one year."

Stromberg calmed his voice. "Let's have the report."

The vice chairman opened his briefcase and passed out thirteen printed, paper-clipped reports along both sides of the table. Then he projected an identical report onto a computerized wall screen from his lap top monitor.

Stromberg lit a fresh cigar as Spencer announced, "Gentlemen, the temperature statistics gathered during the last year produce conclusive evidence that Spaceship Earth's warming more rapidly than previously calculated. I encourage you to offer these figures to any experts for their opinions; thermometers don't lie."

Mitchell read the next eight pages aloud, comparing data from the last twelve months with findings for the previous five years. The totals indicate an average three-degree rise across the Central Province for 2039. Temperatures were collated by region and population in every major city from Honolulu to San Juan, Seattle to Miami, and San Diego to Boston. Measurements of the desert southwest, all central provincial mountain ranges, and numerous hydrodynamic samples over the Atlantic, Pacific, Gulf of Mexico, and The Great Lakes' coastlines were all displayed. The evidence appeared uncontestable. Spencer finished his presentation and scanned for any sign of disagreement.

A full minute elapsed before Matthew Rigby finally said, "It seems to me there's a discrepancy in your analysis."

"What discrepancy, Matt?"

"You say this report constitutes a record of all central provincial cities intermingled with sparsely populated regions and all of our coasts?"

"With a full year's temperatures compared against those of the past five years."

"Why did you include urban centers for this report? It seems to me that adding the inflated temperatures of large cities would artificially skew the results. Those—"

Mitchell erupted, "Are you accusing my staff of fraud, Rigby?"

Max belched smoke. "That's enough, Spence! Go ahead, Matt."

"Yes, sir. I was saying that major cities recycle the same initial amount of solar radiation many times over by radiating light and heat repeatedly off of glass, cement, asphalt, and steel surfaces. Cities cannot produce a natural temperature record because of what they are constructed from. However, temperatures over oceans, mountains, forests, and lakes are not inflated artificially. Obviously, combining their rural averages with the artificial heat indexes of metropolitan areas might skew the accuracy of our TDI analysis.

"In fact, I'm surprised your boys didn't come up with an even higher result. Three degrees would be a catastrophe if the average hadn't been inflated with temperatures from urban areas. I'll wager that if you throw out the inflated recordings, you would come up with a very different conclusion."

Sam Thomas sat forward; his respect for Matt Rigby suddenly skyrocketed.

Mitchell insisted, "Our conclusion's correct. Greenhouse gases like carbon dioxide are produced mainly by the industrial activity of major cities and millions of automobiles abroad. Our TDI must now regulate the output of these gases. Since King Oil's still the primary source of energy our people use, our purpose remains to reduce pollution. If we reduce pollution, we reduce greenhouse gases and thereby might get a handle on global warming, which, if continued unchecked, could spell disaster for Spaceship Earth and our posterity. Is that clear enough for you, Matt?"

Rigby crossed both arms. "Very clear, except you evaded my question. I was asking you about the inflated temperatures of major cities, but have it your way. You say you're concerned about the abnormal warming of the earth due to the carbon dioxide we inject into it. I assume that when you say global warming, you are talking about the entire surface of the world, including oceans?"

"Of course."

"Then what good are urban temperatures if your objective is to measure the average for an entire province along with the rest of our world?"

Spencer blasted, "Are you a climatologist, Rigby? Do you have any expertise in the field of meteorology? No! You're just here because you're daddy's an old friend of Max's!"

Rigby remained undaunted. "Sometimes distinguished scientists make mistakes. They can't see the forest for the trees. But the error of this experiment was too blatant for any honest scientist not to have noticed; therefore, they must have deliberately added urban heat indexes into their experiment! Common sense dictates that if you want the average temperature of a house, you don't include steam from a boiling pot in the equation! Someone's pursuing a hidden agenda and I intend to find out who they are! This report's a farce! Don't bother firing me, I quit!

"But before security escorts me out, I'll say one thing more: I may not be a climatologist, but my father used to work for the United States Department of Meteorology and I've studied their records for years. The average, collective temperature of the United States hasn't changed more than plus or minus two degrees in the last 180 years! I loathe fraud! You people can shove this job!"

Rigby kicked both double doors open before disappearing into the hallway.

Max chuckled before saying, "Well, Spence, Matt certainly said a mouthful."

"Do you agree with him?"

"He put forth a very logical argument before he blew a gasket. I think Matt would make a very good Chess Roulette opponent."

Mitchell barked, "That goddamned game's all you ever think about lately! Ever since Atlanterran President Xavier donated it to the TDI, you've been hooked! You play it every chance you get!"

"I don't play Chess Roulette every day, but I might if I could entice you into a match. So far, only Frances Snell and Warren Miller have taken me on."

"Blast it, Max, don't start on me again! Aren't the president of Fraser Provincial Freightlines and the former President of the United States enough for you?"

Stromberg crushed his latest cigar. "It's just I think you might enjoy fighting me in some other arena besides the boardroom. I know I'd love to have a full scale war with you."

"What's that mean?"

"Don't bunch your panties; I only want you to enjoy yourself. And Barry Xavier's given me such a fascinating game, it's hard for me not to play it."

"Forget it, Max! I don't know how to play chess anyway! Now, whose side are you on regarding my report?"

Stromberg narrowed his eyes to slits before yelling, "Rigby's side and I'll tell you why! We've had a good thing going here; we've extorted $500 billion in citations and fines from American motorists since TransTrak went on line. No outsider has been the wiser about our little racket. But if your annual report's made public, other citizens may start asking the same question that Matt tossed in your lap. I don't want your report publicized! I don't give a tinker's damn whether it's accurate or not! I don't want The TDI to rock its own boat! Be satisfied with the status quo, Spencer! Be content with—aaaagggghhhh!"

Mitchell's rage disintegrated at the sight in front of him.

Stromberg hit the floor while convulsing. His eyes bulged with needle sharp pain as his heart rate and blood pressure soared. Agony pulsed a ruby flush under the skin. His ears and throat throbbed hard enough to cock his head from side-to-side with each pulse beat. Max endured daggers of pain through every nerve as his voluntary muscles continuously twitched as if enduring a full electrocution. Then he abruptly blacked out.

Spencer screamed for security into the tabletop intercom as everyone else gathered nervously around their quivering chairman. "We've got an emergency in the boardroom! Call an ambulance! I want white coats up here fast!"

Mitchell pushed men out of his way to reach the chairman. Stromberg writhed like a worm before abruptly stopping. He oozed blackened blood out both eyes, ears, and nostrils while gushing a mouthful of fresh red gore. Spencer turned Max on his right side to clear the mouth before placing him onto his back. He closed Stromberg's gory nose, propped his chin and head back, reluctantly clamped his mouth over the victim's, and blew in to expand Max's chest. Mitchell released as the chairman regurgitated thickening, blackened blood from his ruptured body core. The vice chairman wiped a shirtsleeve across his mouth and depressed Max's chest with crisscrossed palms. Stromberg failed to respond from half a dozen attempts before Spencer finally gave up.

Sam asked Spencer, "Are you assuming command?"

"Max's lying dead and you're probing me about rank?"

"Andre Roget was celebrating in Virginia last night. Since we're so close here in Washington, I'm assuming our new Minister of Travel will pull a surprise tour."

Mitchell roared, "Satan's scimitar! How about some genuine respect for the dead, huh? So why don't all you guys haul your sickening apathy out of here?"

As eleven inspectors departed, three white-uniformed men charged into the boardroom.

Mitchell bitched, "It's about goddamned time! The chairman's dead! His brain's probably cold oatmeal by now."

The trio knelt down and began standard procedures. The head physician noticed bruises on the corpse's chest during defibrillation before glancing up at. Spencer anticipated his question, "That's right, pal. I tried to resuscitate that sculpted slab of quivering meat in front of you!" The doctor nodded before draining Max's mouth and throat and inspected them for clot blockage. Then he examined the left carotid artery swollen to a half-inch diameter from the base of the skull to the jawbone with an overlapping network of purplish, blue, and black splotches. The physician immediately stripped the corpse before locating identical networks of ruptures all over Max's inner thighs, torso, armpits, wrists, earlobes, and the soles of both feet.

Standing up, the doctor motioned his companions to remove the body while commenting, "A valiant effort, Mr. Mitchell, but no one could have saved this man."

"Are you a doctor or just a paramedic?"

The doctor bowed, "Charles Edmonds, M.D., at your service; my twin companions are paramedics."

"How'd you know my name, Doc?"

"One of your security people reported the emergency and who called it in."

"Why didn't security escort you up here?"

"Exactly my question after we entered the lobby. Security said their team was under orders to guard the building's perimeter; they simply told us which floor to take."

"That's my fault, Doc. In my hurry to get at Max, I yelled to security for an ambulance. That's all I told them. Since they had no other specifics, they followed their primary function of intruder control."

Edmonds frowned. "That doesn't do much for anyone needing medical attention."

"You've got a point, Doc. When Minister Roget shows up, I'll discuss your suggestions with him. Is there anything else that you want from me?"

Edmonds lowered his voice. "I didn't mean to snap at you. I hate to lose a patient."

"No sweat, Doc, can you tell me what killed him?"

"Those purplish, black marks all over the body's circulatory areas indicate that this man died from a hyperactive heart; the organ was literally pumping blood so fast that the victim's circulatory system ruptured under the strain from a hundred different areas."

Spencer asked, "What about the blackened blood?"

"Must be some type of metabolic disorder that I've never heard of. Something that induced hyperactive blood clotting from simultaneous clusters of internal bleeding."

"You mean Max's veins and arteries ruptured apart like an internal dam bursting?"

"That seems a fair analogy at the moment. I want to secure the medical history on this man. He may have had some type of exotic disease I'm not familiar with."

"Would a hyperactive heart cause muscular convulsions, Doc?"

"What kind of convulsions?"

"The kind that spasms every muscle at once like a fatal electric shock."

"I doubt it. Was this man an epileptic?"

"I've known Max for years; he was a triathlete."

"Triathletes are screened too thoroughly to conceal epilepsy; their tests wouldn't miss any circulatory anomalies either."

"Max went through everything I just described before dying."

Edmonds asked, "The decedent's name was Max?"

"Maximillian Stromberg, former chairman of the Triumviral Department of Intermodalism. It's ironic that he dropped dead on the first day of his new triumviral position; he didn't even get a chance to meet our new Minister of Travel."

"Who's in authority here now?"

Mitchell extended his right hand, "Vice Chairman Spencer Mitchell at your service, Doctor. You can call me Spencer."

Edmonds shook hands answering, "Call me Charles. I'm happy to meet you. By the way, here's my card. This man's death is so extraordinary that I might need some more input from you concerning how he died. If you think of anything else, please call me right away. I'm attending the autopsy of this one myself. If my superiors allowed it, I'd do the dissection too."

Spencer accepted Charles' card.

The doctor's Media Palm signaled another emergency; he excused himself before jogging out of the room.

Mitchell sat alone at the table and poured himself a drink before activating the tabletop intercom. Security answered, "TDI Main Security, Tom Martin speaking."

"Marty, this is Spencer Mitchell. The crisis is over. I assume that the medicals have already made it to the lobby with the body of the chairman."

"Yes, sir, but they haven't left yet; the building's still sealed."

"Security access can't help now; open the building again."

"At once, sir."

"Marty, is Matt Rigby down in the lobby?"

"No, sir. He may be in his office or in the cafeteria."

Mitchell located Matthew Rigby, who was drinking coffee in the cafeteria two floors below the boardroom. Rigby looked at him contemptuously while sipping his drink.

Spencer admitted, "Matt, I owe you an apology and an explanation. All I ask is a minute of your time. Will you hear me out?"

Rigby nodded.

"First of all, I admit that I treated you badly in front of the committee. I'm sorry. I have no excuse. Your urban heat question bowled me completely over when we were back in the boardroom. But in retrospect, I realize that it makes logical sense. I won't blame you if you refuse my apology, but I don't want us to part as enemies. What do you say?"

Matthew stood up and shook Mitchell's hand saying, "I don't apologize for my question, only my manners. I'll apologize formally in front of Chairman Stromberg if you wish."

Mitchell's smile dropped.

Rigby asked, "What is it?"

"Max's dead, Matt."

"What happened?"

"He started to bawl me out about the way I handled you, then he had some kind of an attack and died right in the boardroom."

"The chairman? But he had a heart like a hammer. If it wasn't for that look on your face, I'd suspect you were pulling my chain."

"I'm not kidding, Matt. Max's dead."

Matt's brow furrowed, "My little tirade cost the chairman his life. I didn't know he was sick."

"It was something freakish. Maybe it was those stinking cigars of his."

Rigby got up, emptied his coffee into the sink, and returned rubbing both eyes.

Spencer regained composure, "As the acting chairman until Roget appoints another, I'm promoting you to my former rank."

"But I'm the junior man around here!"

"And the only one who spoke his mind against my report. I need a right-hand man with some integrity. None of those departmental yes-men will give me that. The vice chairmanship's yours if you want it."

Matt smiled. "What's my first assignment?"

"You've given me suspicions about our global warming analysis. I am an environmentalist, but I don't want to be an ostrich with my head in the sand! I want you to interview every expert available regarding this subject. Take Sam Thomas with you. He seemed interested in your arguments. I want only objective evidence. We both need to know the truth."

Matt nodded and tapped Mitchell's shoulder before bounding out of the room.

Spencer's Media Palm rang the moment he entered his office. He answered, "Triumviral Department of Intermodalism, Spencer Mitchell speaking."

"Good day, Mr. Chairman. Congratulations would be in order if it weren't under such depressing circumstances."

"Who's this speaking?"

"Minister Andre Roget."

"Yes, sir! What can I do for you?"

"I was just informed about Chairman Stromberg's bizarre demise. Please accept my condolences; I understand you were the man who tried to save his life. Very commendable, you may be a man I can deal with. Until further notice, I am promoting you to TDI chairman; you will move into Max's office as soon as possible."

"As you wish, sir, and thank you."

"There's no need. If you were Max's right-hand man, then you've earned his old position. Now, I want you to broadcast the latest TDI temperature records from your new office this evening."

"I...I don't understand, sir."

"One of the responsibilities of chairmanship includes speaking as the TDI's figurehead. The Triumviral Environmental Guardians want your report to broadcast all over North America by eight tonight; your new office will be prepared beforehand. Do you have a problem with that?"

"No, sir, it's just I wasn't aware that Max Stromberg ever did TDI broadcasts."

"He didn't. The responsibility begins with you, Mitchell, unless you want someone to do your job."

"No, sir, I'm more than willing to handle the job."

"Splendid! I'll look forward to watching you tonight. Simply read your report word-for-word and the television people will handle the rest; obey their instructions implicitly."

"Certainly, Minister. Any other instructions?"

"You can call me Andre, Mr. Chairman. Have Stromberg's furniture removed immediately, but leave the Chess Roulette Cube where it is. That item stays with the chairmanship; it's such an excellent ice breaker when visitors come to call."

CHAPTER EIGHT

Encounter

Mickey Broderick was twenty-two minutes late. Although not his fault, he'd probably be penalized one way or another. The truck driver sat in his North American Motors *SleeperTrak* waiting for the Atlantic Shellfish Confederacy to get their conveyor platforms moving again. The loading system had shut down when Mickey's double trailer was only three-quarters full. The front section was packed but his rear trailer was only half-loaded. A trio of cargo workers were now playing cards alongside the docks.

Mickey's rig was parked in Stall Number Five. The remaining eleven bays were occupied with local, short-haul pickups upon his arrival; however, each one managed to depart with full loads before the latest break down. Broderick was currently in Hampton, Virginia District. When fully loaded, this shellfish run will eventually take him across the Potomac River into Washington, D.C., the overlapping capital for both the Central Province and the Third Triumvirate itself.

Broderick shuddered at the thought of his beloved United States now being obsolete. North America was completely annexed to the *Planetary Pandect* of the Universal Regions Council and its three bureaucratic subsidiaries: the *Tribune Assembly*, the *Planetary Court*, and the *Martial Protectorate*.

Mickey tapped his steering wheel with both hands before checking his wristwatch; the loading delay was now at thirty minutes. He jumped out of his cab before ambling with boredom toward the loitering workers.

One of the card players asked, "Hey, Long Haul, want to take a hand?"

"No thanks. I've never had much luck with cards."

"You must be happily married then."

"What makes you say that?"

"Because bum luck with cards usually means great luck with love."

Mickey admitted, "I've been married to the same beautiful lady for twenty-seven years."

"I knew it! Another dead giveaway was that you weren't cussing and pacing the docks like a caged lion waiting for those asinine conveyors to start up again. Name's Norman Ramsey, what's yours?"

"Mickey Broderick."

Ramsey abandoned his cards and stood up from the wooden crate he had been squatting on. He stretched out and shook Mickey's hand before answering, "Glad to know you. There's a coffee machine at the other end of the warehouse; it's on me."

"Thanks, don't mind if I do."

The two men walked the interior length of the corrugated iron building. Ramsey shelled out two dollars for his visitor's cup, then vended himself another. Broderick gratefully sipped the steaming beverage.

Ramsey asked, "This delay's costing you some big money, isn't it, Mickey?"

"Not so much me as my company. My only trouble's that it might screw up my next route and I had my sights on a load heading west."

"Are you trying to make it home?"

"I live in Clatskanie, Oregon District."

Ramsey reacted, "Wow! That's almost to the Pacific Coastline! How long you been on the road?"

"About six weeks. When you drive for the only remaining commercial truck company in The United Sta—Central Province, you go home only when they say so."

"Hell of a note, isn't it? Now that the United States is now the *Untied States* and since we're all mixed together with Latins and Canucks, it may even be a longer trip."

Mickey replied, "The Untied States, that's an interesting phrase."

"I picked it up listening to the SOL Radio Network. Have you ever heard of it?"

"No, but it sounds interesting."

Ramsey said, "It's for anyone who questions authority, especially political authority."

"Do you mean our Third Triumvirate or the Universal Regions Council?"

"What difference does it make? All triumvirates relinquish sovereignty when they sign the URC's *Planetary Pandect*. Anyway, The SOL Network runs at 1580 AM around this area; a live show will be on at nine this morning."

Mickey grinned before asking, "You don't belong here, do you?"

"What makes you say that?"

"You seem too experienced and well informed to be content with loading oysters."

Ramsey paused before saying, "I used to be a reporter."

"And a damned good one, I'll wager. What the hell happened?"

"I tangled with the U.S. Department of Intermodalism or *DOI* before the Third Triumvirate annexed it. I'd been working a story on the alleged connection between Frances Snell and the DOI. A reliable source showed me documented proof that the truck company owner was a silent DOI partner."

Mickey took another sip before asking, "What happened?"

"My source and his documentation died suddenly in a hotel fire along with thirty other people. I tried to have my employers at the *Richmond Banner* print the story anyway; I was sacked for my efforts. I spent the next month e-mailing my resume to mainstream media outlets across what's now known as our Central Province, but I'd been blacklisted. I ended up taking this job to survive. So much for freedom of the press, eh?"

"Why did you try to print your story after the fire?"

"I believed our people had a right to know what little information I did have. The fat cats knew I didn't have any proof myself; that's probably the only reason I'm still breathing. Oh well, I'm a busted down dockworker, but at least I'm still alive. That's more than can be said for my barbecued collaborator."

Mickey drained his cup before asking, "Norman, why did you tell me this? You don't know me from Adam. I even drive for Frances Snell's trucking empire."

"I can usually sense a kindred spirit when I meet one, Mickey. Besides, sometimes I feel like I'd go crazy if someone else didn't hear me out!"

"I appreciate that, pal. It's not often I'm given the trust of a total stranger."

"Anytime, trucker. Let's get back to the docks; the delay should almost be over."

"You can approximate how long a breakdown runs?"

Ramsey instructed, "Sure, we average three delays a week at about forty-five minutes a shot."

The conveyers were running again by the time Mickey reopened the back trailer doors and climbed up into his cab. He pulled a cranberry juice bottle out of a small refrigerator before propping both feet on top of an eight-inch square, stainless steel, TransTrak monitoring cube; its metal skin seems to gleam back defiance under his dome light. The device's unblinking, pale-green LCD display remained locked onto the vehicle driver's position. TransTrak's circuits were permanently connected to the speedometer, odometer, transmission, fuel tank, driveshaft, wheel axles, and both vertical exhaust pipes.

Mickey was in command of one of Fraser Provincial's newest trucks: a 2039 SleeperTrak equipped with mandatory TransTrak accessories when it rolled off of the assembly line last year. A lot of Fraser Truckers coveted his rig, but Broderick wasn't very impressed with it. His new truck and trailer had been a bonus to his fifteen-dollar-an-hour pay raise when he received a five-year safety plaque from Fraser Provincial Freightlines. Broderick would have been happier keeping his old Freightliner tractor, but President Snell wouldn't allow that; he'd personally awarded Mickey the plaque. TransTrak's sensor array was permanently uplinked and locked into a solar-powered, geosynchronous, suborbital platform-monitoring system that never deactivated. Fuel consumption, vehicle speed, engine output, lubrication levels, and even tire wear were under twenty-four-hour scrutiny. Mickey felt like a bug in a bell jar whenever he was on the road.

The Atlantic Shellfish Confederacy was five miles behind when he summoned his dispatcher over the TransTrak unit at eight A.M. A pleasant, female voice answered, "Fraser Provincial Dispatch, Cora Sanders speaking. What's the story, Mickey? You're almost an hour late."

"Sorry, doll, the shellfish boys had a delay that cost us forty-five minutes. It looks like I won't be in Washington until eleven A.M. What's the penalty this time?"

"You're lucky today, sweetie; there are currently no excursions scheduled from Washington, D.C., to any point toward the Rockies until two P.M. But you know that our status is always changing."

Broderick answered, "Well, maybe I can bag a West Coast load."

"My board shows we have fifty-seven trucks heading into Washington with ten of them arriving ahead of you. But they've all been driving at least seven hours; none of them will rate another load before eight P.M."

"What about the remaining forty-seven?"

Cora replied, "They're just short hauls that spent last night in their sleepers."

"How many have homes west of the Rockies?"

"Only ten at the moment: Cheyenne, Denver, Santa Fe, Las Vegas, Los Angeles, Salt Lake City, Pocatello, Missoula, Seattle, and an impatient fish hauler who lives in Podunk."

"That's Clatskanie to you, sister."

"What's the difference? I still had to scope out a platform map to locate the stupid place. You live about sixty miles northwest of Portland, Oregon District. Right now, you probably wish that home was closer to Portland, Maine District, instead."

"Not a chance, doll. Oregon's God's Country to me, or was before we got our noses pierced with computer chips."

"Is the proud driver of a new SleeperTrak mashing sour grapes?"

Broderick retorted, "You're just as uncomfortable under TransTrak as I am."

"You're supposed to step on truck pedals and not soapboxes."

"Being a trucker doesn't mean I have to hang my brain on a meat hook."

"Only kidding, sweetie. My board's buzzing. Call me when you've unloaded, bye."

Mickey switched off the speaker before suddenly realizing he hadn't set the cruise control before bantering with Cora. Fear trickled cold sweat between both shoulders as his speedometer read 82 mph; he quickly coasted back to the legal limit of 75. He wondered if a $200 TDI fine notice would be waiting in his home e-mail bin when he finally got home. State Troopers, radar guns, and local speed traps no longer operated within the Central Province. High-speed computers now detected and transmitted traffic violations via the Internet. A citation could already be processing at the local DMV office in St. Helens, Oregon District, which was his home county seat.

Police and Paramilitary patrols combined armed authority on the roads today; one of their many functions was to combat the insurgence of truck piracy that had risen to epidemic proportions within the former United States. The thought of murderous *Blacktop Buccaneers* suddenly stung Mickey with a familiar dread, which catapulted his memory back to a childhood experience at the age of six.

Mickey was the youngest sibling of Roy and Angela Broderick. He had three sisters and an older brother of five years named Alan. As a child, Mickey shared a room with Alan. It wasn't much fun having an older roommate, particularly when Alan played practical jokes on him.

In the summer of 1998, Roy and Angela had taken their children into the Cascade Mountains of Washington State for a weekend campout near some foothills at the base of St. Helens. The family always slept in three separate tents: one for the parents, one for the three girls, and the last one for the Broderick brothers. On the first night, Alan had told Mickey about an eight-foot-tall ape-man who allegedly stalked upright through the Northwest Wilderness and only prowled at night. The regional tribal word for this giant was *Sasquatch*, but the popular vernacular was *Bigfoot.* After Alan finished the story, he promptly went to sleep.

Still scared awake, Mickey's imagination converted every sound into the moonlit, predatory calls of hairy, eight-foot giants. Each time he peeked out the tent flap, the misty, moonlit night gave form to all kinds of evil hairy monsters that seemed to crouch just beyond the perimeter of the Brodericks' camp. Pale, gray light mixing with the moist, black shadows of trees, rocks, and underbrush betrayed the images of advancing ape-men; some were crawling, others slithered noiselessly across the dirt, and some were standing erect beside clusters of timber. The wind rustled while Mickey sobbed just loud enough to awaken his brother.

Alan sat up and broke the silence. "Mick, why the hell are you awake?"

"I think I saw some Bigfoots around our camp. You you think they're hungry enough to eat us all?"

"You're full of shit, runt. I never said that they eat people; they roam around in forests where they're hardly ever seen."

"But that's why they are hardly seen, Alan, I know it. They eat most of the people that see them. That's how they stay hid. I think I saw some of them move closer to Mom and Dad's tent. Can't you hear them?"

Alan scolded, "Cripe, Mick, that's the wind. I'll get my flashlight and prove it."

"No!" croaked Mickey.

"Stifle it, runt. You want to wake up Dad? I made up that story about the Bigfoot; I was just trying to scare you."

Alan found his flashlight and crawled through to the tent entrance before switching it on; the artificial beam overwhelmed the moonlight as it penetrated the swirling mist. Alan led Mickey outside by the hand. The two boys walked into the center of the family camp. Alan beamed his light in every direction, taking care not to shine it into the other tents. All of Mickey's monsters had miraculously transformed into trees, rocks, and underbrush.

Then both boys heard some heavy thumps behind their backs. Mickey's lungs cramped as if punched in the stomach. Alan whirled around, shining his light on their tent. The sound stopped. He whispered, "Mick, I'm turning off our light. I want to see what happens, okay?"

Mickey nodded with a shiver. Both brothers listened in the lunar darkness for the eternity of a full minute. The sound didn't return. Alan walked toward the opposite side of the camp while dragging Mickey along. Then he crouched in front of a boulder while sitting his brother down in some soft weeds.

Alan whispered, "Mick. Do you hear anything?"

"No. Just some wind and the splashy sound of the lake."

The thumping returned but farther away this time. Alan relaxed as the noise grew fainter with occasional popping sounds as if the intruder hadn't bothered concealing its movements any longer. Alan wanted to investigate, but Mickey threatened to wake up Dad if he tried. When they returned to their tent, Mickey insisted on sleeping with his brother. Alan reluctantly zipped both their sleeping bags together before the pair slept the rest of the night through.

Roy got up at dawn and headed toward the edge of Spirit Lake to wash his face and catch the sunrise while Angela started breakfast. Her husband returned ten minutes later and knelt silently beside her. Despite the morning fire, his face was pale.

Angela asked, "Roy, honey, what's wrong?"

"I've always wondered if they were bogeys or real. Now, I'm sorry I know. Angie baby, we're packing out of here right after breakfast. It isn't safe."

"There's nothing out here that's ever given us trouble; besides, you've got a pistol in your gear."

"I know, honey, but we're leaving anyway. We can head for Long Beach and spend our last day there; you and the kids love the seashore anyway."

"Roy, what the Sam Hill's going on?"

"There are bare footprints along Spirit Lake that are twice the size of mine, Angie. They look human. The tracks came from the direction of our camp. Whatever made them was close enough to spit on us last night. We'll break camp as soon as we can. I'm going to check our perimeter."

Angela begged, "Please tell me this is one of your miserable practical jokes."

"Do I look like I'm kidding?"

"Momma, Daddy's not kidding; there was a Bigfoot last night."

The Brodericks whirled around to see their youngest son Mickey fully dressed with matted hair that looked electrified.

Roy knelt down before asking, "What made you say that, son?"

"I heard you talking to Momma about tracks you saw at the lake. Alan and me heard but never saw him. Daddy, did a Bigfoot make those tracks? Do Bigfoots eat people?"

Roy ignored the questions. "Why didn't you boys wake me up last night?"

"Alan said you'd be mad. He said that the noise came from some normal woodsy animal. But it was a Bigfoot, wasn't it, Daddy?"

"Is your brother up?"

"He went down the hill. He said that he wanted to walk down to the lake. He said that it was all right. Bigfoots don't move around in the daytime."

Roy raced into his tent and came out with a pistol. Then he ran toward the lake trail before stopping hard. Alan suddenly came into view while walking toward him.

Roy reached his son before blurting, "Alan! Thank God you're all right, son! What the hell made you go off alone like that?"

"I've gone down to Spirit Lake alone before. You said that it was safe."

"Yes, but you still need permission before traipsing off!"

"Sorry, Dad, I thought I'd be back before you woke up."

Roy escorted Alan back to the campsite where they both sat down by the fire.

Angela picked up two frying pans and handed one to Roy while commanding Mickey to awaken his three sisters. Soon the family packed up their camp after a hot breakfast of scrambled eggs. Mickey's sisters were confused about leaving; their father explained that Momma wanted to see the beach before they went home. Then Roy took point and bypassed his family away from the lake during the hike back to their car. Alan had brought up the rear with little Mickey walking alongside while frequently asking, "Alan, did you see any Bigfoots?" Alan answered silently by constantly looking over his shoulder.

Mickey didn't know whether Bigfoots existed or not. Daddy and Alan were practical jokers and only Daddy claimed to see those footprints. But he also knew that Daddy was still carrying his pistol in plain sight and Daddy never did that before. Mickey gave up asking questions when the family safely reached the car and drove away.

Roy Broderick took the secret of that event to his grave when he died in 2033. So did Alan, who had succumbed to a retroviral infection in 2036; he had been the victim of a newly mutated, airborne virus.

The trucker's mind returned to the present for an incoming TransTrak dispatch. "Broderick here. Did you folks change your mind about my route? Do I have to go somewhere else first before I volley Washington, D.C., with a salvo of shellfish?"

"It's Cora, Mick. I called you because Carl Logan's missing."

"What do you mean missing? Has he been in a wreck or something?"

"I don't think so. His TransTrak box should have transmitted a breakdown. His signal has gone blank as if his unit was disconnected. But that's grounds for termination of employment."

"Where did you track him last?"

"He was in the New Mexico District just outside of Raton. He was heading north to Denver, Colorado District. He had a load for some weather outfit."

Broderick offered, "I'd like to go off line and search for him on my own time."

"Talk sense! You're on the Eastern Seaboard and not within a thousand miles of New Mexico!"

"Right, I only love Carl Logan like a brother; he's only my best friend in the world! Why should I want to help find him?"

"I understand, but getting yourself fired won't help Carl either. He and his rig are classified as missing, not dead. We've got the New Mexico District Police checking out his last position. I'll keep you posted. It may simply be a glitch in our TransTrak system."

"Forget about steering me for home! I want something heading for Denver!"

Cora sighed before answering, "I'll see what I can do."

CHAPTER NINE

Initiation

Mike Parker parked near the White House North Lawn Access Gate. The officer slowly walked out of the shack recording his visitor's license number. Parker rolled down his window as the armed, leather-laced guardian sidestepped around an access barricade and stood alongside the driver's window. "Good afternoon, Mr. Vice President. Welcome to the White House. President Brady's expecting you. Produce your Coherence Card please."

Mike handed over a thin, plastic, credit card-sized, silvery gray wafer. The upper right corner displayed a photograph of his head and upper torso. A holographic image of his right retina was encoded directly below it. The left side bordered a sensor file containing all vital statistics including Parker's medical records and individual DNA. The guard retracted a maroon laser gun opposite his pistol holster before scanning the card.

Parker quipped, "Well, officer, you resemble a two-fisted, pulp western gunslinger."

"Afraid so, sir, but I prefer using this gun; no one ever died from a laser scan. Now, if you would kindly focus both eyes on my uniform badge."

Mike stared blankly until the officer's laser gun butt produced a locked, greenish-yellow, liquid crystal image.

"The match's absolute. You're free to enter, sir."

"You can call me Mike."

"My name's Rick Jackson. I'm glad to know you."

"I'll wager you never thought you'd be packing something resembling a sci-fi sidearm."

"A laser pistol's nothing new to me. Only a non-lethal one is."

"Are you a Marine, Rick?"

"Affirmative. And standing guard here's a hell of a lot better than marching with a Martial Protectorate force."

"I wouldn't know about that; I've never been in military service. Have a good day, Rick."

"Have a safe day, Mike."

The Vice President parked in the White House's north lot while admiring a nearby fountain. Then he peered through the windshield as two armed guards advanced rapidly with a German shepherd leashed between them. Within seconds, a leather-gloved hand knocked on his driver window just before he rolled it down again. A monotone voice issued from between a helmet and visor, "Good morning, Mr. Vice President. Step out of your car please."

Parker quipped, "Am I under arrest?"

"Oh no, sir, all vehicles are routinely searched for explosives. Our four-legged friend's going to inspect your car. Please unlock the hood, all four doors, and your trunk."

Mike obliged before stepping out; his car passed inspection within two minutes before the point guard closed up and rejoined him.

"Please raise your arms, Mr. Vice President. We need to scan you for weapons."

Mike complied with a yawn. Once satisfied, the guard unit departed rapidly. Parker then passed by six armed sentries before stepping through the north White House entrance. A well-groomed woman met him in the hallway. "Good afternoon, Mr. Vice President. My name's Wilma Marsh. I'm President Brady's Executive Secretary. This way, please."

Four of the six entrance sentries bracketed the pair as they penetrated the bowels of the central building, turned right, and then traversed down a long corridor toward the West Wing. The sentries then released their two charges to four other guards flanking the entrance to President Brady's Triad Office.

Parker inspected the sentinels before commenting, "Thanks for the escort, Wilma."

"Have a good day, sir."

Mike watched Wilma take a seat behind her desk as the squad leader announced, "The door's open, Mr. Vice President; you're expected." Parker nodded and stepped across the threshold. A surprise greeted him as the door closes from behind. The room held none of its previous historic paintings, tapestries, sculptures, or a single piece of traditional American furniture. The rape of the former Oval Office appeared complete.

A trio of giant portraits hung from the walls: Alexander the Great riding in the foreground with a vast army stretching behind him; Attila the Hun seated on a stone throne atop a mound of human skulls with a skull and vertebra scepter in his right hand; finally, Napoleon Bonaparte astride a white horse while a nearby squadron of cannons targeted a rural village.

Every window was framed with royal purple drapes while North American President Garth Brady was sitting in red leather behind an oak desk with his back to the office door. He faced a window while talking on a telephone. Parker advanced to the center of the Triad Office to examine a curious, three-foot-square, table height cube with a cluster of chairs surrounding it.

With every other side encased in polished cherry wood, the cube's top surface displayed an exquisite chessboard design of four-inch squares in alternating plates of stainless steel and brass with a two-inch border of cherry wood framing the outside edge. There are also X-shaped grooves running diagonally through the entire length of each board square bisecting in the center. Mike sat down before studying it carefully; the X's gold-colored lines resemble cracks instead of mere decoration.

"Beautiful, isn't it, Mike?"

Parker whirled around to see President Brady standing five feet in front of his desk with both hands folded behind his back.

Garth added, "Good morning, Mr. Vice President. Do you like it?"

"I don't know; all I recognize is the chessboard design."

"It's a gift from Atlanterran President Barry Claude Xavier; he just called to offer personal congratulations and asked if his present had arrived yet."

"That's one hell of a chess table; the gold X's appear to be cracks."

Brady motioned with his hand, "Have a seat, Mike, let's try it out now."

Parker frowned. "Shouldn't we be attending to more important matters?"

"I've got half an hour before my next meeting."

Mike looked around the sides. "I don't see any pieces."

"Sit in the chair opposite me. You'll find a white, dime-sized button along the cube's right side; press it and all the pieces will emerge from twin deposit bins at our feet."

Mike obeyed before retrieving a mixed set of stainless steel and brass chessmen while Garth unloaded his open bins as well. Both twelve-inch-tall kings were seated on magnetic bases emitting a gentle, humming, vibration when placed upright on the metallic board. The tabletop armies were assembled in less than a minute.

Parker moved first pushing his king pawn forward one square. Garth advanced his brass queen's pawn forward two squares. Mike finished placing his king's knight in front of a vacant pawn position when the square suddenly collapsed and dropped the knight through an open trap door; then the square closed again.

Garth laughed. "You jumped like a shot deer! Did you think your knight was going to bite you?"

"What the hell was that?"

"The grooves in each square open and close at random intervals during the game; any piece swallowed up is permanently dead unless you can get a pawn to an opponent's back row to resurrect it. Barry Xavier calls this game Chess Roulette. It adds random attacks to keep each player thinking on his feet. The king bases are magnetized to prevent their squares from collapsing under them; the vibration comes from an internal power cell that increases the magnetism when the base contacts the board. After all, chess can't be played without kings."

The square below Garth's queen's rook suddenly devoured his piece.

Mike blurted, "This game's excellent; it should never play the same way twice!"

Several minutes later, Parker was still commanding one queen, two bishops, a rook, and three pawns surrounding his unmoved king. Brady's army had dwindled to his king, a single knight, and five pawns; the last four trap doors had claimed his queen, one pawn, and both bishops. The President finally surrendered when the Vice President captured his remaining knight with a tandem bishop assault. Parker stood up raising both his hands in victory just as the square beneath his queen suddenly banished her to a trapdoor purgatory. Both executives howled with laughter while storing the chessmen away again.

Brady returned to his desk, motioned Mike to sit in one of the visitor's chairs, and announced, "Chairman Spencer Mitchell of the Triumviral Department of Intermodalism is my next appointment. I'd like you to stay and meet him."

Mike nodded as Wilma Marsh contacted Brady's Media Palm. The president answered, "Yes, Wilma?"

"TDI Chairman Mitchell's here, sir."

"Thank you, Wilma; please send him through."

Mitchell stepped inside carrying a black leather briefcase. President Brady met the chairman halfway before vigorously shaking his hand. "Good morning, Chairman Mitchell. The Minister of Travel informs me we have a serious problem on our hands."

"Yes, Mr. President."

"By the way, meet Vice President Mike Parker. I wanted him to hear this too."

Mitchell extended and shook Parker's hand before all three men sat down around the Triad Desk like equal points of a triangle.

Garth asked, "What's the bottom line on your global warming field report?"

Spencer opened his briefcase, gave both executives a copy, and allowed them some time to ponder the data.

Three minutes later, President Brady lamented, "It does look bad. Are you positive about this three-degree rise in the summary?"

"Absolutely, Mr. President. It's our contention that our Third Triumvirate be subjected to stricter transportation controls. We just can't keep pumping carbon dioxide into our atmosphere at the present rate. If we do, we'll barbecue ourselves in less than two decades."

Garth said somberly, "It looks very thorough. What do you think, Mike?"

"I am contemplating the future horror a global heat wave might spawn twenty years from now. It isn't a pretty sight."

Then Brady blustered, "That's why immediate and drastic action must be done! I'm delivering an emergency address at nine tonight. It will be a triumviral wide broadcast. Spencer, your staff will provide a workable set of proposals I can announce over the air."

The chairman stood up and grabbed his briefcase before answering, "We'll have them ready by eight tonight, Mr. President." He quickly walked out of the office.

Mike remained seated while Garth paced around the game cube with folded arms. Thirty seconds of dead silence ensued before the President shattered it. "Do you think I acted impulsively?"

"It's your prerogative to institute any executive order you wish provided it doesn't violate URC authority."

Brady barked, "Blast it, man! You're better than that weak-ass answer!"

"Okay. You pride yourself as an environmentalist and yet you took that upstart's word at face value. Why?"

"By feigning urgency, I lit a fire under Chairman Mitchell's ass for pertinent information."

Parker propped both hands against his sides, "Shrewd move, chief, but why tonight's broadcast? If you suspect this report's biased, why would you immediately address our public with it?"

"I didn't say this report's necessarily biased, Mike. I merely suspect its accuracy because researchers and recorders can make mistakes. If the data's correct, we have a big problem. If the results prove subjective, then no harm's been done."

The President removed a presidential Media Palm from his vest pocket and touched its screen; his secretary replied, "Yes, Mr. President?"

"Wilma, I want a visual conference call with all of the municipal temperature research authorities from all three provinces; I want them to produce average temperature readings from North America's coastlines, all continental mountain ranges, the Great Lakes, and the Gulf of Mexico for good measure. Include the chairmen of all three triumviral television networks too. I'll preside over this conference in my office at five this evening. Do you have all of that?"

"I'll arrange it immediately."

"Excellent, my dear! Now, the Vice President and I are taking a personal tour of the White House; I'll be back in my office by four P.M."

Parker was flabbergasted while asking, "Garth, are you sure you didn't let me win that Chess Roulette game earlier? You manipulated Chairman Mitchell masterfully; Machiavelli would have been proud."

Brady chuckled. "Unkind! I would have appreciated a more dignified comparison than to the man who preached Divide and Conquer!"

"I thought Divide and Conquer was appropriate considering the infamous portraits currently haunting your office walls!"

Garth eyed the portraits before retorting, "Infamous? Why?"

"Because all three men were ruthless conquerors."

"I hung those portraits because they're the favorites from my collection. I love the magnificent styles in which they were painted. Besides, seeing fearsome historical figures might inspire my visitors not to embark on policies that would encourage such tyrants back into power."

"As long as it doesn't induce fear about what you might do!"

"Forcing feelings into the open only strengthens people's understanding; that helps us avoid wars. Besides, you know nothing gives me greater pleasure than testing the mettle of my fellow man."

"What about my mettle, Garth?"

"You passed. Now, let's get out of here. I have something else to show you."

The President escorted his partner out of the Triad Office and onto a nearby elevator. He confided as the cubicle descended, "We're headed to the basement. My office isn't the only command center around here."

Garth extracted his Coherence Card from a breast pocket and pressed a green button on the elevator control panel; an emerald laser beam suddenly activated three feet above the floor. The President crouched down on the pads of both feet. He brought his right eye in level contact with the laser until a red indicator flashed. Then Brady placed his card up to the monitor to confirm a match. All panel lights went out as the elevator moved steadily downward for several seconds before opening.

The President led his partner into an immense, fifty-foot-wide, octagonal room. Mike couldn't believe his eyes. Each wall mounted twelve titanic, visual monitors displaying infrared, ultraviolet, visible and spectroscopic suborbital platform images; multiple communication uplinks; and banks of automated computer printers with perpetual surveillance capability for not only North America but the rest of the world.

Garth sat his partner down in one of a dozen chairs positioned in the center of the room before walking to the nearest computer terminal, picking up a black plastic remote control unit, and sitting down beside his partner. Then Brady pointed his remote toward alternating groups of wall monitors all over the room. Each targeted monitor rapidly changed images while collectively displaying scientific data collectors; foreign news broadcasts; and surveillances of The New York, Tokyo,

Hong Kong and Rome Stock Exchanges, along with telescopic images of star groups flashing across the walls.

Suddenly Garth turned off the other wall monitors, leaving the largest rectangular screen on in front of them; it locked onto the image of a transport truck towing twin cargo trailers. The rig was pulling a steep grade. A magnified picture revealed the license plate number. Brady pressed another button and the location of the rolling transport was digitally transposed over the original image. It read *Fraser Freight number 547 Southbound on Interdistrict 25; departed Denver, Colorado District at 9:30 A.M., Mountain Time. Vehicle en route to Pueblo, Colorado District. ETA 11:45 P.M., Mountain Time; present speed holding at 26 mph; current exhaust emission remains nominal. TransTrak compliance reveals no citations pending.*

Then the President encoded another remote sequence. The central monitor scanned the files of the Triumviral Department of Meteorology and immediately collated average temperature records for the Central Province's one hundred largest cities into seasonal lists. When the readout yielded a printed hard copy, Brady retrieved it, sat down again, and dropped the data in Parker's lap.

Finally, Garth produced the image and sound of a TDI meeting in progress. Chairman Mitchell was speaking, "Gentlemen, our new taskmaster from the Triad Office has issued his first commandment. We are to gather up all modified TransTrak proposals. I want a concise, workable list of directives on my desk by six tonight. I realize most of our proposals are already in print, but I want them to be updated for tonight. Vice Chairman Matthew Rigby and Inspector Sam Thomas are not available to assist; they're on a special TDI mission. I hope our presidential puppet appreciates these proposals; his support should put the neck of the North American Motorist under our boot heel permanently."

Brady turned off the surveillance monitor before boasting, "I have access to information generated anywhere in the world by computer, microwave, laser, telephone, radio, television, or even closed circuit camera transmissions. I guess that makes me one of the most powerful hackers on Spaceship Earth. I can track any registered vehicle in the Central Province. I can eavesdrop on any triumviral bureaucracy and any closed circuit television whose access code I have on file. We'll be able to decipher the TDI's annual data now, eh, Mike?"

Parker bellowed, "What gives you the authority to spy on private citizens? How long has this electronic bullshit been operating? I had no idea TransTrak was a sub-orbiting terrorist extorting citation money from motorists for violating arbitrary transportation regulations. Do our people know they're under your microscope?"

The President threw the remote across the room before standing up and yelling, "Don't be so goddamned self-righteous! You sound like one of those moronic Hebrew prophets who warned ancient Israel about the penalties of disobeying a god they couldn't even see! Do you really believe that a majority vote implements genuine reforms? Visionaries who understand their enemies are the pioneers who come out on top! How else could a government direct the destiny of its people? You think North America will progress because six hundred million people participated in an automatic, electronic, presidential popularity poll?

"This is 2040, Parker! Technology's here to stay! Besides, this facility has been here since 2017! Do you still believe governments are supposed to function according to the dictates of uneducated rabble instead of sophisticated and dedicated people who can help mankind progress despite the masses?"

Mike yelled back, "Judas Priest, Garth! You sound like the goddamned collectivists! Only the elite should be in charge, otherwise nothing important gets done? That's a load of rancid bullshit! Absolute power would corrupt the Virgin Mary herself! You can't be serious about this elitist brand of reform you're spitting in my face! What you're defending is feudalism with our people as compulsive serfs!"

Brady's Mars-colored flush of anger suddenly drained away. He drew a long breath before confessing, "I'm not an elite advocate. I was engaged in the childish act of striking back at the attacks of a close friend; your condemnation hurt me deeply. I do believe in the private freedoms of men and women as long as their exercise of that freedom doesn't jeopardize society. Forgive me, Mike."

Parker cooled off. "I'm sorry too. I realize you didn't build this monstrosity. It's just I never wanted to believe such complete surveillance was possible. I just found out the fictional horrors of George Orwell's Big Brother are now scientific facts of life. Are you sure this device is necessary?"

"This system informed us the TDI bureaucrats have been clenching at the bit to expand their power. Also Chairman Mitchell referred to me as a puppet."

"I'm afraid you're right, Garth. If this station has been in existence for twenty-three years, then our enemies must possess it as well. God knows how many other places in the world it's functioning."

Brady smiled weakly. "Technological secrets are the most fleeting of all. We can't be guessing what our adversaries might be doing; the world has become too small for isolation. Our citizens look to us for protection and leadership; surveillance remains a necessary evil in the Information Age. We must monitor both friends and enemies."

"You mean the Surveillance Age now, don't you? I wish you hadn't showed me this, Garth. When did you find out about it?"

"Last night, after I drove all the way from your place at two A.M. I was too excited to sleep when I entered the Triad Office and found none of my furniture had arrived yet. I was daydreaming about redecoration when my quartet of bodyguards entered the room unannounced with former United States President Warren Miller. I was immediately informed that it was time for me to accept his top secret, presidential authority; he seemed most eager to relinquish it."

"Warren Miller was waiting in the White House for you?"

"Yes, the whole thing seemed damn bizarre until I realized what was happening. Miller cleared the Triad Office of guards and showed me a floor safe under the carpet; he had me stare into a green laser below the safe's tumbler while he manipulated a numeric code on its facial keypad. Then the safe opened and he acquainted me with its contents: there were executive, military, financial codebooks, and information about this Scansat Station."

"This *what?*"

"This room's called a Scansat Station, which is short for *Suborbital Scanner Satellite Station.*"

Parker replied, "I'm surprised you granted me access, Garth. This station's probably more top secret than your floor safe. But surely you can't maintain this station alone."

"This station does have assigned personnel, but only when they're needed. I wanted us to be alone when I brought you here because you're not only the Vice President, you're my best friend. I felt that the responsibility for this surveillance station would be easier for me to bear if you were aware of it too."

"I'll wager the URC would be pissed off if they found out you brought me here."

"Probably, but sharing this responsibility will help me sleep at night. Let's go get some lunch; you've seen enough for one day."

Max Stromberg's autopsy began. Dr. Quentin Black started an inch above the brow line while operating a pneumatic saw to penetrate the bone; he sliced a lateral incision around the cranium's circumference. He severed the brain stem and unsheathed the entire organ from Stromberg's truncated skull. The absence of fluid between the brain and the inner skull was puzzling. Then he precisely dissected the medulla, cerebellum, key areas of the cerebrum, the hypothalamus, and finally the pituitary gland. Dr. Charles Edmonds stood in attendance and observed in disbelief as every section of tissue displayed massive trauma from severe dehydration.

Edmonds muttered, "What in the name of epilepsy's going on?"

Black replied, "This isn't the aftermath of any Grand Mal Seizure I've ever seen. What made you ask that?"

"An eyewitness observed violent muscular convulsions during the time of this man's death. I've examined his medical history file. He never suffered from seizures; in fact, he was a triathlete."

"Epilepsy doesn't barbecue the brain, Charles. Look at this man's tissue; it's as though it was microwaved from the inside out. The subject's pituitary gland, which controls adrenal and endocrine functions, looks to have ruptured from over-stimulation. The hypothalamus, which regulates the body's temperature, has literally exploded. This triathlete must have broken the world's record for bodily temperature before he died."

Edmonds crossed both arms. "Thanks for the refresher course in brain anatomy, Quentin."

"Sorry, Charles, I'm used to dumbing things down for the police."

"Forget it, Mr. Wizard, let's get on with it."

Black smiled weakly before continuing, "I'll wager the pancreas, thyroid, and adrenal glands were forced into collapse as well. Let's proceed to the chest cavity."

Max Stromberg's rib cage was bisected at the sternum and pried open to reveal a heart devoid of external fat, but the coronary arteries and veins along its outer walls were ruptured in a dozen different places. Then Dr. Black severed the septum and bisected the heart. The right ventricle was abnormally strained, the inner walls were expanded and torn, and the valve to the atrium has ruptured.

Quentin glanced over at Charles, who shrugged both shoulders without making a sound. The coroner speculated, "Judging by the valve and ventricular damage and a par boiled brain, I would suspect this man was the victim of some super rheumatic fever."

"You took a throat culture, blood, and urine tests before dissecting; there wasn't any indication of infection. This man didn't have any scar tissue in his heart; the damage was fresh. He didn't have any history of rheumatic fever either. It looks as though he literally burned himself up with some weird type of metabolic overload. The victim's brain dried out. The heart muscle's stretched like an overinflated balloon. There are ruptured veins, arteries, and capillaries all over the body. What the hell's going on here?"

"Let's check out the lungs. You told me this man was a smoker."

Dr. Edmonds answered, "He was a stogie puffer, Quentin! He never inhaled!"

Black resumed the dissection in silence. Both sections of the bronchus revealed a plethora of ruptures, along with tears in hundreds of bronchial tubes and alveoli. The diaphragm was pock marked with rips. There was no surfactant fluid remaining and the lobes of the lungs were dehydrated as well.

"Mother of God," whispered Dr. Black. "What?"

"Could this stiff have inhaled any biological weapons where he was?"

Charles replied, "He was in a government building in the heart of Washington, D.C. He was the chairman of the Triumviral Department of Intermodalism. He was also with a dozen other men who didn't suffer any ailments. Besides, the blood and urine analysis revealed no narcotics, alcohol, medications, or toxic chemicals besides traces of caffeine and nicotine."

The coroner paused before adding, "However, I didn't examine this man for nerve toxins."

"He wasn't alone, Quentin! Forget the covert war games scenario, will you? There has to be another reason why this man's dead. Keep pushing that knife!"

Edmonds helped Black remove both kidneys; they were ruptured. The adrenal glands are also dehydrated. "Blast it!" barked Edmonds. "What new kind of medical threat's floating free out there?"

Dr. Black theorized, "You've dismissed my nerve gas scenario. What nightmare are you conjuring up now, Charles? This man looks as if he died from some type of metabolic overdose, which wore out all the vital organs simultaneously. This death is weird, but I'll wager it's probably from natural causes."

"Natural causes, my ass! Something threw this man's body into hyper drive and vapor locked it almost to the burning point! And I'm running it down if it's the last thing I do!"

"You're not a licensed coroner, Charles. I'll have to report this."

"Don't pull rank on me, Chum! Just because you're giving up doesn't mean I have to. I'm going to pinpoint this meatloaf's cause of death if it's humanly possible!"

"Very well, Doctor Edmonds, I wash my hands of the whole damn thing. You have until tomorrow morning. Lock up when you leave, but I still have the last word on the death certificate, got it?"

"Fair enough, Doctor Black. If I find anything, I'll leave it on your computer. Don't worry, I won't sign a thing. I'll make sure you get the proper credit."

Quentin replied, "I just don't want malpractice trouble from sue-happy relatives. Goodnight!"

Dr. Edmonds spent the next two hours checking and rechecking blood, urine, mucus and various tissue samples from every ruptured area; no foreign substance was detected.

Charles reluctantly stopped his futile examination at eleven P.M. and typed out a disgruntled capitulation on his colleague's computer monitor: *Quentin - Examined all major organs and fluid samples again - Results negative on foreign substance hypothesis - You win - Death was by natural causes.*

Edmonds' mind was still in a whirl as he departed the morgue. He walked briskly toward his car while his footsteps echoed loudly off the concrete of the basement parking garage.

Charles grasped his door handle before being pierced in the back of his neck. The doctor's brain stem seized in white-hot agony as a roiling wave of nausea swept across his abdomen while spilling stomach acid into his esophagus. The cement floor pitched and yawed in front of his swimming eyes as his inner ear cramped with paralysis. Voluntary muscles went numb as he fell violently forward. Edmonds' eyes locked open as his face bounced off of the cement; the oozing blood from a dozen facial abrasions and a shattered nose began matting into his trimmed brown beard.

Charles stared through lacerated corneas as the assailants turned his motionless body face up. He unblinkingly saw three dark silhouettes shimmering under the ceiling lights. Edmonds sensed a powerful hand removing the steel dart whose venom had frozen his muscles, heart, and lungs. The dying doctor's starving brain soaked in suffocating horror while his impending murderers tossed his rigid body into the trunk of an idling Lincoln Continental.

Three Protectorate agents were soon driving after their freshly executed assignment. Senior Agent Moses Richmond sat to the right of the driver and affectionately caressed the emptied dart between his right thumb and forefinger. Then he received a call from his hand-held Media Palm.

"This is Scansat Eleven, please enter personal number code."

Moses touched the palm screen. A few seconds later, his wait was rewarded.

"Code verified. Go ahead, Mose."

"Inform Commissioner Quimby our assignment was successful. The good Dr. Edmonds will never get the chance to dispute another autopsy. His body's in our possession and we're traveling to the drop site per previous instructions. We will be dumping him at Piscataway Park within forty minutes."

"Commissioner Quimby's already aware of your mission status; he's been monitoring Dr. Edmonds since the start of the autopsy. Max Stromberg was our first test subject; the results are most encouraging.

"What's our next assignment after this garbage run?"

Eleven relayed, "Return to the White House and resume presidential observation."

"Acknowledged, Richmond out."

CHAPTER TEN

Lesson

Officer Rick Jackson raised the gate while recognizing Victor DeSalle's massive, silver Rolls Royce. His titanic, baldheaded, black chauffeur was unmistakable as the old man's private taxi stopped smoothly near the standing guard.

Jackson remained silent, remembering the President's personal briefing regarding any visit from Victor DeSalle: *No* Coherence Card scan, *no* license plate check, *no* log in of the visit, *no* explosive inspection, *no* personal pat down for either DeSalle or anyone in his company, and finally, there'd be *no* disobedience toward any order issued by this eighty-eight-year-old VIP. Rick bowed as the chauffeur opened his driver and left passenger windows at the same time.

DeSalle initiated, "Good morning, officer. I thought I'd come in and chew some fat with Garth for a while. Is he in?"

"Yes sir, Mr. DeSalle. He's been up since seven A.M."

"Our new world leader seems industrious. Is he alone?"

"No sir, the vice president's with him; he arrived at 12:20 "

"It seems both of our new executives want to hit the ground running. Are there any other visitors currently within the White House? I wouldn't want to horn in on some scheduled meetings."

"No sir. TDI Chairman Spencer Mitchell arrived at one P.M. and left by 1:25."

"It seems I won't be disturbing the President's calendar after all. Good-bye."

"Good-bye, Mr. DeSalle. I hope that you're having a good day."

"It may turn out better later on. Let's roll, Milton."

The chauffer acknowledged with a nod.

At the north White House entrance, the bald, black, 450-pound chauffer stepped out and stood beside the left passenger door. Victor lounged in the back while dominating a transatlantic conversation with Atlanterran President Barry Claude Xavier, who listened from his First Triumviral Capitol of Rome, Italy District. The old man continued, "Look Barry! I don't give a flying damn what your schedule is. I want you here to meet with Garth as soon as possible!"

"But I've already made plans to see him next month."

"That won't cut it, Buster! Today's Thursday and you'll be here no later than Friday noon!"

"Yes, Mr. Chairman. I suppose Walter Mallory can handle things while I'm gone. However, it's a very sensitive time for our First Triumvirate. I feel we're getting ready to annex Greater Africa, but Walter's a good man."

DeSalle barked, "I don't want Vice President Mallory to handle anything while you're away; I don't trust him anymore than Mike Parker! Why did you boys insist on choosing running mates outside of the Cupola in the first place? I was against it from the start and won't relax until I'm certain both Parker and Mallory are team players!"

"Please don't distress yourself, Mr. Chairman. Before any triumviral elections, you agreed that all of the presidents should pick running mates outside of the inner circle. We still had powerful dissenters in our own political alliances that would suspect a coup if every candidate emerged exclusively from well-known, international, dynastic families. It was the only way to appease our enemies long enough for the URC to establish our initial triumvirates. Atlanterra, Indoasia, and now North America are finally locked in. What trouble could Parker or Mallory cause? They are not in power and none of the current triumviral presidents will ever be assassinated."

Victor's voice cracked. "Listen to me, Upstart. I *am* the Cupola! My vote carries the lion's share of the others! What I say goes, period! I reluctantly agreed to have foreign running mates only after our flag officers pleaded your case! But remember this: anything the Cupola creates it can also destroy! Don't you ever patronize me again, Xavier! The Cupola assassinates targets based on expediency and not bloodline. You watch your step, my friend, or you're expediency rating's going to soar!"

"I ask forgiveness, Mr. Chairman. I forgot my place. I have no excuse except that I instinctively wanted to defend Walter. I humbly implore you to consider giving both vice presidents the benefit of the doubt until you're satisfied of their status."

DeSalle smirked with deep-seated crow's feet. "Apology accepted, President Xavier. You may call me Victor. I understand your concern, but don't anger me again. I assure you, the Cupola will not take action as long as you're running mates remain team players; a silent man is a secure man. Now, did Garth receive the Chess Roulette Cube you sent him?"

"Yes, Victor, I talked with him this afternoon. Garth said he would initiate Mike Parker as soon as possible."

"Excellent, Barry! I'm feeling better about North America's vice president already! When are you going to initiate Mallory in Rome? He's stalled long enough!"

"Walter doesn't know how to play. We've been using ordinary chess games to indoctrinate him."

DeSalle's smile sagged. "What do you mean *we?*"

"Three of my ministers have been encouraging him. They told Walter that it would please me immensely. But Walter refuses to play Chess Roulette until he feels he's ready."

"See that he plays soon, Barry. Then I'll feel better about Walter Mallory too. Good-bye."

The old man snapped his fingers while tucking his Media Palm back into a vest pocket; the passenger door opened immediately. Victor stepped slowly out of the car and braced himself on an intricate, antique, ivory cane. Milton remained motionless alongside the open door while scanning his gaze in all directions.

DeSalle toddled through the north White House entrance door while Milton remained at the limousine. Then Victor shuffled along a familiar pathway without any escort before stopping to rest upon one of the hall sofas. He lingered ten minutes before nodding off to sleep.

Garth and Mike were alone in the Regional Dining Room. President Brady enjoyed Fillet Mignon and a broiled lobster tail in garlic butter, a baked Idaho District potato smothered with sour cream and chives, and a Caesar salad freshly dusted with ground pepper. His partner had a small chef salad along with a ham and cheese sandwich.

Both executives returned to the Triad Office by 2:30 P.M. Brady immediately insisted on another game of Chess Roulette. Parker agreed before selecting his brass army. The randomness of the game continually amazed them. The first eight minutes passed without a single square opening. Then Garth moved to capture a jeopardized knight with his queen's bishop, only to see his target drop down the first trapdoor of the match.

The next three ambushes opened under vacant squares before Garth pushed one knight to line up with his other knight when the Triad Office door opened. The President looked up and instinctively cringed; he wasn't expecting Victor DeSalle today. Mike puzzled over a visitor admitted without any announcement as President Brady stood and bowed to the old man before gesturing him toward a game table guest chair. DeSalle obliged.

Parker studied DeSalle's ivory cane. It displayed a spiraling serpent entwined around the trunk of a naked woman's torso. Intricate details of the carving seemed sublime and grotesque at the same time. The serpent's eyes were twin blood rubies reflecting an almost hypnotic luster.

Garth started the introductions. "Vice President Michael Parker, may I present my grandfather, Mr. Victor DeSalle."

Mike rose while offering his hand.

DeSalle refused while resting his upon the cane. "Forgive me, Mr. Vice President, but I never shake hands."

Parker sat back down and inquired, "Mr. DeSalle, do you play chess?"

"I never indulge, but I enjoy watching. Don't stop on my account."

Mike watched his king's rook pawn collapse from a trapdoor ambush. Then Parker castled with his king's rook, which had suddenly lost pawn protection. DeSalle cleared his throat. Parker ignored him. Garth positioned his king's knight behind an advanced pawn; a trap door swallowed the pawn.

Then Mike captured the naked knight with his brass queen. Garth withdrew his king's bishop two squares backward to interpose between his king and the enemy bitch. DeSalle coughed mildly. Garth tightened his jaw. Parker moved a bishop to threaten Garth's queen beside her king's left flank. Three squares opened at once, simultaneously plunging both queens and Mike's remaining rook out of sight. Then Garth checked Mike's defenseless king with a rook.

Parker gasped as the magnetic king suddenly locked his grip in a painful, electric shock. He desperately leveraged his left foot against the cube before eventually falling backward over his chair. The momentum launched the magnetic king back over his head.

The old man remained motionless while Brady rushed to his friend and screeching, "Oh my God! Mike, are you all right?"

Parker slowly stood up and reset his upended chair before exclaiming, "Hot damn! Now I know what a wall socket feels like! What the hell happened?"

Garth blurted, "Damned if I know! That game must be defective. The trap door motor must have shorted, giving your king some nasty amperage! You sure you're all right?"

"I'll live, but where's the king?"

Brady pointed a finger behind Parker and yelled, "Satan's Scimitar!"

All three men beheld Napoleon's horse with the renegade chessman impaled in its backside. Mike howled with laughter as Garth watched his grandfather.

DeSalle clacked his false teeth while nearly hissing, "Moloch's Mud Whore! That painting's been in my family for the last century! I gave it to Garth when he became a U.S. Senator! Get that goddamned toy out of Melange's ass! Goddamnit, Parker, I said move!"

Suddenly Victor wheezed like a punctured bellows before coughing uncontrollably while spewing lemon yellow phlegm. Garth caught the old man as he slumped in his chair while wiping DeSalle's mouth with a pocket-handkerchief; Victor's head bobbed with each racking cough.

Parker opened his vest Media Palm before contacting Wilma Marsh. The secretary answered. "Yes?"

"This is Mike Parker. Get the White House Medical Unit in the Triad Office right away. Victor DeSalle's having some kind of congestive seizure. Have those doctors haul ass!"

Within seconds, five white smocked medics entered and laid the old man on a canvas cot. One medic injected a leathery left arm while another strapped an oxygen mask under DeSalle's eyes. The chairman's spasms relaxed and he was resting easy within sixty seconds of their arrival.

Mike gingerly removed the chess king from Napoleon's portrait and cleared the board again while DeSalle sat up and pulled off his mask before slowly propping up to a stand on his ivory cane. He snapped his fingers; the emergency team departed.

Victor now shuffled to his grandson, who had buried his face in both hands. DeSalle raised Brady's head up by the chin and assured, "It's all right, Garth. I've just endured a chronic condition that's plagued me for the last five years. The phlegm and coughs look and sound worse than they actually are."

"It just hit me that you won't always be around, Grandfather. What am I ever going to do if I lose you?"

"I'm not dying for a long time yet." DeSalle managed a wrinkled smile. "I never do anything without planning ahead."

Mike lamented, "Mister DeSalle, I'm truly sorry about defacing a family heirloom. I will gladly pay for any repair work."

"That's not necessary, my boy, and anyone who witnesses my ailment is entitled to call me Victor."

"Mike."

"Thank you. Mike, it is."

Parker asked quietly, "Would you like to be alone with your grandson?"

"That might be a good idea. It's bad for morale to see the President of North America this vulnerable. He and I need some quality time. I'll contact his secretary when we're finished. Good-bye."

Parker nodded before leaving the Triad Office.

Garth stood up and informed Wilma not to disturb him until further notice. Then he pressed a dime-sized button on the inside drawer of his desk. The Triad Office door immediately locked while every window sealed with steel shutters and an electromagnetic scrambler neutralized any electronic surveillance capability within.

Brady sat along one corner of his desk, crossed both arms, and smugly commented, "I think our charade went off pretty well, Grandfather. Mike's *metabolic signature* should've been filed. But I didn't expect such a nasty power surge. Chess Roulette's supposed to massage the hand of the target, not electrocute it. By the way, you didn't startle when Mike got blasted with that abnormal shock."

"I was struggling to maintain control after ingesting my expectorant earlier; it was manageable until the portrait was impaled. But Parker sure made you jump."

"Barry never said a word about any possible injury risks. Maybe Chess Roulette's too dangerous to operate. Our targets aren't supposed to be assassinated when we add their signatures to our metabolic files."

"Chess Roulette's potential more than justifies the risks."

"Your performance was convincing, Grandfather, but wasn't that risky as well?"

DeSalle sat down before suddenly throwing his cane over the President's head while snarling, "Watch your mouth, Garth! You're no longer speaking from a secure position! The president of North

America is only one of many puppets the Crimson Cupola dangles in front of global rabble for diversion like a mobile above an infant's crib!"

"Forgive me, Grandfather, I meant no disrespect. I love you."

"Moloch's Mud Whore, boy! Let's get down to the real reason I'm here!"

Brady furrowed both eyebrows. "I assumed you were here to size up Parker."

"Although you knew I would test him the first time we met, you didn't know I was coming today. My real purpose was to reprimand your conduct in the basement this afternoon. I'm very disappointed in you."

The President grew pale while slinking into his chair like a dog eyeing a rolled newspaper. He trembled while bracing both arms against his desktop.

DeSalle continued, "You weren't given the clearance to allow a potential enemy admittance to a Scansat Station! Now Mike Parker knows all about them!"

"Grandfather, how did you know about that? I thought Scansat Station interiors were immune to outside surveillance."

"Behemoth's Belly, boy! Save such rancid piles of rumor and propaganda to condition the moronic serfs who slave for us worldwide! Only Cupola flag officers remain exempt from surveillance; that's the reason you won't be punished for scrambling this office right now! However, if you try to use your scrambler without authorization again, I'll make you the guest of honor at one of Sebastian's charcoal roasts! I'm beginning to wonder if we made a mistake choosing you to figurehead the Third Triumvirate. I thought you were loyal to the CC's destiny."

Brady grew pale and said, "I am loyal, Grandfather, I just wanted someone else to see how truly powerful I was. It was a moment of vain glory; it won't happen again."

DeSalle ambled behind the President's chair, raised his cane, and savagely bludgeoned his grandson five times across both shoulders while Brady silently endured. Then Victor sat down while nearly screaming, "That's strike one, Garth! Mike Parker's heir to the Parker Oil Fortune!

His family's current holdings are worth over $10 billion! It's hard to believe the Parkers acquired that much money honestly without leeching dividends from the Federal Reserve Bank of New York! Blast it! I should've had Sebastian peel that bitch Irene Tupik for exposing our Federal Reserve System; it served us well for over a century! I wish we'd possessed the Chess Roulette five years ago! Tupik's family wouldn't have even suspected her murder by natural causes!"

Chairman DeSalle calmed his voice. "I protested Tupik's appointment to your cabinet, but you curried a flag officer majority to apply pressure until I finally agreed. I'm sorry for that! The rest of your ministers seem like morally obedient serfs except possibly for Williams and Martinez; I haven't decided about them yet. But Parker and Tupik openly question authority. The most dangerous human beings that walk the earth are people who think for themselves!"

Brady listened while throbbing daggers of pain raked both collarbones.

Victor resumed, "Remember, Garth, three strikes and you're out permanently."

The President rose up and knelt to his seated dictator before bowing his head. "Chairman DeSalle, I repent of my error. What are your requirements for restitution? If you wish, Mike Parker will die immediately."

DeSalle replied while smiling with receded gums, "Parker's death may not be necessary; he displayed genuine humility toward me today. Besides, the Chess Roulette has initiated Mike's signature into our metabolic files. The human body is like a radio transmitter and the CC can receive and jam those codes anytime we choose. There's no place on earth he can hide from our Scansats.

"Now, my boy, I am giving another chance to prove your loyalty once again. We listened to your meeting with Mitchell today and you will endorse and implement the TDI's TransTrak upgrades on triumviral television tonight. TransTrak will soon control all of the motorists on this continent and not just the commercial boys. You'll expedite your initial triumviral order to fully fund TransTrak."

Garth cleaned his own blood off his grandfather's cane with a pocket-handkerchief and replied, "Yes, Grandfather."

"That's my boy! Alexander the Great, the Roman Empire, Genghis Khan, the Holy Roman Empire, Adam Weishaupt, Napoleon, Abraham Lincoln, Albert Pike, Woodrow Wilson, the League of Nations, Winston Churchill, Franklin Roosevelt, Joseph Stalin, Mao Tse Tung, and the United Nations would've all split themselves with envy over the Crimson Cupola's present accomplishments! But that's nothing compared to what *we* will do!"

CHAPTER ELEVEN

NACAM

Richard and Carmen Franklin snuggled naked beneath a wool, calico quilt along their living room sofa after some intense, newlywed passion. Ravenous with hunger, Carmen got up to prepare them a quick meal. Richard remotely activated their HoloTel mounted in the center of the room. He watched a documentary on South American snakes for a few minutes before the image and sound suddenly faded.

A rapid scan of several different channels produced the same results. Then a solid blue, cylindrical background emerged between the HoloTel floor and ceiling projectors with a bold, white text message accompanied by a loud voice:

THIS IS A TRIUMVIRAL EMERGENCY BROADCAST. PLEASE STANDBY FOR A PRESIDENTIAL ADDRESS.

"Carmen, sugar!" hollered her husband, "you better come and see this. It looks like Garth's delivering an emergency announcement."

The minister of enforcement came out of her kitchen holding four bologna and cheese sandwiches on a plate in one hand and a chilled carton of milk plus two empty glasses in the other. The amorous shine in her eyes was suddenly gone. She handed Richard the plate before placing everything else on the coffee table in front of the sofa.

Their grandfather clock chimed nine times before the broadcaster continued, "We interrupt all other programs for an emergency announcement: The Third Triumvirate has suffered an environmental catastrophe. President Garth Brady and Vice President Michael Parker have been in emergency session with advisors from the Triumviral Environmental Guardians and the Triumviral Department of Intermodalism. Our President expects to address both the press and the North American people from the Rostrum within the west wing of The White House. Please stand by."

Richard held a sandwich in one hand while holding his wife's palm with the other.

Turning a stony face to her mate, Carmen asked, "Richard, is there a war coming?"

"Relax, sugar, you're not used to the tactics of our mainstream media. They love to exaggerate; suspense always sells the best. Besides, I don't think that this so-called emergency's military; the voice reported some kind of environmental crisis."

"A nuclear winter following a Third World War would qualify, darling."

"Spoken like a true tactician. Sugar, you'll make an effective minister of enforcement."

"But the HoloTel's silent now."

Richard assured, "Baby, the networks are reeling all of us in with a pregnant pause; they want the emotions of their viewers to be at fever pitch before they transmit."

"Aren't you apprehensive about this impending crisis?"

"Let's just say that I don't trust talking heads who all scream the same opinion."

Carmen asked, "But you do trust Garth Brady?"

"I wouldn't have endorsed your cabinet appointment if I didn't."

Richard kissed Carmen gently on the cheek; she kissed him back hard on the mouth.

Then the HoloTel projected a flawless, three-dimensional image of the White House rostrum as the same voice continued, "President

Brady's about to address our citizens concerning an environmental disaster. The press will be free to ask questions afterward."

At least fifty reporters and television journalists were seated at the front of the chamber below a platform containing the presidential podium. Then President Brady walked onto the platform to a raucous applause before standing behind his podium. He politely waited for the tumult to die down.

Garth looked pale as his words resonated, "My fellow North Americans, I have the sad duty to inform you that our world's in the grip of an accelerated global warming. Both I and Vice President Parker have been in conference today with the chairmen of the Triumviral Environmental Guardians and the Triumviral Department of Intermodalism; both The TEG and TDI report that the average temperature of our Central Province has risen three degrees above the previous year..."

Carmen raised both eyebrows while biting into her sandwich. Her husband smirked while reaching for the milk.

"...my meteorological staff has collated and triple-checked the findings of this report. Unfortunately, the initial results have been confirmed. Therefore, it's my primary responsibility to enforce revolutionary clean air policies to reduce North American emissions of manmade greenhouse gases that are being pumped into Earth's atmosphere. We must act at once in order to avoid impending cremation.

"I now declare the North American Triumvirate to be in a state of *Executive Emergency*. The following list of regulations will be identified as the *North American Clean Air Mandate* or *NACAM* for short; these regulations will take effect immediately:

"Article One: TransTrak will be expanded in every non-commercial motor vehicle to transmit constant status to the Triumviral Department of Intermodalism including location, engine condition, exhaust output, speed, and the citation status that each individual vehicle has accumulated. Minimum engine efficiency will now be upgraded to seventy-five percent. Central Provincial motorists have six months to comply with these conditions; the Northern and Southern Provinces will have an entire year. Failure of compliance will result in vehicle confiscation and a mandatory jail sentence of two years per offense. The North American Government will pay for all vehicular modifications."

"Article Two: The maximum speed limit will still be 75 mph on all provincial highways. Every violator will automatically be detected and penalized by the *Triumviral Department of Motor Vehicles* via TransTrak suborbital platform surveillance; there will be no appeals. The first violation will cost $100. The second violation is $5,000, two years in jail, and permanent revoking of the perpetrator's license. The third violation incurs deliberate motorist blinding to prevent any future violations…"

Carmen coughed after swallowing. "*Blinding?* The President can't be serious!"

Richard frowned. "Garth's being strong-armed about this."

The televised speech continued.

"Article Three: All paramilitary units and municipal law enforcement officers will establish random blockades to inspect any vehicle for TransTrak compliance. The following mandates will prevail over all passengers of illegal vehicles and perpetrators of stolen illegal vehicles: All passengers over sixteen years of age will incur a $500 fine and a thirty-day jail term. All underage passengers will be escorted to the nearest police facility where their parents or legal guardians will be notified to pick them up. All parents or legal guardians of underage violators will incur a $500 fine per child. Upon conviction, all violators of stolen vehicles will be blinded along with serving any other convictions at the judge's discretion. After processing, the impounded vehicle will be returned to the rightful owner.

"Article Four: After the grace period ends, all civilian motor vehicles with a minimum three-passenger capability including automobiles, recreational vehicles, pleasure boats, and private aircraft will be under a mandatory passenger pool restraint. All vehicles so classified will travel with a minimum of three people (driver included) or will incur an automatic TransTrak traffic citation for noncompliance. All commercial vehicles are excluded from mandatory passenger pooling. The Triumviral Department of Intermodalism will regulate and issue *Privacy Permits* if circumstances regarding the vehicle owner warrant special classification. Fees for the awarding of Privacy Permits will be determined on an individual basis; the Triumviral Department of Intermodalism will collect all fees. All violating vehicle pool passengers will incur a $500 fine and a revoking of their driver's license. Violating pool drivers will incur a $5,000 fine and a two-year jail term. Upon conviction, all drivers of stolen vehicles will be blinded while serving any other convictions at the judge's discretion. All impounded vehicles will be returned to their rightful owner.

"Article Five: All aircraft are to be connected to TransTrak status surveillance. Maximum private aircraft speed will be 500 mph. All commercial aircraft are exempt from the mandatory speed limit. All initial violators will incur a $10,000 penalty plus a two-year jail term. Repeat offenders and pilots of stolen aircraft will be blinded to prevent any future violations. Any impounded aircraft will be returned to their rightful owners.

"Article Six: All commercial vehicle operators will maintain their current standard of restriction; no additional NACAM regulations will apply.

"Article Seven: All passenger railroad coaches must have no more than five vacant seats before traveling. All passenger train speeds will not exceed 80 mph. Non-complying train crews will receive a mandatory two-year jail term; the owners of said train will be fined $100,000 for each offense and a two-year jail term. Paramilitary units and municipal law enforcement officers will have authority to board any train for random passenger inspections.

"Article Eight: All heavy construction and farm machinery engines will be installed with TransTrak sensors; their engine efficiency will also be a minimum of 75 percent. There will be no speed limit on these vehicles. There are no passenger restrictions on these vehicles.

Noncompliance for engine standards will be $100 for the first citation. The second violation is $500 and a thirty-day jail term. The third violation will incur deliberate blindness to prevent any future violations.

"Article Nine: Every small internal combustion engine will be equipped with TransTrak surveillance. Minimum small engine efficiency will be 75 percent. The first violation will cost $100. The second violation will be $500 and a two-year jail term. The third violation will incur blindness to prevent any future violations.

"Article Ten: All Martial Protectorate military forces, triumviral paramilitary units, municipal law enforcement officers, and essential emergency personnel are exempt from NACAM while performing their duties. I will now accept questions from the press."

The press core erupted with unanimous outrage.

Garth snapped his fingers. One hundred Martial Protectorate foot soldiers suddenly poured into all six rostrum entrances at once. Each soldier was clad in royal purple combat fatigues, contrasted with gold helmets, buttons, epaulets, and braids. Their gold-colored shoulder insignias displayed a semicircle displaying Third Triumvirate landmasses embossed in royal purple.

Richard was trembling mad watching his HoloTel; he'd never witnessed a military coup on live television before. Carmen finished her sandwich. Their naked bodies cuddled as they kept watching while President Brady pointed toward the upraised arm of a press core newcomer.

The reporter asked, "Mr. President, I don't understand why you've deployed protectorate forces here tonight. Did you anticipate a mass attack from the press core?"

"Certainly not, Mister…Mister…"

"Martin Wagner, sir. I'm a reporter for *The Washington Witness*. This is my first time covering a presidential press release; I'd say it's already been memorable."

"I am pleased to meet you, Mr. Wagner. I repeat that there's no reason I felt that I needed Martial Protectorate intervention tonight.

This military display was orchestrated simply to prove that I'm serious about enforcing NACAM. I want all of our citizens to get a good look at these uniforms; they'll be seeing a lot of them in the future."

"I see. Then it was a mere coincidence of timing that brought these armed brutes storming into this chamber unannounced?"

"They chose their own method of entrance. I only chose the timing. The North American people are probably as impressed with them as me."

Wagner commented, "To continue, sir, I would like to understand why this environmental emergency's being dispatched with such swiftness. Surely there's time for a scientific collaboration to examine the TEG's and the TDI's findings. Why don't you sanction a triumviral televote to decide this matter?"

Garth frowned back his retort. "Because this crisis is too serious for a political poll; this abnormal heating must be stopped. The best way to make these facts known to the rest of the world is to lead by example. Don't you think I realize this step will make me unpopular with our citizens? But it's suicide not to prepare for the worst-case scenario! My duty's to protect our people, which includes doing our part to protect the earth we live on!"

"What does NACAM stand for again, sir?"

"The North American Clean Air Mandate."

President Brady pointed to another upraised hand.

Jennifer Scott of the *New York Guardsman* was recognized. The forty-year-old reporter was a veteran of fifteen years of Washington, D.C. interviews. She was no stranger to Garth Brady. She asked, "Mr. President, you said the NACAM Directive will be enforced in the Central Province within six months. Is that correct?"

"That's right, Jennifer."

"How do you expect to convert over five hundred million civilian motor vehicles in only half a year?"

Brady answered, "The combined auto repair resources of our triumvirate will accomplish it. A large contingent of my forty million paramilitaries will assist in this project as well. We will also employ all qualified people of the Triumviral Highway Department and all air quality monitoring stations to provide additional facilities to perform the operation. All auto repair businesses will be installing TransTrak upgrades by the end of next week. After our Central Province's relatively quick conversion, all Central Provincial resources will assist the Northern and Southern Provinces to speed up their compliance time."

Jennifer continued, "You said that virtually all Central Provincial auto repair facilities will have modified TransTrak equipment by the end of next week, but it's impossible to mass produce the amount of components needed from scratch in just ten days. Obviously, the Central Province was in possession of this equipment before you were notified of this impending global crisis."

"This isn't a conspiracy, Jennifer. All commercial vehicles within the Central Province have previously been under TransTrak surveillance. We have massive stockpiles of TransTrak equipment to compensate for commercial breakdowns and new vehicle manufacturing. I am simply commandeering that equipment to accommodate our NACAM Directives. There's nothing sinister going on here."

"Then why are you mandating a blindness penalty against any three-time losers who refuse to surrender their right to travel as they please?"

"I'm not a barbarian, Jennifer. That brutal mutilation policy's recorded in the NACAM Articles because I don't want any North Americans to treat them frivolously. No one will take a punishment like blindness lightly. I have no intention of blinding anyone unless they deliberately violate the law enough to incur the maximum penalty. Then they'd be guilty of blinding themselves because they knew beforehand."

"I see. Mr. President, when are Triumviral World Citizens going to be branded with a triple six laser scan on either their foreheads or hands?"

Brady smirked before answering, "Although I'm an atheist, your flippant, biblical remark to the *Book of Revelation* is familiar to me. But I am not the Antichrist, Jennifer. As I understand it, the Antichrist's Satan himself and will not be born of a woman. I assure you that I have a mother. Also, according to some biblical traditions, Satan must be released from heaven by Michael the Archangel and will arrive on earth with many of his fallen angels to masquerade as Jesus Christ. That way, he can allegedly deceive the people of Earth into the *Great Apostasy* before the return of the true messiah."

"For an atheist, you seem to know a great deal about the Bible, sir."

"I enjoy studying the religions of many cultures; their self-righteous ravings tickle my fancy. However, I neither believe in the devil or in Almighty God. If your comment is meant as a joke, it's fallen flat on me. If you're serious, I suggest that you seek some kind of psychiatric help. Any other questions?"

Jennifer countered, "One more. I'm acquainted with a group of scientists who claim that abnormal global warming's untrue and they're prepared to prove it scientifically. I ask you now, in front of the North American people, will you allow a debate between the Global Reaction Alliance and a panel of your environmental experts on triumviral media? I believe our people should have the right to decide what evidence they agree with. What's your answer, President Brady?"

"It's a waste of time to debate the existence of abnormal global warming when the current three-degree rise has become an established fact. I am aware of the GRA's evidence, but the question has been rendered academic."

"How is it you know of the Global Reaction Alliance? The GRA's been denied any legislative, executive, or judicial audience in Washington, D.C. for the past ten years."

Brady paused before leaning heavily on his podium, "As a senator of the former United States Congress, I've exchanged information with a GRA member in the past. I found his evidence to be thought-provoking but not sufficiently conclusive to be of any practical use."

"Would you be kind enough to reveal his name?"

"Those senatorial meetings were confidential; my informant isn't here for me to ask permission to break that confidence. I respect his privacy."

Jennifer retorted, "I smell an evasion, sir. What's a minor privacy matter compared with this serious global crisis you keep talking about? You know very well that your informant would love some public exposure! The GRA has been struggling to be heard for years. My employer's forbidden me to print a single word of their evidence or even to mention their name. As a matter of fact, I'll probably get fired for touting them on live triumviral television tonight. But you, sir, have forced me into it. This NACAM assault on North America's mobility makes the Red Shield's financial strangulation of Europe look like a surprise party!"

Garth paused before answering, "My GRA contact was Dr. Rudolf Zadock; he's chairman of the Global Reaction Alliance. We discussed his evidence when I was chairman of the *Congressional Environmental Task Force* from 2034 to 2036. I listened to his complete presentations and received copies of all the GRA's current data at the time. I compared it openly with many other environmentalists in the political sphere, which violently disagreed with the GRA evidence. That was the end of it. I'm no scientist. Are there anymore interrogations, Miss Scott?"

Jennifer almost shouted, "Will you allow an open global warming debate if the North American people demand it?"

"If the majority of North Americans wish it, I'll bow to their demands. I will conclude now by saying that I made an environmental emergency decision with the NACAM Directive. I personally believe that the danger's horribly real. If we are to escape worldwide extinction, we must now endure some scathing restrictions. Good night."

The signal terminated before Richard switched off the HoloTel. He chuckled before commenting, "Well, sugar, it looks like Garth's bitten off more than he can chew. I hope he doesn't try any more drastic reforms or you'll be commanding multiple maiming squads to blind criminal motorists from the Arctic to the Caribbean."

Carmen asked, "What do you mean, darling?"

"I mean that the majority of North Americans will resist the NACAM directives; they love their freedom of travel too much. Garth Brady has just declared war on the American Dream. I sadly anticipate a second Civil War. It will be interesting to see if paramilitaries and municipal cops will prevail against human wave assaults from millions of outraged North Americans. If I know our people, they'll fight to keep their right of free passage just as the Old Confederacy valiantly fought to defend their right to exist as sovereign states."

"Richard, you're not making a lot of sense to me. The North American People will understand that this emergency's real; they are too civilized to rebel en mass."

Richard nearly howled with laughter before answering, "Sugar, your native Cuba rebelled against tyranny long after Castro's natural passing. You fought for it yourself and I consider you extremely civilized, but you're also extremely tough. However, you're going to have your hands full with this situation. You'll most likely have to kill a lot of people to maintain order."

"Darling, I have no wish to hurt anyone, but I will carry out my triumviral duty no matter what my personal feelings. The President's executive orders must be enforced."

Richard caressed her while whispering, "That's why you're the best choice for Garth's top soldier. Let's go to bed, sugar. You're not due back until Monday morning.

Franklin stood up with his bride in both arms and headed for the master bedroom. He muttered, "I hope Garth knows what he's doing; he's opened a Pandora's Box on steroids."

CHAPTER TWELVE

Escape

Eric Wilford trembled with rage after hearing President Brady's radio address. To him, the NACAM atrocity was an excuse to seize both political and military control over North America's transportation. He wondered if all North Americans were as pissed off as he was. Maybe the GRA evidence was correct in spite of the President calling it a waste of time. A waste of time for whom?

Eric relished Jennifer Scott's tenacity about a debate; he felt she was a kindred spirit. But he also pondered if Garth Brady would allow any triumviral vote to settle the matter. The inventor stopped tinkering on his Bipolar Drive. The machine ran flawlessly under the hood of his 2038 North American Pegasus Sedan.

He thrilled with enthusiasm watching his creation draw electromagnetic force out of thin air and convert that energy into kinetic motive power. Then he suddenly trembled again at the idea of being eliminated to keep this new invention off the market. Wilford had never gone in for conspiracy theories before, but this NACAM coup was too big to ignore. He locked up and walked toward the house under a crisp, starlit night.

One thousand yards away, three black, spandex-clad men focused Spectrum Goggles from a forest summit. Thermographic sensors and listening devices penetrated the walls of the Wilford home as they recorded any open conversations, Media Palm, and computer discourses with equal efficiency. Under normal conditions, any two-way HoloTel would have done all the eavesdropping for the CC, but Alvin Wilford had stubbornly kept a 2025 Visor Projection System in his home and HoloTels weren't produced before 2032. A fourth man monitored all recordings inside a windowless utility van fifty yards deeper into the woods.

Surveillance was boring work, but every Cupola agent attending knew the penalty for dereliction of duty and their idea of a pleasant evening sure as hell didn't include being entertained by Sebastian Singh in the *Pit of the Damned*. The trio's eyes stayed transfixed to the thermograph monitor perched on a tripod behind the leafless winter skeleton of a nearby maple tree; they locked on Eric's heat signature as he stepped through the back doorway. Then their infrared specter walked into the living room. Alvin was sleeping in his rocking chair. Eric sat down grasping a Media Palm from his pocket and made a call.

A woman's voice transmitted from Eric's Palm. "Vermont Information Exchange. Which area do you wish?"

The inventor answered, "New York City Information."

"One moment, please."

Eric was connected five seconds later.

"New York City Information, may I help you?"

"Patch me through to the New York Guardsman switchboard."

"Sir, you will save money if you dial it directly."

"Just patch me through!"

"One moment, sir."

Eric drummed his free fingers across one knee.

"New York Guardsman information exchange. Press one for the personnel department. Press two for the managing editor. Press three for the news desk. Press four for dispatch. Press five for public relations. "

Eric pressed number five.

"New York Guardsman Public Relations, may I help you?"

"Yes, ma'am, how do I contact Jennifer Scott?"

"She isn't here at the moment, sir. May I take a message?"

"Certainly. Tell her my name's Eric Wilford. She doesn't know me, but I have some fascinating information pertaining to the global warming crisis. I live in Bolton, Vermont District; that's about twenty miles northwest of Montpelier. I am now leaving for Hartford, Connecticut District, on Saturday morning. I will meet her at the Hartford Chamber of Commerce next Monday at four P.M. If I don't show up by five, I'm either abducted or dead, end of message."

"I'll see she gets your message."

Eric closed his Media Palm and went upstairs to pack without waking his father.

Alvin was still asleep when Senior Agent Justin Phillips and two others entered through the back doorway. In seconds, Phillips injected an anesthetic into the old man while one of his cohorts inserted a pre-recorded disc into the living room stereo before the whole surveillance team exited the house, loaded up the van, and drove away with their unconscious hostage within four minutes.

Eric spent fifteen minutes packing before hauling two suitcases downstairs; his blood chilled after discovering Pappy missing. He searched the whole house; there was no sign of his father. Checking the living room again, he spotted the power light functioning on Pappy's stereo. He played the available disk and listened. A stranger's voice declared, "Go anywhere or inform anyone about this abduction and we'll peel your pappy like an onion. You will be contacted later."

Eric bloodied two knuckles on the power button before unlocking the safety on the handgun tucked inside his belt. He grabbed both suitcases and walked out the back door before reaching and unlocking his metal-skinned workshop. Then he slammed and locked the steel door behind him.

The inventor's 2038 Pegasus prototype was in prime condition as Eric mounted Pappy's license plate tags to both bumpers. He stuffed both suitcases in the back seat before raiding his pantry. He gathered three bags of food and three gallon jugs of refrigerated well water onto the front passenger seat. Then he removed every computer disc in his files before viciously shattering the monitor and hard drive with a ballpeen hammer.

Eric turned out the lights and walked outside before crouching silently under the shadows of a naked maple tree. He grasped his gun and waited five minutes while straining both eyes in vain for intruders. Clenching a penlight between his teeth, Eric pried up a fifty-pound boulder before uncovering a hole. He grasped a corner of plywood lodged under a false dirt bottom and yanked up. A one-inch layer of soil came with it revealing a burlap sack three feet below the ground surface. The inner plastic sack contained 125 one-ounce, gold American Eagle Coins currently worth $2,200 apiece on the open market; their total value tallied at $275,000. Wilford replaced the covering and laid the coin bag onto the Pegasus' passenger floorboard. He opened the garage door and sat in total darkness behind the steering wheel. A full minute passed without any sign of company.

Eric switched on the penlight to examine his instruments. A dashboard lever controlled the electromagnetic field intake and connected directly to a super conductor, which collected sufficient static to jumpstart the engine's polarity chamber. Eric waited another minute to hear nothing but rustling wind. Then his bipolar engine hummed to life. He pressed the accelerator lightly and drove his prototype out through the garage doorway before locking up behind him.

All four studded tires crackled and gouged along bare asphalt as the inventor drove onto the main road. He attained 40 mph before finally activating his exterior lights. Eric headed toward Denver, Colorado District, starting a two thousand-mile journey trying to reach the Global Reaction Alliance. He shivered for several miles before his car heater kicked in.

CHAPTER THIRTEEN

Arrival

When President Garth Brady began his NACAM address at nine P.M., Eastern Standard Time, Atlanterran President Barry Claude Xavier was just leaving Rome, Italy District. His *Augustus One* sub-orbital jet covered the four thousand miles to Washington, D.C., with amazing speed. By 11:42 P.M., President Xavier had already dismissed his twelve bodyguards at Dulles Airport and chatted with Victor DeSalle in the old man's silver Rolls Royce while Milton the Mountain drove them toward DeSalle's rural estate in Manassas, Virginia District.

Xavier yawned while DeSalle snarled, "You can sleep when I've dismissed you! Now, as it turns out there's no longer any need for you to meet with Garth and Parker."

The Atlanterran President nodded acknowledgement.

DeSalle blustered, "But we still have a problem, Barry. It appears that Garth has become a liability. He declared an environmental emergency and authorized the NACAM Directive as per orders, but he has committed two strikes in a single day. And the Cupola only allows three before dereliction of duty applies, no matter who the perpetrator may be!"

"What's he done, Victor?"

"Garth revealed the White House Scansat Station to Mike Parker earlier this afternoon without authority."

"Does Mike act like he's going to break with the information?"

"He hasn't had time to do anything, has he? It's hard to believe that Garth could be so careless. That was strike one, but it'll be all right as long as Parker remains a team player.

"Strike two was agreeing on a triumviral-wide debate over global warming if our North American serfs collectively vote to demand one. Chances are, at least four hundred million North Americans will witness a battle of environmental evidence between our triumviral scientists and the GRA opposition, who believe they possess valid evidence to win."

"Do they?"

DeSalle bellowed, "Of course, you moron! The TDI's been inflating average temperature readings in North America for years. We need those measurements to beguile the populace into allowing restriction on their mobility. Now that TransTrak's the vehicular law of the land, our NACAM directive can be fully enforced. But the Global Reaction Alliance suspects that somebody's trying to pull a fast one!"

"I hesitate to say this, Victor; I don't want a blind date with Sebastian."

"If you're going to slur my grandson for blatant incompetence, don't bother! That nosy bitch Jennifer Scott already did that in front of all North America!"

Barry asked, "Who is Jennifer Scott?"

"She's political editor for the *New York Guardsman* and practically branded Garth a liar on triumviral television. At the moment, she has no proof that someone's covertly trying to restrict North American mobility. But if that debate goes through, she may get all the proof she needs."

Xavier crossed both arms. "Why not dispose of the lady?"

"No, she's too well known. If she died right now, it could backfire hideously and cast more suspicion toward the North American government; those damn citizens are probably pissed off over NACAM enough as it is. They could rebel and our plans don't include a domestic revolt right now."

Xavier continued, "I don't intend any disrespect, but..."

"Moloch's Mud Whore, Barry! What are you babbling about? Relax, I'm not going to cane you for speaking your mind as long as you ask my permission first. Go ahead! Spill it!"

Xavier rubbed his right shoulder on reflex while glancing at the ivory scepter before calmly asking, "Is it possible that Garth's neither as inept nor stupid as you imagine?"

"What's that supposed to mean?"

"Could he be playing a two-sided game? You know him much better than I do, and I've only been around him occasionally for over thirty years. But it seems to me that anyone articulate and forceful enough to be elected president might not be the idiot you take him for."

Victor chided, "Since when have Americans actually elected any man or woman of their choice? Citizens have been voting for our political puppets ever since we pocketed the news media. The only serious candidates in any major election are leaders that the Cupola backed financially! It requires billions of dollars to get elected to any federal public office.

"But sometimes once elected, presidential puppets spawn agendas of their own. Like that time in the nineteenth century when we impeached and ejected President Andrew Johnson for second guessing the real purpose behind the 14th Amendment to the now defunct U.S. Constitution! There hasn't been his like since, except for that idealistic Irishman from Massachusetts who dared to print non-interest-bearing United States currency to compete against our Federal Reserve Notes! We showed him what happens when a presidential puppet tries to cut his own strings!

"As for your notion that Garth's playing us for suckers, that warrants further investigation. I've never contemplated the possibility that my grandson might have a contrary agenda to ours; I've raised that boy since he could walk. He knows the penalty for dereliction of duty, but he did show a mound of nerve showing Parker our Scansat Network. That would be a supreme irony, wouldn't it? Garth Brady secretly opposing the agenda of his mentors? That would be cunning worthy of Napoleon himself!"

Barry commented, "Garth's cunning would be more in the style of Machiavelli; he may be attempting to divide and conquer the Third Triumvirate for his own purposes. Of course, it's just a theory. Our flag officers would demand proof in order to chastise him."

DeSalle stopped romanticizing. "One more strike and Garth will be peeled like an onion anyway. The Pit of the Damned always welcomes fresh meat; at times, the thought of Sebastian chills even my blood. If I have to eliminate Garth, it's a comfort to know that our Chess Roulette Cube initiated Mike Parker in case his political power becomes unmanageable. In fact, I think that I'll check Mr. Parker's metabolic signature status before Milton reaches New Corsica."

"You named your North American estate New Corsica?"

"Certainly, my boy. I've long admired Napoleon. It's fitting that my North American estate should be named after the French Emperor's birthplace, don't you think so? After all, The Crimson Cupola financed Napoleon's thirst for conquest and his British opposition at the same time; shrewd financiers always milk profits from both sides in any war. Our organization's been amassing wealth and power since our ancestors monopolized purple dye to cover the cloaks of roman emperors. The only real fun the Cupola's enjoyed between Rome and Napoleon were the Crusades, the European conquest of the Americas, and the Spanish Inquisition."

Xavier reminisced, "Ah, the Spanish Inquisition was always my favorite subject in history! I envied those clergymen with the power to condemn any enemy to inhuman tortures in the name of their god; that's when our traditional Pit of the Damned was conceived! Religious power must be more fun than mere military might; a dictator can conjure and enforce any belief system he wishes."

The chairman pulled out his Media Palm before connecting with the nearest Scansat Station in three seconds.

A voice responded, "Scansat Eleven, please confirm authorization by encryption."

DeSalle touched his screen and the voice acknowledged, "Yes, Mr. Chairman, how may I serve you?"

"A new roulette target was initiated yesterday afternoon in the Triad Office. It was Vice President Mike Parker. Both his fingerprints and metabolic signature should be recorded on our database. I want to track his exact location at this moment."

"I am collating, sir. I find no record of any metabolic signature acquired yesterday in the Triad Office, but there's record of a defective power surge within that particular Chess Roulette Cube that disabled its encoding system. Our sensors indicate that the cube still operates only as a game. Shall I affect repairs, sir?"

DeSalle barked, "Yes, do it now! I don't care what time it is! Has President Brady been informed of the machine's defect?"

"Certainly, sir. He gave us prior instructions not to touch the unit until further notice. However, your supreme authority outweighs any common president."

Victor answered through clenched teeth, "Are you saying President Brady initiated contact with you yesterday? You didn't alert him first regarding the defect?"

"Yes, sir, it was most unusual. Roulette procedures specify only flag officers can initiate contact with active Chess Roulette monitors. The President said you authorized it; we logged it as such."

"I want twenty-four-hour Scansat surveillance on Garth Brady. After he retires, I want a technician to repair the game cube. Senior Agent Richmond's squad has the expertise; contact him as soon as I finish with you. But do not inform President Brady of the repairs; if he circumvents protocol again, call me."

"Yes, Mr. Chairman."

"Goodnight."

DeSalle hung up and snarled at Xavier, "That disloyal, cowardly, treasonous little worm! How dare he contact the Roulette Monitor without prior authorization? I'm liquidating that miserable little wretch!"

He breathed deeply before pocketing his Media Palm. Then he pressed every fingertip slowly together. "But first, he's going to perform one last task for us."

Barry asked, "What do you have in mind, Mr. Chairman?"

"We're going to New York City. I'm calling an emergency session of the Universal Regions Council. Milton, park the car at Citadel. Wake us when we arrive."

Milton the Mountain nodded and changed course immediately; they arrived in New York City by four A.M. The titan awakened his master.

DeSalle yawned before pressing his Palm screen again.

A female voice responded, "Yes, Mr. Chairman, how may I serve you?"

"Good Morning, Minerva. I want you to call the monitor of the Cohesion Cluster, the Martial Protectorate commissioner and the chief magistrate of the Planetary Court. Inform those three officers of the Universal Regions Tribunal that I want the entire audience of URC representatives present in the forum by one P.M. today for an emergency vote. Both the Atlanterran President and I will be attending; I'll not accept any appeals."

"Yes, sir, I'll notify them at once."

"Thank you, Minerva, good-bye."

"Good-bye, sir."

CHAPTER FOURTEEN

Confession

Garth and Mike departed the rostrum with six Martial Protectorate agents after the last reporter departed the White House at 11:45 P.M. Parker snapped, "Why the hell do we need these soldiers now? All of those big, bad, unarmed reporters have left the building after that damned NACAM edict!"

"I thought you're supposed to be the silent man; we'll talk about it later."

Within two minutes, both executives were standing inside the Triad Office with their automatic weapon clad escorts deploying outside on the grounds. All remaining paramilitaries joined the perimeter defense while conventional security maintained their stations.

Garth motioned Mike to his side while pulling open his desk drawer. Parker started to speak, but Brady cut him off by raising his right hand. The President pointed toward a small, white button in back of the drawer while motioning his partner to press it; Parker obeyed.

Garth sighed relief before assuring him, "We can talk now without being monitored by the Crimson Cupola."

Mike whirled around, now watching all of the windows disappear behind steel shutters while the Triad Office entrance door locked automatically. He blurted, "What's with this cloak and dagger horseshit?"

"That white button activates a random, oscillating series of electromagnetic pulse frequencies shielding this room against any electronic surveillance devices, including Scansat Stations."

Mike blustered, "Marvelous. Now what the hell's the Crimson... *what?*"

"The Crimson Cupola, Mike. Both words have specific meanings: *Crimson* means blood red. *Cupola* means a vaulted, rounded roof. I'd say that the domed ceiling of an Islamic Mosque bears a good example. Its members belong to an ancient organization made up of multi-trillion dollar, dynastic families. They're the most powerful people on Earth."

Parker flopped into a chair before retorting, "A conspiracy group? You've got to be shitting me!"

"The Cupola controls the utilities of all First-World Nations. They're also stockholders and board members of the largest central banking houses in the world. This society sets the price of gold, silver, platinum, oil, precious gems, foodstuffs, and controls computer technology, pharmaceuticals, durable manufactured goods along with all corporate media empires. Although these financiers don't control every business, they do rule the mainstream activities that make modern businesses possible: Energy, credit, raw materials, and distribution systems. Now the Cupola covets control over the mobility of every industrial citizen on Earth, and NACAM's their crucial step toward that agenda."

Parker crossed both arms. "Are you part of this atrocity?"

Brady sat down despondently before replying, "I was, until midway through our presidential campaign. I am the grandson of the Crimson Cupola chairman; my mother's one of Victor DeSalle's daughters."

"You mean that scrawny old man who vapor locked during our chess game is...?"

Brady interjected. "Is the single most powerful man on the face of the earth. DeSalle's orders are immediately obeyed without question. All triumviral presidents are CC members. You don't believe me, do you, Mike?"

"No."

"What would it take to convince you?"

"For openers, if you're part of this so-called power structure, you must've been indoctrinated at an early age, right?"

Garth confirmed, "Certainly. I wasn't allowed to create a personal destiny! My presidency formed from Cupola edicts! Global politicians are the puppets dangled in front of audiences while their masters manipulate from the shadows! It's the unseen hands that buys elections and wields real power. I'm nothing more than a slave, but I used to be content with that. I really believed that the masses should be controlled for their collective welfare as well as the Cupola's.

"As I drew closer to the presidency, I began noticing changes in the Cupola's attitude toward me. I suddenly resented being under surveillance. As a Cupola elite, I felt that I warranted better treatment than global serfs. I began questioning a world system that treated both allies and enemies with equal contempt.

"Then a mutual friend introduced me to Dr. Rudolf Zadock of the GRA; his ideas were compelling enough for me to reconsider the evidence I haphazardly dismissed as a senator from Virginia. Rudy's my new mentor; I would die for that man. I constantly fear for his safety, but I also mentored him about Cupola operations in the spirit of reciprocity. After all, knowledge will always be power. Tonight, Jenny and I collaborated to introduce Rudy to the triumviral media spotlight. Celebrities are less likely to be assassinated because the Cupola thrives on secrecy."

"If you're opposing this Cupola, why did you implement NACAM tonight?"

Garth exclaimed, "Grandfather ordered me to implement NACAM after you left us alone in the Triad Office! His seizure was bogus and staged for your benefit!"

"What about my electric shock?"

"I rigged that game cube to shock you on command. By the way, don't ever play Chess Roulette again or your life may be forfeit."

Parker blurted, "Why?"

"Because that machine isn't just a game! It's the most insidious tracking device yet conceived. It's a thousand times worse than any Scansat Station!"

Mike furrowed his brow. "What does this Chess Roulette do?"

"Every human being transmits a unique metabolic signature of brainwaves and bodily rhythms. The game kings record these signatures and transmit them to monitor stations where they're stored on a database. With this database, the Cupola can locate filed individuals anywhere by locking onto their metabolic signature. That is, except under an electromagnetic scrambler like the one we're shielded with now. Then these *Metabolic Monitors* transmit an overload signal to a target until their body literally burns out with hyperactivity. But in order to transmit a lethal signal, these monitors must tie into one of the suborbital booster platforms above each pole. Without polar boosters, Double M's can only record and locate, but they cannot kill.

"Polar boosters also channel the main power supply for the TransTrak and Scansat Networks. That's why New Genesis deploys polar hypercraft to constantly maintain Cupola suborbital equipment; their surveillance monopoly emanates from the sky."

Parker barked, "But why did you push Chess Roulette on me in the first place?"

Brady's mind flashed back to his first Pit of the Damned ritual before answering with a vocal tremor, "I had to follow orders or be murdered."

"But how could a machine overload a person's body by remote control? It's not possible! Your organization's probably employing some mythical terror tactic."

Garth shook his head from side to side, "The technology does exist. A Scansat Station observed former TDI Chairman Max Stromberg refute the TEG temperature report in front of his entire staff. The Cupola ordered Double M to murder Stromberg at once. Spencer Mitchell witnessed the incident but didn't know a murder was committed. Only high-ranking Cupola officials and flag officers are privy to Double M's existence. I don't know how many Chess Roulette Cubes have been constructed, but I do know all three triumviral presidents have one."

"Then I'm already as good as dead!"

"Negative, Chum, I told you I raided the game. Your signature's not on file with the Metabolic Monitor; I contacted them illegally to be certain."

"Illegally?"

Brady nodded, "I contacted Double M without receiving any flag officer authorization. Grandfather probably knows about it already and that will give me strike three on his perverted scorecard. I suspect you're going to be the new President of North America very soon."

"You're still Chairman DeSalle's grandson."

Garth exhaled thoughtfully. "Back to the subject at hand. When Victor ordered me to implement NACAM, I talked with Jennifer and set up my mock presidential roast to get the GRA some mass media attention. Then I informed Rudy as well; his staff's already collating evidence and preparing for the upcoming debate. The GRA's headquartered in Denver, Colorado District."

Mike stood up asking, "Does the GRA know you're giving me this information?"

"No one does, partner. I want to protect you and your family if I can."

Parker grasped Garth's right hand, smiling. "I believe you, Garth. But what will happen to you if the Cupola discovers what you told me?"

Brady released the grip. "Both of us would likely become Sebastian's guests of honor to the Pit of the Damned. These people are capable of the most sadistic acts of satanic torture imaginable. And these blood-drinking bastards fancy themselves as elite human beings! Many of the Martial Protectorate's training exercises include human sacrifices. The rituals they perform were spawned out of Babylonian Mystery Schools. In fact, all Cupola flag officers are practicing pagans who worship a Canaanite god dating back centuries before the Hebrew Old Testament. That's why I've never subscribed to religion of any kind. Since age twelve, the rituals I've witnessed have jolted me by déjà vu back to the Pit of the Damned whenever considering any religious doctrine or concept!

"Cupola tradition even includes a form of ancient gladiatorial games that they call a Geodesy Gauntlet, but such a celebration's only declared at the whim of whatever chairman's in power; these games are scheduled completely at random."

"Jesus H. Christ!" exclaimed Parker.

Brady shuddered before suddenly whispering, "You mustn't tell any of your family what I just told you, not even Margaret. Do you understand?"

"Yes, Garth. But how long has the CC been in power?"

"That depends on what you mean by power. This dynasty has existed since the reign of the Roman Empire. The Crimson Cupola started out as Mediterranean merchants who cornered a monopoly on purple dye for the adornment of royalty. They had wealth and influence back then but not on the worldwide scale of today. Absolute power didn't gestate until the Roman Catholic Church. My ancestors manipulated countries from the shadows the same way they do today. Ancient merchant wealth purchased power for centuries over historical popes, clergymen, kings, queens, and key military leaders.

"The Cupola initiated the Crusades, Spanish Inquisition, European Conquest of the Americas, Triangle Slave Trade, and both American and French Revolutions. Cupola banks financed the thirteen original American Colonies and Napoleon Bonaparte respectively along with all opposing forces at the same time. They've amassed unimaginable wealth from the misery of mankind. Am I overwhelming your mind, Mike? Do you want me to stop?"

Parker stretched, walked over to the wall panel, and opened the camouflaged bar. He poured two glasses of beer and served President Brady before returning to his seat, still holding the second glass. He finally answered, "Garth, I could listen to you all night. You always give me a new perspective on things I thought I already knew. Go ahead, pal, vent your spleen."

Brady smiled before continuing, "After the Revolutionary War,

America still wasn't free; they possessed political independence but not financial freedom. The Bank of England upheld every single lien and liability they contracted against the United States of America. Another key to American bondage occurred during the Civil War, which was never fought over the issue of slavery, as most textbooks preach. It was fought over the issue of sovereign states having the right to make and exercise their own laws by majority sovereign citizen vote. The southern states were the injured party in that war.

"After states' rights perished with the Confederacy, the 14th Amendment was ratified to the U.S. Constitution; this piece of legislation declared that all American Citizens were now subjects of the U.S. Corporate Federal Government instead of sovereign citizens of sovereign states."

"Holy shit, is that really true?"

"Certainly. Look up the history of the time and verify it through the writings of people who lived through it. Collectivists always use the false sanctity of the public good to crush their enemies."

"What about—"

Garth interrupted, "More history another time, Mike. Right now, I've got to tell you what new executive order I'm planning for tomorrow evening. Listen, I'm going to declare Minister Carmen Valdez-Franklin the commander over all North American Paramilitary and Police Forces. This ploy's designed to enrage our citizens so badly they will openly rebel, which should help retard NACAM operations in the process. Hopefully my new edict will be enough for North Americans to demand triumviral secession from the Planetary Pandect.

"Atlanterran and Indoasian military forces would likely invade North America to reestablish URC rulership over their Third Triumvirate. As the next president, you must be prepared for these upcoming scenarios. I have no intention of enforcing the NACAM directives, but this second executive order should provide the catalyst we need to eventually break the URC's chains on our people."

Mike's eyes widened. "But how will domestic executive orders affect the URC? They have no jurisdiction over this NACAM thing. There's nothing in their bylaws to give them authority to intervene on North America's NACAM directives."

Brady paused before answering, "Grandfather intends to incorporate NACAM into the Planetary Pandect. Victor confided that when I was ordered to implement the directive. I'm betting that he already knows about our current surveillance blackout. I understand how his mind works; he'll probably order a URC emergency forum in New York City within the next day or two. He'll command me to attend and use my presidential vote to help endorse the NACAM agenda, which will likely be my last official act as President.

"Now, the only way to implement my second executive order is for Grandfather to believe it's to his advantage to appoint Carmen military commander of North America. He mustn't believe it's my idea; otherwise, he may smell a trap. Before I turn my scrambler off, I will take a fountain pen and scratch the wooden drawer frame surrounding the white activation button to lend credence to our charade about an accidental alarm. After our scrambler is off, I want you to encourage Carmen's sudden promotion after we convince Scansat that our blackout was an accident. We'll pretend to start another roulette game. Then we'll stop suddenly, because you will still be too nervous to try again. Are you with me so far?"

Mike sipped his beer before answering, "You're doing fine, pal."

"Okay. Then we're going to have a drink while discussing the reactions of the press crowd to NACAM. I want you to come up with some logical reason for promoting Carmen. I will openly reject it. That'll give Grandfather some incentive to embrace the idea. This stunt may also help endear you into his confidence."

"Does Carmen already know about this?"

"No. As soon as we've laid the trap, I'll call and order her to attend an emergency TDI meeting, at ten A.M. this morning. Before she gets there, I'll brief her about our little charade. Then I'll have her drop the bombshell on Spencer Mitchell and his boys."

"Are you going to tell Andre Roget?"

"No, Andre's a Cupola member. Don't trust him with any critical information."

Parker asked, "Then why did you appoint him Minister of Travel?"

"I didn't. Victor DeSalle did. Andre was his choice for my running mate. The only way to get him to accept you was to keep Roget close at hand. Andre's also Cupola Overseer for TransTrak. That's why we will invent tasks that will keep him out of as many Cabinet meetings as possible."

Parker finished his beer and asked, "What else do you want, Garth?"

"Right now, the Scansat Station will be alerting Grandfather about this unauthorized blackout. When the blackout lifts, Scansat will scrutinize our role-playing in this office. After I reject Carmen's promotion, you will admit it was a joke. Your idea will be on Scansat file when Grandfather gets the message. I'm gambling that he'll use your joke against us. He'll command me to implement the order. I'll act dejected and reluctantly agree. At nine tonight, I'll announce this executive order over triumviral-wide media. Do you think that you can bait your side of this trap?"

"I'll do anything to stop these elitist assholes!"

"Thanks, Mike. If our people learn the truth about world collectivists, maybe they can take their government back. I wish I could live to see it."

Mike squirmed, "Scansat must be going crazy; we've been off the air a while."

"I know. It was a bit longer than planned. I'm turning off the scrambler; just follow my lead."

The President impaled the antique wood of his desk drawer repeatedly with a fountain pen point, winked cheerfully at his best friend, and then deactivated just before yelling, "Balberith blast it, Mike! Be more careful! You crushed my pen against the alarm button when you jammed my desk drawer!"

Mike bellowed, "What was all that steel shudder bullshit? You scared the hell out of me!"

"The button's an intruder control alarm. White House Security's probably sealing off the building. I'll call their extension to disregard the alert."

Garth grabbed his Media Palm. "Marcus, this is President Brady. No, I didn't spot any intruders through the windows. I jammed a pen against the alarm button by accident. Yes, everything's fine. Tell security to stand down. I'm sorry about the false alarm. Thanks, Marc; good night."

Parker lamented, "I'm sorry, Garth, all I wanted was pen and paper to scribble down a new chess strategy; mine went dry."

"Forget it, Mike. I'm sorry those steel shutters freaked you out. It sure took a bit of time to pry my drawer open again. Are you certain you want to play again? That was a nasty shock you got burned with earlier."

"No sweat, boss. I've been looking forward to another game since before tonight's speech."

Garth set up the board rapidly before teasing, "All right, Vice President Pigeon, this time you've got the stainless steel."

Brady pushed his king's pawn forward one square.

Mike countered with his queen's knight placing it two squares in front of the queen's bishop. Mike's king's bishop pawn dropped down a trap door. He flinched while expecting an electric shock.

Garth advised, "Maybe we should forget the game for now."

"You're probably right. Do you want to call it a night?"

"No, not for a while. Since it's around midnight, let's just sit here and relax. Got anything on your mind, partner?"

Parker groaned before replying, "I'm wondering what the general public reaction will be to your NACAM directive. I saw how those news hounds responded. However, I doubt that they'd make an accurate barometer for our people. Some reporters seem like professional rabble-rousers to me. Bad news sells best and all that."

Garth sighed. "I realize my order was a drastic step, but I suspect the majority of citizens will understand the reasoning behind NACAM. After all, it's for our collective survival. I even placed triumviral staff cars under NACAM jurisdiction. I only hope that people won't become three time losers; I'd hate to have to blind anyone."

"You're actually serious about that maximum penalty?"

"Deadly serious, partner. Do you have any qualms?"

Mike confessed, "It was a shock to me, but I knew that something had to be done. The TEG reports proved a pretty deadly instrument. I lament that freedom of mobility is dying in North America, but I suppose that's better than death by a roasting earth."

Garth shuddered.

Mike continued, "NACAM must succeed with a minimum of resistance. After all, we'll never convince the other triumvirates to adopt it if we are suffering mass rebellion in our own provinces."

"I'm glad you agree with me, Mike. By the way, we have a cabinet meeting at seven A.M. on Monday morning. I imagine they'll have plenty of questions regarding NACAM. Irene Tupik will pepper me with objections, but we cannot surround ourselves with mere yes people, can we?"

"No. By the way, how's Victor?"

"He's all right. A little run down, but a coughing jag that severe would incapacitate anyone for a while. Grandfather's still very strong. He'll be around for a good long time yet. Speaking of family, did you talk to Margaret today?"

Parker replied, "I called her after I left you and Victor. She's just fine, but that was before the NACAM announcement."

"Maybe you should call again like a dutiful husband."

"She's probably already asleep. Besides, she trusts your judgment."

Garth emptied his glass and sat it down on an end table. "Well, it's nice to know that I'll still have one supporter after the next opinion poll. I just hope our citizens will comply voluntarily; otherwise, I'm afraid that Carmen and her paramilitaries will have an awfully bloody row to hoe."

"It'll be all right, Garth. Carmen denotes a true professional. I'm sure that her department will maintain order as far as her jurisdiction permits. But I'm curious about who's overseeing the NACAM directives? This project's so big that there's no way that any of our ministers will be able to concentrate on it. I suspect you'll need another minister specifically added to the cabinet."

"You're forgetting that NACAM will be linked into TransTrak. Every citation will be exacted automatically. Physical enforcement's the only concern. I have confidence that Carmen will maintain order. You just said so yourself."

Mike inquired, "Isn't Carmen required to maintain order for all crimes and not just traveling violations?"

"Yes, so what?"

"We have six hundred million motor vehicles in North America with only forty million paramilitaries on active duty with another twenty million recruits for next year. I don't think Carmen's units are capable of maintaining order in North America if we incur an open revolt. Instead, a solution may be to commandeer all North American law enforcement agencies under triumviral control. That way, paramilitary units and civilian police would coordinate with each other to avoid wasted effort and resources."

Garth countered, "I don't know about that, Mike. Such a military intrusion would streamline enforcement, but do you think our citizens or even the police themselves would allow such an invasion in their private lives?"

"You're the President of North America. You just issued an edict without a majority vote. Issue another one."

Garth countered, "I don't think I like what I'm hearing."

"Gotcha, I just wanted to see if NACAM had gone to your head. I don't believe North Americans would ever stand for their local police being placed under triumviral jurisdiction. If you declare such an edict, I believe restoring order would be damned near impossible."

Garth sighed, "You had me worried for a moment, Mike. I thought you might be serious about a military coup."

"I'm more serious about going to bed. I think I'll say good night."

"Good night, Mike. I'll be hitting the sack myself pretty soon. See you in the morning." Mike yawned, "It's already morning. Its pushing 12:30 A.M. Later."

Garth reclined at his desk after Mike departed.

Scansat Eleven awakened Chairman DeSalle in his New York-bound limousine to brief the old man on his grandson's current activities.

Xavier pretended to sleep while hanging on Victor's every word.

After the full report, Victor called Brady directly with a shriek, "Moloch's Mud Whore, Garth! What the hell's going on?"

"What do you mean, Grandfather?"

"Don't hand me that, boy! Why'd you use the scrambler tonight? Scansat Eleven just relayed a full briefing!"

"Then they should have told you that it was an accident. Mike Parker crushed a pen against the scrambler button when he closed my desk drawer. It took several minutes to pry it open again."

"What was he doing in your desk?"

"He was after some pen and paper to scribble down a Chess Roulette strategy. I'm afraid that the drawer's permanently scratched."

DeSalle snarled, "Who cares about that goddamned drawer? I just wanted to hear what happened from your own mouth. Now, regarding Mike Parker's police commandeer proposal, authorize it at once!"

"B-But Grandfather! That was a joke! It would be political suicide for me!"

"I didn't ask your opinion! Blast it, Garth! Do what I tell you! You'll inform your citizens about the order tonight."

Brady paused a moment before answering, "Yes, Mr. Chairman."

"That's better, whelp! Now, there's one more thing. I'm holding an emergency session of the URC Forum this afternoon at one P.M. You will attend."

"Yes, *sir*. Is there anything else?"

"Are you getting smart with me, boy?"

"I'm just tired."

"Go to bed then. I want you fresh for that session. And I want you wide awake when you announce that second executive order tonight!"

DeSalle closed his Media Palm and went back to sleep.

Xavier had remained awake without moving a muscle.

CHAPTER FIFTEEN

Sebastian

lvin Wilford awakened on a bare mattress, rubbing both eyes. He beheld a ten-foot-square stone cell surrounding his metal-framed bed. A dingy, white toilet and sink were positioned in the corner opposite his headboard. The cell had no windows. An enormous gate of iron bars blocked one side of the perimeter; the rest of the walls, ceiling, and floor were ancient stone and musty mortar. Outside the cell door, a naked, white light bulb illuminated the shadows of iron bars across the length of the floor while icy cold walls glistened with intermittent pockets of slime.

Alvin cursed arthritis while placing his bare feet against the rough floor, noticing that he was wearing a smock and drawstring sweatpants the color of bleached bones. He staggered toward the iron gate like a balancing seaman in a typhoon. Pappy grabbed twin handfuls of bars while staring into the hallway beyond. A succession of suspended ceiling bulbs ran in both directions as far as his perspective could see.

Then he whirled around toward the sound of scurrying claws. Pappy quickly removed his smock before crouching on one knee. He looked under his bed. Nothing was visible in the black void, but he heard the grating sound of a sliding metal bolt.

An enormous weasel suddenly charged out from under the bed. It was the largest, slimiest, and foulest smelling varmint he had ever encountered; the beast must've exceeded twenty-five pounds. Pappy fell onto his back as the creature sank fangs into his right calf muscle. Alvin rolled onto his left side to grasp the attacker, but the weasel released before sidestepping out of reach. The old man regained his feet as the weasel slowed to a stalking pace. Pappy clenched his smock before lunging toward the animal. The weasel scampered out of reach again. Alvin slipped on some floor slime and fell just as the varmint sprang onto his back, sinking its fangs repeatedly with ravenous fury. Pappy dropped his smock in the center of the floor before standing again with the weasel dangling by its jaws and rending open flesh with all four claws.

Alvin repeatedly shoved his back against the nearest wall before finally crushing the wretched creature. He flung the dead animal into a vacant cell corner. His mangled back throbbed while washing his wounded calf in the fractured porcelain sink.

Another slide bolt grated. Alvin screamed and jumped backward as a muscular Plymouth Rock Rooster gouged him with razor sharp claws after charging through an open door beneath the sink. Pappy couldn't believe the bird's size. It easily exceeded thirty pounds and stood over two feet tall. The cock suddenly stopped in the center of the cell, expanded its clipped wings, and crowed defiantly.

Alvin seized his smock off the floor. The rooster lunged again aiming for its target's left thigh. Pappy kicked the bird in the breast, hurling it onto its back. He dove to the floor enclosing the smock around it, but the rooster flapped free to land on both feet. The bird sliced the old man's nose, chin, and left cheek before its target finally rose off his belly. Alvin pushed his smock over the bird's body again until the animal's maneuvers shredded his makeshift net to tatters.

Pappy grasped the rooster's right leg with both hands the instant the bird got free. He slammed its back against the nearest wall, its head against the edge of the sink, rammed its breast into a metal bedpost, and finally pounded the monster against the sink until it mashed into bloody pulp. Alvin sucked a deep cold breath before tossing the creature's corpse into a corner. He picked up his tattered smock and swooned onto the mattress, trembling with cold while covering his frigid feet with the cloth.

Another slide bolt grated. Alvin's sweated chilled into icicles while pulling both knees to his chest and sitting upright. An enormous raccoon lumbered out through an open door near the iron gate, reached the rooster, and sucked blood from its limp, oozing neck. Alvin watched without moving a muscle. Then the beast suddenly sat up on its haunches and sniffed the air rapidly. Pappy suppressed a scream with his fist before locking eyes with the animal. It snarled back at him with foamy, bloodstained teeth before charging.

Then a single gunshot blasted the animal dead to the floor. Pappy looked up seeing the silhouette of a man standing outside the gate of his cell with a gun, smoke pungently wafted through the bars.

The silhouette commanded, "Come with me."

Alvin was too exhausted to lift his body off the mattress. He simply melted down into a lying position. The shirtless gunman produced a key, unlocked the gate, and stepped into the cell wearing a mat of hair across his chest and back. His bare feet gripped the slimy floor with familiarity. The six-foot-six-inch gunman packed a pistol in his left hand and repeated, "Come with me." The old man remained immobile looking up into twin, red eyes recessed into a clean-shaven face with a thick bush of black eyebrows joining at the center of his captor's forehead. Grasping Alvin's torn right hand, the gunman fired three bullets through Wilford's palm. Pappy passed out as the brute slung him over one shoulder and departed the cell with his burden.

Pappy awakened on a wooden chair. The floor below him patterned a checkerboard of black and white linoleum. He scanned the enormous, forty-foot-wide, circular room. A twelve-foot-high ceiling displayed massive, wooden moldings carved into images of upright pigs, goats, and dogs dancing around multiple dome-shaped monoliths that were three times each animal's size. The room was pleasantly warm. There were other wooden chairs randomly scattered all around him along the length of the floor.

Then he spotted an elderly silver-haired man occupying a large, oak desk at the opposite end of the room. Alvin's shooter suddenly entered through a set of double-swinging doors; he was still bare foot and shirtless with his pistol now tucked inside his pants. The giant brute quickly picked Alvin up over his head by the neck and ass, walked the length of the room, and violently slammed him onto a three-legged stool in front of the desk. The silver-haired man ignored him while currently performing paperwork.

Five minutes later, Alvin Wilford lost his temper. "All right, you old fossil! Where the hell am I?"

Finally finishing his paperwork, the silver-haired man stood up and spoke, "Mister Wilford, your son's abandoned and placed you in deadly danger. I will only question you once; you will answer truthfully and without hesitation. Otherwise, you'll die most unpleasantly. Do you understand me?"

"Yeah, Warden *Hell spawn*, I get the picture. But how about answering my questions first?"

The brute fractured Alvin's right collarbone with his pistol butt. Wilford hit the floor in a fetal position with bone shards protruding upward through his shoulder skin.

The silver-haired man continued calmly, "Now are you ready to answer my questions?"

"Aaaagggghhhh!—Yes!"

"That's fine. Sebastian, please reseat our guest."

The sadist seized and dangled his burden in midair before slamming him onto the stool again.

The silver-haired man resumed, "Where has your son gone?"

"I didn't know that he went anywhere. I went to sleep at home and then found myself in that slimy, vermin-ridden shit hole." Alvin nodded toward the giant. "Where from the pits of hell did you dredge up this monster?"

Sebastian raised his pistol, but an upraised hand from the interviewer stopped him.

The silver-haired man continued, "What was your son working on?"

"A new car engine."

"What kind of engine?"

"I don't know. He never let me inside his place."

"Come now, Mr. Wilford. We know you've a pretty good idea what was inside that workshop. Our organization's been randomly monitoring your home for the past two years ever since your son earned $50 million for his PVC engine designs. We know that he was experimenting with electromagnetism but don't have any specifics. Now talk."

"All right! Just keep this shithole ape off my ass!"

Sebastian tucked his pistol back before clenching both of his fists.

The silver-haired replied matter-of-factly, "I'm still waiting."

"Eric was experimenting with an engine that ran on electromagnetic fields. He called it a Bipolar Drive. It doesn't need any liquid fuel to run; it only needs a slight amount of lubricant for its moving parts."

"A Bipolar Drive? You mean his engine could extract energy out of thin air and channel it to the wheels of an automobile?"

"That was the general idea."

"Did he get it to work?"

"I don't know. I never saw him road test it."

"You mean this prototype is already attached to a functioning automobile?"

"I said I never saw it! It's possible he could have bought a cheap car to rebuild himself. My son's a pretty fair mechanic."

"What model of car was it?"

"You got wax in your ears, prune face? I've already told you I don't know anything about that! He was very secretive about certain phases of his experiments. He would discuss theory with me, but that was all. He seemed to think that I would be safer if I didn't know too much!" Alvin glanced painfully up at Sebastian. "Ain't that a laugh?"

The interviewer continued, "Do you have any idea where your son might have driven his prototype?"

"Goddamnit! I'm not sure he's got a prototype!"

"Trust me, Mr. Wilford, he has. The workshop's now empty and he certainly didn't carry a car engine away on foot. His registered vehicle is still in your garage. He also destroyed his computer; there were no data disks found. Where could your son have gone?"

"He's rich enough to travel anywhere. If Eric's trying to escape you bastards, then he's disappeared off the face of the earth."

"Do you believe your son will try to contact you?"

"Not if he's running away. He'd anticipate surveillance."

"Thank you for the information. Proceed, Sebastian."

The brute pulled and jammed his pistol through the clenched teeth of his victim. Pappy spewed blood and bone as Sebastian shoved his gun barrel against the back of Alvin's throat before pulling the trigger. Alvin Wilford was dead before his twitching body slumped to the floor.

The silver-haired man commanded, "Have maintenance clean this mess up. Sebastian, you may salvage the corpse if you wish."

The brute grinned rows of chipped yellow teeth before slinging Alvin Wilford's decapitated body over his right shoulder and lumbered out of the room. Pappy's freshly draining corpse swathed a crimson trail diagonally across the linoleum.

The silver-haired man sat down, extracted a Media Palm from his vest, and touched its screen. A female voice answered, "Martial Protectorate. Good morning, Tau."

"Good morning, Mary, I need to speak with Commissioner Quimby."

"Commissioner Quimby's not in his office. He's en route to attend a URC emergency session in New York City scheduled for one P.M. today."

"Then I won't intrude. Inform him we're still on the Wilford trail, but the inventor's father proved a dead end. We are expanding our search to a five-hundred-mile diameter. Also inform him that the senior Cupola Agent who allowed Eric Wilford to escape has been consigned to the Pit of the Damned as today's object lesson."

"Good hunting, Tau. This Wilford fella is important, isn't he?"

"With any luck, he won't be for long."

Tau Singh returned the Palm to his pocket while leaving his interrogation room. Five minutes later, Singh walked onto one of thirteen private, stone-carved, outer wall balconies, reserved for any Crimson Cupola dignitaries attending the local Pit of the Damned rituals. Each balcony was suspended twelve feet above the surface of a serpentine stone floor spanning forty feet in diameter. As Protectorate Security Chief, Tau happened to be the highest-ranking official for today's activities. He walked to the edge of the booth and gazed down.

The center of the floor displayed a circular bed of cold charcoal spread evenly over its ten-foot-diameter to a depth of twelve inches. Two four-foot-tall, eighteen-inch-diameter, steel posts were anchored into opposite points central to the charcoal bed. A high-powered motor was mounted on top of each post within a cube-shaped housing of asbestos; although both housings were bolted down, their three-foot cubic volume betrayed the illusion of top heaviness. A twenty-four-inch stainless steel disk was mounted within each housing that faced one another from opposite sides of the fire pit. Both disks included a pair of steel manacles attached to an inner winch mechanism whose steel cable threaded through each housing wall and attached around a massive steel spool inside both cubes. The diameter of the semi-dark amphitheater was sixty feet with a vaulted ceiling towering thirty feet above the serpentine floor.

Grotesque illustrations of hell fire were painted in towering columns of red, yellow, blue, and orange flames. The paintings lined the stone-walled circumference of the chamber. Intermingled among the gaps in the flames were images of demonic figures like fugitives from a druid's nightmare. Alternating figures displayed gray, black, blue, red, green, and purple skins with the scaly texture of either fish or reptiles. The creatures are wearing the torsos of men and women with cloven hooves and scalp hair of various colors. Animal heads crowned every figure: bulls, pigs, goats, snakes, cats, bats, wolves, bears, and even lizards. Many demons extended forked tongues from slobbering mouths while disgorging fluids of dark red, black, and bluish-green.

Six rows of stair-stepping, stone-carved benches surrounded the central serpentine floor and its fire pit. The amphitheater was about half full of occupants murmuring with anticipation. Between the top layer of stone benches and the inner walls stood a circle of twenty-four full scale and inverted crosses reaching ten feet in height with a tiny cast iron cauldron perched on the top of each one. The vapors within the pots melded incense and sulfur into a pungent odor resembling decomposing flesh.

There were also thirteen gothic-arched windows set near the ceiling, encircling the chamber at equal distances. Each window was stain glassed in a single color: yellow, red, green, blue, orange, gray, cream, gold, silver, crimson, turquoise, rose and royal purple. The sunlight diffusing through them created a mild prismatic effect.

Sebastian's balcony suspended twenty-two feet above the center of the fire pit. From there, the brute could operate all manner of cables, pulleys, chain hoists, and directional booms controlling any Pit of the Damned lifting, holding, and rotating tasks during ritual ceremonies.

Tau remained standing while cheerfully anticipating the festivities to come. The Pit of the Damned was a sacred place for the Crimson Cupola of North America; it had existed since the seventeenth century during the reign of the Massachusetts Bay Colony in New England. However, no non-Cupola members of that colony ever knew of its existence, the CC had constructed it secretly and almost completely underground with timely upgrades over the centuries.

Singh raised his right hand and plunged the amphitheater into obedient silence. He announced, "Servants of the Crimson Cupola, a brother has committed an act of disobedience. Regretfully, it is one of the senior operatives among you. Therefore, an object lesson is mandatory. Former Senior Agent Justin Phillips will now endure Naked Fire. Commence the ritual."

Three men pushed an eight-foot tall, four-foot in diameter, fluid-filled, transparent cylinder mounted on top of a motorized platform onto the serpentine stage before stopping along one side of the charcoal pit. Phillips floated unconsciously while immersed inside; he wore a facemask with a small breathing gas canister beneath his chin. One attendant waved up toward the control balcony.

A set of chained manacles descended from a boom into the waiting hands of the signalman. Holding the chains, he and another man stepped up onto the wheeled platform. While the signalman waited, the other man placed a stepladder beside the tube and climbed up to where his waist was level with the top. He hauled Phillips out and stretched him on his back against stone floor.

Then the signalman brandished a large, razor sharp scalpel before deftly slicing away the skin of Phillips' feet while leaving his toenails unmarred. The skin softening solution had done its work as the satanic surgeon peeled the skin of both legs up to the knees.

Then Phillips' ankles were fastened in boom manacles before Sebastian winched the victim off the floor to an inverted position. The free folds of peeled skin hung downward while Justin suspended three inches above the floor like a freshly slaughtered steer. The victim was then castrated and cauterized for expediency before his scalp was peeled away like the hide of a ripened orange. After the fiends removed his facemask, Phillips' forehead, cheeks, and jaw line skin yielded readily enough, but the eyelids, nose, and lips required a much slower pace. Finally all the facial skin was sliced clean of its covering but displayed multiple nicks from non-chemical skinning.

The signalman gestured again. Agent Phillips was lowered slowly onto the cold charcoal pit. The attendants unfastened the ankles from the boomed shackles before securing them and the victim's wrists to the sets of steel post manacles hanging from both housing disks. The signalman removed a syringe from the pocket of his black smock and injected Phillips' carotid artery. Then Sebastian's butchers stepped off cold charcoal leaving their mutilated handiwork lying alone with plenty of cable slack.

Overhead Sebastian pressed a button on his console; all four limp cables retracted in sync. As their tension increased, Phillips was lifted off of the charcoal and stretched tightly to hang four feet over the center of the pit. Another button activated pneumatic rams within the steel posts while their height extended upward from four to eight feet. Flaming gas jets ignited the charcoal with deep red coals clustering in moments and projecting intense, shimmering heat into the air. Both motors turned now slowly rotating Phillips in a clockwise rotation at six revolutions per minute. The heat assailed the victim's naked nerve endings as the injection eventually awakened him. The human rotisserie began as Phillips fought his instinct to scream.

Sebastian slowly lowered the victim back down to four feet. The heat increased exponentially. Justin's pain became excruciating while steaming tears boiled over the bare muscles of both cheeks. His peeled eyes bathed in searing heat. Unable to pass out due to his injection, he screamed as millions of broiled nerve endings registered immeasurable pain simultaneously. Then Sebastian dropped the rotisserie within two feet of the glowing charcoal. Phillips convulsed uncontrollably as trickles of cooking blood blackened all over his skinless body.

The Pit of the Damned proved itself to be a literal hell on earth, but to Tau Singh, Phillips' throat rupturing screams were music to his ears.

Sebastian lowered Justin within a single foot and continued rotating over the glowing embers. Phillips' eyes melted within their burning sockets. Fresh shrieks launched expanding bubbles of blood out Justin's fried mouth while his whole body blackened like a Cajun steak. The controller raised the pitiful wretch back up to eight feet. Phillips hung here thirty seconds before descending to six feet. After ten more seconds of screeching that would have made a banshee gasp, Justin was returned to the one-foot level again before the man mercifully died of shock and dehydration. But Sebastian continued to evenly cook the blackened hulk like a side of beef at a ranch barbecue. With Phillips' death, today's object lesson was over and class was immediately dismissed; the stone benches were emptied within five minutes.

Tau Singh left his balcony and walked down to the fire pit. Phillips' body was now completely basted black with wisps of fine ash dropping from baked arms and legs. The victim's empty right eye socket began oozing brain fluid to bake within the skeletal hollow above his cheekbone.

Tau smiled while watching Sebastian suddenly elevate the body back to a four-foot height. A pipeline of water suddenly gushed underneath the hot embers now belching both steam and ash into the chamber. Tau sneezed mildly while all of the coals disintegrated. The charcoal pit cooled down and drained within sixty seconds.

Then the controller lowered the fully cooked corpse back against the dead coals. Tau watched the signalman and his partner release Phillips' body before dragging it onto the serpentine floor while crinkled flesh wisped away under the friction.

Then Singh watched Sebastian lower Alvin Wilford's naked body, ankles up on an auxiliary boom, before placing it onto the wet coals. The signalman and his partner released Pappy's corpse from the boom. Then they fastened its arms and legs onto the slackened rotisserie before they departed now leaving Tau and Sebastian alone within the Pit of the Damned.

Sebastian operated more controls from above; the elderly corpse stretched out before elevating four feet above the charcoal pit. He reignited the gas jets while automatically setting his prey at 15 rpm. Alvin's corpse began roasting and turning like an impaled hot dog over an open campfire. Then Sebastian left his balcony before joining Tau near the edge of the burning fire pit. Pappy was already beginning to turn a golden brown.

Tau grinned before asking, "My dear Sebastian, is Alvin Wilford sufficient payment for your services rendered today?"

The cannibal brute articulated, "Certainly, Father. I relish our enemies; their strength will soon bolster my own and I'm going to need all of it to finally defeat Milton at the next Geodesy Gauntlet!"

"I understand, son. But don't let this sporting contest turn into a vendetta. Remember that both you and Milton are on the same team."

"Only outside of the gauntlet arena, Father! Next time, I'm pitching that titanic bastard over the ropes! By the way, join me for a healthy slice of Homo Crematus?"

"No, thank you. Cannibalism leaves me squeamish."

Sebastian reflected, "I know, Father, and that's always amused me. You've taught me everything I know about inflicting pain. You've even assisted in training my cell animals. I would think that a little cannibalism shouldn't bother you at all! By the way, did you enjoy our little amusement in Wilford's cell today?"

"Very much, but it's a shame you had to shoot DeSade. That raccoon's brought us many hours of pleasure."

"I miscalculated the old man's frailty. After all, killing Rikki-Tikki and Talon should have been easier. Wilford simply didn't have enough stamina to face DeSade afterward."

"A pity, son. DeSade proved a more valuable creature than Alvin Wilford."

"Still, the old man defied us even unto death. That's why I want his flesh!"

Tau asked, "What about Justin Phillips' carcass?"

"I can't stomach any traitor, Father; he's meat for my cell beasts."

"You know, Chairman DeSalle hasn't announced a Geodesy Gauntlet for quite a while. You may be waiting a long time before facing Milton again."

Sebastian replied, "True, but our chairman may decree one at any time and I want to be ready. Besides, Homo Crematus tastes better than any other meat, especially when basted in its own blood."

"Don't overeat. Now bend down here."

Tau kissed Sebastian's lowered brow before departing.

CHAPTER SIXTEEN

Double Cross

Matt Rigby and Sam Thomas had collected enough evidence during the last two days to prove the TEG's temperature report was bogus. Matt had cashed in on his father's connections to gain a covert interview with a GRA mole within TEG ranks; his confidant was a former member of the defunct United States Department of Meteorology now living in Washington, D.C., Maryland District.

At eight A.M. on the third day, Matt informed Chairman Spencer Mitchell about his Washington breakthrough and also announced another personal rendezvous pending in Boston, Massachusetts District. After Rigby hung up, Spencer requested a *Protectorate Termination Compact* on both his field officers; the request was immediately authorized by Commissioner Quimby at the standard fee of $100,000 per target.

At ten A.M. Spencer was presiding over a strategic assembly of the TDI and TEG with Minister of Enforcement Franklin attending. TEG Chairman Anthony Rankin was currently declaring to their guest that the President could count on complete TEG cooperation regarding any NACAM enforcement.

Carmen sat adjacent to Chairman Mitchell at the table end opposite Rankin. She had remained silent while taking notes. Her lack of authoritative manner surprised Spencer; if he'd possessed her authority; Mitchell would have been belching imperial edicts just to throw his political weight around. He also wondered why the minister of travel was blatantly absent; Andre Roget seemed the logical choice to represent President Brady for any transportation proceedings.

Rankin's briefing included information regarding upgraded suborbital platform connections and modified equipment for implementing NACAM in order to avoid overloading TransTrak's detection system. At length, the speaker concluded with some personal suggestions regarding NACAM manpower deployment.

Mitchell regained the floor, "You have your assignments. Any questions before we dismiss?"

Carmen raised an arm.

"Yes, Minister Franklin, what is it?"

"I want to know how such surveillance can be done without eliminating the North American Citizen's triumviral rights to privacy."

"The right to privacy only exists for law abiding citizens, Minister Franklin. In the case of NACAM surveillance, TransTrak would alert our department to the commitment of a travel or small engine crime. If a citation and penalty are computed and recorded against a given individual, then any surveillance necessary to apprehend the perpetrator would be under the lawful operation of probable cause. Search and seizure violations don't apply to probable cause."

Minister Franklin paused before saying, "I see. Then any citation generated by your TransTrak Network would be regarded as an established fact even if this system committed any error?"

Spencer countered respectfully, "TransTrak does not make errors, Minister Franklin. It has alternate backups and multiple platform confirmation designed within it. If a crime's detected and registered, you can rest assured that it's genuine."

"Thank you, Chairman Mitchell."

"Spencer," he replied with a mild leer.

"Very well, Spencer. I have another question."

"By all means, Carmen."

"Minister Franklin, please."

"Of course, pardon my familiarity."

Carmen continued, "I'm in the process of recruiting several million volunteers to reinforce the bulk of my troops. After my military forces eventually build up sufficient manpower for NACAM enforcement, are your people going to continue surveillance duties in the field?"

Mitchell retorted, "The TDI exists only to serve the collective good of our citizens. My people are at your disposal, Minister, not vice-versa."

Chairman Rankin interrupted, "As are mine. This operation mandates a team effort in order to succeed. My people have many connections with municipal authorities including domestic police forces. Since you're not authorized to command local police, those ties could possibly act as liaisons between your paramilitary units and police officers."

Carmen stood, replying, "Thank you, gentlemen. I appreciate both of you placing your departments at my disposal. I am now notifying you that President Brady's issuing a second executive order over triumviral media later today. As of midnight tonight, Eastern Standard Time, every North American police officer and triumviral paramilitary soldier will be placed under my direct command. Do you have any questions?"

Nearly numb with shock, Mitchell snarled involuntarily, "Who convinced the President to authorize such a drastic step? We don't know whether North American citizens will revolt against NACAM yet. Why are they being herded under one whip before any trouble has begun?"

Minister Franklin answered, "We must prepare for the worst case scenario; assembling all enforcement officers under a single authority is expedient. I don't know who convinced the President to make this move. Maybe your own temperature report compelled him. As for myself, I follow orders. I would encourage the rest of you to do the same. Any other questions?"

The chamber grew silent.

Carmen declared, "Very well, gentlemen, this meeting's adjourned."

Both chairmen remained in the boardroom after everyone else left. Rankin broke their ominous silence first, "Well, Spence, that Cuban bitch really nailed our slats to the wall! Brady must be convinced by our bogus report, but I never dreamed that fool would initiate such a sweeping order on his own!"

"I'm not sure he did, Tony. He's not a very popular fella right now. We both knew that would happen over this NACAM directive. But we also know that politically correct citizens will comply with anything to avoid violence. Those idiots proved that handing over their guns to the Feds five years ago. President Brady must've been compelled to declare this new order. He wouldn't commit such political suicide without a lot of outside pressure. Who has enough clout to pull President Brady's strings? It can't be The URC; they only preside over collective, triumviral matters. This new bombshell's must be domestic."

Rankin asked nervously, "What are we going to do? We can't have every cop and soldier in North America under the capricious whims of that Cuban twit! How are we going to stop this?"

"We can't stop it, Tony. We're not big enough, but I believe we can fight it. Remember what Brady promised to that reporter last night? He would allow a televised environmental debate with the Global Reaction Alliance if North America's majority vote demanded it."

"What the hell good does that do for us? Nobody outside of a few free thinkers and objective truth-seekers believe what the GRA says. Our media partners have been spoon-feeding citizens since the *Report on Iron Mountain* back in the mid-twentieth century! Now that we've got them conditioned to our way of thinking, we just can't stand up and say, 'Sorry, folks, but we lied to you about the environment!'"

"Relax, Tony. All we have to do is concede the debate based on the scientific truth presented by the GRA. That way, we save face and shoot President Brady's power grab right between the eyes."

Rankin blurted, "But that'll derail our TransTrak scam too! We'd be throwing away trillions in potential revenues for decades to come!"

"We can always perpetrate another scheme later. Most people

believe whatever they're told as long as the message's stamped with a triumviral media seal of approval. But now it looks like President Brady's ambitions are too goddamned big to allow!"

"That's funny coming from you, Spencer. Didn't you have some ambitions of your own? TransTrak didn't accidentally become law, you know. We used up most of Frances Snell's and Max Stromberg's favors to push it through the former U.S. Congress."

Mitchell rolled his eyes, "Look, stupid, I don't need the sanctimonious ravings of a rookie right now! If it weren't for me, you'd still be preparing peoples' income taxes in a rinky-dink cubicle!"

"Sorry, chum, I'm scared. This whole NACAM thing's freaking me out."

"I'm scared too, pal. That's why we've got to keep our heads. What we need is someone who can boost the GRA's credibility on a triumviral wide basis in a hurry. And it's a cinch that none of the triumviral media networks will help us; they're all under one roof of ownership. And I'm not familiar with any alternative Internet sites big enough to get the message out."

"How about independent stations? There must be a few left."

"Independent television stations? Where?"

"I meant radio stations, Spence."

Mitchell huffed before declaring, "Nobody listens to radio anymore except prime networks catering to motorists. We need somebody that will stick his neck out against the mainstream of popular opinion. Unfortunately for now, nobody survives against our media long enough to get an effective message out."

"What about that paltry Richmond, Boston, and Washington, D.C.-based network we spent $20 million trying to shut down awhile back?"

"The SOL Network can't still be around by this time! Max was murdering that business over three months ago by using his connections to perpetually strip sponsors from Peter Wicks!"

"What was the AM setting for that show?"

"I don't remember, but it was close to the right end of the dial.

Try it, Tony."

Rankin walked to an oak cabinet and activated a console radio. Classical music quickly flooded the room.

Mitchell retorted, "No, that's our local FM nerve tonic; switch to AM!"

Rankin adjusted the dial until Mitchell stopped him at 1580. The present spokesman was bashing the NACAM directive with zeal while claiming that abnormal global warming was dubious.

Mitchell almost squealed, "That's it! Old Wicks is still kicking! Maxy must be roiling in his grave!"

Rankin exclaimed, "Incredible! The SOL network's still alive! What do you have in mind, chum?"

"We can pump money into Wicks' message. I'll set up a dummy corporation to transfer an anonymous windfall into his lap; we'll start with $50 million."

Rankin got excited. "Peter Wicks is probably up to his ass in hock. Let's send Rigby and Thomas over to see him; those two Boy Scouts would make perfect liaisons! Let's set it up right away!"

Mitchell's smile suddenly slid off his double chin. He sucked in a labored breath, rubbed his forehead, and somberly said, "Turn off the radio, Tony."

"Why?"

"Turn that goddamned thing off!"

Rankin obeyed while asking in a whisper, "What's the matter? We can use the SOL Network."

"Not with Matt Rigby and Sam Thomas, we can't."

"Why not?"

Spencer paused before answering, "I authorized a hit on them before dawn this morning; they're supposed to participate in a lethal car accident. I didn't want to take any chances with Rigby after he discounted our report; he seemed too sharp for his own good. Sam Thomas was just a faithful dog, but Rigby commanded his loyalty. So I targeted both of them for assassination."

"Oh my God! Call it off, Spencer! We can use those boys now!"

Mitchell yelled, "I can't rescind a protectorate termination compact, you idiot! A Martial Protectorate death squad will liquidate me for malfeasance; no one screws with those maniacs! Matt Rigby and Sammy Thomas will end up meat for the worms just as sure as we're sitting here!"

Tau Singh was batting a thousand today. After leaving Sebastian to feast in the amphitheater, the silver-haired man received a Media Palm message that announced, "TDI Chairman Spencer Mitchell has sanctioned a PTC for his subordinates Matthew Rigby and Samuel Thomas. Commissioner Abner Quimby has authorized the request. Currently, TransTrak has full surveillance on Rigby's vehicle. Both targets are traveling to Boston from Washington, D.C. The compact will initiate after the targets depart Boston; they must not return to Washington, D.C. Exterminate them at your discretion, Tau. End of message."

Singh decided on a Massachusetts deathtrap. Within five minutes, he was being chauffeured toward Boston to personally supervise this murder; the Pit of the Damned had already whetted his appetite. Tau anticipated the most likely route and chose Foxboro, Massachusetts District, as a base of operations. Once TransTrak confirmed the target's specific road, the compact would be consummated. His assassination squad had completely assembled in Foxboro by one P.M.

Matt drove his 2036 Pegasus sedan toward New London, Connecticut District, at 1:30 P.M. Sam was asleep in the back; he'd stayed up half the previous night collating atmospheric data into a concise form for their next contact. Rigby had informed Spencer Mitchell that he was heading for Boston but not that their covert meeting in New London would come first. Neither Rigby nor Thomas had ever met Commander Richard Franklin, but their Washington mole had made them swear not to reveal their Connecticut destination; otherwise, their contact would never show up even though he'd set both the time and place.

Both TDI men were in a New London pizza parlor by 2:14 P.M. Recognizing Mole's description of the newcomers, Richard left his booth and greeted the pair while wearing a gray sweat suit and a Red Sox baseball cap. "Welcome, gentlemen; I'm at your disposal."

"Pleased to meet you, Mr. Shrew. I'm Matt Rigby and this is Sam Thomas."

Richard encrypted, "The pleasure's all mine, gentlemen. *The sun rises and sets every day.*"

Matt answered, "*But there's a hot spot at both dawn and dusk.* You and Mole were really serious about that silly recognition code, weren't you?"

"We're always serious about potential danger; we have families too. Now, why has Mole sent you?"

"Search me. Mole said we had to contact you, but he didn't say why."

Richard held up his right hand and said, "Before we go any further, let's order. The smell of that pizza's driving me nuts. You guys can have anything you want. It's on me."

"Thanks, I'll eat any pizza as long as there are no anchovies. How about you, Sam?"

Thomas smiled. "I'm not much for pizza, but I'll take a salad bar and a beer."

Matt added, "Beer for me as well."

Franklin smiled while ordering a salad, a pitcher of beer, and a large pepperoni and mushroom pizza with extra cheese. The beer arrived just as Sam returned from filling his plate at the salad bar.

Richard continued, "Back to the business. You two are here to save your lives. Chairman Mitchell plans to murder you both."

Sam spilled some beer on the tabletop.

Matt smirked while crossing both arms, "Very funny! Now, what's the real reason?"

"Spencer Mitchell issued a termination compact against your lives; the request came early this morning. Mole informed me after monitoring

Mitchell's Media Palm. Mole also told you that Shrew possessed some very sensitive information, which was in your best interest. I believe that saving your skins qualifies."

"What a load of bullshit! Chairman Mitchell personally sent us on this fact-finding hunt! Why would he do that if he didn't want Sam and me to uncover anything?"

"He wanted you to uncover any potential moles who don't side with your superior's TransTrak objectives. Mole's been monitoring both Max Stromberg and Spencer Mitchell's Palm calls for quite a while. Your superiors suspect they have dissenters. Your enthusiasm at the last board meeting gave Mitchell the idea of using you as a Judas Goat to identify any traitors."

Rigby frowned. "Then why would Mitchell kill us before we informed him?"

Franklin shrugged. "I don't know."

Matt slammed his glass on the tabletop. "This cloak-and-dagger horse shit is nonsense! What's your real game, Shrew?"

Richard replied, "This isn't a game, rookie. Chairman Mitchell set you up for a permanent fall along with your sidekick here! Up until this morning, Mitchell thought that he was going to control the NACAM directives under his personal authority."

Sam interrupted, "You mean NACAM was a TDI objective?"

"Precisely. NACAM is the combined brainchild of the TDI and the TEG. President Brady was ordered to declare it into law."

"Who gives the President that kind of order?"

"The same people who buy triumviral elections all over the world."

Rigby snorted. "Certainly, and they're the same people who covertly rule the world! Oh God, deliver us from the paranoid delusions of secret societies!"

Franklin flared both nostrils. "Can the sarcasm, sonny. You and your partner are marked men. I've told you everything I know. If you don't come with me now, you're on your own."

"That's okay with me, buster!"

Franklin watched the pair stand up and walk out the restaurant door.

Matt never looked back as the two of them climbed back into his Pegasus Sedan.

Sam almost whimpered while Matt stared the car. "What if Shrew's telling the truth? What if we *are* marked?"

"That kind of intrigue bullshit went out with James Bond! This is probably someone's idea of a practical joke and a damned poor one! We're getting the hell out of here!"

"We're not going to Boston, are we?"

Matt exclaimed, "Hell no! I'm not wasting any more time! We're heading back to D.C.! I don't appreciate driving three hundred miles out of my way for some goddamned Snipe Hunt!"

Tau Singh was informed that Matt Rigby's car had reversed direction at New London and was now returning south the same way it came. He frowned while briefing his squad. "Our fox has doubled back. TransTrak reports he's moving south at the legal limit. Any suggestions how we can intercept a moving target now over one hundred miles ahead of us?"

Agent Richmond man raised his hand.

Tau asked hopefully, "Moses, you have a suggestion?"

"Yes, sir. I recommend we use aircraft to intercept him before he approaches Washington, D.C."

"We'd have to backtrack to Boston to acquire some."

Richmond suggested, "Sir, Boston's only thirty minutes away. Rigby and Thomas are moving at the legal limit. If they're heading back to D.C., they're at least five hours away. We have a Mantis Transport at Logan Airport. We could be airborne and landing near Philadelphia at least an hour before they reached it."

Tau tugged his ear. "Maybe, if the aircraft wasn't used to fly Chairman DeSalle to New York." Singh received Palm confirmation in less than a minute. "The Mantis is available. Let's roll, boys."

Forty-five minutes later, Tau Singh's task force was airborne. The

Mantis crossed the Massachusetts/Rhode Island District Line at forty thousand feet flying southwest toward Philadelphia. The deathtrap was set within another hour twenty miles east of Philadelphia on Interdistrict 95 near the town of Hartford, New Jersey District. TransTrak still had Rigby's position locked.

The Pegasus sedan crossed Rancocas Creek five miles northeast of Hartford before spying an advancing Ford pickup gaining from behind. The rear driver strobed both headlights rapidly before veering to his right while paralleling the Pegasus' hood with its own. Matt slowed down to 40 mph as the marauding pickup accelerated away and parked along an emergency shoulder one quarter-mile ahead.

Rigby suspected a road rager while slowing to 30 mph and eventually passing the pickup. Then the Ford accelerated from behind, passing the Pegasus again. Matt got angry; he'd taken a belly full of fun and games for one day. Sam implored his partner to ignore the stalker, but Rigby stomped his accelerator as the Pegasus eventually overtook the Ford on the left at 70 mph.

Then the pickup driver opened his window before firing a sawed-off shotgun toward the sedan. The Pegasus' right passenger window exploded into hundreds of crystalline razor blades. The blast struck Matt in the neck and shoulder while tearing his right nostril. But Sam had caught the brunt and died instantly as both forearms and the right side of his neck were blasted away with buckshot first. Matt steered his Pegasus into the pickup's left side before rolling his attacker over onto a hillside along a stiff patch of frigid grass. Rigby didn't look back while turning on all the heat he had. Then he grabbed his Media Palm and called 911.

A voice responded, "Camden Emergency Exchange. Press one for the fire department. Press two for an ambulance. Press three for the police." Matt touched three and connected to a human voice. "Camden Police Department. Please state the nature of your emergency."

"This is Matthew Rigby. A road rager has shot me. My passenger's dead. I'm wounded but still driving. The assailant's Ford Pickup is lying on its side near Rancocas Creek on the New Jersey District Turnpike; he's five miles north of Hartford and has a shotgun."

"Where are you now, sir?"

"I'm approaching the northern outskirts of Hartford. I'm—"

Rigby was cut short by a remote-controlled tanker truck cruising at 60 mph. The lethal weapon rocketed through a four-way intersection just as the Pegasus was passing through. The truck cab had a freshly murdered man belted behind the steering wheel; Tau's agents had commandeered a total stranger to provide believability.

The tanker slammed into the Pegasus on the right before crushing it beneath its front grill as glass and torn metal sprayed over the pavement. Rigby and Thomas were compacted into bloody pulp before the truck's fuel tank detonated. Then the flaming projectile pushed its imploded target across the intersection while slamming the Pegasus into a four-wheel-drive station wagon with the burning tanker's momentum behind it; within the wagon, a man, his wife, and all three of their children were incinerated instantly. The fire trail spread the width of the turnpike with red, orange, yellow, and white flames before the mass of flaming scrap, glass, flesh, and bones finally came to a stop. Black smoke billowed into the winter air.

Tau was delighted to randomly vaporize an innocent family in the operation; it would lend credence to the accident scenario. The silver-haired man welled tears of joy while relishing his current field assignments. Such spectacles always proved the most gratifying.

CHAPTER SEVENTEEN

PANCAM

Milton the Mountain escorted his two charges into the Universal Regions council chamber. Victor first sat in the visitor section while Atlanterran President Barry Claude Xavier was seated in a reserved front row section alongside Indoasian President Chu Ahn Singh, North American President Garth Brady, and Vice President Mike Parker.

Reginald Masterson, monitor of the Cohesion Cluster; Telia Zendar, chief magistrate of the Planetary Court; and Abner Quimby, commissioner of the Martial Protectorate comprised a presiding tribunal behind an elevated oak bench in the center of the chamber. All three judges faced the executive section.

Masterson announced, "Good afternoon, presidents, tribunes, ambassadors, ladies, and gentlemen. Today, we have a dire emergency. It has come to the council's attention that Earth's greenhouse effect is accelerating. North America has compiled the collective temperature records of their Central Province for the last five years. These records confirm that Mother Earth's temperature has risen three full degrees in just twelve months."

A cascade of shocked murmurs enveloped the chamber as Mike leaned toward Garth before whispering, "This place is as solemn as a church."

Brady replied, "As sacred as the Ritual of Imik."

"Ritual of what?"

"Imik. He's the god that Crimson Cupola dynasties have worshipped since Mesopotamian merchants used clay tablets for contracts over four thousand years ago."

Mike replied, "Tell me more."

"Shhh." Garth put a finger to his lips. "Not now."

Reginald continued, "Now, these North American findings have been checked and confirmed. Many of you heard President Brady's speech last night; his NACAM directive will not be a popular one. However, this tribunal concedes that if Earth is to avoid cremation, this URC Forum must examine NACAM and vote on whether to incorporate the edict into our pandect bylaws. Time is of the essence! Our heralds are now passing out copies of NACAM in case some members aren't familiar with North America's new directive. While NACAM is being examined, does anyone have something else to address this august body with?"

Jerry Argus raised his hand.

"The tribunal recognizes the former Wyoming State governor, who's now the tribune of Wyoming District."

Argus stood up with a frown. "It's no secret all of North America's former sovereign states and nations have defaulted to triumviral districts with every corresponding governor or president presiding as chief administrator. Its also no secret President Brady has usurped any tribune voting majority by dictating an executive order. What I'm wondering is why we North American tribunes were summoned here?"

Masterson replied, "It's true your triumvirate's already locked into NACAM, but as members of the Universal Regions Council you're still entitled to vote in this assembly. Any other questions?"

The forum grew silent again.

Masterson resumed, "Then all members of this council have two hours to study the NACAM proposals among themselves. This emergency forum will reconvene at three P.M. for a formal vote on the matter."

Mickey Broderick wheeled his truck down Texas Interdistrict 45 between Houston and Dallas with both trailers filled with frozen shrimp, crabs, and oysters from Galveston. Brooding about last night's NACAM broadcast, Broderick's mind dwelt on the 30-06 telescopic rifle, pump action cylinder bores shotgun, 357-magnum pistol, and a semi-automatic .22-caliber target rifle hidden under the floor of his rig. He wondered how far President Brady would go with his newfound executive powers. Then he shuddered while wondering how far the URC would push all their triumvirates to ensure worldwide enslavement.

Reconvening at three P.M., Monitor Masterson declared, "Attention. I will now open the floor for discussion on the validity of NACAM for URC pandect adoption."

Indoasian President Singh raised his hand and stood before being recognized. "I motion that NACAM be ratified at once. Everything within this report convinces me of the critical, possibly terminal position our world faces if we don't reduce the greenhouse effect! I admit the NACAM penalties are severe, but I believe leniency on this issue cannot be tolerated if we are to survive."

"A motion for a Pandect Clean Air Mandate standard has been declared. Does anyone second it?"

Atlanterran President Xavier stood up. "I second the motion!"

Masterson declared, "The motion's been seconded and lawfully entered. Are there any dissenting opinions?"

Thirty silent seconds elapsed before Masterson resumed, "All in favor of annexing NACAM into our URC pandect signify by Pandect Media Palm. All opposed will do the same. The voting time limit is five minutes."

Seventeen North American Tribunes were quickly tallied as the only dissenters: British Columbia, Alaska, Arizona, California, Colorado, Florida, Hawaii, Idaho, Massachusetts, Mexico, New York, Ontario, Oregon, Panama, Quebec, Texas, and Wyoming.

After the time limit, Masterson read the vote tally on his desk monitor before projecting it onto an enormous flat screen mounted high on the wall behind him. He declared, "The Pandect Clean Air Mandate, or PANCAM, is ratified by a vote of 133 to 17. Thank you for your expediency and wisdom, ladies and gentlemen.

"The Martial Protectorate will regulate all future PANCAM enforcements. But before we adjourn, I have a separate announcement. All executive members of the Cohesion Cluster, Planetary Court, Martial Protectorate, and all attending triumviral presidents shall remain in chambers after this assembly departs. Thank you. Meeting adjourned."

Mike nudged Garth. "What's coming down now, chum?"

"I have no idea. But since it's informal, there's probably some kind of social gathering coming up. Sorry you're not invited; I'll brief you later."

Parker departed with relief and without hesitation.

Victor DeSalle took Commissioner Quimby's seat at the tribunal bench while the deposed officer sat dutifully in the front row. Milton the Mountain stood with both hands behind his back next to the old man's chair.

DeSalle spoke cheerily, "All right, people! I'm feeling so good about PANCAM approval today that I am declaring a Geodesy Gauntlet! The celebration will be held tomorrow morning at New Corsica at nine P.M. Is there anyone here besides Telia and Reginald who cannot attend?"

The assembly remained reverently silent.

"Excellent!" DeSalle nearly squealed. "I look forward to seeing my presidents there. Then Victor looked directly at Abner before adding, "Commissioner Quimby."

"Yes, My Chairman?"

"Inform Tau Singh and Sebastian. Also, invite all Cupola agents in the region. Then tell our Gauntlet Committee to arrange some novel contests. You know how I crave surprises!"

"At once, My Chairman."

CHAPTER EIGHTEEN

Gauntlet

A clear, crisp, forty-degree Virginia District dawn arched across the sky over New Corsica at 8:55 A.M. The fog rolled over perfectly, manicured lawns and dormant pole lights surrounding an immense, bone-colored, domed structure. Inside, every attending member of the Crimson Cupola elite reclined within a purple leather section separate from the throngs of surrounding subordinates. The massive crowd murmured with anticipation while waiting warm and comfortably within forty concentric, stair-stepped rows of red leather seats lining the four-hundred-foot-diameter stadium within the confines of Chairman Victor DeSalle's 1,500-acre estate.

Today marked the Cupola's first Geodesy Gauntlet in three full years. The private arena boasted many technological conveniences. On hand were digital menus mounted within the right hand armrests of every chair. There were pneumatic beverage carrier transports placed between every pair of seats reminiscent of twentieth century banking tubes servicing drive-through customers. Holographic television images hovered in midair along the inner perimeter of the coliseum offering a pleasant diversion to everyone before the main event. An army of hoverbot waiters, each brandishing six gripping limbs, navigated along tubular beams of laser light while serving patrons free of charge. Everything was on the old man's house today.

Victor DeSalle reclined on a couch within the executive section nearest the center of the arena grounds among his special guests. Atlanterran President Barry Xavier, Indoasian President Chu Ahn Singh, and North American President Garth Brady were assembled on separate couches at the chairman's right hand side with Garth nearest his grandfather.

Abner Quimby sat two chairs away on Victor's left while commanding a squad of protectorate agents stationed around the executive perimeter. Senior Agent Moses Richmond stood nearest his commander wearing a puzzled look while staring at the empty guardian post between Quimby and DeSalle. Milton the Mountain, the chairman's bodyguard, was nowhere in sight.

A hoverbot had arrived while patiently holding a jeweled chalice of Braggot Mead brewed from honey and bitter hops in front of the old man. DeSalle seized it, sipped, and placed it in his cup holder. He glanced at Brady before exclaiming, "Ah, what an ideal time to enjoy some sports! It's been far too long since I sanctioned a Geodesy Gauntlet! We haven't started yet and I already feel like a little boy at his first World Series!"

Singh had digitally ordered Mongolian Kumis fermented from mare's milk while Xavier selected a chilled Sangria mixed with Jamaican Rum and laced with chicken blood.

Garth replied to Victor, "Nearly every seat in the arena is filled; it's nice all your regional subordinates gathered under such short notice." He looked at Milton's vacant seat and asked, "By the way, where's your resident monster? He usually at your side, Grandfather."

"You've a short memory for Gauntlet tradition, my boy. Milton's behind one of the six arena access gates preparing for our festivities. Ah! I love watching my man vanquish all challengers!" Victor glanced at Chu before continuing, "Even President Singh's brutish nephew Sebastian has been defeated during our last two celebrations, but that boy never learns."

Garth digitally ordered a can of common lemonade, which shot up the pneumatic tube beside his recliner in seconds. He popped the aluminum top and sipped once.

DeSalle resumed, "I understand Sebastian may be facing Milton again today along with anyone else who feels lucky."

Garth licked both lips while looking puzzled. "I thought you wanted today's Gauntlet to be novel?"

"I'm confident everything nestled between our traditional appetizer of Practice Targets and the dessert of our non-lethal Malevolent Menagerie climax will prove to be extraordinary; my catering committee hasn't disappointed me in over eighty years."

Brady asked, "But why kill for entertainment, Grandfather? Can't today's participants demonstrate martial athletic skills without having to butcher each other?"

Victor frowned with disappointment. "Since the dawn of history, life and death struggles still remain the most entertaining of all human spectacles. All of our most powerful ancient civilizations understood that. Besides, we only use inferiors for lethal contests; either Cupola subordinates who've failed loyalty or any captured political rebels who openly defied our authority. They're all sentenced to die anyway. Why shouldn't they provide their masters with some diversion before they're finished?"

Garth sipped again before asking, "But must it always be so, Grandfather? We've managed to unite North America, Europe, North Africa, the Middle East, and Asia into three triumvirates under a single political system. Haven't we outgrown the need for gratuitous bloodlust? Doesn't a modern society merit something more progressive than savage, gladiatorial combat strewing carnage all over this arena?"

DeSalle retorted, "A modern society, you say? What in the name of Moloch's Mud Whore is that supposed to mean? The strong have always conquered the weak!"

Singh interjected, "Absolutely, My Chairman!" while accepting a bronze goblet from the hoverbot waiter now in front of him.

Victor quizzed Garth, "Do you think any technical advancements or education on a world scale would ever change that? The only reason any system of government rules is that there's an enforcement arm of violence backing it up! Violence or the threat of it has always been the final authority from which all other authorities have been spawned! There remains only Victor or Vanquished!" The old man lightly thumped his sunken chest. "Personally, I prefer Victor!"

Xavier smiled at the pun while accepting a glass of icy Voodoo Sangria from another hoverbot's grasp.

Garth conceded, "Very funny, Grandfather, and perhaps you're right. It does seem that every time we put down one political rebellion somewhere in the world, another one emerges to take its place; violence does seem to rule our earth."

DeSalle confirmed, "At least we control violence on our terms within the three triumvirates, my boy. But those unruly, pig-headed, unincorporated clusters of humanity still known as South America, Australia, and Greater Africa remain outside of our grasp!"

Barry interjected after wiping a crimson trickle down one corner of his mouth with a handkerchief. "Don't you mean the future sites of Triumvirates Four, Five, and Six respectively, Victor?"

The old man grinned with receded gums. "You make my mouth water, Barry. Ever since antiquity spawned the Crimson Cupola, we've envisioned a time on Earth where all cultures would unify into a super cell of social, economic, industrial, political, and military power under our rule. So far, we've managed to lock half the world within our fist!"

Xavier sat his glass down while commenting, "But the first three triumvirates covertly conquered territories over a long period of time by indoctrinating their populace with corporatism, collectivism, and preplanned divided loyalties.

"Once those people overwhelmingly believed whatever our corporate media spoon fed them, the concepts of individual freedom, national sovereignty, and civil rights went down the proverbial tube. The Phantom Terrorist Oppugn from 2028-37 sealed our power in those regions permanently."

DeSalle sipped his mead and reminisced, "Along with those social coups of 2032 imposing mandatory vehicle transponders, two-way television, and Internet surveillance in nearly every home. And the majority of citizens gradually accepted their every condition under the media guise of national security! What a bunch of lemmings! The Americans especially couldn't see the cliff before plummeting head first with every other utopian sap blindly leading the way!"

Xavier waxed nostalgic, "Ah, the United States! That obsolete bastion of liberty where its citizens foolishly believed they were free simply because their government and mass media told them so, especially when all hard evidence to the contrary hovered under their noses for decades!"

Garth interjected, "Decades? It was a hell of a lot longer than that! You know as well as I do that the Sovereign United States died in 1865 and that the Corporate United States ruled from 1865 through 2039! That was nearly two centuries!"

Xavier added, "Yes, I know, Garth. Just as I also know that the North American Triumvirate now rules this continent. Don't you think I can read between the lines from the same newspapers, history books, and the mass saturation media broadcasts that you do?"

Brady quipped, "You know, it's strange how the majority of Americans back in those days actually believed their news media was unbiased."

Barry conceded, "You have a point, Garth, especially when every talking head on every competing network kept reporting the same news stories at the same time while offering up the same conclusions! And those American dolts refused to believe their mainstream media was censored beneath an ultra-corporate umbrella!"

Victor sipped more mead and chided, "You've a talent for saying the right thing at the right time, Barry. That's why I appointed you President of Atlanterra. But do you think you can maintain control over Europe, North Africa, and the Middle East Provinces without any conflicts?"

Xavier lifted up his blood-laced glass before answering, "Does it matter? I have the combined military prowess of North America and Indoasia as allies to call on in case of insurrection. Rebellion doesn't concern me now. You know, once a triumvirate, always a triumvirate. But regarding South America, Australia, and Greater Africa, our element of surprise doesn't exist. All of them are familiar with Cupola tactics and vehemently oppose our triumviral rule."

The old man sneered. "Nothing to worry about. When the Cupola governs the assets and military power of the former United States, Canada, Mexico, Great Britain, France, Germany, Israel, Iraq, Iran, Pakistan, India, Russia, Korea, China, and Japan. Moloch's Mud Whore—Our list of military muscle's nearly endless!"

Victor finished his mead before resuming, "And also given specific triumviral sanctions of embargoing enough corporate food, fuel, technology, and raw materials from our enemies, in time the people of unincorporated South America, Australia, and Greater Africa will pressure their archaic governments to fall in line with us! What else were multi-national, corporate monopolies designed for?"

Singh quietly savored his warm Kumis.

Barry concluded, "That's hard to argue with, Victor. You make me feel better already. Oh, look! The standards are up now! Everyone's waiting for you to initiate today's benediction!"

The coliseum's hundred-foot diameter, central combat ground displayed a flat, sifted, bone-colored dirt surface. Embedded upright around its perimeter stood six vertical, twenty-foot-tall, twelve-inch-diameter, oak poles forming the intersecting points of an invisible hexagon. Each pole top brandished an identical two-by-four-foot flag displaying the image of a blood red, fully kernelled and wind-blown wheat stock carved into the center of a silver signet ring, superimposed over a field of royal purple. The end of each flag tapered to a point at the center, resembling a medieval coat of arms turned on its side.

DeSalle stood up to a throng of applause. He beamed a great smile now staring directly at a thirty-foot-high set of double oak doors at the opposite side of the arena. Silence ensued as both doors opened slowly, now revealing the rough-hewn, wooden image of an outstretched owl mounted on a rolling wooden platform. It towered fifteen feet high with a manned, electrical pushcart positioned directly behind it. The owl moved forward on cue until the cart driver positioned it within the center of the standard pole area. Then the vehicle backed away until disappearing behind the closing doors again.

Twelve hooded figures clad in royal purple robes suddenly walked out of another access gate in single file carrying burning torches under the bright stadium lights. The center section of the domed roof above them suddenly opened, revealing a rectangular patch of frigid, azure sky.

They assembled around the owl's elevated base with all their eyes on the standing chairman. Surveying the crowd in all directions, Victor savored the sweetness of absolute power before reluctantly sitting back down. Then all torches were tossed onto the owl and rapidly kindled the image into a bonfire as impellers from the open roof drew the smoke straight up and out of the arena.

Every spectator cheered while each torchbearer untied a satchel from every robe and consigned their contents of powdered mandrake root, sulfur, nightshade, hemlock, wolf bane, and copper salts to the flames. The bonfire transformed to emerald green and burned half an hour until consumed to ashes. Then the stadium roof closed as several caretakers finished raking warm ash into the bone hued soil.

Victor raised his right fist with a bent elbow toward Marshall Quimby, who immediately retracted a dark brown, heavy steel gauntlet tarnished and tacky with ancient blood and soil from a crimson velvet packing case at his feet. Quimby approached the chairman before bending on one knee, displaying upraised hands under the gauntlet and waited until Chairman DeSalle christened the tarnished glove with his touch. Then the marshal threw it full force onto the arena floor where an event caterer quickly placed the weapon onto the ashen center of the hexagonal pole region.

A hoverbot arrived before DeSalle while holding a sterling silver platter in two hands. Victor grasped and secured it to his armrests before the six-armed machine accelerated away. The chairman savored his meal aroma. The entrées featured raw oysters on the half shell with lemon wedges, cooked escargot basted with garlic butter plus chicken stock, and a small mound of steamed crab legs.

DeSalle tucked his tray napkin under the liver spots along his chin. He seized a stainless stain tong and an ancient bronze spoon with a pointed iron handle off of the platter, clenched the first snail shell, and speared out the dead mollusk before dipping its steaming flesh into a golden cup of more garlic butter.

Garth Brady mildly shuddered as his grandfather savored the delicacy in his mouth like an orgasmic lover.

A voice suddenly boomed through multiple loudspeakers covering the full perimeter of the arena. "Welcome, Cupola citizens! As it was in the dawn of our faith, so it is today! Mighty Imik approves our celebration with his emerald blessing of purification! Whether friend or foe, those who bleed for us today will do so for his glorification! Hail our Geodesy Gauntlet! Hail the Stemma and the Gem that spawned our ancient order! But most of all, hail to the coming triumphs bestowed upon the Crimson Cupola with Imik's approval of our festivities! Let our practice targets perform!"

Chu smiled while securing his platter robotically set before him. The triple entree included calamari cooked rare, sheep's eyes seasoned with curry and vinegar, along with a baked potato gushing with chives, melted butter, large bacon chunks, and sour cream.

Xavier rubbed both hands after anchoring his food tray featuring a whole game hen stuffed with bacon and goat's cheese, steamed scallops in garlic cream sauce, and a smoldering shish kabob of impaled lamb meat, mushrooms, onions, bell peppers, and pineapple.

Garth wrinkled his nose while quickly swigging some lemonade.

The audience tumultuously cheered as another access gate lifted open. Four crimson-cloaked, bronze-helmeted guards forced a pair of weaponless, leather-sandaled, bare-chested men wearing white cotton loincloths through the open maw to the edge of the arena. Every guard brandished a red-hot element on the end of a narrow, lightweight, six-foot-long electronic bull prod while continuously surrounding their slow walking captives.

Both prisoners had been shaved hairless and stained from head to toe; one contestant was colored magenta while the second displayed silver skin.

They suddenly screamed and sprinted toward the glove on the ground after enduring red-hot incentives against their naked backs. The guards collectively followed as Magenta and Silver now tugged the crusty gauntlet between them.

Magenta kneed Silver in the abdomen to wrench the steel glove away as his opponent crumpled onto his back. Magenta filled dingy, tacky, steel fingers with his right hand before advancing toward the downed combatant with bull prods still surrounding the pair.

DeSalle juiced a whole oyster with lemon before pronged it into his mouth. He savored before swallowing it all at once.

Then Silver laterally spun away before shoulder rolling onto his feet. Magenta reached his opponent and swung roundhouse only to miss completely. Silver upended his enemy with a right leg sweep and backed away giving Magenta time to stand.

Victor frowned while exposing the flesh of a crab leg using a handheld, stainless steel shell cracker.

A guard's bull prod blackened the flesh over Silver's left kidney, penalizing his good sportsmanship.

Singh stuffed a sheep eye into his mouth; it burst between clenched teeth. He sighed before exclaiming, "Damn! I love these things!"

Now enraged, Magenta steel punched Silver's tormenter on the back of the neck below his helmet. The guard fell dead to the ground as blood oozed out both his ears.

DeSalle forked crab flesh and garlic butter into his mouth.

The remaining sentries instantly seared Magenta's groin, neck, and left eye. Triple seizures of agonizing pain collapsed him unconscious to the earth. A fresh guard sprinted from the nearest gate to reinforce the ranks. The sentries viciously backhanded Magenta until he regained consciousness. Soon both prisoners were fighting again.

After missing Silver several times, the steel-gloved Magenta slumped to his knees. Silver quickly kicked him unconscious with a right heel to the chin before removing and placing the gory gauntlet over his own fist.

DeSalle chewed and swallowed a snail before wiping drool from the corners of his mouth with a linen napkin.

Four bull prods now viciously impelled Silver to finish the match quickly. He steel punched his opponent in the nose. A harpoon of broken cartilage impaled Magenta's brain behind it; he died before his convulsing body hit the ground. The crowd roared approval.

Silver was disarmed as a sentry returned the freshly blood spattered glove to a caterer, who quickly arrived at the arena ground directly below the executive section. He gingerly tossed it upward with both hands to Marshal Quimby, who quickly replaced the oozing weapon within its red velvet box and closed the lid without cleaning it.

Silver was escorted back through an access gate while a separate detachment of sentries carried Magenta's bludgeoned corpse through another doorway before disappearing into the bowels of the stadium. Now surrounded by a six-guard contingent, Silver reentered his cell and was granted the customary sixty seconds to verbally atone to Imik. His eyes were then seared and his tongue removed so as not to assail the ancient god with stares or cursing in the afterlife. According to gauntlet tradition for his victory, Silver was mercifully beheaded by an executioner's battle axe without audience observation.

Chairman DeSalle, Marshal Quimby, plus Presidents Xavier, Singh, and Brady emptied their hands and continued clapping with the raucous crowd until the arena was cleared. But Garth's stomach continued to roil while fifty men worked rapidly in and around the standard poles as high technology lights, spike mats, metal frameworks, crane booms, and cable winches assembled for the next event.

The executives passed the time sampling their gourmet platters with relish. Xavier savored a chunk of lamb meat garnished with bell pepper, onion, and mushrooms. Then he forked a naked scallop before consigning it to the cream sauce. Singh worked on his rare calamari with intermittent sheep eye bursts while sipping his Kumis. DeSalle continued staining his bib with oyster and lemon juice, snail drippings with garlic butter and chicken stock, plus the shell fragments of cracked crab legs.

After the caterers finished construction within twenty minutes, the loudspeaker resumed. "Our Chairman, the catering committee humbly hopes that this next contest will prove entertaining; they call it the Corpus Grid. We await your pleasure."

The old man speared another snail while acknowledging by raising his empty fist.

Former CC Agents Titan and Minotaur were immediately escorted up a ladder onto a forty-by-forty-foot, hexagonal grid of transparent, triangular glass sections linked together by an intersecting network of metal frames.

The platform was suspended twelve feet above the arena floor and supported from the sides by steel braces clamped around all six standard poles. A motorized, identically sized, hexagonal ceiling of six-inch-long, needle-sharp, conical steel spikes were mounted twelve feet above the grid by cables. Stationary crane booms supported the ceiling weight as each spike pointed downward to encompass every square foot of the battlefield directly below it.

Titan and Minotaur stepped cautiously onto the game grid with a contingent of sword and spear bearing sentries ushering them to the center; each combatant was carrying a sheathed belt dagger and five-foot-long iron trident with gleaming, razor-sharp prongs under the lights.

Soon every guard departed before retracting a lone exit ladder down the throat of its scaffold. Titan was painted turquoise while wearing a bronze helmet that exposed only his eyes, nose, and mouth. Minotaur's helmet was identical except for two natural, four-inch-long horns attached above the ears contrasting sharply against his orange-tinged skin.

The combat pair watched from above while fifty caterers suddenly issued from the access gates while dragging massive carpets of twelve-inch-long, upright, conical steel spikes carried on metal rollers. The minions rapidly positioned them under the platform and twenty feet beyond the grid perimeter, eliminating either contestant's option of jumping to freedom.

The loud speaker announced, "My Chairman, the Corpus Grid awaits your salute."

DeSalle impaled raw oyster flesh as his pulse quickened. He raised an empty fist again. Both prisoners remained motionless and stared back at the old man with obvious contempt. Victor frowned as the ceiling spikes begin winching slowly downward. Then DeSalle squirted lemon juice onto a whole oyster before chewing it slowly. He spat a tough membrane onto the floor at his feet before swallowing the rest.

Both fighters suddenly launched the struggle; their clashing tridents threw off bluish-white sparks as the ceiling spikes stopped descending. Titan locked Minotaur's trident with his own while pivoting hard right and flinging his opponent's spear onto the surface grid. As Titan thrusted toward Minotaur's throat, the target sidestepped to the right while causing his opponent to miss completely.

Singh grinned with another mouthful of calamari.

Suddenly Minotaur dropped on one knee, pulling his dagger before plunging its blade into the back of his attacker's right thigh, twisting, and withdrawing the gory blade. Titan roared while pivoting clumsily as Minotaur retrieved his downed trident. Titan hobbled a trail of fresh blood across the transparent grid before eventually charging Minotaur's position. Clashing tridents sparked again with Titan straining his wounded stance against Minotaur's two-legged leverage.

Titan freed his right hand for an instant, grasped his belt dagger, and pierced Minotaur's left knee with a full force throw. Minotaur dropped onto his left side while bellowing in razor-edged agony. Titan double-gripped his trident and hobbled in for the kill, but his left leg suddenly collapsed through a trapdoor section of metal framing and glass, which plummeted against the spiked carpet below while leaving a gaping hole in the grid. The startled warrior's leg momentarily dangled beneath the platform surface before he managed to pull back up through the gap.

Minotaur painfully regained his footing, pulled the enemy's dagger out, and flung it into his foe's turquoise muscle mass above the left collarbone. Titan winced while withdrawing the blade as both fighters trickled blood while resting and gasping for air.

The spikes descended twelve more inches and stopped again before Titan thrusted a trident toward his foe. Minotaur sidestepped, stabbed Titan's left side above the hip, and quickly pulled back. Minotaur suddenly dropped his spear against the transparent battlefield as three consecutive triangles collapsed under his feet; the ambushed warrior managed to catch himself while dangling both legs below the newborn gap.

Xavier smiled while cutting into his game hen with a sterling silver knife and fork.

Titan limped toward his downed enemy with a feeble spear charge. Then Minotaur muscled out of the torso trap before grabbing his trident. He pole-vaulted across the nearest floor gap and side-kicked Titan's legs out from under him. The turquoise fighter slammed against the floor. His jarred trident clanged the transparent surface just as the grid floor collapsed beneath it; glass, metal frames, and his weapon plunged down onto more arena spikes below.

Minotaur suddenly collapsed through another trapdoor, dropping up to both armpits. His remaining trident fell through to the spike carpet. The ceiling spikes dropped another foot and stopped before the weary prisoners resumed mortal combat. A dozen segments of open floor now pockmarked the battle grid.

Titan and Minotaur lunged toward each other, simultaneously grabbing each other's wrist below both dagger-clenched fists. The test of arm strength surged until Minotaur tripped Titan's right foot and slammed the turquoise-skinned foe onto his right side. A ten-foot-diameter hole collapsed in the center of the Corpus Grid as both men rolled laterally over each other with both daggers still locked. Minotaur maneuvered Titan to the brink of the nearest hole, pivoted into position, and savagely pushed his enemy's legs over the edge with a hard right kick.

Titan gingerly balanced his washboard stomach against the metal framing, still stubbornly gripping his opponent's wrist. Minotaur slammed Titan's knife mercilessly against the platform before finally wrenching it free. Titan furiously seized Minotaur's right fist with both hands while hanging in midair. Minotaur grasped Titan's loose dagger with a free hand and pierced his enemy's right eye socket. Titan slumped dead onto the ground spikes among all the debris. Then the ceiling spikes began descending again.

Minotaur clumsily crawled across some remaining platform frames before finally reaching the ladder scaffold. The remaining Corpus Grid framework immediately dropped down, leaving Minotaur briefly hanging by both hands along one edge of the scaffold before it collapsed and impaled him on a cluster of ground spikes below.

The crowds' cheers were deafening as the caterers prepare for the next event. Barry teased DeSalle, "Victor, are you sure you didn't know about this Corpus Grid competition? You're an enthusiastic gamester, and that contest smacked strongly of playing Chess Roulette with human pawns."

"I didn't know, but I'm delighted my caterers were so creative! I can hardly wait for what's next!" Singh popped another sheep eye into his mouth before reaching for his Kumis. Brady hard swallowed against a souring knot in the pit of his stomach while DeSalle asked, "What did you think of the contest, Chu?"

Singh wiped his mouth before answering, "Most interesting, My Chairman, but I would've collapsed the scaffold earlier to force the survivor to stay on the battlefield framework until the ceiling spikes nearly touched him. Then I would have stopped the spikes for at least two minutes before forcing them to slowly pierce him. However, I'm growing impatient to watch Sebastian take on Milton again."

Victor assured, "Relax, Chu, we'll get to the Malevolent Menagerie soon enough. After all, that final contest's non-lethal and reserved for loyal Cupola agents alone. We must dispose of our garbage first."

Garth beaded with sweat struggling not to betray revulsion to his peers. He knew they would take it as a critical sign of weakness. Singh savored another sheep eye especially heavy on the curry. DeSalle dug out another snail for his garlic butter.

"What's the matter, Garth?" asked his grandfather, noticing the perspiration beading on his grandson's face. "You haven't eaten anything. Aren't you enjoying yourself?"

Brady swallowed hard before replying, "Certainly, Grandfather, but I feel as if I'm coming down with something." He saturated a linen napkin after wiping his face. "I'm drenching in sweat."

The chairman wiped both hands before pressing a withered palm across Garth's forehead and cheeks. He frowned before commenting matter-of-factly, "Mmm, you're clammy too. Garth, I'm having one of my staff drive you all the way back to Washington, D.C. You'd better spend the next day or so in bed at the White House."

President Brady feigned disappointment. "But this is the first Geodesy Gauntlet in three full years. I'd like to finish watching the spectacle."

Victor baptized another pronged oyster with lemon juice. "Forget it, my boy. It won't do for the North American President to get sick now. I have too many plans for you."

Brady felt his tension unravel while conceding. "Very well, Grandfather."

Fifteen minutes after Garth's departure, the arena was staged for the next event. The murmuring crowd grew silent as the speaker announced, "My Chairman, the next contest is called the Javalena Joust; it requires a brief introduction to fully savor the cultural flavor of the event."

Xavier dipped a scallop into cream sauce and chewed slowly before stabbing another chunk of hen breast. Singh finished all his meat before attacking the baked potato. DeSalle finished his oysters and snails before working on the remaining crab legs.

"Farmers in the past used an elaborate trap to catch wild Javalena Hogs without getting cut up by their savage tusks. They would leave a pile of food in an open clearing while allowing the hog pack to eat freely. The next day they would erect a few fence posts around a second food pile while continuing to allow the hogs to feed unmolested. This process continued until fence posts and rails were built up around the fresh bait pile, which eventually only left an open gate for the hogs to enter."

Singh smiled while mouthing some bacon.

"When the hogs came through the gate, the farmers would suddenly close it and trap the entire pack without incident. The following contest's a creative variation on that same principle. We await our chairman's pleasure."

Victor DeSalle finished his crab, drained his mead, and ordered another cup. Then he raised his fist a third time. Twelve groups of six bull-prod-packing sentries entered the arena simultaneously from separate access gates. Half of them jogged within the flag pole area where six more ten-foot-high, round-notched, perforated oak poles had been anchored thirty feet apart, forming another equidistant but smaller hexagonal shape inside the standard region.

The remaining sentries divided into six squads of six with each unit standing several feet in front of an arena access gate; every captor wore a burlap shoulder bag nearly overflowing with two-inch-diameter, fourteen-inch-long, oak pegs along with a large wooden mallet. On the dirt beside each squad lay a stack of seven twenty-two foot long, seven-inch diameter oak poles with holes on both ends, which matched the predrilled diameters of the inner uprights.

Barry finished the scallops and shish kabob before wiping melted goat cheese off his mouth. He ordered another Voodoo Sangria before finishing the last of his game hen.

Then thirty-six bare-chested, barehanded prisoners clad in white loincloths and leather sandals emerged through a single gate; they were ushered along by a rear group of thirty-six elemental sentries. The captives were rapidly herded into twelve sets of three with a single set stationed at every pole stack.

Then the guards strapped their peg and mallet satchels around the shoulders of each individual captive before fanning out all over the open ground between the pole stacks and the arena walls. This maneuver formed an auxiliary wall to reinforce both the thirty-six guards near the drilled poles and the three dozen sentries scattered along the base of the arena walls. The triple set of bull prodders now totaled the sentries at 108.

A dozen sword and spear packing guards suddenly ushered a pair of leather clad figures into the arena from another gate; both prisoners were carrying full-length, double-edged swords and wearing sturdy helmets of burnished and tarnished bronze. The access gate closes behind them.

All three executives now had their platters removed while enjoying fresh beverages while arena speaker rumbled, "My Chairman, you now see three rings of red-hot elementals dividing this arena into a cage, auxiliary, and a wall perimeter. The wall squad will prevent escape over the top. The cage units control the action around the poles by keeping the warriors inside and providing red-hot incentive for the construction slaves. The auxiliary squad reinforces any skirmishes requiring fresh sentries. These thirty-six peg-carrying prisoners will labor in twelve squads of three while mounting each stack pole rail between the nearest uprights in front of them, which will be fastened by oak pegs pounded through the notched, predrilled holes to secure each rail.

"Their task is to build a six-walled enclosure with a half-dozen rails stacked six inches apart to eventually form a seven-foot-tall holding pen. Since both armed prisoners realize that wall completion means their imminent death, they will try to delay construction by killing any slave they can reach; if either warrior attempts escape out of the pen, he will be branded back into position with bull prods. Naturally, our construction trios won't relish getting near the range of any captive swordsman, so they'll minimize their individual risk by swarming to build every containment wall simultaneously. This procedure will force the two swordsmen inside to literally run in circles trying to halt construction.

"A fresh worker from the nearest access gate will replace any slave that's killed; this will maintain a constant workforce of thirty-six builders. If any construction slave refuses to work, they will be given red-hot incentives. If any warrior refuses to fight, he'll be persuaded to change his mind. Once all six sides of the hexagonal pole cage have been completed, Round One will end and Round Two will be announced. We await your pleasure, My Chairman."

Victor raised a right hand now gripping his chalice within it. Each slave trio moved in unison carrying separate rails toward the inner uprights. Sentries nimbly gave each group the right of way.

Burnish and Tarnish flanked each other while bisecting their hexagonal station; each warrior tried covering three sides at once. Burnish stepped across his boundary to extend his range, but quickly withdrew after catching a red-hot prod against the skin of his left shin. Tarnish remained inside his zone. Then all twelve building groups initially screamed like banshees while charging forward and before attempting to anchor collective bottom rails into place from multiple crouching positions. Tarnish sliced two throats of one squad while suddenly spraying blood across his front.

DeSalle licked spilled mead off his chin as another team pegged their bottom rail into position and sprinted back toward their stack. Fresh slaves entered through the nearest gate to pick up any slack in the action as Tarnish thrusted his sword through a second crouching pair. Yet a third team anchored their bottom rail and helped another group peg their second rail into place.

Burnish kicked a slave in the face with his left leg and pierced another's skull with a right-hand sword thrust. Then he sprinted toward a different position while running one slave through the belly and grappling briefly with another, who had tried to block the warrior with a pitiful mallet. Burnish snapped his enemy's handle and sliced the slave from cranium to larynx before retracting his brain-spattered blade.

Singh wiped Kumis off the corners of his mouth.

Burnish hacked a slave's right arm before rapidly beheading another who had just finished pounding his bottom rail into place.

Xavier filled his mouth allowing the Sangria's subtle coppery taste to caress his palate.

Another rail team cleverly hammered their fourth rail into place to prevent Burnish from performing any full sword swing over their heads. Tarnish slaughtered two more slaves as another team followed suit while hammering their separate rail at alternate fourth level. Tarnish ignored two other teams while they took their comrades' lead by quickly hammering their fourth and fifth rails unmolested.

Burnish glanced at his comrade while yelling, "Move over, partner, I'm backing you up! It's useless to guard more than one opening against this perpetual horde!"

Tarnish smiled wryly as the twin warriors now concentrated their defense on a single gap while ignoring the construction of the other five sides. Within five minutes, five separate rail walls were complete up to the seven-foot mark, while both warriors had butchered another twelve slaves with fresh replacements surging the whole time.

DeSalle and Xavier clapped as the chairman nearly squealed, "I was wondering if those traitors had enough brains to defend a single opening! Now we should see some serious bloodletting, eh, Barry?"

Xavier drained his glass before answering, "Affirmative. But how long do you think those warriors can defend that single gap before they're overwhelmed?"

"Probably quite a while since they've stopped chasing their tails. What do you think, Chu?"

Singh sat his goblet down and pondered, "I think these warriors will probably eliminate at least fifty slaves before facing round two."

"Oh, that's right!" answered DeSalle, "I'd forgotten that my caterers will add something new to this situation after the rail pen's completed. Anyone want to place a wager on how many captives die before Round

One ends?"

Barry interrupted, "You're on, Victor. I'll wager $500,000 triads the carnage stops at—by the way, Chu, what's the current body count?"

"Twenty-two—uh, twenty-five slaves. The tarnished helmet just disemboweled two more on one end while the burnished helmet beheaded a third. The other five teams are being herded towards the cage gap to reinforce ranks. No, my bad! It's to carry the bodies away from the opening so the warriors can't erect some grisly barricade. We've got a few moments; let's set this wager. I will raise Barry and go $5 million triads."

"Now you're talking, Chu!" interjected Victor. "But I'll go as high as $10 million."

"Done," answered Singh.

Barry countered an offer, "Done, Victor, but I'll pay you $25 million if you'll grant me an unusual request."

Victor furrowed an eyebrow and asked, "What's on the First Triumvirate President's mind?"

"If either of those warriors survive both rounds one and two, I'd like you to spare their lives. I could use such competent fighters."

"The Crimson Cupola doesn't give enemies a second chance!"

"You *are* the Cupola, Victor. Ten or twenty-five million triads; it's up to you, My Chairman."

Then DeSalle rubbed his gnarly chin before agreeing, "All right, Barry, if it will add spice to the game. I'll grant those warriors their lives if they survive round two…whatever that is. Now, pick a number; the slave corpse pile's nearly cleared away."

Xavier calmly predicted, "Forty slaves."

Chu countered, "I say fifty-five slaves, especially since our swordsmen have their second wind."

Victor finished, "And I say that they only reach thirty-eight. Now, is anyone still hungry?"

DeSalle ordered a chicken chef salad, Singh chose turtle soup with sea bass, while Xavier selected a small portion of haggis with Scottish whisky chasers. Then they watched a unit of eight slaves grab a single rail nearest the opening and lift it to chest level. The remaining twenty-eight slaves brandished wooden mallets on both sides just beyond either warrior's sword range. The rail carriers slammed their burden against both uprights at the fourth level while some mallet men hammered pegs with others defending wildly against both swordsmen.

Burnish slashed two mallet men across the throat and severed each one's larynx and windpipe with a single swing before jumping sideways to cover the center of the rail; another thrashing slave died after a sword thrust through the navel. Then Burnish leaped back a step to dodge two mallets converging on both sides of him.

Tarnish beheaded his nearest rail man before slashing the abdomens of three others with a double-handed, full-force swing; then he beheaded all three disemboweled targets while they slumped to their knees. Rail four had cost seven slaves to secure. Seven more workers immediately took their place.

All three second course meals swiftly arrived at the executive section.

Rail three was pushed forward at waist level with an identical battle plan. Burnish and Tarnish paused until the last moment before suddenly jumping onto both ends of the new rail while violently swinging their swords. Five startled mallet men fell before Tarnish as he severed two heads and slashed two throats before piercing a fifth slave's abdomen.

DeSalle pushed a fork full of diced chicken breast, raw vegetables, and ranch dressing into his mouth.

Burnish killed four others on the opposite end with two beheadings, one throat shot, and a full chest penetration. Still near enough to smell the sentries' heat elements, every surviving slave pressed on without hesitation. Anchoring rail three had cost nine workers; nine more charged to reinforce the ranks.

Xavier savored his steaming haggis.

DeSalle suddenly yelled, "Moloch's Mud Whore! That's thirty-eight already! Those swine aren't even halfway home plugging that last gap! Oh well, at least those warriors are disposing of excess prisoners."

Singh slurped turtle soup from the bowl and wiped off his chin before replying, "It seems I have a fair chance of collecting today."

Xavier swallowed before asking, "Who wins the wager if all three of us guess incorrectly, Victor?"

The old man instructed after a sip of mead, "Whoever comes closest to the right total of course! Behemoth's Bloated Bowels! There go three more! Looks like you children will definitely decide the winner now!"

Rails one, two, five, and six had cost another sixteen slaves, but now Burnish and Tarnish became too exhausted to stand. Both fighters dropped their swords before crumpling onto both knees in heaving gasps. They helplessly watched rail seven go up without further resistance. Round one ended with a body count of fifty-four.

Victor set his fork down and cheered, "Congratulations, Chu, you were only one off! I'll deposit $10 million triads in the Pandectory Reserve of Tokyo today!"

Singh finished his soup and nodded gratitude before starting on the sea bass.

"Sorry, Barry," consoled DeSalle. "Better luck next time."

Xavier swallowed more boiled sheep stomach filled with liver, heart, lungs, oatmeal, and onions. Then he downed a whisky chaser and answered, "The second half of my wager stands, provided the fighters are still breathing after round two."

The chairman shrugged. "We'll just have to watch and see."

A contingent of twenty-four sentries armed with automatic weapons suddenly poured through an open access door forcing their remaining reinforcement slaves onto the arena grounds. They herded the newcomers and surviving joust builders against one wall before mowing them down with a hail of machine gun fire. Then the Cupola gunmen withdrew back through their access gate while the raucous crowd cheered. In seconds they reappeared without firearms while leading several large, electrical, pilot-driven, flatbed carts. Two sentries had throat-cut three wounded slaves before every corpse was stacked onto the carts and hauled back through the access gate with the loaders eventually following out of sight.

Thirty-six bull prod sentries still circled the bloody pen keeping Burnish and Tarnish inside. Then seventy-two more guards dismembered and opened one rail wall before removing the remnant slave carnage from both sides of the opening. Then they closed the pen again.

The speaker voice returned. "My Chairman, round two will consist of a simple fight to the death inside the hexagonal pen. One of our loyal Cupola gladiators will face both prisoners at the same time. Allow us to muster three of them so you can choose which one will exterminate these disloyal vermin."

Singh and Xavier kept chewing while DeSalle popped in another mouthful before raising the empty fork in his hand.

Three massive, leather clad, helmeted gladiators with purple tunics walked into the arena; they soon stood at single file attention twenty feet away from the retaining wall below the executive section. DeSalle perused the trio. The first man measured six-foot-eight while brandishing a mace and chain with his right hand and carrying a chain mail net in his left. His leather belt sheathed a Roman Short Sword while both feet nestled within open toed sandals. However, Mandible's trademark weapon was a jagged, sixteen-inch-wide pair of tensile strength clamps resembling the jaws of a giant ant. The device fastened along his left forearm extending just short of the wrist to both open wide and close tightly through selective muscular flexes.

Victor's second candidate stood two inches taller while brandishing a six-foot-long tungsten steel trident in both hands; his belt held a throwing knife and both leather boots revealed retractable, three-inch long, flat steel spikes. Sole operated his spikes while displaying a Martial Art combat pattern before resuming his stance.

The final warrior, Colossus, stood seven-feet-tall while gripping a monstrous, four-foot-long battleaxe firmly in his right hand and a thinly edged, four-foot-diameter bronze shield balanced gingerly against his left forearm. He also wore open-toed leather sandals.

Victor stuffed his wrinkled face again before pointing

toward Colossus.

The loyal gladiator lumbered toward the rail cage as every sentry in his path relinquished their right-of-way. Colossus climbed over and dropped inside the pen as Sole and Mandible leaned against a retaining wall to watch their comrade perform. Surging with fresh fear, Burnish and Tarnish flanked their black opponent on two sides.

Singh killed his last bite of sea bass before swilling more Kumis. Xavier finished the petite haggis and his last whisky chaser.

Colossus suddenly charged Burnish with an outstretched axe, and then abruptly flung his massive bronze disk in the opposite direction catching Tarnish savagely in the throat. The flattened, writhing swordsman spewed blood while clutching his crushed windpipe. Then Burnish sprinted forward before leaping towards his opponent while double gripping a sword overhead. Colossus pivoted left, outstretching his double-edged battleaxe.

DeSalle finished the last bite of his salad.

Burnish's forearms shattered against his enemy's weapon. He dropped his sword before hitting the bloody ground. Colossus hoisted Burnish off his feet by the throat with his empty shield hand. Burnish struggled like a salmon clenched in the jaws of a hungry bear. Colossus dropped his battleaxe and slammed Burnish against the ground. Grasping him by both feet, the giant swung the captive over his head like a war club. Then Colossus bludgeoned Burnish's skull against the nearest rails before literally beating it off the stump of his neck. Blood flew in all directions as Colossus tossed the headless corpse over the railings onto open ground.

"Bravo, Colossus!" cheered Victor. "Superbly and savagely done!"

"A most vicious and excellent kill," commented Chu before swilling more Kumis.

"Balberith's Blood!" exclaimed Barry. "It seems that even Milton's baby brother is too much of a monster for a pair of expert fighters. Obviously, it runs in the family."

Chu retorted, "Those fighters couldn't have taken out my Ninja or Ghurka bodyguards!'

Barry countered, "They gave an excellent accounting of themselves when they slaughtered those fence builders!"

Chu asserted, "It's fitting that the last contest was called the Javalena Joust; those two swordsmen died like slaughterhouse hogs at the hands of Colossus!"

Xavier chided, "If your bodyguards are so damn good, it's a pity our chairman couldn't witness a confrontation between Milton, Colossus, and our other resident giants against some of your touted Ninjas and Ghurkas right now; I'd be more than willing to wager on that winner!"

Victor coughed phlegm before declaring, "You may have just named your own poison, Barry. Our Malevolent Menagerie finale always hosts a dozen separate contestants; maybe you'll get the combination you wish. Whatever the lineup, this should prove amusing."

Barry blurted, "I do enjoy watching gangs of wrestlers attempting to remove larger opponents from the ring first only to turn on each other later. But Milton has always been champion since I can remember! I've personally seen him pick up Colossus above his head and throw that younger brother over the top rope. Even Sebastian Singh's been tossed out with a single arm thrust more than once."

Chu frowned. "Unfortunately, that's true. But this outcome may be different."

"Nonsense!" boasted DeSalle. "Milton's the most powerful man alive and can never be defeated!"

"Double or nothing, Victor," challenged Singh. "I'll give you a chance to recoup your loss today. If Milton wins, we're even. But if any of my warriors are victorious, then you'll owe me twenty million triads."

The old man asked, "Aren't you rooting for Sebastian today?"

"Not at the risk of a president's ransom. Come on, Victor. Put your money where your mouth is!"

"You're on. I'll even go one better. If neither Milton nor one of your people wins today, then we'll both pay Barry twenty million triads."

"Agreed!"

Xavier chuckled surprise without saying a word.

Then the chairman asked with a smile, "Is anyone ready for dessert?"

Singh and Xavier eagerly followed DeSalle's lead.

The caterers quickly constructed a hexagonal, thirty-five-foot-wide floor apron; it was covered with a three-inch-thick wrestling mat padding and rose three feet above the arena ground while firmly attached to all six inner posts. Three elastic, turn-buckled ropes, spanning eighteen inches apart, stretched tightly between each corner post. Every rope segment offered enough tensile power to slingshot a large wrestler nearly across the length of the ring. Masses of twelve-inch-thick floor pads overspread twenty feet on the ground past the ring's perimeter to cushion any flying bodies flung out of the apron.

All three executives sampled their desserts while watching the preparation. Victor dug into a Baked Alaska dessert of vanilla ice cream, chocolate cake, and browned meringue. Singh savored fresh fruit and a Bing Moon Cake with red bean paste, while Xavier sliced into a large piece of black forest cake with cherry sauce oozing out both sides.

Eventually Mandible and Sole stretched the second and third ropes tightly before stepping through them and into the wrestling arena; they wore matching pairs of purple spandex loin girdles and red leather boots.

Tau Singh had now arrived and was quickly given access to the executive section before sitting beside his brother Chu.

Sebastian slithered under a vacant bottom rope before shoulder rolling onto bare feet. He wore a faded pair of blue denim jeans frayed at both calves above the hairy knuckles of his bare toes.

Colossus and Milton now entered over the top ropes from opposite sides of the ring with each one wearing red, sleeveless, spandex shirts tucked inside crimson loin girdles and purple boots. Then suddenly seven other contestants, with four wearing gray and three wearing black spandex body suits from heat-to-toe, all leaped over the top ropes from every side of the apron at once; their various five to six-foot-tall sizes seem severely dwarfed by every giant now standing with them inside the ring.

The speaker announced, "My Chairman and all Cupola allies, welcome to our final event of the day. It's a familiar one to many of us. We have a padded, hexagonal wrestling ring where twelve athletes are now assembled. The rules are simple. Anyone tossed out of the ring will be disqualified. The contest won't be over until there's only one competitor remaining inside the hex. This event's non-lethal and barehanded. Acknowledgement to our undefeated champion of twelve successive matches, Milton the Mountain, our beloved chairman's bodyguard…"

Milton paraded to the center of the ring raising a gargantuan arm to the sound of tumultuous applause.

Sebastian glanced at the champion before spitting contemptuously out through the ropes.

Colossus clapped as the idea of finally beating his brother made his mouth water.

Suddenly all contestants stood erect and immobile now facing DeSalle.

The speaker resumed, "As a bonus novelty, President Singh has assembled four gray-clad Ghurka and three black-clad Ninja warriors to contrast the giants. We will see if speed and agility is any match for titanic size and power. We await our chairman's pleasure."

"Excellent, Chu!" exclaimed DeSalle. "What a marvelous idea!"

President Singh stood and bowed reverently to his chairman before retaking his seat.

The old man paused before raising his right hand after eating a fork full.

Every contestant tensed while the champion stood in the center. Suddenly Mandible and Sole charged Milton with each one gripping an arm in both hands and struggling to twist them behind the black titan's back. The champion smiled while lifting both warriors off their feet. Mandible released his grip, hit the floor apron, and shoulder-rolled toward more manageable opponents. Then Milton grasped the back of Sole's neck and girdle before lifting the attacker up over his head and flinging him onto a vacant set of side ropes. Sole recoiled hard against the apron after a string of painful rolls.

Mandible lunged toward the nearest Ghurka, who leaped backward onto a top rope and launched over his attacker's head. Mandible jumped vertically and struck the flyer's stomach with an upraised fist; his opponent crumpled to the apron six feet short of the target rope.

Then Mandible picked up the prostrate Ghurka, walked to the ropes, and threw him out of the ring just as the remaining three Ghurkas collectively launched through the air planting their feet into the small of his back. Mandible propelled frontward against the nearest rope before rebounding toward the middle of the apron. He lost his balance before slamming onto both shoulders. The unsteady warrior regained his feet before quickly charging toward a lone Ghurka near the opposite end of the ring.

The gray spandex acrobat dropped onto his back, places both feet against Mandible's abdomen, and launched him head first through the second and third ropes already stretched wide by two Ghurka comrades. Mandible crashed onto the ground mats below.

Sole seized and tossed both rope Ghurkas headfirst out of the ring; the startled pair landed on Mandible before he could rise.

Colossus quickly grasped Sole's neck and girdle from behind before flinging the suddenly disqualified warrior over the ropes. The remaining Ghurka retreated to a neutral corner now catching a breath. Suddenly Colossus was struck in back of both knees by two flying Ninjas; he collapsed onto his back against the apron. Milton leaned against a turnbuckle while cheerfully watching his baby brother regain his feet and charge both Indoasian bushwhackers.

Sebastian leg-whipped Colossus as he passed by; the wrestler slammed face first against the apron. Colossus rose up while eyeing Sebastian with his back toward all three black spandex opponents.

The fresh Ninja pushed full force against the ropes before launching through the air to wrap both legs around Colossus' neck from behind. The lone Ninja's leverage flipped Colossus onto his back again near an apron edge. Quickly releasing, the lone Ninja jumped backward and pushed against the opposite ropes before flying hard into the downed opponent with both feet. The other two Ninjas stretched the bottom rope high enough to accommodate the dazed behemoth as Colossus slid dizzily out of the hexagonal ring.

Sebastian stood up facing all three Ninjas only to be side-kicked by the rejuvenated Ghurka; Tau Singh's muscle man bounced the left side of his face off the apron.

Milton advanced behind the kicker without any stealth. Ghurka bridged up onto both footpads and pivoted 180 degrees to whip an extended right leg against Milton's left shin. Ghurka's right tibia shattered as if striking a steel pole. Milton gingerly picked up the maimed contestant by the front collar while taking the weight off his broken leg and slowly dropped him over the top rope as gently as possible into the waiting arms of his disqualified comrades.

Sebastian charged Milton from behind before side-kicking the small of his back with both bare heels. The champion slammed hard into the ropes. Then Sebastian shoulder-rolled to his feet as the ebony giant's bulk strained every rope before eventually rebounding him back toward the center of the floor. But Chu's nephew miscalculated by ineffectively bouncing his extended right heel off of Milton's washboard abdomen; the giant grabbed his Chinese opponent's right leg by the thigh, lifted, and inverted him completely off the apron. The black titan contemptuously glared into Sebastian's bulging eyes.

Suddenly the Ninja trio blindsided the champion. One wrapped both legs around Milton's neck while another side-kicked into the back of his knees as the last one toe-kicked him behind the right elbow. Numbing spikes ascended through Milton's stunned arm as he clumsily dropped Sebastian onto both shoulders.

Milton pulled the struggling Ninja off of his neck with one hand, swung the captive twice, and threw the now disqualified fighter over the top rope. Both remaining Ninjas leaped to a neutral corner as the champion flailed numbness out of his right arm.

Sebastian elbowed Milton's tingling funny bone before raking the champion's eyes with both hands. Milton went down on one knee and swung a reverse left, catching Sebastian in the chest and hurling him toward the Ninja corner. Sebastian tried to regain his wind as both Ninjas rolled his body laterally toward the bottom rope. At the apron's edge, Sebastian seized a Ninja by the sole on one foot and launched him through the second and third ropes onto the padded ground.

The last Ninja dodged Sebastian's charging leg dive; the brute's own momentum pushed him face-first against the apron again. Sebastian snarled and regained his feet as Ninja backed against some opposite side ropes. Singh charged his black spandex opponent again. Ninja slingshot off the ropes before clipping Sebastian's feet out from under him and sending his bulk slamming against an apron edge. Ninja sprinted toward the prostrate foe before side-kicking him with full force under the bottom rope and off of the apron.

DeSalle finished dessert before saying, "One on one now, Chu. There's no way your puny Ninja can take Milton alone!"

The Singh brothers glanced at each other before Chu replied, "I'll wager another twenty million triads."

DeSalle wrung both hands. "You're on. This is like taking candy from a baby."

Ninja rested while waiting for Milton to clear his blurred vision. Then the champion charged with outstretched arms. Ninja sprang backward onto the nearest top rope and launched deftly to the opposite side of the ring.

Xavier killed his last bite of cake before chiding, "It looks like Spider Man is wrestling Godzilla out there!"

Milton reversed direction and advanced toward Ninja again. Ninja continued riding the top ropes while never allowing the giant to close in before easily escaping time after time.

Angered by some laughter in the seats, Milton furiously charged again. Ninja launched from the top rope, planted a flying boot heel against Milton's jaw, and pushed off his left shoulder with the opposite foot. The ambushed champion slipped onto his right side while crashing mercilessly into a turnbuckle pole. The crowd cheered thunderously. Ninja waited for Milton to regain his feet while keeping the length of the ring between them. Milton looked up at his frowning master who was folding both arms in disappointment.

Chu finished dessert, but Tau ordered nothing.

Then the ebony giant cautiously advanced within eight feet of his foe before charging hard. Ninja waited until the last moment before springing backward onto the top rope and triple somersaulting over Milton's upraised arms before deftly touching the apron with both feet. The giant's momentum propelled him against the straining ropes again before snapping him backward toward the center of the ring. Ninja laterally rolled with full length before knocking Milton's legs out from under him without stopping. The mammoth champion fell backward before bouncing his head off the platform.

Ninja waited again as Milton stood up and rubbed both eyes while finally shaking off the cobwebs; he charged once more. The challenger sprang toward the ropes to the right, but this time the giant dove into the air with outstretched hands.

Milton clipped his right hand across Ninja's left knee toppling his foe belly first against the apron. Then the black titan grabbed Ninja's right leg, stood up, and flung the challenger toward a top rope. Ninja twisted in midair before snagging the rope behind both knees, arched upward at its tightest stretch, and recoiled into a steep angle before somersaulting backward to the center of the ring. Milton shook his head with both hands on his hips as the crowd tumultuously cheered. Then the giant crossed both forearms across his massive chest while signifying a rare but official timeout.

Victor was furious watching Milton walk over and shake the challenger's right hand before returning to his initial position to resume the action.

Milton smiled before charging within eight feet of his target. The challenger launched off the top rope and came down with both boots against Milton's sweat-glistening shoulder blades. Then Ninja pushed off hard, sending Milton crashing forward into the nearest ropes. The impact collapsed the ring perimeter, sending the former champion out of the hexagon onto some ground padding.

Ninja upraised a victorious fist before removing the black spandex cowl to an ecstatic audience. Suddenly the cheers dwindled to murmurs. The new Malevolent Menagerie Champion was female: a slender, black-haired, almond-eyed Indoasian woman.

"Moloch's Mud Whore!" roared DeSalle. "We've *never* had a woman in the gauntlet before! Who is she?"

Chu answered. "Her name's Chameleon; she's my most experienced assassin. She was the only survivor of that Mike Parker assignment you compacted last Election Eve."

DeSalle clenched his clattering false teeth and yelled, "But that bitch failed!"

Chu furrowed his unibrow. "The hell she did! Her bathroom poison gas trap was set. But because you didn't let Moses Richmond in on your plan, his security sweep of Parker's house detected and destroyed our gas canister in advance!"

Victor didn't answer.

Agent Richmond silently squirmed in the executive section while Milton eventually regained his feet, climbed back onto the apron, gently lifted Chameleon onto his left shoulder, and paraded her around the ring.

The old man snarled, "Chu, you don't seriously think I'll award our traditional platinum laurel to some Indoasian bitch, do you?"

"A win is a win and a bet's a bet!"

Tau nudged his brother; Chu shut up immediately.

Victor commanded President Xavier, "Barry! You present that woman with a platinum band. I haven't the stomach for it."

Xavier acknowledged, "I understand, My Chairman."

Agent Richmond escorted DeSalle toward an executive exit. Victor took a few paces before turning back toward both Singh brothers and said, "Enjoy your newfound wealth and celebrate your female champion's victory, gentlemen!" He lowered his voice to a whisper,

"While they both last."

The Singh brothers bowed and Chu flushed hot needles of anger, which contrasted Tau's chills of icy fear.

Milton continued parading Chameleon. The spectators began cheering again. Then the ebony giant waved until the cheers returned to a raucous level. He finally set Chameleon's sleek form back on the arena floor before bending down on one knee and kissing her right hand. She ran an open palm along his cheek and smiled before slowly pulling away.

Chameleon headed toward a makeshift rope ladder now bridging the gap between the arena grounds and the executive section. Milton looked up seeing his master scowling. Then the old man abruptly turned away while Agent Richmond escorted him out of the giant's sight. Then Milton watched Chameleon climb to where Barry Xavier awaited to crown the Cupola's new Malevolent Menagerie champion.

CHAPTER NINETEEN

Interruption

The rostrum was filled to capacity with restless reporters. Garth stood at the podium waiting for the media cameras to activate. No paramilitary units were present tonight, but the collective apprehension of impending calamity oppressed the air. Two trusted subordinates flanked the President's position from ten feet behind him. Vice President Mike Parker was on Brady's right with Minister Carmen Franklin seated beside him, scanning the room continually.

Garth began on cue. "Ladies and gentlemen of the press and the myriads of North Americans who are tuned in tonight, welcome to another broadcast from the White House rostrum. As your president, I have another announcement concerning our collective future. I'm sure it seems a trifle strange to hear me again so soon, but this message is as critically important as my last address.

"My staff has evaluated the imperative steps introduced with NACAM. It has come to my attention that another executive order will be necessary to properly implement the first. I hereby command that as of midnight eastern time, all North American domestic police forces will be under the direct command and jurisdiction of my Minister of Enforcement, Carmen Franklin. I immediately promote her to the ultimate rank of Triumviral Commissioner."

Then Brady remained silent while the press core murmured with anger, shock, and outrage. Mike held his breath, expecting Garth to summon soldiers, but the President did not oblige.

Parker leaned over while whispering, "Carmen, where are our soldiers?"

She whispered back, "The President ordered that all paramilitaries stand down away from the rostrum out of sight of the cameras. I argued with him about it earlier, but he stood firm. But if anyone approaches our president, I have enough firepower on me to start one hell of an argument."

"Is that why he ordered you to appear with him tonight?"

"No. Garth wanted our North American people to get another clear look at me for future public recognition. Protecting him was my own idea; he didn't know that I would appear armed to the teeth tonight with concealed weapons. But with this potential mob frothing with rage, I am glad I'm packing."

"Did you know Garth was going to promote you?"

"No idea."

"You really are a cool customer."

"I don't make rules; I only enforce them."

President Brady resumed after his visitors quieted down. "Thank you for your attention again, ladies and gentlemen. I realize that this second executive order might seem more shocking than NACAM itself. But I have not entrenched domestic police forces into the triumviral paramilitary units to invade your homes. This order's specifically designed to expedite NACAM enforcement. There are over eight hundred million citizens in North America, which are far too many for either enforcement arm to handle separately. By working together, I believe these officers can avoid wasted effort and man-hours as an efficient team.

"The NACAM directives were evoked for our mutual survival. This new North American Collective Enforcement Order, or NACEO, is designed for our citizens' mutual protection. None of us can predict the future; we have no way of knowing how much insurrection will erupt over NACAM. The NACEO directive will assure the most efficient use of our triumviral police to help quell any violent or criminal acts. Now it's time for questions."

A familiar front row reporter raised her hand.

Brady responded with a smile. "Good evening, Jennifer. I see you're back for another round of verbal boxing. So be it."

"Mr. President, were you pressured into ordering NACEO?"

"Why do you ask that?"

"This second executive order closely resembles a stroke of political suicide. The NACAM directive hasn't had time for compliance yet, but our triumviral polls indicate that you're a very unpopular fellow. Right now, the chances of you making a political recovery range from slight to impossible. Therefore, my common sense dictates that you were forced into this."

"The NACEO directive is my own idea."

Jennifer blurted, "Then why did you do it? I haven't heard of any reports of riots over NACAM. Why do you find it necessary to group every law enforcement officer under one whip when no threat has yet appeared?"

"This order's a preventative action to maintain order in case of a mass rebellion. It's good policy to hope for the best and prepare for the worst, Miss Scott."

"Absolute power corrupts absolutely, Mr. President. You have single-handedly enacted a program of governmental control that has never been done on this continent before. You and Commissioner Franklin, in the brief span of forty-eight hours, have both become taskmasters over our mobility. You have abolished the framework of the North American Republic. With no consul assembly yet elected to challenge these two executive orders, your actions smack of a military coup."

"I explained our global crisis last night. NACAM was an imperative first step to stem the tide of planetary cremation. NACEO is the next logical course to safeguard compliance of said regulations. This triumvirate must protect its citizens from domestic insurrection."

"Then I believe that you're in for a shock, Mr. President. May I answer your response with some personal observations?"

Garth smirked a moment before saying, "By all means, Jennifer."

"Citizens want their elected government to protect them from violence and suffering, but I doubt they're willing to renounce their rights of personal privacy and passage to obtain it. The right of passage is something that Americans have enjoyed for a very long time. The right to be protected from unreasonable search and seizure is another. Your TransTrak tyranny will restrict their collective right to take private journeys wherever they choose.

"Now, the NACEO directive will homogenize all municipal police into triumviral storm troopers. These newly hardened soldiers will only obey the edicts of one commander and not the goals of common citizens. The main objective of NACAM enforcers will now be to hunt down and punish TransTrak criminals whose only crime is that they didn't recognize a single man's authority to regulate their mobility.

"An electronic poll was sanctioned by your voting staff and tabulated by HoloTel earlier today. The results are now a matter of triumviral record. They support a televised debate on abnormal global warming by a 75 percent majority vote. So I ask you again, Mr. President, as I did last night in front of the entire continent: will you permit a televised debate between the members of any governmental, environmental agency, and the Global Reaction Alliance?"

Garth smiled before announcing, "If our citizens want to collectively decide on this abnormal greenhouse effect for themselves, then I won't impede their wishes. The answer is yes! However, that doesn't neutralize the NACAM or NACEO directives; they still stand at least until the outcome of the debate. Is that fair enough?"

A cluster of round, steel pellets suddenly exploded straight up in one precise direction from inside the podium. Wood paneling splinters and ball bearings shredded the President's head and upper abdomen while blowing him straight up off both feet. President Brady was dead before he hit the floor, spattering blood, brains, and clothing swatches onto the rostrum ceiling before oozing downward onto the floor.

Carmen lunged and pinned Mike Parker while using her body as a shield. Taking out a command link from her pocket and a pistol from her thigh, she ordered the rostrum sealed. The room flooded with fifty uniformed paramilitaries within sixty seconds. Once her charge was enveloped with bodyguards, Commissioner Franklin ran over to scan Garth's corpse; half of his pulverized head was still attached to the shredded neck by gory strands of fibrous flesh.

She scanned the press core. Some screaming reporters had bolted only to be returned to their seats by armed guards. Then Carmen stood back up before watching the lead cameramen, who handed her a microphone and gave her a thumbs up. She spoke without hesitation. "Citizens of North America, President Brady has been the victim of a brutal assassination. Please watch closely."

Carmen as she knelt down over Garth's mutilated body and removed the presidential Scansat disk from his vest pocket. She motioned Parker to join her before transferring the disk to him and announced, "Mike Parker is now President of North America. All executive orders will be carried out at once unless lawfully rescinded at a later date. This broadcast is ended."

The cameras died as Carmen escorted the new President out of the rostrum under armed guard, while ordering her remaining soldiers to detain the audience in the Regional Dining Room until further notice.

Jennifer prayed President Parker would have the courage to oppose this newly formed triumviral police state, or at least have enough sand to stand up to North America's new military dictator.

CHAPTER TWENTY

Exclusive

Jennifer Scott sipped her third cup of espresso while lounging comfortably inside the Regional Dining Room for the last ninety minutes. Personal chefs, steaming buffet trays, white linen tablecloths, and the presence of twenty armed paramilitaries completed the ensemble of the elegant prison cell.

Commissioner Franklin entered the room in full uniform. The dining room occupants went silent. She announced, "Ladies and gentlemen, each one of you will be permitted to leave the White House as soon as you are separately briefed regarding Garth Brady's untimely murder. My department suspects everyone and no one; I will question you myself. Since most of you are engaged in eating, I'll start with this woman sipping a cup of coffee. Miss Scott, will you please come with me?"

Carmen personally escorted the editor into one of the small secretarial offices adjacent to the President's. They sat down facing each other across the polished surface of a black walnut desk. A digital clock displayed eleven P.M. Carmen gazed at the reporter while trying to read her eyes. Jennifer didn't bat an eyelash.

The soldier spoke first. "Miss Scott, do you know anyone who wanted Garth Brady dead?"

"Commissioner, I don't know anyone who wanted him dead, but there are millions of us who wanted him stopped."

"I understand their resentment. However, there aren't many citizens who have open access to the White House without being searched first. I'm sure you can attest to that."

The reporter exclaimed, "You got that right, sister! The security force practically sifted me like wheat before they allowed me access tonight. That's why I don't understand the reason for our press core being detained now!"

"Don't be alarmed, Miss Scott. This so-called interrogation's just a simple pooling of knowledge. I'm simply trying to round up any possible leads. As a journalist, I'm sure that your staff frequently runs across unusual characters with questionable behavior."

"Why single me out?"

Carmen replied, "Because you're the uncrowned leader of the rostrum press core. The rest of them look to you in times of stress. Your colleagues will be released as soon as we finish our chat, but they don't know that. So, are you positive there's nothing you can tell me that might help?"

"Well, I did receive an unusual message at my office two nights ago on Wednesday. A man claimed his life was in danger and kept spouting some story about a revolutionary invention."

"What story?"

"It had something to do with blowing the lid off NACAM."

The commissioner raised both eyebrows. "I'm surprised you're taking me into your confidence. Aren't you afraid of military reprisals?"

"Reprisals for what?

"I'm the new Commissioner of North America. It's now my responsibility to enforce the NACAM and the NACEO directives; your contact might be construed as an enemy to those orders. I could also consider you his accomplice. Aren't you afraid I'll lock you up?"

Scott laughed before continuing, "Look, cookie, there aren't any male hormones to impress in this room right now! By the way, you can call me Jennifer! We can be ourselves now! The answer is no, I'm not afraid! I suspect you dislike this NACAM/NACEO atrocity as much as me! I don't doubt you'll carry out your duty, but you're not going to imprison me for trying to help you."

The commissioner smiled. "Call me Carmen."

"Thanks, Carmen. Are you going to hold me for voicing opposition to Garth's executive orders?"

"If President Brady didn't arrest you last night, why should I do it now? Freedom of speech hasn't been rescinded yet."

"The Global Reaction Alliance might disagree with you. Even my boss forbids me to print their environmental evidence. The rights of bearing arms and free passage are now dead issues, just like the now defunct United States Constitution. Now it's damned near impossible to get any opposing views against radical environmentalism on prime time media these days. Our world leaders seem to be trampling over each other to get these drastic environmental laws ratified before the common citizen realizes what they're up to."

"What are they up to, Jennifer?"

"The same old masculine lust; global power over humanity. Any boob can see Garth Brady wouldn't have ordered these edicts on his own, especially when he previously promised an environmental debate. I hope President Parker doesn't renege on that."

Carmen smirked. "He won't. The new President wants all of the environmental facts to come out too. He's hungry for some answers just like everyone else."

"You mean Mike Parker has never met the GRA or been given access to their data?"

"Not that I know of."

Jennifer hunched forward, suddenly excited. "If he wants evidence, I have copies of the GRA's data. He's welcome to them at any time."

Carmen replied, "I'll pass the word. Is there anymore you can give about your phantom caller?"

Jennifer pointed toward a desktop device. "Turn on that recorder. I presume that you'll want a record of this for Gar—I mean President Parker."

The commissioner smiled weakly while obliging her guest.

The reporter began, "The caller's name is Eric Wilford; he lives in Bolton, Vermont District, and claims he's invented an engine that operates on electromagnetic fields. He wants to meet me at the Hartford, Connecticut District, Chamber of Commerce tomorrow at four P.M. I intend to be there."

Both of Commissioner Franklin's eyes now twinkled with excitement. "If he's on the level, Jennifer, then he has neutralized this world's alleged need to control greenhouse gases, even if the GRA proves they were never necessary! How much security do you want?"

"Hold it, Carmen! He's expecting me to come alone! I don't think this guy would meet me in a public place just for a chance to do me harm!"

"You misunderstand me, Jennifer. Assuming that he isn't dead already, I intend to protect you both."

"Assassination? Why would anyone bother killing me? I'm just a civilian! I don't have any power to change political policies!"

"Your voice projects reasonable opposition to the global powers-that-be, especially after you cornered Garth Brady into sanctioning a media environmental debate. I suspect your enemies already know about the Wilford rendezvous. If they want Eric Wilford silenced, it's obvious you may be next on their agenda if you meet him. Now, how many soldiers do you want?"

"I'll leave that up to you, but don't smother me or my contact won't show."

Carmen affirmed, "My people are never seen until needed. By the way, I'm brand new at this job. Why would do you trust my military judgment?"

"You shielded Mike Parker with your own flesh. As a reporter, I hate to admit this, but actions always speak louder than words. Besides, Garth Brady trusted you and that's good enough for me."

"But I thought that you didn't like Garth Brady?"

"We were allies, Carmen. We preplanned our televised environmental arguments in advance; that way he had an official reason to authorize a televised environmental debate."

The commissioner cocked her head and smiled again. "I like you, Jennifer; you're brave enough to speak your mind. Now, I'm going to do you a favor, but first we'll have to leave this room."

"Why?"

"Trust me."

Carmen led Jennifer out of the office and down a hallway. Four armed bodyguards collectively saluted the commissioner when both ladies stood in front of the Triad Office door.

Carmen commanded, "I want permission to enter the Triad Office with my guest; please inform President Parker."

Colonel Bushnell replied, "That won't be necessary, Commissioner. We have standing orders to allow you in anytime tonight."

"Thank you, Colonel. Now have the press core released immediately."

"At once, Commissioner."

President Parker was sitting on one side of the Chess Roulette Cube staring at the portrait of Napoleon and talking tenderly into his Media Palma when both women entered. Carmen closed the door loudly to announce their presence.

Mike motioned his guests to seat themselves before eventually hanging up. Then he finally reclined behind Garth's old desk and said, "Well, Commissioner Franklin, I notice you have a guest with you. Welcome, Miss Scott. Now, why are you here?"

Jennifer nodded toward the commissioner. "Ask *her*."

Carmen interrupted the discourse with an upraised palm.

Mike pointed his right thumb up answering, "It's all right, Carmen, I haven't deactivated the scrambler since tonight's cabinet meeting. But I deactivated the shutters and the door lock manually. We're free to speak openly. I am sure the Crimson Cupola will be pissed off about that. But that's tough shit!"

Franklin answered, "I'm convinced we can trust Jennifer Scott. She seems capable of handling your impending revelations. Since she has some covert information related to NACAM, she should know about PANCAM."

Jennifer blurted, "What's PANCAM? And what's this cloak-and-dagger routine?"

Parker informed calmly, "There's a round white button on the outer left side of the center drawer to this desk; it controls a scrambling device shielding this office from all electronic surveillance."

"Shields you from whom?"

"The puppet masters, Miss Scott. May I call you Jennifer? It seems only fitting that all of us should be on a first name basis."

"Only if I can call you Mike. Please go on."

"Thank you, Jennifer, but I must first caution you that the puppeteers may kill you if they find out what you're about to discover. You may leave now if you wish to. In the Triumviral Age, it's much safer to live as an ostrich."

Jennifer Scott paused before answering, "I'm a journalist. Come on, Mike, spill it!"

"The Planetary Pandect of the Universal Regions Council controls all the triumvirates of Earth. But The URC is merely a smokescreen for the most powerful covert organization in the history of the world, which is known as the Crimson Cupola. They also go by the CC or Cupola for short.

"This alliance of dynastic families has been molding and shaping political and financial policies on a global scale since the Roman Empire. The organization began as a merchant cartel controlling the distribution of purple dye, which was a precious ancient commodity. It was used exclusively to stain the garments of worldwide royalty. The Cupola wielded power initially over Caesars, then eventually over European kings, Holy Roman emperors, and Popes through the outlet of the Roman Catholic Church.

"Their power grew steadily over the centuries until it reached a milestone during the Napoleonic Wars. They originated European Banking Houses that supplied capital to both Napoleon and his adversaries during the Little Frenchman's reign as Emperor of France.

The Cupola also spawned the Industrial Revolution and financed the groundwork for Great Britain's Imperial colonial expansion. This organization manipulated key members of European and Asian aristocracy through multiple murders, bribery, blackmail, and terrorism."

Parker paused a moment before saying, "Please let me know if I'm throwing too much information at you, Jennifer. I don't want to glaze you over."

The editor sat on the edge of her seat. "Are you kidding? I'm eating this up!"

Mike beamed a smile before continuing, "When the United States of America won independence from England, that victory only comprised political liberty. Even after the Revolutionary War, United States Courts continued to uphold all commercial loans and liens owed to the Bank of England. The United States has been financially manipulated by these covert power brokers along with every other First World Nation since Napoleon's time.

"The CC propagated the American Civil War; they blueprinted the tyranny of the Federal Reserve System; they manipulated conflict and financial control over both sides during World Wars I and II; and they established the defunct League of Nations, United Nations and now finally spawned the Universal Regions Council.

"Also since 1945, this secret society's incited every so-called police action or regional war by collectively herding countries into obedient camps through the false terror of nuclear annihilation. I say false terror because the Cupola was financing the Cold War on both sides just as they had done during both previous World Wars. They extorted trillions of dollars from United States citizens for decades. The plunder took the form of Federal Reserve usury fees and a mandatory income tax to send financial aid to the Soviet Union. In essence, the American people unknowingly financed their own perceived nuclear enemy.

"Once the CC amassed a large enough military force supplied by the arms race of both superpowers, the threat of global nuclear annihilation miraculously ceased. Incidentally, when Garth Brady told me that, I almost cried. The Crimson Cupola has inflicted immeasurable suffering on the people of the world; they consider outsiders as collateral property that exists only to serve their goals. Do you still want me to go on, Jennifer?"

"For God's sake, don't stop now!"

During the briefing, Carmen walked over to the bar and poured herself a cup of hot chocolate after bringing some to both her companions.

Mike resumed, "The chairman of the Crimson Cupola is Victor DeSalle. The tribunal officers of the URC reads like a family tree: Reginald Masterson, the monitor of the Cohesion Cluster, is Victor DeSalle's cousin. Telia Zendar, the chief magistrate of the Planetary Court, is DeSalle's widowed sister-in-law. Abner Quimby, commissioner of the Martial Protectorate, is a member of a dynastic Crimson Cupola family, which controls all the gold and diamonds produced in South Africa.

"Chu Ahn Singh, the President of Indoasia, belongs to an Asian Cupola family that has dealt directly with European members since the advent of Marco Polo. Chu's brother, Tau Singh, is a high-ranking security chief in the Martial Protectorate under Commissioner Quimby's personal command. Atlanterra President Barry Claude Xavier's a dynastic Cupola member whose family controls majority stock in several European banks serving the DeSalle's and other First Level Families since Napoleon's time. Garth used to say that Victor DeSalle's especially fond of Xavier and treats him like the son he never had. Incidentally, Garth Brady was Victor DeSalle's grandson; his mother was one of Victor's daughters.

"Garth also informed me that triumviral presidents chose Cupola outsiders as running mates to help alleviate political suspicions of an elitist coup. Nicholas Martov, Walter Mallory, and I are non-Cupola officials. I don't know if these vice presidents can be trusted, but I will find out at my first opportunity.

"Now comes the kicker. The Crimson Cupola possesses virtually unlimited surveillance capability with very few exceptions all over the world. There are some inner chambers in South America, Greater Africa, and Australia that aren't exposed to their scansat station network, but the overwhelming majority are."

Jennifer was still hunched forward. "What are scansat stations, Mike?"

President Parker sipped his cocoa before continuing. "They're sub-orbiting, electromagnetic relay and recording platforms that have covert access to microwaves, lasers, telephones, radio, computers, three dimensional HoloTels, and the equipment on New Genesis, which is a CC north polar military base safeguarding their scansat network. I don't know how many scansats are in operation, but there's one in the White House basement. Garth Brady patched in my retinal code access manually the last time we visited there. The man was apparently a closet electronic genius.

"Anyway, I've already showed this basement scansat station to Carmen and the rest of my cabinet earlier this evening, which unfortunately included Andre Roget."

Jennifer probed, "Why unfortunate? Roget is your minister of travel. Garth Brady handpicked that French Canadian himself, didn't he?"

"Negative. Roget's a Cupola man and has a direct channel to the chairman himself. Andre Roget cannot be trusted, which is why I was disappointed seeing him appear for our cabinet meeting this evening. He was scheduled to be at home nursing what he said was a sinus infection. But Chairman DeSalle probably orchestrated the Roget's miraculous recovery. Since my plans for disclosure were already set, I reluctantly chose to enlighten my staff regarding scansat. Roget is probably announcing that exposure to his superior as we speak. Incidentally, Carmen, have you released those poor journalists from their VIP prison?"

The commissioner nodded silently.

Parker continued, "I know I've slammed you with a lot all at once, but there's still more. Do you want it, Jennifer?"

She sipped her cocoa before answering, "Wild horses couldn't drag me away!"

"Okay. At the last emergency forum of the Universal Regions Council, a majority vote ratified the NACAM directive into their Planetary Pandect. NACAM now commands jurisdiction over all three triumvirates; they must comply with all NACAM policies within a single year. The Universal Tribunal converted NACAM into PANCAM, which translates into the Pandect Clean Air Mandate. As a result, I can't rescind NACAM for North America. It's now become Pandectory Law, which supersedes the authority of the North American Constitution. That is, as long as we remain a triumvirate."

Jennifer inquired, "I see. Are you going to rescind NACEO?"

Parker sipped again before calmly answering, "No."

"Why the hell not? I thought that you were against these dynastic bastards!"

"Keeping Carmen in command will enable me to maintain enough presidential authority to organize resistance against the PANCAM Amendment. If I rescind NACEO, the Cupola will snuff me like a candle in a whirlwind. The longer DeSalle thinks I'm playing ball, the longer I'll stay alive to work this office. When the time comes, we'll kick those CC elitists right in the groin. Besides, keeping NACEO active will keep North Americans mad as hell and they'll need that anger to defy the Universal Regions Council."

Jennifer was puzzled. "Why are you trusting a reporter with this political dynamite?"

"I'm weary of this secrecy garbage. Covert societies like the Crimson Cupola thrive on it. Maybe if we expose them even in a small way, it may weaken their strangle hold on North America. What I'm trying to do's just a pinprick, but if we spread the word, maybe more pinpricks will follow. The Crimson Cupola's an organized, ruthless, and merciless organization controlling most of this planet's wealth, but they're still only people; people are not invulnerable."

Jennifer shrugged. "I'm not even sure I can get this information published."

"You probably can't. However, word-of-mouth advertising still remains the best way to persuade people. Just be damn careful who you confide in."

Mike suddenly welled up tears, thinking of Garth. "After all, one martyr for this cause is enough; I don't want to see you dead, Jennifer."

"You don't even know me, Mike."

"I knew you when you stood up against triumviral authority. Just as I knew Carmen when she instinctively risked herself to keep me from harm. I am on the side of anyone who questions authority or acts on his or her own initiative. The Cupola's like a hive of drones. Their interdependence betrays weakness. None of their agents make a move without commands from flag officers, who in turn don't move without the blessing of Chairman DeSalle.

"Our initiative and strength may enable us to overcome this enemy assuming that we can survive long enough to exploit their weakness. This PANCAM atrocity spawned from environmental lies. But we can't eradicate mental cancer with force; we must fight this idea with another idea. If you know anyone in the Global Reaction Alliance, I would love to meet him or her."

Jennifer beamed a wide grin. "I know the chairman personally, Mike. Dr. Rudolf Zadock would be delighted to talk with you. He probably watched tonight's speech and is likely forming his debate team as we speak. If I know Rudy, he'll come here as soon as possible. This opportunity to be heard is too precious to delay."

"Excellent! I was hoping you had a connection! By the way, I thought you had a train to catch?"

"Not if I can get a lift from Triad One."

"Welcome to the team, Jennifer! Commissioner Franklin, will you see that Miss Scott has an escort to New York City?"

Scott countered, "You better add the City of Hartford to my New York hop; I'll tell the President why."

Carmen bowed before departing the office. Jennifer relayed her story about Eric Wilford to President Parker, who was the one now hunching forward in his chair. When she finished, the President almost howled. "Hallelujah! That's almost too good to be true! Has Carmen arranged to protect you both in Hartford?"

"She said she'd handle it. Do you really think I may be in danger?"

"I'm afraid so. This conversation's unknown to the Cupola, but they always know when they're being blacked out. It's a small matter to find out who was occupying this office during such blackouts. However, as President, I have no intention of turning the scrambler off again. Garth instructed me regarding this device and I'll know if it's been tampered with. The CC will soon discover that you were privy to a presidential conversation they couldn't hear; they won't like that. But I suspect that it's too soon after Garth's murder for them to try something on me directly. However, they would have no qualms about liquidating you. Right now, I believe Carmen's vital to your personal survival."

"Why do you trust her, Mike?"

"Maybe it's the way she quietly exhibits authority without bullying subordinates; maybe it's the ice water in her veins during a crisis; maybe it's the understanding way she looked at my wife and myself during our election party; or maybe it's simply because Garth Brady trusted her. I don't really know. I feel it more than know it. But I do know that I have to start trusting someone or our enemies will win. If I'm wrong about her, then I'm meat for the worms. But isn't it better to go down fighting for something you believe in than just giving up with a whimper?"

Jennifer quoted impulsively, "Evil can only thrive when good men do nothing."

"By God, Jennifer, you *are* a journalist!"

"Thank you, Mr. President. But if you're wrong about Carmen's loyalty, then we'll both end up as toast. What about your personal bodyguards? How can Carmen be convinced of their loyalty?"

"As I said, we have to start trusting someone, don't we?"

Jennifer smiled weakly and shrugged both shoulders.

Commissioner Franklin returned before closing the door behind her and announced, "Triad One's standing by, Mr. President. Jennifer can leave whenever you give the word. I have selected eight soldiers to accompany her."

"Thanks, Carmen. I believe I've said everything I intended. Are there any questions either of you ladies want to ask?"

"I'm still a reporter, Mike. Have you decided who the new Vice President of North America will be?"

"Yes, but he doesn't know it yet. The man's on his way to Caracas, Venezuela."

"Who's that, Mike?"

"Jocquin Martinez, my Minister of Trade. I've sent him to the headquarters of the Fourth Triumviral Annex Committee in South America. He's attempting to reveal the PANCAM conspiracy to the delegates before they sign in the dotted line. I hope he's successful. It'll be hard enough to oppose two full triumvirates without Commissioner Quimby getting his meat hooks into South America's assets!"

"Thanks for the exclusive, Mike. I've got a plane to catch. I'll contact Rudy Zadock on your behalf. Good-bye, Mr. President, and good luck to us all."

Jennifer left the Triad Office with Carmen and an escort of uniformed soldiers before they walked to the White House rooftop. Eight other soldiers in plain clothes were patiently waiting for them at the helipad.

CHAPTER TWENTY-ONE

Remorse

Chairman DeSalle and President Xavier witnessed Garth Brady's second triumviral address at New Corsica by HoloTel. Recent events were weighing heavily on the old man. The Cupola had scored a massive victory with PANCAM, but Victor couldn't ignore the murder of his grandson, even if he had been a wretched turncoat. DeSalle had reluctantly ordered Garth's murder at four P.M. Commissioner Quimby had obediently detonated the podium bomb from New York City while watching Brady's address and crushing an empty beer can.

DeSalle and Barry Xavier had watched Garth's speech inside the chairman's private study. The ornate room was pentagonal, which displayed a teakwood parquet floor, gothic vaulted ceiling arches, and twelve-foot-tall shelves filled to capacity with hardbound volumes of antique books, music, and videos. There was also a mahogany desk and communication array with a laser fax, stereo system, personal scansat station, and a remote control.

After the broadcast, the chairman sat and buried his face in both hands before commanding half-heartedly, "Barry, I need my sonic tonic. Play *The Planets*. Right now only Holst's classical music can soothe me. Inform Milton I will sleep in the study until awakening on my own. He's free to go to bed as well. Don't wake me up unless there's a Crimson Crisis."

Xavier nodded and activated the CD player.

The London Symphony Orchestra soon cascaded exquisite harmonies signaling the melodious approach of the "Planet Mercury," which was the first of eight different planetary strains created by the famous German composer. There was no ninth composition; the Planet Pluto was unknown when Holst had composed his masterpiece. Despite his remorse, the exhausted old man fell asleep with rasping snores before Mercury's song waned.

Barry remained in the study to await his favorite melody: Mars, the god of war. Blood pounding strains of dominant brass and percussion transported his imagination to the vistas and plains of the red planet. A voracious reader since twelve, Barry Claude Xavier was familiar with many of the classic adventure stories of Edgar Rice Burroughs. *Tarzan* had left an indelible impression on his psyche, but the *Lord of the Apes* played second to *John Carter of Mars*. This powerful and heroic character battled fantastic creatures on the surface of *Barsoom*, which in Burroughs' imagination was the Martians' collective name for their native planet.

As he listened, President Barry Claude Xavier reflected on the Cupola's current Chess Roulette strategy. Twelve cubes existed now with only four in use. One was inside the White House Triad Office. A second was at Chu Ahn Singh's Typhoon Palace. The third was in Chairman Spencer Mitchell's boardroom at the TDI, and the fourth was at the Renaissance Rectory inside the Octavius Palladium Mansion in Rome. The remaining eight weapons were yet to be assigned.

Xavier abandoned DeSalle after the digital concert, relayed his mentor's message to Milton the Mountain, and climbed the stairway to his guestroom. He felt Milton's eyes probing before disappearing from the giant's view. Despite Victor's relayed message, the black titan remained on guard outside the study like a colossal statue. The guardian frowned while wondering to himself if Xavier was somehow planning to usurp his chairman's throne.

After an hour of guarding the silent study, Milton walked into an adjacent, encoded, steel-vaulted chamber concealed in the hallway wall near the study door. He scanned a cache of weapons from machine pistols to plastic explosives, from chemical launchers to hypersonic stun mines, and from flame-throwers to Cerberus Pulse Cannons.

Milton strapped on one custom-sized cannon, closed the chamber, and padded upstairs. After confirming Xavier was asleep in bed, the black titan locked the guest inside with his household skeleton key before returning to DeSalle's study door. He contacted New Corsica's main entrance security squad by Media Palm.

A voice quickly answered, "Templar Gate Security, Colonel Phipps here."

"This is Milton, Colonel."

"Yes, sir, what can we do for you?"

"The chairman's asleep in his study. I'm standing guard at its entrance on the main floor as we speak. Since President Brady was murdered, I'm feeling a little anxious about New Corsica's security tonight."

"We're absolutely secured here tonight, sir, as with any other night. We have one hundred soldiers armed to the teeth to keep it that way. Besides, Brady was terminated at our chairman's command."

Milton continued, "Call it my gut then, Marv, but I need to vent my spleen a little. I want your squad to assemble some field targets beyond the west lawn. I'm going to be firing my weapon from the sliding door adjacent to the master's study. That way I can practice while still standing guard."

Phipps confirmed, "As you wish, sir. What weapon will you be discharging?"

"My Thunderbolt Trigger. Since the master study's soundproof, the noise shouldn't disturb him."

Colonel Phipps was impressed by sliding out a long and deliberate whistle before replying, "I'll have my squad round up some hardcore targets. Do you want to annihilate anything in particular?"

"Just some replacements targets similar to the ones I creamed last month."

"Acknowledged, sir. It should be quite a show; I've never fired a Cerberus myself. They only allocated those to the cream of the Cupola's guardians like you."

"Then how about giving me some competition? I'll school you on its use."

Marv said cheerfully, "I was hoping you'd offer."

"I'll have a standard issue waiting for you when you get here. But make sure that you approach the house from the west lawn so I don't mistake you for an intruder."

"I'll have my troops set up a dozen targets."

"Music to my ears, Marv."

"See you soon."

After shading his master's room, the giant activated all west lawn lighting brightly enough to play a football game. Later, after briefing his comrade, Milton stood bald head and shoulders above Colonel Phipps' blond-haired, blue-eyed, six-foot-two-inch frame as both marksmen trained their sights on a target range that had taken forty minutes to set up.

The Templar Guards had mounted upright plates of four-foot-square, two-inch-thick steel, iron, titanium, and bronze respectively; a one-ton, flatbed, pickup truck; an abandoned tank; a black, cylindrical railroad tanker car drained of fuel; the upper half of a corroded steel oil derrick; and a four-by-six-foot wall of eight-inch-thick cement blocks reinforced with steel bars.

Milton announced while taking aim, "I'll focus on that titanium sheet first."

The black titan launched a bluish-white sphere of compressed energy out his four-inch nozzle. Laser guidance aimed the projectile dead on target. On impact, the implosion cluster expanded in size to envelop the titanium plate in a rainbow effect before the bulk of the metal reduced into haphazard piles of brittle flakes. The titanium had literally powdered.

"I *love* this thing!" commented Marv after rendering the bronze plate into tan sand flecked with green.

Milton fired his next sphere engulfing the front of his military truck target head on; half the hood, engine, and grill granulated to the ground.

"Imik's wrath!" blurted the colonel. "Too bad about the limited expanding capability, but it sure gnawed a big chunk out of that deuce-and-a-half!"

Milton instructed while his partner took aim, "A maximum four-foot-diameter energy sphere can still bring down a plane or sink most any ship afloat."

Marv fired at the left side of a stationary tank from 150 yards; his implosion cluster rain-bowed a four-foot-diameter hole clear through the center before leaving powdery residue all around the impact point. The black giant grinned. "An awesome shot, Marv! How about firing at will to finish the rest?"

"You're on, Milton!"

The target grounds beyond the west lawn strobed rapidly with prismatic radiance until there wasn't a solid remnant left to shoot on the open ground. Multiple pulses against each target had gradually strewn powdered elements into drifts like the remnants of a sandstorm. Twenty minutes of continuous firing hadn't drained either cannon below 80 percent power.

Phipps was grateful. "Thanks, Milton, for a taste of the Cupola's latest update in foot soldier ordinance! That was even more fun the watching you kick ass in today's menagerie match."

The black titan unslung his Thunderbolt Trigger before answering, "I may have kicked ass, but I didn't win."

Marv continued, "That slender ninja was sure full of surprises, especially after revealing to the crowd that she was a woman. I was even more surprised watching you carry her around for a victory lap within the apron. You actually enjoyed parading that agile Asian warrior on your shoulder."

Milton shrugged while admitting, "I was overwhelmed. I'd never been defeated before today."

"You never relished defeat at anything and I've never seen you betray a single romantic impulse in my life—that is, until today."

The black titan powered down his cannon before answering, "I was just briefly impressed with Chameleon's superior skill."

Marv interjected mildly, "And risked Chairman DeSalle's wrath by helping the little lady celebrate. I saw the way he glared at you before leaving the arena. He also broke tradition by refusing to bestow the platinum laurel on Chameleon's brow. He made Xavier pinch hit for him instead."

Milton glanced up toward the ceiling above them for a moment before declaring, "What the master did wasn't right, Marv."

Phipps unpowered and set down his CPC before concluding, "Milton, you're in love."

The black titan wrinkled his forehead and nearly snarled, "You're nuts, Marv!"

"Come on, pal! We're friends! I've known you for years! I've never heard you openly criticize the chairman before! No problem, Milt. I'm happy for you! The lady seems dazzling!"

"Marv! She…she doesn't even know I'm alive! I'm a colossal brute and she's the most beautiful, delicate, skillful creature I've ever seen!"

Phipps patted Milton against one arm and countered soothingly, "My friend, she seemed pretty pleased with your company today."

"Let's drop the subject, Marv."

"You're secret's safe with me, pal. I'm honored that you shared this with me."

Phipps was amazed seeing shallow tears well up in Milton's eyes before the titan nodded his head affirmatively and returned Marv's pat on the arm.

Then Milton declared, "Thanks, Marv, I appreciate it." He wiped both eyes with his shirtsleeve before composing himself. "Well, playtime's over. Back to the salt mines."

Andre Roget arrived at New Corsica after midnight while driving his 2037 North American Bayonet convertible with its top sealed against the January night. DeSalle's perimeter squad detained him at the main gate with a bristling array of automatic weapons. Then Colonel Phipps contacted Milton while detaining the minister of travel.

Now back on guard and carrying conventional firearms, Milton responded, "What's up, Marv?"

"Andre Roget's with me at the Templar Gate. He claims a Crimson Crisis, requesting an audience with Chairman DeSalle immediately."

Milton countered, "If it's a Crimson Crisis, why hasn't Roget already contacted the master by Media Palm or scansat?"

"The minister claims that he's been trying since departing the White House. Shall I admit him?"

"Send him through. I'll escort him myself."

"Acknowledged. Minister Roget was searched as we spoke. He has no weapons, chemicals, or unauthorized electronics; he's as clean as a plucked chicken."

"He'd better have a genuine emergency or he'll be as dead as one. Out."

Andre rang the front doorbell and was admitted by some New Corsica servants before Milton escorted him toward DeSalle's study. Roget asked, "Why are you wearing so many pistols, Milton?"

"I was expecting trouble; then you arrived."

"Good God, man! What trouble could happen in *here*? I've seen you lift Sebastian Singh off the floor with a single arm! I've seen you kill a tiger barehanded! I've even seen you gut a Nile crocodile with a pocketknife! But today that ninja twit sure cleaned your plow!"

Milton stopped halfway down the hallway, stared down into Roget's widening eyes, and said with icy control, "Malign Chameleon again and I'll shove your head against a belt grinder until the back of your scalp is matting in my hand."

The minster remained dumbstruck while pair continued down the hall until reaching the study door.

Milton resumed, "The master's asleep inside. Wait outside until I awaken him."

The French Canadian entered five minutes later after the black titan opened the door for admittance. Then Milton left the room, closed the door, and stood sentry again.

Victor sat up, now fully awake, in his favorite chair saying, "Have a seat, Andre."

Roget obeyed without a word.

"All right, Minister, now what's so goddamned important?"

"President Parker called a cabinet meeting last night. He was surprised to see me arrive for it."

"I already know that, dimwit! I sent you in the first place!"

"Parker introduced all of us to the White House scansat station."

"Moloch's Mud Whore! How did Parker acquire the access code?"

"Garth must have added Parker's retinal code into the system. I have no idea when."

"I do," muttered Victor. "Since the rest of Parker's cabinet's fully informed about scansats, we've got a real security problem on our hands. You were very prudent in declaring a Crimson Crisis tonight, my boy. My compliments to you."

Roget smiled weakly. "I thought perhaps your already knew, My Chairman. Milton's wearing a lot of guns tonight."

DeSalle sighed before replying, "Sometimes, he just gets anxious."

"Why?"

"I suspect it has something to do with my grandson's death. My bodyguard's as faithful as a hunting dog, but sometimes he's as moody as an old biddy. But one of the reasons he excels at protecting me is that he trusts his instincts, whether they're logical or not."

Andre pressed his fingers together. "*That* explains why he threatened me tonight."

"About what?"

Roget continued, "Milton threatened my life when I jested about how Chu Ahn Singh's ninja tart had bested him in a fair match. Your loyal sentry told me to shut up about that or he would rub my face off on a belt grinder."

DeSalle blurted a brief belly laugh before responding, "Indeed? Apparently my former champion's more despondent about his defeat than I realized. He may be itching for a rematch. I may have to accommodate his wishes soon."

"Milton wasn't very despondent when he paraded Chameleon on his shoulders."

DeSalle scowled. "Don't remind me! He was still carrying that Chinese bitch when I departed the arena!"

Andre shifted gears and asked, "What are your instructions for me this morning?"

"Don't do anything for now, Andre. Your information is appreciated. Now, I need my sleep. Dismissed."

Jocquin Martinez was flying with one hundred other passengers at fifty thousand feet. His aircraft was cruising at seven hundred miles per hour. The Aztec had departed Dulles Airport at 11:30 P.M., Eastern Time, en route to Caracas, Venezuela, via New Orleans, Louisiana District. The minister of trade had insisted on flying in a civilian aircraft with common passengers because his trip might prove less conspicuous to any scansats monitoring random flights.

President Parker had reluctantly agreed.

CHAPTER TWENTY-TWO

Encounter

Mickey awakened to the sound of quiet rustling, irregular thumping, and loose crunching of gravel outside his stationary SleeperTrak. The dashboard read 3:30 A.M. He continued listening while surging adrenaline and wondering if some Blacktop Buccaneers were surrounding him. Broderick's blood pounded while he yanked a loaded .357 magnum pistol from under his pillow. Then the sounds stopped.

The trucker crept off his bunk, slid behind the steering wheel, and started the engine. The SleeperTrak flashed on all exterior lighting as Mickey drove his tractor in a slow circle. Two startled adult raccoons abruptly scampered in tandem across his path toward the nearest patch of darkness. Broderick sighed relief and touched a memorized number code on his Media Palm.

"Fraser Triumviral Distribution, good morning, Sleeper 223."

"Good morning, Paul, Mickey Broderick still commanding. When did Snell rename our company?"

"Hi, Mick, the name became official about thirty minutes ago. You sound pretty alert this morning. Did you sleep well for a change?"

"Yeah, I'm in fair shape. The tractor's still parked in Dallas, but I'm sure that your surveillance board already shows that. Where's my first fare?"

"Albuquerque, New Mexico District, pal. Some boys in the New Mexican desert want a load of computer software and meteorological equipment delivered to Denver, Colorado District."

"Cut that district reference, Mr. Henderson. It makes my skin crawl."

"Can't help it, Mick. All dispatchers and drivers have to convert to the new triumviral vernacular; our supervisor issued a direct order. I don't like it any more than you, but my family still needs to eat."

"May God help us!"

"Amen, Reverend Broderick, your load will be ready at one, which gives you about nine hours to cover six hundred miles, via a short pickup in Lubbock, Texas—"

"—District, I know. Anything else?"

"Not at the moment, but Lubbock's load can fit in a grocery sack. No sweat."

"Acknowledged, dispatch. Pilot to navigator, please relay our course."

Broderick immediately received the destination addresses for cities, the contact persons' names, the nominal route for Lubbock and Albuquerque, and a twin city electronic map courtesy of TransTrak. The trucker locked his equipment onto all vital statistics and replied with mock cheer, "Mission accomplished, Paul. Thanks for the fare. Anything else?"

"Just a personal question."

"What maggot is boring your brain this morning?

"You don't know, do you?"

"What the hell are you rambling about?"

Paul Henderson paused before relaying, "President Garth Brady is dead, Mick. He was murdered in the White House rostrum. It was televised in front of the whole damn triumvirate. Someone had rigged a bomb to his podium; he died in pieces on prime time media. It made JFK look like a vaudeville comedy act."

Broderick nearly yelled, "Holy shit!"

"It happened last night at 9:15, Eastern Time."

"Why did the President make another broadcast so soon after his first one?"

"Brady promoted Minister Franklin to the rank of commissioner over all the civilian police forces of North America. It's called the NACEO directive; it stands for North American Collective Enforcement Order. It became law last midnight, Eastern Time. Now, Commissioner Franklin commands all the cops and all the triumviral soldiers combined."

Mickey punched his dashboard, "Sonofabitch! That tears it! People must be mad enough to kill!"

"You got that right! The only good thing about Brady's address was that he gave the okay for an environmental debate. President Parker reconfirmed the debate and scheduled it for Monday night at seven P.M., Eastern Time."

"What was Brady saying when he bought it?"

"A funny thing about that, the bomb exploded the instant he sanctioned that debate."

Mickey calmed a bit, "Hmmm. Anyway, thanks for the info and the fare."

"No problem, cowboy. Take care. There are masses of angry citizens out there. Call us when you've grabbed the Lubbock parcel. Got other calls to handle; my surveillance board's lit up like Christmas morning. Later."

As his SleeperTrak rolled toward Abilene, Kansas District, Mickey now felt guilty about previously wanting President Garth Brady dead. But he sensed an impending political storm on the horizon. Whoever eliminated the President now seemed a far greater threat than any single egocentric politician with delusions of triumviral dictatorship.

Caracas

Dr. Rudolf Zadock and his senior staff shuddered in icy horror in the GRA's parlor after watching President Garth Brady blasted to pulp in front of their eyes. The HoloTel's flawless, three-dimensional image projected phantom blood, flesh, and debris straight up toward the ceiling from the center of their sanctuary. Vicky Taylor and eight other people covered their faces and screamed while six others wept.

Then twenty-five people fell silent in Denver, Colorado District, at 11:15 P.M., Mountain Time. Garth's address had seemed like the fitting end to an extremely productive day. The Global Reaction Alliance had spent the last twenty-four hours coordinating environmental ammunition for their much-anticipated debate. But now, their presidential savior has been splattered on live television. Silence persisted as Dr. Zadock's intellectual warriors watched Commissioner Franklin transfer the presidential mantle to Mike Parker.

After the broadcast Rudy turned off the HoloTel and wiped his runny eyes. "I want to thank all of you for the teamwork you provided to get our data ready for the triumviral debate. We can thank Almighty God that President Parker has confirmed authorization for our group to still debate next Monday night. It's a pity all of you can't come with us, but I told Garth that five panel members would be enough to get our point across. Does anyone want to say anything before I go to bed?"

Vicky blurted, "Those ice-blooded bastards! What a vicious and cowardly assassination! When are we leaving for Washington, D.C.? It's time to nail those false, environmental vermin to the wall!"

"We're departing at six A.M. tomorrow. The debate's five days away and I don't want those Greenhouse Effective team to see us coming. We need time to scope out our enemies on their own turf. Does anyone have anything else to say?"

The GRA staff bowed their heads in reverent silence.

Dr. Zadock sighed and walked toward his sleeping quarters; every subordinate followed suit and fell collectively asleep within an hour. Thirty minutes later, Zadock jolted awake from a ringing Media Palm on his night table. He answered while rubbing both eyes. "Hello?"

"Rudy, its Jennifer Scott. President Parker's personally informed me that Monday night's debate's still on; you will not be cancelled."

"How'd you rate a private discourse with our new president? He must be smothered with soldiers."

"It's a long story, Doc. Listen, Mike's sending over a presidential aircraft to pick you and your staff up. Triad Three will land directly at GRA Headquarters at four this morning; prepare your schedule accordingly. The plane's a Mantis Vertical Transport; they can land that machine on a basketball court. Make sure everyone is ready to leave immediately after landing."

Zadock rubbed his eye again. "Sounds like ancient Cold War stuff. By the way, when did you start calling President Parker *Mike*?"

"I'll explain later. The President has a dinner reception for you at the White House tonight; I'll see you then."

Rudy asked, "Aren't you meeting us on the Mantis?"

"No, I'm in New York City and on my way to Hartford, Connecticut District. Just trust me on this, okay?"

"Of course. Why do we need an escort to participate in a media debate?"

"President Parker won't leave anything to chance regarding this debate. After all, Garth was murdered after agreeing to it."

"All right, Jenny, we'll be ready. Good-bye."

"Godspeed, Rudy."

Chairman Zadock contacted his five panelists within ten minutes; they acknowledged the message and pledged to be standing ready on their resident football field by four A.M. Scansat Twelve fully recorded Jennifer's call to Denver. The monitor immediately called Commissioner Quimby.

Andre Roget was still asleep at New Corsica as Milton the Mountain extracted his master's Media Palm from the sleeping old man's vest pocket before answering quietly, "Chairman DeSalle's resting in his study, Commissioner Quimby."

"This is a Crimson Crisis, Milton."

"I will awaken him."

Quimby waited until Victor DeSalle's voice was on the line. "What is it, Abner?"

"The Global Reaction Alliance is scheduled to leave Denver today at four A.M."

"You issued a Crimson Crisis for *that*? You must be getting soft, Abner. I've already granted you authority to prevent those potential rabble-rousers from reaching Washington, D.C. When they're airborne, kill them; any casualties on board with them are irrelevant."

"But President Parker has dispatched Triad Three to transport them."

DeSalle sat up abruptly. "Why the hell did he do that? Never mind! Is Parker going to ride that plane?"

"No, but twenty of his military bodyguards are."

"Then intercept the GRA on their way to the airport. Set up a convenient accident."

"But Parker's dispatched a Mantis to collect them directly off GRA property."

"Moloch's Mud Whore! Parker must suspect some form of ambush.

I suppose Garth's death has made him overreact. Never mind, Abner. Let that transport carry out its mission unmolested."

Quimby countered, "We may never get a better chance to kill the GRA leaders."

"Behemoth's Bowels, Abner! Do what you're told! Obviously broadcasting Garth's murder was a giant mistake! That's what I get for ordering an assassination on impulse! Carry out your orders, Commissioner! Leave that plane alone!"

"Yes, sir, but I have some different information."

Victor leaned back. "Make it brief."

"President Parker sent out one of his private helicopters last night with Jennifer Scott aboard. She's on her way to Hartford, obviously to rendezvous with Wilford."

"Goddamnit! Any *more* good news, Abner?"

"I have units staking out the Hartford Chamber of Commerce now. If Wilford shows, what do you want me to do?"

"I want that would-be Nikola Tesla and his newspaper broad dead as dirt!"

"Yes, sir. Do you want me to eliminate Commissioner Franklin too?"

DeSalle sat up again. "What's that Cuban bitch got to do with this?"

"Parker sent her to guard Miss Scott along with eight other presidential soldiers. All of them are armed to the teeth. They could annihilate a small army."

"Balberith's Bloody Balls! What the bloody hell's going on? I go to sleep for a few hours and my organization loses ground? Why is Franklin guarding Scott?"

"We don't know why. But we do know that Parker, Franklin, and Scott were together in the Triad Office after Brady's elimination; the scrambler's still on. Then both women boarded a chopper on the White House roof."

DeSalle snarled, "Obviously Scott sought a private audience with Parker telling him about Wilford. Since the new president's involved, I want all units to leave both targets alone. Monitor their activities, but don't move in. Do you understand, Quimby?"

"Yes, My Chairman."

DeSalle disconnected abruptly only to see Barry Xavier cross his study threshold clad in a purple robe and shuffling silver slippers. The guest asked, "What's the problem, Victor?"

"What are you doing up, boy?"

"I sensed something was wrong. So I came to see if I could help."

DeSalle muttered bitterly, "That was Abner Quimby. He told me that Parker's protecting the GRA debaters and Jennifer Scott with Carmen's elite military guards. These new presidential soldiers are outside of CC ranks and I don't like it! Our agents can't move on Parker's friends without risking exposure! The last thing we need right now are more suspicions in the imbecilic minds of North American serfs just when we need their obedience the most!

"Killing Garth in public backfired on us, Barry. I thought his death would terrify the populace so deeply they'd capitulate without defiance. I also assumed President Parker would oblige us with the same fearful attitude; I miscalculated. Mike Parker hasn't been subdued by the surveillance terror of scansat. Garth's death hasn't neutralized his initiative. It's seems to have strengthened his resolve, but resolve toward *what*?"

Xavier replied calmly, "Maybe Garth spilled his guts to Mike before Quimby killed him. Maybe Mike knows all about our Crimson Cupola. He may know about the Chess Roulette's real function. I'll wager Parker even knows about the Triad Office scrambler."

Victor denied it. "There's no proof of that, Barry."

"One of the first things you taught me is that there's no such thing as a coincidence. Is it a coincidence that Parker sends Jennifer Scott to Hartford under armed, military escort? Is it a coincidence that Parker would send a military unit to safeguard a bunch of civilians flying to Washington, D.C., for a triumviral debate? Obviously Mike believes political insiders murdered Garth and not some radical protest group that hasn't any access to the White House rostrum. If he thought otherwise, he wouldn't fear for the GRA members' lives, which would be natural allies against NACAM. I believe that Parker expects an attack."

"If you're right, when could Garth have enlightened his partner about us? We've been monitoring both men twenty-four hours a day. We know everything they talked about, even when they were inside the White House scansat station."

Barry theorized, "Except when the two of them were scrambled inside the Triad Office two days ago after Garth dropped NACAM on the populace."

"That blackout was an accident. The Triad scansat monitor informed us that our former vice president had wedged a pen into Garth's desk drawer while looking for something to write with. That blackout only lasted for a few minutes. When the scrambler deactivated, Garth chewed Mike out for inadvertently pressing the white button. Garth told Parker that the button was a silent security alarm. I had our people check out that drawer later. Our investigators seemed satisfied with what Garth claimed to have happened; the evidence bore him out."

Xavier crossed both arms. "Garth might've been putting on an act for our benefit. He could've deliberately pressed that button to use what few minutes he could risk to confide in Mike about our organization. With Parker going along with the act, he could've inscribed those marks himself and then deactivated the EMP umbrella."

"Aren't you grasping at straws, Barry?"

"Not if Garth Brady was the clever turncoat you now believe him to be. I suspect he planned every step of his reverse coup against us. I also believe he knew he was going to die. So what would prevent him from telling Parker about us?"

DeSalle countered, "He loved Mike Parker like a brother. Why would he deliberately endanger Parker and his family by revealing our dynasty to him? Garth knew what we would do if Mike was aware of our existence. The Parker family tree would be pruned past his wife and three children."

"I hadn't thought of that angle. You may be right after all. It is possible Parker's just acting rashly because it's the only way he can handle dealing with Garth's murder."

Victor smirked. "Don't sell yourself short, boy. You pitched some persuasive arguments as well. But for the time being, we'll give the President Parker the benefit of the doubt. Besides, I've already initiated a plan to keep Mike Parker in his place no matter what happens. Since we're both awake, how about a nocturnal banquet? I'm hungry."

Barry smiled. "I'll join you after I've grabbed a quick shower. By the way, I'd like to return to Rome today with your permission. I'm sure Walter's anxiously awaiting my return to the Octavius Palladium."

"Permission granted, President Xavier. You and the other presidents have completed your tasks in New York City for the time being. The PANCAM directive's now triumviral law. I'm sorry that you dislike my company so much and wish to rush off."

"You know better than that, Victor. Besides, I have a Chess Roulette initiation to perform. I hope my ministers have groomed him properly."

"That's my boy."

Eric Wilford laid out ten Golden Eagle coins in front of a surprised currency exchange teller at the St. Louis, Missouri District, branch of the Bank of North America. The teller excused herself and located the branch manager. A slender, gray-haired man returned with her and rapidly scanned the disheveled-looking gold bearer. The manager inquired, "Excuse me, sir, what's your name again?"

"Ross, Herbert Ross. Is there some problem with my gold?"

"No, sir. I can tell immediately that they're genuine. It's just that we're not used to exchanging so many coins at once. As a matter of fact, gold and silver have become so scarce among the general public in the last few years, it's a real oddity to find a customer with a single Golden Eagle let alone ten of them. Are you a collector, sir?"

"My father was. May I have my money now?"

"Certainly, sir. The current market for gold is $2,200 an ounce, minus the customary five percent handling fee. Miss Raffin will assist you. Good day."

Eric watched with bloodshot eyes while Miss Raffin calculated the total.

She politely observed, "I see that you're quite tired, Mr. Ross. You look as if you've been driving a long distance. May I suggest you take out a room and rest? Sleepy drivers can't be too careful these days with TransTrak surveillance and Black Buccaneers."

"Thanks, but I have to get to Chicago as soon as possible. My money, please."

"Certainly. Ten coins at $2,200 apiece make a gross amount of $22,000. Deducting five percent, or $1,100, from the gross gives you a net total of $20,900. Any particular denomination you prefer?"

Eric yawned before saying, "I think one hundreds, fifties, and twenties will do nicely."

The weary inventor propped both elbows on the counter as Miss Raffin headed for the vault. Several minutes later she returned with a leather pouch concealing the currency. Then, as discreetly as possible, she informed, "I'm sorry, Mr. Ross. The only way to give you your cash was to include twenty-eight $500 bills. Is that acceptable?"

"I suppose it'll have to do."

Eric watched the teller count out twenty-six hundreds, sixty-one fifties, sixty-two twenties, and a single ten dollar bill before he departed with a stuffed money pouch. It was 10:30 A.M. when the fugitive inventor checked into a motel room near the Interdistrict 70 Freeway, just west of St. Louis, Missouri District, within the Northwoods Community. Pulling off the false beard after he locked the door behind him, Wilford plummeted into the welcome arms of a soft bed.

Jocquin Martinez arrived safely in Caracas, Venezuela, unobserved. He wasted no time petitioning for and being granted an emergency audience with the board members of the South American Triumviral

Annexation Committee. Upon entering, Jocquin noticed that his fourteen Latin American brothers, representing all of South America, were surprised by his sudden intrusion. Martinez bowed courteously to his impromptu audience now seated around a circular mahogany table.

Eduardo Del Rio, Annexation Chairman and delegate of Brazil, was first to speak. "Minister Martinez, we trust your lack of protocol harbors an acceptable excuse behind it; we're not used to being interrupted in this fashion."

"My humble apologies, Mr. Chairman, to you and all the Annexation Board Members, but there's no time for the customary amenities. I've been dispatched here at the direct command of President Parker."

"Yes, we witnessed President Garth Brady's abominable murder. Large portions of our population, including all the members of this board. All of us extend condolences for your loss. Please continue."

Jocquin continued, "Thank you. I've been sent here to warn this committee, as well as the South American people, that the Universal Regions Council is covertly attempting to enslave your respective countries. Yesterday, at three P.M., Eastern Time, the majority in the North American Tribune Assembly—all three triumviral presidents and with the unanimous support of the URC Tribunal—incorporated a restraining edict for all triumviral regions known as PANCAM."

"Is that any relation to the tyrannical NACAM directive President Brady issued two nights ago?"

"Yes, sir. PANCAM stands for the Pandect Clean Air Mandate. The Universal Regions Council accepted the NACAM directives into their Planetary Pandect by a majority vote of 126 to 22."

Del Rio frowned. "We in South America don't agree with former President Brady's environmental conclusions; they seem dubious, to say the least. But why are you in Caracas informing us?"

"May I ask the committee a question, Mr. Chairman?"

"If it'll speed things up."

"Were you made aware of this new pandectory law that was voted into effect yesterday?"

"No. In fact, I don't recall seeing anything about this new law mentioned in either the newspapers, broadcast media, or on the Internet."

"That's because this vote was a closed door session unknown to the public yet. They haven't reported a thing about it to *anyone*, Mr. Chairman."

"Then how'd you know?"

"President Parker informed his entire cabinet after President Brady died."

Del Rio asked, "Why does that concern us?"

"By covertly adopting the PANCAM directive into their bylaws, the Universal Regions Council can now enforce it on all of its triumvirates. Since no one has contacted your committee regarding this new law, North America believes that the URC wants to sandbag South America after you're annexed under their authority."

Del Rio stood up, bristling with outrage, while scanning his colleagues. The board nodded back to Del Rio in collective defiance. The chairman regained composure and said, "South America now understands your urgent mission, Minister. We are in North America's debt and your president's for sending this information in time. You were indeed sent by Providence."

"I don't understand, Mr. Chairman."

"My colleagues and I were here today merely to sign and ratify South America's annexation to the URC. If you had delayed your warning by even one more day, it would have been too late to back out and we would've been locked into PANCAM retroactively as the Fourth Triumvirate. Thank God you caught us in time!"

"Then my mission is a success?"

Del Rio spoke defiantly, "We certainly are not going to pledge allegiance and grant authority to a geopolitical organization that demands NACAM compliance! We thank you again, Minister Martinez. Please observe."

Jocquin nearly wept with joy watching Chairman Del Rio pick up the annexation document from the mahogany table, produce a cigarette lighter, and incinerate the paper for everyone to watch. A tumultuous cheer erupted from the committee as ashes wafted both into the air and onto the white marble floor.

Every delegate now swarmed around their visitor while shaking his hands and patting his shoulders from several directions at once. The celebration took several minutes, then Chairman Del Rio stared at Jocquin while pledging, "Tell President Parker that he's made powerful allies in South America. If there's *anything* we can do for him in the future, all he need do is ask."

"President Parker will be honored and grateful, sir. I suspect that North America may have need of its brothers' help to the south very soon."

"Now please celebrate with us. Caracas is an excellent place to enjoy yourself!"

Jocquin declined, "As a Latin, I'm eager to join you. But as a loyal member of my president's cabinet, I must go and rejoin my colleagues."

"I understand, Jocquin. *Via con dios.*"

Martinez departed and was soon taxi-bound for the Caracas Airport. As per previous orders, the Aztec would not contact President Parker until they were together within the Triad Office again.

CHAPTER TWENTY-FOUR

Reunion

President Xavier was rapidly approaching the Azores at suborbital velocity en route to Rome at four P.M., Eastern Time, while a Mantis vertical transport had launched from Denver, Colorado District, with their GRA scientists as five Cupola Agents observed from a cluster of thick forest one mile away.

Mike Parker had assembled a partial cabinet of his ministers inside the Triad Office. Minister of Justice Tyrone Williams pointed toward the Chess Roulette Cube while asking, "Mike, I'm fascinated by that game table. Garth never mentioned the thing to us. It seems to be a restricted subject. Why? It's a chess game, isn't it?"

"Yes, it is. But how'd you know that?"

"Before Garth's last cabinet meeting, John, Jocquin, Irene, and I had arrived early before anyone else. Garth motioned us to wait in his office. He was engaged in a private Media Palm conversation while pacing the West Wing hallway. You hadn't arrived for the meeting yet, so the four of us were quietly waiting. After a few minutes, I walked over to the game table and poked around; the other three soon joined me. We found the storage bins for the chessmen and activated the game.

"Jocquin, Irene, and I set up both armies while John watched. Our

Aztec friend and I were about to start a match when two of the squares dropped open like trapdoors. Needless to say, we were startled. Not knowing what else might happen, we put the pieces away and turned it off about a minute before you walked in."

Mike's face mingled with anger and terror. He sprang from his chair and leaned his right shoulder against the cube before toppling it onto its side. The President returned to his chair and buried his face in both hands before sobbing. Irene stood up and walked to his side before cradling his shoulders in both her arms while leaning her head against his. Mike slowly regained control before Irene silently returned to her chair.

Parker asked, "Ty, think carefully: who handled the kings on the Chess Roulette Game?"

"Jocquin, Irene, and I set up the pieces. I've already told you that."

"The *kings*, Minister Williams. I won't ask again!"

"Jocquin and I did."

"Are you positive?"

"Yes, Jocquin handled the brass and I the stainless steel. Irene set up pawn structures for both armies. Why?"

"Was there anything unusual about the kings?"

"Like what?"

Parker bellowed, "Answer my question goddamnit!"

"The kings vibrated. It was like getting a finger massage. Both kings were magnetic too; they stuck to the board surface."

"Then someone repaired that game cube without informing either Garth or me. We thought the satanic thing was still defective! Listen to me, Ty. Both you and my new vice president have been targeted for potential assassination."

"You mean Jocquin's your new successor?"

"Yes, but he doesn't know it yet. At any rate, that's not what's important. Garth told me that the Chess Roulette Cube's more than just a novel game. It's some type of metabolic signature tracker. Any person who handles the kings may get their bodily rhythms scanned and recorded on a monitor device. This monitor cannot only locate you by locking on to your unique metabolic signature; it can also transmit an overload signal to short-circuit your life functions. The brain and heart are particularly vulnerable. In essence, a metabolic signature monitor can murder someone by what appears to be natural causes. It's the ultimate murder weapon; there are no wounds, no toxins, and no one to attach a motive to. The builders of this game now have a fool-proof way to eliminate their enemies provided their signatures are on file."

"You bastard! And you left that thing lying around?"

"Yes, but Garth and I had disabled the kings by removing their power cells. Obviously someone had made them functional again. I'm sorry."

"Damn you! That's like leaving a loaded gun in a nursery school!"

"The game was a gift to President Brady from Atlanterra President Barry Xavier. Neither Garth nor I was sure how to handle this situation yet. Then we thought leaving the damned thing in a restricted area like the Triad Office was the safest thing to do. I would have never allowed anyone to use it around me. Unfortunately, whoever repaired it didn't notify Garth or myself of its current status. I'm sorry again."

Tyrone calmed a bit. "Lovely, Mr. President. That means that Jocquin and I could be murdered at any time."

Mike confessed, "Although we can't be certain that your signatures were recorded, we have to assume the worst. That's why I had to tell you, Ty. I'll tell Jocquin when he returns."

"*If* he returns, I won't be around to see it. My resignation from office is effective immediately!"

Parker lowered his voice. "I don't blame you, Ty. But you need to know two things before you leave: One is that you're free to return to your appointment anytime that you wish in the future. Two is that I implore you not to reveal Chess Roulette to the public. You'll be murdered if you do. Your only chance for survival is anonymity. Forgive me."

Williams yelled while storming towards the exit door, "Piss on forgiveness! That's what I get for trusting strangers! Just stay the hell out of my face!"

President Parker sighed as his door slammed.

Suddenly four soldiers came in escorting Tyrone Williams with them. The squad leader asked, "The minister left here very angrily. Are you all right, Mr. President?"

Tyrone barked, "Tell these assholes to get their meat hooks off of me!"

Parker obliged, "It's okay, Major. Minister Williams has every right to be upset with me."

"*Ex* minister to you!"

"Release him, Major."

"Yes, Mr. President." The major rejoined his squad and escorted Tyrone Williams back out before closing the door behind them.

Mike commented sadly, "I hope Jocquin was successful in his mission. If no one else has anything to say, meeting adjourned."

John, Andre, and Irene left the White House grounds without a word.

Mike entered his living quarters to join Margaret and Geoffrey. Parker thought about his children as Margaret tenderly kissed him. Then Geoffrey disappeared as the President hungrily caressed his wife. Mike carried Margaret into their bedroom for some tender loving care. It had been a lonely four days for them both.

CHAPTER TWENTY-FIVE

Discourse

Jennifer Scott had waited for Eric Wilford at the Hartford Chamber of Commerce from 3:30 P.M. until its closure at 5:00; then she walked the building's perimeter several more minutes looking for any sign of an approaching stranger. After 5:30, Carmen reluctantly persuaded her charge to return to Triad One. Convinced that only his death would prevent him from meeting her, Jennifer mourned a total stranger. Within thirty minutes, Triad One reloaded its passengers and vertically climbed above the tree-lined perimeter of Hartford's municipal airport.

Carmen touched Jennifer on the shoulder while bringing a cup of coffee. The reporter accepted gratefully as the commissioner of North America sat beside her. Jennifer sniffled mildly before taking an initial sip.

Carmen queried, "You think our transportation savior's dead, don't you, Jenny?"

"What other reason would prevent him from meeting me? After all, he's the person who set this up!"

"Which is probably why he's not dead."

Jennifer stared at her with widening eyes. "What do you mean?"

"If I were Wilford and wanted to escape from enemies who monitored my communications, I would use you as a decoy to draw their attention away from my genuine escape route."

Nearly spilling coffee on her suit, Jenny gasped. "You think he's still alive and gone underground?"

Carmen shrugged. "I have no idea, but it's certainly possible, especially if this man's as clever as both you and Mike suspect. I only know we could make superb use of his invention if it isn't a hoax."

"Then I may still meet with this inventor after all!"

"I said that it's possible, not definite. At any rate, we'll be landing back at the White House very shortly. I'm very curious to meet the leader of the GRA." Carmen smiled mischievously. "We Cubans are naturally fond of rebels."

"Thanks, Carmen."

The Global Reaction Alliance landed on the White House roof without incident. President and First Lady Parker greeted Dr. Rudolf Zadock and his staff directly, surrounded by an escort of thirty armed soldiers. Commissioner Franklin and Jennifer Scott were also in attendance as the group descended into the West Wing before arriving inside the Regional Dining Room by nine P.M. A squad of ten soldiers remained inside while the rest deployed to other stations.

Mike and Margaret seated themselves at the main table while cueing the rest of their guests to get comfortable. The President had Margaret on his right with Chairman Zadock on his left. Carmen sat on the First Lady's right with Jennifer on Dr. Zadock's left.

Mike raised his wineglass toasting, "To the advancement of Man's knowledge instead of his ego. And to our honored guests, who have sacrificed much to preach the plain, objective truth of physical reality, even if that message isn't popular today."

Dr. Zadock stood up and reciprocated, "And to you, President Parker, for allowing us the opportunity to present our side of the upcoming abnormal global warming debate. We're in both your and Garth Brady's debt. We drink to you and his memory."

Everyone drained his or her toast glasses.

Rudy resumed, "Now, sir, with your permission, I would appreciate the opportunity to thank our Lord for this bountiful meal."

The President was flabbergasted. The last thing he expected was a scientist to say grace, but Parker recovered quickly. "Certainly, if you wish."

Jennifer smirked.

Rudy gazed straight up, closed both eyes, and began, "Our Heavenly Father, Creator of all that we see and can't see. We are humbly grateful for this generous bounty. We thank you for the labor of the people that produced and prepared it. We ask your blessing on them all. Help us to never forget that we are mere people and make mistakes. Help us to live our lives in a manner that would be pleasing to you. Help my staff and me in the upcoming debate to present evidence that is unbiased and objective. We don't want to make people's minds up for them about the environment, but seek only to present information they can use to decide for themselves.

"Be with our new triumvirate and president. Protect him from harm along with his family. Protect us all from the earthly minions of the Prince of the Power of the Air who do the work of satanic deception against their human brethren whether their victims realize it or not. Help us to free the tortured spirits and minds of your children who have been beguiled by intellectual snobs who are also unwitting pawns in a spiritual war.

"Finally and foremost, Dear Father, I and any other believers around this table thank you for reconciling us and all creation through the sacrifice of your Son, the Lord Jesus Christ. We eagerly anticipate His glorious return but also ask for spiritual strength to withstand the world deception of Antichrist, which must come first before the Anointed One claims His Kingdom, amen."

Dr. Zadock reseated himself and began eating.

Parker couldn't help but stare at the head scientist.

Rudy noticed before saying, "I hope I haven't offended or bored you by giving thanks, Mr. President. Ask my staff: I have a tendency to be long winded in prayer. Do you have a question?"

"I thought that you were a scientist, Doctor. Jennifer Scott told me that the Global Reaction Alliance was dedicated to the truth."

"We are."

"Then how can you believe in God? A being that by definition can't be comprehended by the mind of Man?"

"I have faith in the things I cannot see because of the things that I can see and confirm. There are many things in our world that we can dissect and observe, which lead to the rational conclusion that the cosmos is truly designed. It is not the haphazard product from a random explosion of volatile gases. There's no order from chaos; there's only chaos from chaos."

Mike asked, "Are you saying there are rational, objective, scientific arguments for God's existence; that God isn't an extension of the superstitious fears our ape-like ancestors acquired after walking upright?"

Rudy chuckled after swallowing, "Mr. President, may I call you Mike?"

"Certainly, Doctor."

"Rudy. But to continue, do you really believe all life on Earth evolved from inorganic soup?"

"My teachers did. They had diagrams, examples of genetic mutations and changes in existing animals, Carbon 14 dating techniques for fossils and the generally accepted concept that anything's possible if given a long enough period of time."

"Do you believe *anything* is possible?"

"It makes sense to me, Rudy."

"Does it? Do you believe I would fall to the ground if I jumped off the top of the White House?"

"Of course! You would splatter like a ripe melon!"

Margaret retorted while grabbing her napkin, "Mike, what a thing to say during our meal!"

The other guests laughed.

Rudy answered, "It's all right, Mrs. Parker, I find Mike's analogy quite colorful."

"My name's Margaret."

"Thank you, Margaret. But to continue, Mike, you're absolutely right. No matter how many times I jumped off of the roof, I would fall to the ground. Why's that?"

"Gravity, of course. Any child can understand that."

"It's technically the Law of Density, but we'll use the common notion of gravity if you'd like."

Mike laid his fork down and retorted, "Notion of gravity?"

"Correct. But I digress. Anyway, even if that jumping experiment were carried out indefinitely, as long as the present conditions on the earth existed, the result would be the same, right?"

"Right."

"That's one example of definite limitations to our physical world. All the eons of time an evolutionist could imagine wouldn't alter the outcome of that experiment in density as long as the conditions for that density remained constant on Earth."

Parker countered, "But the earth *does* change, Rudy. It never stays the same. It's constantly altering its structure."

"That's true. But it can only change within the parameters of established physical laws. Without those laws, there's no physical reality."

"You lost me, Doctor."

"In other words, laws of density, buoyancy, and electromagnetic attraction, or what people incorrectly refer to as the mass of gravity, will never change as long as the present conditions remain constant. This world can only change within the boundaries of basic physical laws, which cannot be ignored. Follow me?"

"I agree that physical laws cannot be ignored. Go on."

Rudy smiled. "All right, let's take your example of evolution. When we study the theory of evolution, we only use physical laws because evolution denies the concept of a conscious, personal, spiritual Creator."

Parker mildly sighed relief. "Now you're talking. Forget the mumbo-jumbo. Let's talk hard, tangible reality, okay?"

"Agreed. Are you acquainted with the Law of Entropy?"

"Enlighten me, Rudy."

"That law simply means that complex objects, if left to themselves, will decompose and deteriorate into their basic components. For example, if you left your car unprotected from the outside elements, it would break down over time. Rust, sunlight, moisture, and so forth would slowly but surely destroy that car. It would eventually break down into its basic elements. Corpses of plants and animals decompose into chemical dust. Even minerals decompose. Every complex object on the earth breaks down over time into its simple elements. Follow?"

"Anyone with eyes knows that."

Zadock resumed, "However, the theory of evolution declares that complex life forms over time evolved from simpler life. A random group of elements became an amino acid, an amino acid became a cell, that cell became a simple plant or animal, and that simple life form became more complex over time all the way up to the notion of mankind springing forth from apes. Evolution makes a fascinating theory, but it's impossible on Earth."

"Why?"

"Because of the Law of Entropy, or what's commonly known as decomposition. This earth of ours is subject to physical laws. Simple elements cannot develop into more complex ones by natural processes. Therefore, simple life cannot develop into more complicated life. The theory of evolution requires that the law of decomposition be erased in order to work."

"Then why have educators been preaching evolution as fact?"

"That's a good question, Mike. I'm not sure. For some reason, our governmental leaders in the past wanted to erode the general public's entrenched belief in a Creator. I don't pretend to know their reasons for this action. I simply confirm the action itself."

Margaret interrupted, "Then what about mutation?"

Rudy answered, "Mutation's an established physical fact. However, mutation doesn't support the theory of evolution either. Mutation's the natural change in plants and animals due to repeated exposure to changing environments on a hereditary level. It is the result of minute alterations in the chromosomes of life forms during reproduction. From time to time, there are aberrations in nature like two-headed calves and so on. Some parent organisms of random species have reproduced slightly different offspring from themselves as long as creatures have lived on Earth."

Mike retorted, "Rudy, aren't you defending evolution by saying that over time, due to changing environments, natural selection takes place slowly to help animals survive. Isn't that the basis of evolution?"

"No. It's a fact that many animal species over time can reproduce slightly different offspring through environmental changes in heredity, but there's no scientific evidence to support the idea that organisms can transcend boundaries between different species. A fish never becomes a frog; a frog never becomes a lizard; a lizard never transforms into a bird or ape, and an ape never straightens itself into a man. More often than not, mutations in plants and animals are detrimental to the creature's survival."

"Do evolutionists know this too?"

"Certainly. They've taken a natural but exceedingly limited process of life on Earth and projected it backward as radically as possible to support their claims of evolution. I'm not saying that every present evolutionist has done this deliberately; many do not know why they believe in evolution. They simply accepted it on faith from teachers in the past that did know better. Now, the theory of evolution's been around long enough to be assumed as factual. You proved that yourself tonight."

"I see your point."

Margaret interjected again. "Darling, the good doctor will never be able to finish his dinner if you keep after him like this; he's barely been able to steal a bite."

Zadock smiled. "It's no problem, Margaret. I find intelligent conversations much more stimulating than a mere steak. Your husband is curious. I don't have all of the answers, but I would be delighted to inform him of what I do know. Are you curious about anything else, Mike?"

"You were specific about Jesus Christ when you gave thanks tonight. Are you—what's the common expression—a Born Again Christian?"

"It depends on what you mean by *born again*, my boy."

Parker said, "Isn't that some kind of spiritual rebirth or something?"

"Why yes! I'm delighted to see you use the proper scriptural meaning!"

"What other meaning could there be? A person can't be born again physically."

Rudy resumed, "Of course not, but try explaining that to people who adhere to the fallacy of reincarnation by believing a person's spirit can be recycled after death like an aluminum can! But forgive me, Mike, I was digressing again. To continue, yes, I am a Christian. I believe in the Divine Inspiration of certain sections of the Old and New Testaments within the Bible."

President Parker quizzed, "Only certain sections of the Bible, Rudy?"

"Yes, my boy, but like the fallacies of gravity and dark matter, that's a subject for another time. At any rate, when the Bible declares Jesus Christ to be the *only begotten Son of God* and insists that only the *blood of Christ* can forgive sin, I believe it. Also, when that same book teaches that a person's eonian status with Almighty God depends on the completed work of the Lord Jesus Christ, I believe that as well."

Parker blurted, "But that's *blind* faith, Rudy! None of what you just said can be proven in the laboratory. Where's your objective reasoning now? You seem to be a mass of contradictions: First you talk about the reality of physical law. Now you're calmly preaching about the invisible aspects of some type of metaphysical philosophy as if they're as real as the earth we walk on."

"I understand your confusion, Mike. Tell me, do you find mathematics to be a concrete, scientific subject?"

"I most certainly do."

"What about the mathematical Science of Probabilities?"

"You bet. Probability's an excellent tool to locate averages and a reliable method of computing random chance. What's your point?"

Zadock continued, "First, let me say that I haven't always been a convert of the Scriptures. I'm sixty years old but have only been a Christian believer for the last five. However, I was never an atheist. The intricate mechanisms and balances of our dynamic world always convinced me that reality was the product of some kind of creative design. Evolution never made sense to me for some of the reasons that I've just explained. But the belief in a personal, loving, and sovereign Creator had eluded me. I thought one religion was as good as another regarding worship of whatever Creator orchestrated our world with its perfect checks and balances.

"Being a native-born German, I'd been exposed to both the Catholic and Protestant faiths of my forefathers, but I never blindly believed what they taught me. The reason was that they never explained *why* I should believe their doctrines. Despite what you may suspect, Mike, I'm not a person of blind faith. I refused to hang my mind on a meat hook whenever I studied any subject. That list of subjects eventually included Christianity. I admit that in metaphysical matters I have genuine faith, but that's only because my studies of tangible reality have guided me toward that position. I'm not boring you, am I?"

"No way, Rudy! I've never heard anyone combine physical science with spiritual faith. Please continue, but have some more dinner first."

Zadock obliged his host and continued speaking moments later. "One of the strongest claims that both Christians and Jews have regarding Divine Insight rests on the Bible's uncanny ability to correctly prophesy future events."

"Prophecy? None of those Biblical predictions ever came true, did they?"

"On the contrary, hundreds of them have been confirmed by history. Do you want some examples?"

"I'm all ears, Rudy."

"Splendid. But if I drag too long, please tell me. I have a weakness for long-winded discourses. That's one of the reasons why my trusted colleagues are with me to assist on the upcoming debate; they control their tongues much better than me."

Chairman Zadock glanced at his four colleagues, who smiled back. He continued, "First of all, are you familiar with the military campaigns of Alexander the Great?"

"Only generally."

"Do you recall his historic battle against the City of Tyre?"

"Only that it was one of many cities he destroyed in his push for world conquest in the third century B.C.E."

"Correct, Mike. You seem a good student of classical history. But were you aware that the Old Testament Prophet Ezekiel foretold the destruction of Tyre in the sixth century B.C.E. three hundred years before it happened?"

"Bully for him. Predict the death of a city and given enough time it'll come true. What does that prove?"

Rudy swallowed another bite before saying, "You misunderstand, Mike. When I say that the Bible predicts future events, it provides specific details that no man could know in advance. It doesn't spew forth generalities and broad statements that can apply to any individual person like some contemporary horoscope. Ezekiel gave specific details regarding Tyre's destruction."

"Like what?"

"In the Old Testament, the Book of Ezekiel, Chapter 26:4-5, the prophet declared that Tyre would be attacked and destroyed so completely that its towers would be razed to the ground. The very dust of the ground on which it stood would be scraped to resemble the top of a rock. Ezekiel also described that the ground where Tyre once stood would become a place for fishermen to spread their nets. Now, when Alexander the Great laid siege to Tyre, its inhabitants evacuated their main city via the Mediterranean Sea. They escaped to an auxiliary refuge erected on a small island a short distance from the shoreline.

"Since Alexander had no navy, the men of Tyre felt that they'd reached safety. They were wrong. Alexander leveled the deserted city on shore. The Greeks literally scraped the ground of mainland Tyre so that it resembled the top of a rock. Then Alexander's forces threw all the rubble into the sea to construct a causeway between the shore and the auxiliary island so he could destroy Tyre's fugitives. Today, part of the ancient site of mainland Tyre's as bare as Alexander the Great left it. To this day, Mediterranean fishermen use the area to stretch out their nets. The prophet Ezekiel made a detailed, accurate prediction of an event that would happen three hundred years later. This prediction was fulfilled by a Macedonian military power ignorant of any Hebrew scriptural prophecies."

Mike exclaimed, "Holy cats! Is that really true, Doctor?"

"Archeology has confirmed it as a historical fact."

"Why don't biblical preachers and teachers spread that around? It's a very strong example."

"I don't know. But don't just take my word for it; confirm it with your own research."

"That's amazing! It's too bad the identity of Jesus Christ couldn't be confirmed similarly."

Zadock looked into the President's eyes before resuming his meal.

Parker exclaimed, "Don't tell me that the Bible also has prophecies specifically pointing to Jesus of Nazareth as the Biblical Messiah. That's not possible. If it was, then there would be no doubt about the existence of God and the supernatural."

Rudy silently finished his steak before eating part of a baked potato. Then he sipped some more wine, wiped both corners of his mouth, and replied, "The Bible has dozens of prophecies concerning the Jewish Messiah that were fulfilled specifically by Jesus of Nazareth."

"I'd like some specifics please."

"There are many prophecies concerning the Jewish Messiah in the Old Testament, which the New Testament fulfilled to the letter centuries later. I am going to give some examples, but remember, Mike, I don't have *all* of the answers. Seek out and confirm your own research; otherwise what I'm saying will never be real to you. They'll only be the opinions of an old Christian scientist. I don't believe that Almighty God appreciates mindless robots.

"To continue, in the sixth century B.C.E. along with the prophet Ezekiel, there was another Jewish man of God named Daniel. In the ninth chapter of his Old Testament book, the twenty-fifth verse, Daniel recorded a prediction given him by the Angel of the Lord. I have the passage memorized from the New International Version of the Holy Bible, *Know and understand this: From the issuing of the decree to restore and rebuild Jerusalem until the Anointed One, the ruler, comes, there will be seven 'sevens,' and sixty-two 'sevens.'* Hebrew scholars have established that the meaning of Daniel's 'sevens' corresponds to literal years. It's also been historically confirmed that a foreign king named Darius allowed his captive Israelites to rebuild their City of Jerusalem in 450 B.C.E. Still with me, Mike?"

"Absolutely, keep going."

"According to Daniel's prophecy; that order to rebuild Jerusalem started the countdown to the Jewish Messiah's appearance. A foreign king ignorant of Jewish scriptures also issued that building decree 150 years *after* Daniel wrote about it in the Old Testament. Now, if we take sixty-nine *sevens* in Daniel's prophecy and multiply them out, we get a total number of years to be 483, or sixty-nine times seven years. If we take 450 B.C.E. and add 483 years or sixty-nine *sevens* to it, we end up with 33 A.D. That's the same time of Jesus of Nazareth's ministry, triumphal entry into Jerusalem and his subsequent crucifixion. Archeology and history have confirmed these dates."

Carmen interrupted, "Excellent, Doctor! Do you have any other messianic predictions about Jesus?"

"Certainly, Commissioner Franklin. By the way, I was very impressed with the way you handled yourself after Garth's assassination. You're very efficient at what you do."

"Carmen to you, Doctor. Please continue."

"Since there are so many Old Testament prophecies confirming Jesus of Nazareth as the Jewish Messiah, I'll only state some that were fulfilled beyond Jesus' personal control of circumstances. Then we won't be hampered by claims that Jesus fulfilled his own prophecies to claim Messiahship. The following Old Testament prophecies are: Micah 5:2, which establishes the birthplace of Messiah in Bethlehem; Jesus was born there. Hosea 11:1 says that Messiah would be called out of Egypt. Jesus' parents fulfilled this when they took the child to Egypt to escape King Herod's assassination squads. Isaiah 53:12 foretells how Messiah would die by crucifixion or *poured out his life unto death*. It also predicts that Messiah would be *numbered with the transgressors*; Jesus died between two thieves. Psalm 22:16-17 foretells how Messiah had his feet and hands pierced and how people would cast lots for his garments. The Romans fulfilled both prophecies by crucifying Jesus and casting lots for his clothing. These Romans had no conception of Hebrew prophetic teachings, but they fulfilled them just the same. A spear was thrust into Jesus' side as he hung on the cross fulfilling the prophecy of Zechariah 12:10. Judas Iscariot, the disciple who betrayed Jesus, was paid thirty pieces of silver for his crime. The exact amount of betrayal money foretold in Zechariah 11:12.

"These are only a scant few of the messianic prophecies that Jesus of Nazareth fulfilled in both life and death. There are many others concerning his ministry and miracles. As to Jesus' resurrection, it's a matter of historic fact that Jesus' tomb was discovered empty three days after his death. Roman soldiers guarded that tomb, thereby making it extremely unlikely for Jesus' disciples to carry away his body. Because of the Biblical track record of Jesus' fulfilled messianic prophecies, I consider it logical to accept what the Bible also declares about things I cannot directly examine. Mathematicians have calculated the probability of a single person fulfilling all Old Testament prophecies concerning the Messiah as one chance in 8 x 10132 or to the 132nd power. That number would be an eighty with 132 zeroes behind it. The odds of accidental prophetic fulfillment are nothing short of astronomical. It requires blind faith to believe in evolution, which contradicts physical law. But I consider it inescapable logic to accept the idea of a personal

Creator communicating to mankind through some authors of the Bible. Much of that book simply possesses a track record that cannot be honestly ignored. The mathematics of probability easily bear that out."

Rudy returned to his dinner.

Mike trembled with a fresh sense of wonder like a child gazing up at the stars. The world suddenly seemed a much larger place. Then President Parker regained composure and said, "Thank you, Rudy. You've definitely given me some food for thought. I reserve judgment on what you just told me until I examine it for myself. Now, about the GRA's stand on abnormal global warming..."

CHAPTER TWENTY-SIX

Hijack

Eric opened both eyes after a twelve-hour block of sleep. His luminous watch displayed 10:45 P.M. on his bedside table. The inventor stretched beneath two blankets, sat up, put on his shoes, and walked out of his room fully clothed. The motel office was still open as the fugitive paid his bill, returned the room key, and walked directly toward his prototype. The inventor was cruising down Interdistrict 70 within five minutes.

Four and half hours passed before Eric crossed the Missouri/Kansas District Line. Wilford's watch read 3:20 A.M. as he passed through the heartland metropolis of Kansas City and reached Topeka an hour later. By ten A.M., he approached Goodland, twenty miles east of the Colorado District border. Wilford stopped to sleep in his car ten miles west of the Colorado/Kansas District Border near Beaver Creek. For the first time since leaving Bolton, he began to believe he might reach Denver after all.

At 1:15 P.M., Mickey Broderick was in Albuquerque exchanging a Lubbock grocery bag of circuitry for a full load of meteorological surveillance equipment packed into a single trailer. He left at 1:40 bound for Denver. Twenty minutes later, Mickey's sense of fatigue forced a detour. The SleeperTrak pulled off the Interdistrict Freeway and stopped near the town of Corrales, twenty-five miles north of Albuquerque, New Mexico District. Denver would have to wait as Broderick was snoring by 2:15, still wearing boots and keeping within reach of his .357 Magnum.

Broderick opened his eyes at 11:30 P.M. to the sound of broken glass. He clutched his pistol, lurched forward on his bed, and sat up on both knees to stare out through his windshield. The darkness was intense even under a clear canopy of stars. He strained to catch any sound. Keeping below the windows, Mickey slid onto the passenger seat before pushing the door open with the sole of his right boot. The cab dome light flashed on. Mickey jumped to the ground and closed the door before scrambling beneath his trailer chassis.

Five eternal minutes of silence passed before the twin orbs of approaching headlights loomed approximately two miles away. Mickey scanned for invaders in the oncoming lights. Nothing but scrub brush, sand, and the white lines of the highway were visible. Mickey fished out a flashlight from his trailer box and examined his rig closely; the broken glass came from a driver's side headlight. A .22-caliber bullet hole was drilled half an inch to the right of the broken bulb socket. Mickey had apparently been hit by a drive-by gunman. Broderick puffed both relief and anger.

Then gravel crunched behind him. The intruder pistol-whipped Mickey across the back of the neck setting off a parade of psychedelic stars inside the trucker's eyelids. Then a needle prick rendered his jaw, ears, and scalp numb all at once before he crumbled onto the desert sand. The attacker frisked his victim, retrieved his keys, and walked to the rear of the trailer where four companions are waiting. The trailer contents were then destroyed and all five intruders departed within ten minutes.

Broderick awakened looking into the face of a New Mexico District Trooper. Mickey's jaw is still numb. "Wha the ell ith goin ahh?"

The officer replied, "I was hoping that you could tell me. My partner and I found you like this. We've been here about fifteen minutes. You don't seem to have any broken bones. Unless you've got some internal injuries, I think you'll recover. I wish that I could say the same for your cargo. What happened?"

Mickey's numbness began ebbing away as he rose clumsily to his feet. Then he spoke clearly again, "I don't know what the hell happened. The last thing I remember was a light show inside my skull after some bastard slugged me. Did you say that my cargo's toast?"

"Afraid so, Mr. Broderick. You've still got a full trailer, but now its high tech junk. It's been deliberately trashed."

"How'd you know my name?"

"Had plenty of time to check your identification while you were impersonating Sleeping Beauty. Your wallet still has money in it. Here."

Broderick took his wallet with an unsteady hand.

The trooper advised, "I wouldn't move too fast. You're as unsteady as a fly in a wine glass."

"Thanks. Officer..."

"Greco. Hector Greco. Sergeant. New Mexico State...er, District Police, Sandoval County Division, and headquartered in Los Alamos."

"Los Alamos? That's seventy-five miles from here."

"We have jurisdiction for the entire district. My partner and I were on our way to Albuquerque when we found you. Where were you going with this load?"

"Denver, Colorado District. This stuff was for an outfit called the Global Reaction Alliance. My dispatcher said it was some kind of weather gear. What's the matter?"

Greco scowled. "This is the fourth time in six months the GRA has lost property. But this is the first sign of deliberate destruction. The last three were accidents: one on a bus, another by plane and the last one was a wrecked freight truck four days ago.

"What happened?"

"The bus was hit by a commercial truck that ran a red light in Santa Fe. The airplane crashed into the Southern Rockies before it reached

Denver. The third was a truck that went over a cliff near Raton. The driver's still missing."

"My dispatcher informed me about that. That driver was my best friend. His family must be going crazy. Do you think those so-called accidents were deliberate?"

"Not the first two, but that one with your missing friend, I wonder."

Mickey and Officer Greco walked to the back of his trailer. The mass of twisted sheet metal, broken plastic, and glass silhouetted in the dim cargo box resembled remnants from a gang of sledgehammers.

The trucker's blood heated. "Goddamnit! These people play for keeps! But why didn't my assailants waste *me*?"

"Who knows? But President Brady opened Pandora's Box with his NACAM directive. Now this NACEO thing's pushed people over the line. I personally know that New Mexicans are furious about their local police being drafted under triumviral jurisdiction."

"I hear you. What's the standard procedure about this hijacking?"

"We return with your truck to Albuquerque and hand it over to the District Police. Do you need a Media Palm to call anyone before we go?"

"I've got one in the cab. By the way, what time is it?"

Greco replied, "It's eight A.M. Hell of a way to spend a Sunday morning. You sure you're all right to drive?"

"I feel okay now. I'll need a couple of minutes to prep my truck, and then I'll honk my horn when I'm ready to roll. Okay?"

"Sounds like a plan. Good luck with your superiors; you'll probably need it."

"I don't give a damn. I value my skin a lot more than a lousy load of microcircuits."

Mickey locked up his trailer doors, climbed into his SleeperTrak, checked his instruments, and contacted his company. Cora Sanders responded, "Fraser Triumviral Dispatch. May I help you?"

"Hi, sweetheart, this is your prodigal son."

"Mick! What's the story? We've been trying to call you for hours! Sir Frances wants your eyeballs for earrings!"

"I got bushwhacked. Last night some vandals got the drop on me and trashed my cargo bound for Denver. They shot out my left headlight to wake me up. When I left the truck to investigate, somebody took me out with some damn drug. I woke up on desert sand at eight this morning with a New Mexican District Trooper standing over me. We're headed back to Albuquerque. You better take me off line until I'm done with the police. Better inform the GRA their cargo's toast."

"Who's the cop involved?"

"Sergeant Hector Greco, Sandoval County Division headquartered in Los Alamos."

"I'll inform the GRA myself. Call me when you're ready to roll again. Bye."

Broderick blasted the horn to start his escort back to Albuquerque.

CHAPTER TWENTY-SEVEN

Return

A report of the GRA equipment loss reached Commissioner Franklin through her Media Palm. She and Jennifer Scott were attending President Parker and his GRA guests in the Triad Office at 10:30 on Sunday morning.

Carmen raised her hand, interrupting. "Mr. President, I regret to inform you that a shipment of GRA equipment on route to its Denver Headquarters has been intercepted and destroyed near the New Mexican town of Corrales, twenty miles north of Albuquerque, New Mexico District. However, the truck and driver were unharmed."

Zadock asked, "All of our equipment?"

"The police report a total loss. But I'm curious why Blacktop Buccaneers would leave a witness alive."

Jennifer blurted, "Well, I'm getting this vandalism story printed even if I have to rape my editor-in-chief! Carmen, can your people get me the full scoop on this southwest hijacking?"

"Certainly."

Parker interjected, "Carmen, should you ladies leave my scrambled office, your Palms call could be intercepted by the CC."

"If the New Mexico District Police and NACEO Central Command briefed me about this attack, they know already."

"Agreed. But make sure Jennifer doesn't go to her New York

office alone."

Carmen nodded before escorting the reporter out of the room.

Rudy asked, "What went down in Hartford, Mike?"

"Jennifer went to meet some Vermont inventor who claimed the perfection of a prototype engine that runs on electromagnetic fields."

"You mean someone's finally tapped electromagnetic force for kinetic power?"

"This inventor claims his life was in danger; he didn't show up for his Hartford rendezvous with her yesterday. I had Commissioner Franklin and eight subordinates provide her military protection. We're afraid the CC may have already taken this inventor out."

Rudy lamented, "I'm sorry to hear that. Scientists have been working on electromagnetic energy extraction for decades, but this is the first time I've heard of someone making it work. If this inventor was telling the truth, then we could slash NACAM's proverbial throat."

"If he was in earnest, Rudy, then the CC has probably already poured him into a concrete foundation."

"What was the poor lad's name?"

"Eric Wilford."

"If he was telling the truth, then he deserves a seat beside the great Nikola Tesla."

The President suddenly answered his intercom. "Yes, Myrtle. What is it?"

"Minister Martinez has arrived at the security gate."

Mike welled up in tears. "Give immediate access to Vice President Martinez!"

"Vice President, sir?"

"Correct, please inform the White House staff. Jocquin will be moving into the vice presidential quarters as soon as I've vacated them! Thank you, Myrtle, you've made my day!"

The Aztec walked into the Triad Office three minutes later. Mike and Jocquin embraced while sharing private whispers before inviting the GRA to sit down with them.

President Parker formally announced, "Members of the Global Reaction Alliance, this is Jocquin Martinez, the new Vice President of North America. Jocquin, these good people starting on my right are Chairman Rudolf Zadock and Doctors Victoria Taylor and Vitus Baronov. To my left are Doctors Ernest Goldberg and Simon Hoskins. These are the handpicked members of the GRA triumviral debate panel; they have donated their valuable time to enlighten our citizens that the sky's not really falling. They're staying here with us until tomorrow night when we broadcast from the rostrum."

Martinez bowed gracefully. "I'm delighted to meet all of you. Mike tells me you can be trusted and already know about the CC, scansats, PANCAM, and my clandestine trip to Caracas. I'm happy to report South America has relinquished petition for triumviral annexation. They despise PANCAM and swore to fight and die before succumbing to the Universal Regions Council. South America has pledged to help us. We need every ally we can get. Therefore, Mr. President, I want to speak with the leaders of both Greater Africa and Australia. Since these regions are not under URC jurisdiction, we may find allies there as well."

Parker confirmed, "President Masai Gampu of Greater Africa and Prime Minister Virgil Tasman of Australia are scheduled to be here by six A.M. tomorrow. I've already dispatched two sub-orbital military transports to pick them up in Sidney, Australia, and Khartoum, Sudan."

Jocquin raised an eyebrow. "But we're an active member of the URC now. Why would those dignitaries voluntarily come here?"

"President Gampu wants to discuss the future sale of North American grain for the drought ravaged regions of his African Confederacy. Prime Minister Tasman will be here regarding my offer of leasing both Guam and the Marianas Islands as future military bases for their naval and air forces. Both leaders were eager to accept my invitations."

Rudy laughed. "Wait until Old Man DeSalle hears about this; he'll have a stroke!"

Mike smiled, "Greater Africa and Australia need allies as much as North America. My job is to persuade them that we're on their side.

Maybe they'll believe us after our South American success. I'm only sorry that it took the death of Garth Brady to give me ammunition to fight the URC and the Cupola. May the Lord God Almighty have mercy and give my best friend rest."

CHAPTER TWENTY-EIGHT

Surprise

Reginald Masterson was apprehensive about calling his chairman on Sunday morning, but the news couldn't wait. DeSalle screeched, "Behemoth's Belly! What was South America's reason for backing out?"

"Chairman Del Rio claims that his populace had a change of heart because of Garth's NACAM broadcast. Now his people want more time to consider their position."

"But we spent months coddling those Latin peons toward our way of thinking! Damn Garth Brady anyway! That impudent bastard's damaging the Cupola even *after* he's dead!"

Masterson asked, "But wasn't NACAM our idea, Victor?"

"Of course it was! But Garth seemed to have a talent for throwing monkey wrenches when he was obeying orders! He instituted NACAM under orders, but then that miserable worm suddenly promised North America an open debate on global warming! His compliance with our NACEO edict seems to be backfiring too; Commissioner Quimby reports open triumviral rebellion in response to that order! The last thing we need's a collective outbreak of American loyalty; it could set our timetable back half a century!"

"*What* report, sir?"

"Seattle, Boston, Atlanta, Phoenix, Los Angeles, and some other cities are all witnessing incidents of sabotage to some police vehicles along with a number of destroyed DMV offices. There have been drive-by shootings aimed against triumviral police stations, paramilitary armories, and the private residences of a few provincial politicians. Damned if I know where these rebels are getting their guns, but I suppose it's impossible to uninvent gunpowder."

"You anticipate more trouble, Victor?"

"Of course! Garth tricked us into instituting a policy that North Americans refuse to live with. We lost control when his fear of death evaporated. Now, President Parker isn't showing any intention of rescinding Garth's debate commitment." DeSalle grasped and slowly twirled his Serpent Scepter. "Maybe he and I should have a chat before that debate."

"In the meantime, Victor, is there anything you want the URC to do?"

"Not at present. It seems everything we do lately bites us back in our ass."

Masterson asked, "Are you going to allow that debate tomorrow?"

"Reggie, if you can figure a way to stop it without fueling even more insurrection, let me know."

"Since Parker has replaced our White House bodyguards, none of our protectorate agents can get near him, his new vice president, the GRA debate team, or even Jennifer Scott."

"What was that about a new vice president?"

"President Parker appointed Jocquin Martinez his new vice president."

Victor yelled, "That muscle bound Aztec with shoulder length hair? Satan's Scimitar! What the hell can happen next? Something's got to be done about that right now! I won't allow a Latin peon to back up the President! My other flag officers must be shitting razor blades!"

Reginald advised, "We do have an option."

"Let's hear it!"

"When you sanctioned repairs to the Triad Office Chess Roulette, we were able to record and file Jocquin Martinez' and Tyrone Williams' metabolic signatures."

Victor smiled thin lips and receded gums before saying, "But we can't assassinate him yet; right now every eye in North America's concentrating on whatever happens in Washington, D.C. Martinez' sudden death may only trigger more rebellion and generate sympathy for the Global Reaction Alliance. But it's nice to know that we've got a trump card regarding that greaser; that's the first good news I've heard today."

"Is there anything else, cousin?"

"Hang up, Reggie."

Victor headed into the study for another dose of Holst's planetary concert when a scansat station contacted him. DeSalle acknowledged, "What is it now?"

"This is Scansat Three, sir. I have an updated report on the GRA."

"Spill it."

"There has been an incident of blatant vandalism in New Mexico. A high tech shipment of GRA equipment has been destroyed, but neither the driver nor the truck itself have been harmed."

"Who authorized such an operation? I ordered that nothing be attempted against Zadock and his people until after that environmental debate; it would only serve to magnify their cause!"

"This was an independent act of sabotage committed by an unknown party, Mr. Chairman."

"Who besides us would sabotage their cargo? This wasn't a random act of robbery if both the driver and truck are still intact. I want to find out who did this! Make sure Commissioner Quimby checks it out."

"Yes, sir, but there is also something else."

The old man blustered, "*Now* what?"

"Jennifer Scott knows about this. We scanned her when she contacted her newspaper in New York regarding the incident. Minister Franklin's still keeping her under armed escort."

"Blast it! That Cuban tamale's still dogging her! Don't take any action against Scott until further notice, but command her editor to kill the story."

Scansat replied, "It's too late, sir. Scott also used the President's public relations staff to get the story out. When they announced Jocquin Martinez' promotion, they also broadcasted the New Mexico incident."

"Moloch's Mud Whore! Tell Quimby to keep me posted, DeSalle out!"

The old man quivered with fresh anger while pressing a Palm button. Milton the Mountain appeared inside the study doorway; he was a tower of silence. DeSalle commanded, "Milton, get the silver rolls ready; I'm are paying a call on the new President."

"Immediately, sir."

It was one P.M. before Mickey started his SleeperTrak again. Cora was still on duty. "Fraser Triumviral Dispatch. May I help you?"

"It's Mick in New Mexico, doll. The police just sprung me. Any fares?"

"I have orders to send you straight to GRA Headquarters, in Denver, Colorado District; they want to interrogate you themselves. They also want you to pick up some freight at Colorado Springs on the way. I don't pretend to understand why they're paying a full truck rate for one lousy banker's box, but that's their business. I'll send you the information now."

"Beam it in. I'll check in when I've loaded up."

Sanders added, "Good luck, Mick. Try to do this done without a purple heart."

"I'll do my best, Cora."

Broderick eased his SleeperTrak Tractor onto Interdistrict 25 and departed Albuquerque. He was eager to depart after traveling between Albuquerque and Corrales three times in twenty-four hours.

Carl Logan was happy with the New Mexican sabotage mission. Intercepting Broderick's truck had been simple after Logan had converted his old TransTrak box into a receiver before plunging his own truck over an arroyo in northern New Mexico last Wednesday. However, he didn't enjoy drugging and leaving his old buddy unconscious on the desert floor, but his feelings didn't carry much weight as the newest member of the Citizen Reaction Alliance. It proved difficult to destroy a truckload of equipment to an organization they swore to protect, but the CRA believed this latest publicized act might generate sympathy and recognition for their friends before Monday's historic debate.

The ten-man interception team was now back across the Colorado District border riding in a Chrysler Minivan, a four-wheel drive Ford Explorer, and a full size, canopied Chevrolet pickup with Logan riding in back alongside another man. The TransTrak receiver between Carl's knees had just finished relaying Cora Sander's latest message to Mickey Broderick. Carl unlocked the selector as it randomly scanned for other Fraser transmissions. He glanced at Titus McCoy while snickering, "Do you believe this? Old Mickey lost a load of cargo and now the GRA's sending him on another errand."

McCoy suggested, "Maybe we ought to intercept him again. You wanted Broderick to join us. Looks like you'll have another chance."

"Mickey wasn't expecting trouble when we took him out the first time. But he's got more firepower than a single pistol. If we tried again tonight, someone might get shot!"

"You know that hitting Broderick's rig again is a good idea. Admit it."

Logan confirmed, "All right, chief, I admit it! But please try to handle my friend with kid gloves, will you?"

Titus smiled before sliding open a window between the pickup bed and cab while issuing an order to his driver. "Call the boys and tell them we're taking a detour to Greenland, Colorado. I've decided to pay Carl's trucking buddy another visit."

CHAPTER TWENTY-NINE

Reunion

The SleeperTrak departed Colorado Springs at 6:30 as the sun telescoped for another night under the optic law of perspective. Time passed as Mickey paralleled the eastern foothills along the Rocky Mountains. Suddenly both front and eight rear tires exploded a split second before his SleeperTrak slammed into a soft roadside hill. Broderick's safety harness carved into his right shoulder while restraining his whiplashing head from smashing into the steering wheel. He rubbed the back of his neck and pulled his magnum pistol out from under the driver's seat.

After killing the truck's lights, he scanned the darkness outside while reaching toward his Media Palm mounted on the dashboard; the device had jarred loose and was missing. Still grasping his gun, Mickey startled at the sound of a familiar voice blasting through a distant bullhorn. "Mick, don't be afraid and don't shoot! It's Carl Logan. I am unarmed and I'm coming over to talk! I won't get any closer than you allow! Turn on your outside lights!"

Mickey obliged before yelling out his opened driver window, "Prove you're Logan or I'll splatter your brains!"

"You're pistol's a .357 Magnum revolver, which's your favorite choice of weapons. You also have a 30-06 telescopic rifle, pump action cylinder bores shotgun, and a fifteen shot, semi-automatic, scoped

.22-caliber target rifle.

"Come on over, Carl, but do it alone!"

Logan crossed the highway before standing directly in front of the SleeperTrak. Mickey illuminated him with a spotlight and barked, "What the hell's going on, Carl? You've been missing since last Wednesday!"

"First let's get some flares and cordon off this wreck before some trucking brother runs over it in the dark. Hand me your road kit."

Broderick tossed down six flares and cautiously watched Logan set them one hundred yards away from both ends of his wreck. Then the trucker noticed the cause of his multiple blowouts in the rose-colored haze: there was a long, thin, rectangular spike pad stretched across his northbound thoroughfare of Interdistrict 25.

Carl returned before asking, "Mick, can I come inside? I don't want to end up road pizza."

"First, empty your pockets and toss your jacket on the fender. Come through the driver's door while I shift to the other end with my back and passenger door against the hillside. Then we'll talk, Carl, but if anybody else comes near us, I'll ventilate your brains."

"Fair enough, pal."

Logan emptied his pockets and threw his jacket before slowly climbing behind the wheel. He saw Broderick's pistol aiming for his head. "Okay, Mick, it'll save a lot of time if *you* ask the questions."

"Did you set up my tractor?"

"Of course. My organization doesn't want your cargo to reach Denver."

"What organization?"

Carl resumed, "Let's just say that we're on the side of the common North American. We're vigilantes fighting the establishment that wants to destroy our right of passage with that NACAM crap. We also oppose the Universal Regions Council. To us, a triumvirate's nothing more than a police state."

"Why are you attacking the GRA? They're against NACAM too."

Logan drummed some fingers against the steering wheel. "We

are only getting their names into the media. We've never assaulted them directly."

"You guys hit my rig last night, didn't you?"

"Yes, I'm sorry about that syringe in Corrales, but my leader wanted you out of the way while we trashed your cargo. I've been using my TransTrak box as a scanner after disabling its homing device. The GRA doesn't know us, but we're operating as their guardian angels."

Mickey retorted, "Angels like you are about as welcome as leprosy!"

"We've given them the biggest publicity boost they've ever had. The vandalism in Corrales has granted them a sympathetic look by the public. That New Mexican truck attack has been reported on all the news services. They will appear to be the injured party when they participate in that debate tomorrow night. By incurring sympathy for their cause, people might be more inclined to consider the GRA's sincerity."

"Who thought that one up?"

"Titus McCoy, our leader. Anything else?"

"Why are you telling all this to me?"

"I know how much this NACAM and NACEO atrocity must fester in your gut. I'm offering you the chance to join our little group."

Broderick's eyes widened. "You want me to oppose my government and incite rebellion? You want me to vandalize private property to sway public opinion against the URC? You want me to help you set collectivism back one hundred years?"

"Yes, Mick."

Broderick handed his revolver over before asking cheerfully, "Where do I sign up?"

Logan sounded three horn blasts. Five men moved across the highway, armed with screwdrivers, crowbars, wire cutters, and side arms hanging from their hips. Each man was also carrying a large pack on his back.

Carl and Mickey jumped out of the cab before three men climbed inside to deactivate and remove Broderick's TransTrak Box from the dashboard. They also removed the banker's box, first aid kit, road flares, recovered Media Palm, and all the documents in the glove compartment. Another man removed and rolled up the highway spike pad.

Mickey announced, "Fellas, I've got two rifles and a shotgun under the false bottom of my bed and five thousand rounds of ammunition for each." His new teammates retrieved them while tossing Mickey his loaded .22 scope rifle.

Then Broderick followed Carl and his new comrades on foot across the highway and down a steep slope.

Eric Wilford awakened from a peaceful, revitalizing slumber at seven on Sunday evening to a foot of fresh snow all over Beaver Creek. The frozen Colorado blanket proved a natural camouflage against Commissioner Quimby's scansat system, which had expanded its search pattern from Vermont by two thousand miles. Eric chained his tires and rolled through a side road before unchaining for the bare pavement of Interdistrict 70 by 7:45. He stopped briefly in Burlington long enough to use a drive-through breakfast window. Denver was now less than two hundred miles away.

The inventor was five miles east of Genoa when he passed a thirty-foot-long, silver-colored bus meshed in hundreds of small, gleaming metal plates resembling a crocodile's hide as it cruised in front of Eric's Pegasus sedan. After passing safely on its left, Eric reentered the right hand lane in front of the vehicle. Then the bus strobed both headlights while bathing his eyes with afterimages through his rearview mirror. Eric veered back into the fast lane so the Crocodile Bus could cruise by; but it paced him while remaining parallel to Pegasus.

Horror seized the inventor as he spotted the stalker's open driver window in winter, which offered the foreboding of an impending gunshot. Wilford accelerated back to sixty-five as the bus resumed pacing Pegasus. Then the inventor locked his brakes as Crocodile abruptly passed by before gradually stopping a quarter-mile ahead on the right shoulder.

Eric suddenly burned rubber before quickly blowing by his stalker. The bus attempted the pursuit but was soon outdistanced. Eric entered the town of Genoa before quickly parking behind a service station. Crocodile eventually sped past his position still heading west. Wilford sat thirty minutes before moving ahead and eventually moving through the town of Limon. Then Crocodile suddenly reengaged him from beneath a railroad trestle. Pegasus rocketed away doing 100 mph, but his stalker was gaining. Then Eric pushed his prototype past 120 mph.

Ten minutes later, Crocodile managed to parallel Pegasus again while the inventor ignited a road flare; one lucky toss dropped it through his stalker's open window. Eric readjusted his rear view mirror while watching Crocodile suddenly pitch onto its right side while spraying a jet of sparks as metal ground mercilessly against asphalt. The bus somersaulted end-over-end before exploding fuel, glass, metal, fire, and its driver's remains all over Interdistrict 70. Wilford watched the inferno shrink steadily into the distance.

TransTrak Fourteen's monitor detected Pegasus' 90 mph in a 65 zone within a microsecond. Applying manual override, Eric was zoomed in, scanned, and recognized by facial software identification. Commissioner Quimby was contacted directly.

Abner licked both lips before replying, "Excellent, Number Fourteen! Fortunately, we've already planned for a GRA scenario! The trap's already laid! However, you'll forsake all other vehicles while keeping a lock on Wilford's car exclusively!"

"At once, Commissioner."

"I'll contact the chairman; he could use some good news!"

Eric reached the GRA's main security gate at 11:30 P.M. with his engine still running. After finishing a Media Palm conversation, the security officer stepped out of his gate shack. Wilford was ecstatic, but his demeanor plummeted as the officer pointed a pistol in his face.

Wilford squawked, "Good God, man! That gun isn't necessary! I'm here to see Chairman Zadock!"

The guard commanded, "Turn off your engine and step out of the car."

"What the hell for?"

Eric howled a frigid, visible breath as the guard fired a muzzled shot through his left hand. The officer repeated, "Mr. Wilford, turn off your engine and step out of the car."

Eric stomped his accelerator. Pegasus lunged forward, clipping the officer's gun from his hand while knocking him to the ground. The plan to abduct Eric Wilford had failed as the undercover Cupola agent stood up before sprinting across the main roadway and diving through the open passenger door of a parked sedan, which immediately sped out of sight.

The bleeding trespasser never looked back as he reached the main building entrance. Pegasus' oncoming headlights had alerted the main lobby security officer, who'd witnessed the incident at the front gate from a distance. The officer called his superior. Eventually parking in front of the main building, Eric dizzily made out two blurred outlines running toward him before he swooned against his steering wheel. A horn blared steadily into the Colorado night.

CHAPTER THIRTY

Debate

All preparations for the media-wide debate had been completed an hour before airtime. Every square inch of the chamber had been scrutinized for any weapons, explosives, booby traps, and covert electronic devices of any kind. Commissioner Franklin's squad had remained inside after inspection to safeguard secure status. Then Mike Parker entered the room with presidential guards deployed in equal distances around the perimeter while absolutely bristling with weapons.

Mike completed a pair of important tasks earlier today. One was to confide to his new vice president the terrifying truth behind Chess Roulette. Jocquin had shrugged and said, "That's all right, Mike. It was our fault. Besides, I'd already given myself up for dead when I was flying toward Caracas."

The President's second task had been a genuine pleasure. He'd refused Victor DeSalle admittance to the White House when the old man had arrived at eleven this morning. The Cupola chairman attempted to circumvent Parker's authority by having Milton the Mountain crash the gate but retreated when seven armed soldiers sprang up out of camouflage aiming from every direction toward the silver Rolls Royce. Officer Jackson had marched to the driver's side announcing, "We have orders to shoot any gate crashers. And when President Parker says shoot, he means *kill*." DeSalle had frowned hatefully before Milton drove him away.

Jennifer Scott sat in the front row of the press core near the Greenhouse Effective debate panel already in attendance. Carmen occupied a chair in the front row to the left of where President Parker would be seated after his official announcements. Margaret had bracketed Mike's chair on the opposite side; there was no way she would miss this event. The GRA team sat directly below her position with Rudy gazing upward over his shoulder before giving her a reassuring wink.

Every rostrum camera activated as President Parker began at nine A.M., Eastern Time. "Citizens of North America, welcome to our televised debate on the subject of abnormal global warming. We have two debate panels, whose members have drawn opposite conclusions regarding this subject.

"On your left we have the Greenhouse Effective team that insists on the subject's reality; I will ask them to stand as they're introduced. First, Dr. Boris Hindemann, chairman of the Universal Regions Department for Atmospheric Studies. Next is Spencer Mitchell, chairman of the Triumviral Department of Intermodalism, which operates and regulates TransTrak. The third member is Oscar Livingston, doctor of climatology and environmental studies for the Universal Regions Planetary Protectorate. Fourth is Dr. Barbara Rubenstein, meteorologist, geologist, and chairman of the Spaceship Earth Reclamation Group. The fifth member is the acting panel captain. Dr. Miles Anderson, climatologist, astronomer, botanist, chemist and chairman of the Triumviral Department of Atmospheric Integrity in Phoenix, Arizona District.

"On your right are scientists who all claim membership in an organization known as the Global Reaction Alliance, which refutes abnormal global warming as a myth based on manipulated data from subjective computer models. They will stand as introduced. First is Dr. Simon Hoskins, marine biologist, oceanographer, and consultant for the North American Institute of Aquatic Science. The second is Dr.

Victoria Taylor, climatologist and senior meteorologist for the North American Aeronautical Engineers. Third is Dr. Vitus Baronov, senior botanist for the Planetary Photosynthetic Preserve. Our fourth member is Ernest Goldberg, chief engineer for the NORAM Construction Company and chief consultant for the Triumviral Military Corp of Engineers. Finally, Dr. Rudolf Zadock occupies the center chair; he has doctorates in chemistry, climatology, geology, and environmental studies, and is chairman of the Global Reaction Alliance. He's the other panel captain. Incidentally, GRA headquarters is located in Denver, Colorado District.

"Each panel will begin with an opening statement. Then the distinguished members of our rostrum press core will act as moderators by interviewing and addressing any members of either panel that they wish. Earlier this evening, all forty members drew numbers to decide the order in which questions will be asked. Each journalist will have the privilege of only one question.

"Procedural guidelines mandate a particular panel member to answer each question with a five-minute limit, and then any member from the opposite camp will have equal time for rebuttal. If the press core runs short of inquiries, connective Media Palm, Internet, and laser fax lines will receive and transmit questions from North American citizens on a first come basis. Our contact numbers will appear at various intervals during the first two hours of this debate. But only previously unasked questions will be used.

"The third hour will be reserved for both panels to cross examine each other one member at a time but also to a five-minute time limit; I will personally act as moderator for the final hour."

President Parker paused a moment before continuing, "As your president, I'm authorizing an electronic televote for qualified triumviral citizens. Our people are going to decide which policy North America will follow after concluding this debate. By executive order, this broadcast's declared a lawful quorum. I will abide by our citizens' votes, but only if we acquire a majority to authorize and ratify the outcome. Media Palm televotes can be registered anytime during the debate using personal encryption codes; I encourage all our people to vote their own mind."

Mike alternated looks between panels and asked, "Do both teams understand and agree with the format?" Miles Anderson and Rudolf Zadock nodded. "Then we'll start with the Greenhouse Effective Team first."

The President descended the platform before sitting between Margaret and Carmen.

Dr. Miles Anderson spoke first. "Citizens of North America, the record's clear. Since the intensive activity of the Industrial Revolution began in the nineteenth century, the atmosphere of our world has been radically altered by the buildup of substances commonly known as greenhouse gases. These gases consist not just of carbon dioxide, but methane and carbon monoxide as well.

"Billions of metric tons are deposited into the atmosphere per year. Spaceship Earth's volume of air is not infinite. By circulating higher concentrations of greenhouse gases all over the globe, the threat of global warming has now become a planetary crisis. This is something that must be dealt with in a sober manner if our posterity is to avoid planetary cremation. Serious problems demand serious solutions. That's why our first triumviral president instituted both NACAM *and* NACEO. We must comply with these progressive programs or Mother Earth's doomed. Thank you."

Then Dr. Rudolf Zadock spoke from his seat. "Fellow citizens, the captain of the Greenhouse Effective panel's correct when he says that industrial activity has injected billions of metric tons of pollutants into our atmosphere for over two hundred years. That's not even counting the numerous volcanic eruptions that have produced massive quantities of greenhouse gases, but volcanoes are beyond our control.

"What our panel contends is that this gaseous pollution does not threaten Earth with what our adversary's term as 'global warming.' My group prefers to call it abnormal global warming, which is a more accurate term because solar warming's the natural process where sunlight warms Earth's surface by penetrating through cloud layers. Sunlight converts to heat, but then those same cloud layers prevent a large portion of that heat from escaping back into space.

"We *need* solar warming; elimination of the greenhouse effect would cool Earth below its capacity to sustain life. When my respected opponents postulate the threat of global warming, they are telling a half-truth. It's true that earth does warm worldwide through the greenhouse effect. It isn't true that this natural process is now malfunctioning and threatens our earth. It's our safeguard, not a curse. The Global Reaction Alliance intends to demonstrate through the accumulation of objective, scientific data that abnormal global warming is both a misnomer and a myth. Thank you."

Mike and Margaret held hands while Carmen scanned the rostrum for anything unusual. The President's bodyguards remained motionless with shallow breathing their only evidence of life.

The first reporter launched his inquiry. "I want to ask the Global Reaction Alliance the following question: If you contend that there's no abnormal global warming, then why has the average temperature of our Central Province increased three degrees in a single year?"

Zadock nodded to Dr. Victoria Taylor. She replied, "Dense industrial areas such as large cities produce accumulative temperatures. Cities are constructed of glass, steel, concrete, and asphalt. People who live there all know that these particular surfaces both absorb and partially reflect the same initial sunlight from one surface to another and another, and so forth. This process enables eggs to fry on sidewalks during peak summer months. Therefore, cities average abnormally high summer temperatures, which don't provide accurate climate measurements.

"When these inflated temperatures are added to computer models, it raises the regional average beyond any natural solar-heating process. It's very easy to juggle the inflated temperatures of densely populated cities to reach any conclusion desired for a computer model. The GRA contends that such a manipulation has been deliberately done to enforce restrictive laws such as TransTrak, NACAM, and NACEO on

North American citizens. There appears to be a concentrated effort to regulate and restrict the activity and mobility of the common North American; we don't pretend to know the reason why."

Miles Anderson tapped Spencer Mitchell on the shoulder. He rebuffed, "That's not true! Our temperature studies weren't recording data from cities alone; we've measured temperatures from rivers, lakes, mountain ranges, ocean surfaces, deserts, and beaches, and added their findings into our calculations."

The second reporter inquired, "But it seems logical that once inflated city temperatures are mixed into the data pot, then any conclusions based on that data would be inflated above normal no matter how the other recordings were factored in. If the Department of Intermodalism and the Triumviral Environmental Guardians have added inflated urban temperature readings to natural environmental averages, wouldn't their calculations still be in error?"

Mitchell turned pale before replying, "That's something that would have to be determined. But I do not believe the subtraction would be as significant as theorized."

Zadock nodded to Ernest Goldberg. The engineer announced, "Since the Greenhouse Effectives have offered no documented evidence to support their temperature claims, our panel would be happy to offer some of our material to the press."

Goldberg picked up a stack of GRA reports and had them distributed within the press pit. Two other GRA members mounted enlarged copies of the identical report on tripods in case any cameraman wanted to zoom in for television viewers to compare.

Then Goldberg walked in front of the center camera, steadily held up a normal-sized copy of the report, and continued, "These calculations are precisely the same data issued in annual reports from both the Department of Intermodalism and the Triumviral Environmental Guardians for last year; our press guests and citizen viewers will notice both bureaus' official seals on these normal-sized documents for verification in the upper right corner. As you can see on our enlargements, all official DOI temperatures are in red. GRA calculations are paralleling each red number with a blue counterpart in a separate column. My organization has collated last year's average temperatures for the Central Province using only official DOI and TEG report data. However, we intentionally deleted the summer temperatures of our fifty largest cities only allowing each urban area's spring high temperature into the equation, plus an added ten degrees to account for summer averages.

"We also retained every single summer temperature for all of the various regions outside of urban areas including the deserts. Only inflated city temperatures were eliminated. The DOI's own data concludes that last year's average temperatures for the Central Provinces are only one degree higher than the figures published over a century ago in 1900."

A murmur of mild anger and disapproval reverberated among the press. Throngs of North American viewers stayed at attention wherever they were while watching or listening.

Dr. Goldberg returned to his seat.

Reporter three asked, "Dr. Zadock, is your panel trying to convince us that none of the successive record breaking temperatures in the decades of the 1980s, 1990s, 2010s, 2030s and this last year have anything to with an abnormal greenhouse effect?"

"That is correct. Specific and isolated temperature records have been broken at random intervals since such records started being kept. It is true that our province suffered record-breaking heat waves in the all the previous decades you've mentioned, but it's also true that many areas in America retained very mild temperatures during alternate years. I must point out that those previous record temperatures had still been inflated by urban heat index sprawl.

"Isolated weather conditions for various regions of our triumvirate always produce remarkable weather over time, but long-term, climatic temperatures still remain static. Remember that weather's merely a snapshot of a specific condition on a given day. Climate is the accumulation of average temperatures and broad weather patterns for that same area over massive spans of time. The GRA cannot find any objective, scientific evidence that supports abnormal global warming."

Anderson nodded to Dr. Oscar Livingston. "Greenhouse Effectives agrees that climate is a more accurate indicator to evaluate atmospheric patterns than isolated weather incidents. However, it cannot be denied that there are much more concentrated amounts of greenhouse gases in the atmosphere now than before the Industrial Revolution.

"Atmospheric Carbon Dioxide gas levels were first measured accurately in 1956 by a scientific pioneer named Charles David Keeling. He used vacuum spheres to determine that CO2 levels in Earth's atmosphere were approximately 315 parts per million molecules of air. In 1980, it was 341 parts. In 2015, it was 404 parts and last year it reached 440 parts per million. These facts are uncontestable. Since CO2 is a heat trapping gas, greater concentrations of it must increase Earth's greenhouse effect while retarding more and more solar heat from escaping into space at night. Therefore, an abnormal greenhouse effect must be the result!"

Reporter four quizzed, "I would like to ask the GRA that if the concentration of carbon dioxide in our air is higher than normal, then how can you claim that abnormal global warming is false?"

Dr. Taylor responded, "Obviously CO2 is much higher now than it was in 1956. Dr. Livingston is correct to credit Charles David Keeling for setting the standard for accurate atmospheric CO2 measurements by tabulating averages for the month of April each year consecutively since then. The molecular density of this gas has indeed risen from 315 parts to 440 parts per million today. However, my opponents are declaring another half-truth by implying that CO2 is the principal gas in Earth's atmosphere that regulates the natural greenhouse effect. That statement is inaccurate. CO2 and other heat trapping gases such as methane only make up less than two percent of the greenhouse gas volume in our atmosphere. Ninety-eight of Earth's greenhouse effect is performed by simple water vapor, which is the reason that higher CO2 and methane levels haven't caused any appreciable effect in Earth's average climate.

"The answer to your second question is yes. Historical records of Earth's climate indicate that from 1890 to 1940 average temperatures rose by 0.9 degrees Fahrenheit. From 1940 to 1975, it cooled half of one degree when contemporary, political environmentalists officially predicted an approaching ice age at the time. Between then and now, there has been another 1.6 degree rise. Therefore, Earth's current average is only 1.1 degree higher than the one back in 1940. In essence, long-term climatic averages appear to be cyclical of time; objective evidence offers no other conclusion at this time."

Anderson signaled Dr. Boris Hindemann; the elderly German scientist obliged. "I personally resent the assumption that our Greenhouse Effective team's lying. Dr. Taylor claims that increases in CO2 are negligible because it represents less than two percent of our present greenhouse gas levels. But the earth's ecosystem's a very delicately balanced mechanism. Dr. Zadock also admitted that our planet couldn't survive without the greenhouse effect; he is correct. However, the GRA's wrong in claiming that artificially produced greenhouse gases are so slight that they can be ignored regarding Earth's climate.

"Let's assume that these added gases are negligible for the present. Does that mean they would remain that way in the future if continually increased? Each year billions of metric tons of pollutants are wafted into the air; their concentration may be small now, but they never go away. More decades of minute increases could conceivably result in a large enough concentration to cause catastrophic climate changes. Because of life's delicate balance, we must not artificially alter the earth's climate.

"Many of our URC computer models have produced some startling theories regarding even a small increase in average temperatures over long periods of time. One created a scenario of coastal areas of the world being devastated upon the melting of Earth's polar caps. The raised levels of oceans could push freshwater rivers farther back, thereby reducing available drinking and irrigation water and initiating widespread droughts and famines in the process. No one knows for sure what the exact amount of temperature increase is needed to trigger such a catastrophe.

"But it's prudent not to take chances, especially with the world we live on. It's possible that, for the moment, the earth's average temperature is only a single degree higher than it was a hundred years ago. But suppose that tiny increase is maintained over the next few decades and brought about shrinkage of the polar caps? The devastation would be both unstoppable and long reaching for centuries. Can the people of our earth really afford to take that chance by playing atmospheric tag with our planet?"

Reporter five inquired, "Dr. Hindemann, you mentioned the earth's polar caps. I've been informed that deep glacier ice core samples have been extracted from Greenland since the 1980s. I'm also told the reason was to measure the ancient atmosphere our world had between Ice Ages? Is that true?"

"I'll let Dr. Rubenstein answer that; it's related to her expertise."

Barbara Rubenstein replied on cue, "Core samples taken from both Greenland and Antarctica have revealed that the trapped air inside the ice contains much smaller amounts of Carbon Dioxide. Glaciers are comprised of 10 percent air. In colder ages, the count centered between 190 and 200 parts per million molecules of CO_2 within the imprisoned air. In warmer ages, the count was up between 260 and 280 parts per million. None of the previous ages measured displayed any quantities of CO_2 remotely close to our current levels. Industrial emissions have boosted CO_2 levels higher than anything seen on the earth for the last 160,000 years. We went from a prehistoric level of 280 to 495 parts per million within 150 years. I believe that the GRA's posturing about so-called negligible CO_2 isn't relevant."

Rudy nodded to Dr. Simon Hoskins for a rebuttal. "As a marine biologist, I'm always interested in Earth's water systems; that includes ice. I've studied the Greenland and the Antarctic time capsule ice core findings extensively; they appear to be extremely subjective.

"There has been a contention for decades between both Arctic and

Antarctic scientists regarding the chemical nature of glacial ice over long periods of time. Some postulate that trapped glacial gases undergo natural, chemical changes altering specific concentrations locked inside, which includes CO2. If that's true, then any extracted gas from the glacial ice cores wouldn't produce an accurate representation for any atmospheres in Earth's prehistoric past.

"But even if ice core scientists are exactly correct, what difference would that make regarding this present debate? Both panels tonight have conceded that current CO2 levels are higher than any other time in recorded history. But the fact that these gases comprise less than two percent of our atmospheric greenhouse levels and have not demonstrated any objective evidence for abnormal global warming. CO2 atmospheric levels remain irrelevant to this debate. In fact, I fail to comprehend why our opponents insist on covering the same ground again unless they're attempting to confuse the issue. My colleagues and I anxiously await any objective evidence for their claims of abnormal global warming."

Dr. Rubenstein started to yell, but Miles Anderson stopped her response by clutching her right hand. The irate scientist reseated herself.

Reporter six launched, "Dr. Anderson, actual CO2 levels aside, I understand a byproduct of this situation's the rapid deforestation of our jungles, tropical rainforests, and temperate forests due to land development. I have also been told that rainforest extinction along the equator will substantially deplete our oxygen production worldwide by eliminating dense regions of oxygen producing plants. Could you elaborate on this subject?"

Miles Anderson clearly sighed with relief. "Certainly. Our world's an interdependent planet. Sir Isaac Newton proved that for every action there's an equal and opposite reaction. The crisis of South American rainforests strongly echoes that physical law. Most people know that plants absorb carbon dioxide and release oxygen, which is the exact reverse of animals.

"But people don't seem to realize that this source of oxygen is finite. There are only so many plants in our world. When mankind clears the land and eradicates plant life without laboring to renew the resource, he's unknowingly cutting his collective throat. World population increases while plant density decreases. It's difficult to say when the problem will reach life-threatening proportions with demand for oxygen finally outstripping the supply. Vast sections of plant life also help regulate a stable, global climate with massive absorption of CO2. Without those forests, we would be in a very life threatening situation."

After Anderson sat down, Zadock nodded to Dr. Vitus Baronov. "Since botany's my field, I'll rebuff Dr. Anderson's latest set of half-truths. Mankind couldn't eradicate the planetary oxygen supply if he tried. Dr. Anderson's half right when he says that our oxygen supply is finite, but dead wrong when he implies that terrestrial plants produce the majority of it.

"If every square inch of our landmasses were choked with flowering plants, it would still be impossible for their meager numbers to enshroud the earth with the levels of oxygen we now possess. Seventy percent of the earth's surface is covered with water. The dynamic process of evaporation, condensation, and precipitation of water vapor pump masses of oxygen into the air. Besides, terrestrial plants are feeble in oxygen production compared with the astronomical masses of algae populating all of Earth's waters; they are the single highest source of plant oxygen on our world.

"Also, plants are not the annihilators of CO2 that Dr. Anderson claims. Plants have two different gas processing systems. Most people are only familiar with daytime photosynthesis, which absorbs CO2 and releases oxygen back into the air. The second system is known as *respiration*, which operates at night while releasing absorbed CO2 back into the atmosphere. Because respiration is a slower, more constant process than photosynthesis, the average plant expels much of the same volume of carbon dioxide that was absorbed during each twenty-four-hour cycle. It's true that plants produce oxygen, but they don't decrease long-term CO2 levels significantly. Climate is not dependent on plants; plants are dependent on climate. Warm and cold fronts traversing the planet, initiated by the sun's constant energy upon our oceans and landmasses, are what drives our climatic systems."

The rest of the contest proved increasingly difficult for the Greenhouse Effectives as the Global Reaction Alliance steadily gained credibility. Dr. Anderson and his team were being pushed against a wall of scientific debate. But even though the GRA held the objective ground, their opponents were experienced enough in pseudo-scientific evasiveness to bob and weave with each new argument while escaping a blatant deathblow.

President Parker remained alert and interested but also glad when the debate finally ended. He stretched with pleasure, stood up stiffly, and returned to his podium. He smiled and dabbed his forehead with a handkerchief before proclaiming, "Well, citizens, the final decision is up to you. I have been informed that millions of votes have already been tabulated electronically, but North America requires even more to make any decision lawful through an overwhelming majority. I thank everyone who participated in the debate; I found it most enlightening. The press pit, both debate panels, and I will remain on the air for another hour; then we'll broadcast the final vote tally. Almighty God willing, the count will achieve validity."

CHAPTER THIRTY-ONE

Abigail

Mike Parker's mother Abigail wanted to finish enjoying the debate she had been watching for the past two hours, but the seventy-year-old lady was losing her battle with drowsiness. She transmitted a favorable Media Palm televote for the GRA, activated her disc recorder, turned out the parlor and hall lights, and ambled towards her bedroom; it was midnight in Corpus Christi, Texas District. All three of her grandchildren—Nathan, age ten; Melissa, age eight; and John, age five—had long since gone to bed.

Scansat Sixteen maintained Abigail's HoloTel in surveillance mode while continuing to record every image and sound inside her parlor. Now that the Parker family matron was leaving the parlor area, the monitor contacted one of the four Cupola agents covertly gathered on the second floor of her home. "Sixteen to Number Four."

"Go ahead."

"The old lady's out of my line of sight; she just killed the parlor lights."

"No shit."

"Cut the comedy. She must be heading your way toward the stairs. Commissioner Quimby wants her taken alive."

"Why else would my team still be hanging around since we already have the kids? No sweat, Sixteen, I'm ready for her."

Abigail started up the central staircase heading for her master bedroom on the second floor. The Parker ancestral mansion had three bedrooms downstairs, but the mistress of the house refused to occupy any of them. Abigail always kept the room she had shared with her husband until his untimely death; besides, climbing the stairs was her best daily exercise. The lower bedrooms all operated as servant quarters.

She ascended the first ten steps before pulling out her humming Media Palm back out from under the wool sweater she was wearing. The silent, flashing red light on security mode either indicated a malfunction or an intruder was in her home. Abigail turned around and crept back down the steps, inwardly praising the Lord for six secret service agents patrolling her grounds at all times. The matron padded to the main floor balcony left of the parlor while praying to glimpse one of her protectors, but no one was visible.

Scansat Sixteen's HoloTel picked up the old lady's dark, trembling image by thermograph and relayed her current position. Number Four crouched at the top of the dark stairs answering in a whisper, "I'm still ready for the old broad; she's mine as soon as she moves into position."

"But she's standing by the balcony; she seems to be scanning for bodyguards."

"Those clods are all dead as mutton."

"Now she's heading toward the butler's bedroom. I can't see her any longer."

"Her servants have been neutralized too. Convert your monitor to battery power and tell the boys outside to cut all the electricity. I want to see what she does."

"Acknowledged, Number Four."

Abigail's blood chilled the moment her house went black. She reversed direction and shuffled quickly back into the parlor.

"Scansat Sixteen to Number Four."

"I'm still at the top of the stairs."

"Stand down. That old battleaxe just returned to the parlor in a hurry; she's not interested in the stairs anymore."

"She will be. All of her grandkids are up here with us."

Abigail walked to the parlor desk, pulled a key ring out of her sweater pocket, and opened the middle drawer.

The monitor relayed, "Number Four, Old Lady Parker's getting something out of a desk drawer. I can't tell what it is yet."

The matron withdrew a .38-caliber revolver from the recess.

"Number Four, she's got a gun! Repeat, the old woman's packing a revolver. Watch yourself, this crone looks scared half to death."

"What's she doing now?"

"She's walking out of my camera range. She may be moving toward the stairs again. I think she means business."

Number Four answered, "No sweat, so do I."

Abigail remounted the stairs toward the bedrooms of her grandchildren. As she ascended to the top, a green thread of laser light locked on her right arm before a searing, white-hot pain blasted the pistol from her grasp. Her right hip shattered as she crashed to the floor. Grandma's dim eyes captured the silhouettes of four adults moving among the dark shadows of the second floor hallway. All were momentarily illuminated while passing across an enormous, moonlit, octagonal bay window above the staircase. Their faces were never exposed, but she could tell the first three were carrying bundles wrapped in blankets.

Abigail groped blindly along the carpet and got lucky. Clutching both the gun handle and trigger in her left hand, the matron squeezed off two rounds into the retreating hulk of darkness trailing the other three carriers. One bullet penetrated the back of the intruder's right calf by rending flesh, spattering moon-blackened blood and splintering bone. The second round fractured the two bottom ribs on his left side while passing out through the front.

Number Four cursed as he hit the floor before hobbling toward his attacker with murderous fury. The old lady had just enough strength to squeeze again. The bullet whizzed past one side of the intruder's head only to blast half the cartilage off his left ear. Number Four's face and neck was soaked with fresh blood before he reached Abigail. She saw his silhouette crawl over her before she fainted and dropped her gun to the floor.

"Miserable, stubborn, wrinkled, blue-blooded, old bitch!" growled Number Four, now savagely bludgeoning her repeatedly across the face, head, and neck with the butt of his automatic pistol. Abigail's nose, jaw, and right cheekbone were mangled. Not satisfied yet, Number Four shoved the gun muzzle into his victim's shuddering abdomen and fired twice. Then the gunman staggered up on one knee while looking down on his handiwork, exclaiming, "*That's* what you get, bitch! This is the price of defiance! It's a lesson you'll have time to think about with a writhing belly wound!" The agent thought a moment before resuming, "Or maybe I should show respect for my elders and put you out of your misery like *this*!" Number Four kneels back down while straddling Abigail's blood oozing stomach and wedged his gun harshly against her left temple.

Then he changed his mind, shoving his gun under her shattered chin while laughing. "Maybe I should blow what's left of your brains out the top of your head, eh?" Next, he jammed the pistol into the old lady's left ear, saying, "Or I'll push a bullet in one side and out the other. How would that be? Well, come on, you bloodthirsty bitch. Answer me! I want you to choose which way you're going to die! Wake up, you toothless crone! I want you to see this coming!"

Abigail kept both eyes closed while gripping her gun and firing twice. Both bullets pierced the sadist's liver, right lung, and heart as the Cupola man slumped onto her chest with his pistol rolling over the edge of the stairway and firing as it hit the floor.

Moses failed repeatedly to reach Number Four before contacting the residential observer as his car, men, and captives sped away from the estate. Then the scansat monitor answered his call. "Scansat Sixteen."

"This is Moses Richmond."

"Voiceprint positive. Go ahead, commander."

"The children are ours, but Abigail Parker and Number Four are dead."

"That explains the gunfire. Are you sure he's dead? I never got any images."

"Number Four didn't answer any contacts and I'm not hanging around to find out why. I'm sure plenty of neighbors heard the old lady's shots and the local police are probably moving on it. I'm on my way to the Oubliette with my priority passengers. Maintain HoloTel surveillance on the old woman's estate until further notice. Commissioner Quimby will want as much information about any police investigation as possible."

"Yes, sir. Shall I inform the commissioner of our success?"

"I'll take care of that myself."

Victor DeSalle had grown furious in his study watching the Greenhouse Effectives make monkeys out of themselves in some hilarious process that resembled mental devolution. The final tally of Media Palm encrypted televotes were being electronically tabulated on live television when his personal Palm rang.

It was Abner Quimby's voice. "I report partial success in Corpus Christi, My Chairman."

"*Partial* success? What *exactly* happened, Abner?"

"We've bagged all three of Parker's brats. They're on their way to Protectorate Command in Salem. But we had to kill Mike Parker's mother. She pulled a gun and made a fight of it. Number Four was killed."

Victor calmed a little before replying, "Feisty little bitch for having the audacity to own an illegal gun to defend herself and her home. But Abigail's death may actually work to our advantage. Once he gets our ransom demands, Parker will know we won't hesitate to kill our hostages if he refuses. We're there any witnesses?"

Quimby replied, "No, sir. The estate guards were assassinated by long-range snipers before we killed the servants. Two were whacked with syringes while the third was eliminated in his bed with a silencer. We have them in cold storage for Sebastian; he excels at corpse disposal.

But due to the time factor, Moses Richmond fled the estate with his charges leaving both Abigail's and Number Four's body inside her house."

"Moses knew the kids had priority. Besides, he wouldn't have left an open invitation to the police by remaining too long. Nice work, Abner. That's the first good news that I've heard all day. I reserve the privilege of informing the president regarding his family tragedy. Good night."

DeSalle hung up now watching the President's television image. Mike Parker was standing in front of the podium again holding a computer tabulated total of North American televotes; their result was now official as he displayed the tally in full view of all three cameras.

He announced, "Citizens of North America, a confirmed total of 389,789,512 votes were collated within the mandatory time limit. Out of that amount, the Greenhouse Effectives received 36,112,081 votes. The Global Reaction Alliance received 353,677,431. Our people have passed judgment with overwhelming validity. By the power vested in me by our lawful quorum of voters, I now rescind both the previous NACAM and NACEO Executive Orders. TransTrak will be shut down and dismantled immediately!"

The rostrum audience erupted with cheers as Carmen and Margaret hugged each other. Jennifer ran onto the platform and embraced Rudy Zadock with tears streaming down both their faces. The defeated discussion panel sulked in silence.

Eric Wilford shook his bandaged hand with most of the GRA's skeleton crew in Denver after the televote was announced. A few die-hard technicians were too busy examining his miraculous Bipolar Engine to join the celebration.

Mickey Broderick and Carl Logan embraced as brothers outside of GRA headquarters along with twenty comrades from the Citizens Reaction Alliance. The group was scattered in pairs around the perimeter as they watched and listened by Media Palm. Their televotes had unanimously sided with the majority. The CRA presence there had been the result of Wilford's gate assault earlier in the night. One of their scouts had observed the incident through binoculars. In response, Titus McCoy had sent armed volunteers to defend GRA headquarters.

Abner Quimby snapped a pencil between some fingers at his New York City home. He wanted Mike Parker dead so badly he could taste it, but the thought of killing Parker's children by slow torture made his mouth water even more. The commissioner crushed an empty beer can against the floor with his right foot.

North America was inundated by the honks of truckers, whose horns split the night air in a million different places at once. TransTrak boxes were being torn out of dashboards by the tens of millions. None of the drivers seemed to give a damn how Francis Snell would react to intentional destruction of his company property.

Jocquin Martinez, John Blackfeather, and Irene Tupik were in the Regional Dining Room attending with President Masai Gampu and Prime Minister Virgil Tasman while witnessing Mike's final announcement over a HoloTel. Both visiting dignitaries shook Jocquin's hand agreeing to form an alliance immediately. North America would need the help of South America, Greater Africa, and Australia to survive any URC Police Action the Planetary Pandect would mandate.

President Parker rejoined his new allies in the Regional Dining Room while bringing along all of his bodyguards, GRA officials, press core attendees, and the First Lady to continue the celebration. All five Greenhouse Effective panel members politely declined the invitation and were escorted off White House grounds.

The party finally dwindled at two A.M. when the last of the press core departed. Carmen had fallen asleep on a twin bed in an auxiliary guest room. The GRA and Mike's foreign visitors have already retired. Vice President Martinez was resting in his new suite. Finally, President Parker escorted his tipsy wife into their bedroom. Margaret giggled as she plopped onto their bed while fighting the desire to pass out. Mike undressed and rolled his wife under the blankets. His eyelids were closing when the Media Palm on his end table rang.

Mike's spine tingled at the sound of Victor DeSalle's icy, bloodless, authoritative voice. He answered, "What do you want, Victor? It's past two A.M. A bit inconsiderate, even for you!"

"No more than denying me access to your presence today. You know, that's the first time that I couldn't enter the White House whenever I wanted; that was very rude of you, dear boy."

Mike smirked. "I'm sure you're not calling to congratulate me on my first executive order. What do you want?"

"I want you to reinstate NACAM, NACEO, and our wonderful TransTrak system immediately."

"You are getting senile, old man! Nothing your mind can conceive of will force me to do that!"

"Your mother Abigail lies dead at her home in Corpus Christi, Mr. President."

Parker paused before saying, "Not even the CC would be that blatant!"

A moment's silence on the other end passed before the icy voice returned. "I suspected you knew about us, Mike. Now that you've confessed, I feel much better. Where are your children tonight?"

Parker oozed cold sweat down his forehead, cheeks, neck, and the full length of his back. "What've you done to them, you feeble, garbage-brained, aristocratic asswipe?"

DeSalle countered, "Watch your mouth, sonny. My protectorate has abducted them. They were in Corpus Christi with Grandma, chum. Now, they're in our pleasant company. Your brave matriarch was shot to death trying to stop us."

"You'd better be bluffing, skull fucker, or I'll kill you myself!"

DeSalle continued, "Contact the Corpus Christi police, Mr. President. Have some of your people confirm what I say. But don't try to implicate the Cupola or your progeny's toast."

"What do you want for their lives, Mr. Chairman?"

Victor paused to savor Mike's verbal surrender. "That's better. You sound like a president again. I suspected your paternal rage would subside once you learned I held all the trump cards. You'll make another public address tomorrow at ten A.M. You'll abort your executive order against NACAM, NACEO, and TransTrak. Furthermore, you will renounce Jocquin Martinez as your successor; there's no way from Balberith's Blood that I'll allow some Aztec's progeny to occupy the White House."

"He already has, DeSalle."

"You know what I mean, smartass! Andre Roget shall assume the vacant post of vice president. Then you'll resign from office yourself, which will place Roget in charge of the Third Triumvirate."

Parker replied, "I already knew that Roget was your man; Garth told me before you had him murdered."

"The Cupola had to have one of their own in the president's cabinet. Andre was my personal choice for vice president, but Garth insisted on you."

"How does it feel to have ordered the murder of your own flesh and blood, DeSalle?"

The old man roared, "Shut up, you sanctimonious bastard! I've got your own flesh and blood by their eyeballs!"

"Touché, Mr. Chairman, but what if I refuse your terms?"

"Then I'll mail your children back to you a piece at a time; those innocent little angels will beg Sebastian for death a hundred times over before he finishes them in the Oubliette."

Mike asked, "What's the deal if I concede?"

"Then your children will be returned unharmed at a time and place I will specify later."

"All right, Victor, I will broadcast tomorrow. But it can't be at ten A.M. I have an ironclad agenda with foreign dignitaries all day. I can't make the announcement until seven "

"What dignitaries?"

"The president of Greater Africa and the prime minister of Australia."

"What are those wretched rebels trying to pull?"

"President Masai Gampu's here negotiating the price of grain for his drought ravaged African Confederacy. Prime Minister Tasman is negotiating for the leasing rights to Guam and the Marshal Islands as Australian Military Bases."

"You can't do that! North America's subservient to the URC now! Those rebels must be forced to deal with us directly! You have no sovereignty over your continent; you're subject to our Planetary Pandect!"

"I am the President of North America and have the power to negotiate any of North America's assets to the highest bidder. That is, as long as it doesn't contradict our triumviral constitution."

DeSalle commanded with a hiss, "You will cease your negotiations at once or the URC will impose police actions against North America. I control the URC. Your triumvirate can't stand against the combined military forces of Atlanterra and Indoasia."

Mike paused before answering, "You underestimate what six hundred million angry citizens can do if they have a common enemy. But I won't initiate the destruction of my people in order to resist protectorate police actions. All right, Mr. Chairman. You seem to be holding all the cards."

"Cheer up, rookie; at least you got me to delay the broadcast until seven P.M. I'm so glad that we had this time together, Mike. I've enjoyed it immensely. Good-bye for now."

Parker stormed out of his suite wearing a purple bathrobe and bedroom slippers as he padded toward the Triad Office. A trio of bodyguards intercepted him while keeping pace on three sides. Colonel Bushnell asked, "Mr. President, you seem to be in a daze, sir. Are you ill?"

"No, Lionel, I just want to get to my office. Have my switchboard call up Vice President Martinez, Commissioner Franklin, and Chairman Zadock immediately. If they're asleep, then wake them up and have them assemble there as soon as possible.

"At once, sir."

"Maintain all White House security forces on full alert until further notice."

"I'm on it, sir."

CHAPTER THIRTY-TWO

Counterplot

The President confirmed scrambler operation and sat on his desktop with red eyes as the trio walked in at 2:30 A.M. Mike sniffled before saying, "Sorry I awakened the three of you, but Victor DeSalle's informed me that my mother's been murdered and the killers abducted my children. DeSalle's threatened to torture and murder them if I don't accede to his demands."

Carmen bristled while displaying a rare lack of control through furious eyes.

Jocquin embraced his leader as Mike cried, "I'll entertain *any* idea for getting them back!"

Rudy asked, "What exactly were DeSalle's demands, Mike?"

"He wants NACAM, NACEO, and TransTrak reinstated. Then he wants me to depose Jocquin, appoint Andre Roget to take his place, and finally to resign leaving Roget President of the Third Triumvirate."

Zadock continued, "Why depose Jocquin? I thought that the CC had his metabolic signature tracked?"

"DeSalle said no Aztec's progeny would ever inhabit the White House."

Jocquin and Rudy looked at each other before belly laughing. Martinez quipped, "The New World Order's still very Old World minded about some things."

Mike didn't laugh. "I want my kids back! There's no way I'm going to rescind last night's televote! I only feigned agreement to buy time. There's going to be a broadcast at seven tonight, but I'm revealing the Crimson Cupola to our people before asking them to vote regarding North America's succession from the Universal Regions Council. I will not shoulder the responsibility alone; *they'll* have to make that decision."

Rudy smiled, "Good for you, Mike. DeSalle will not expect you to betray him. Now, let's do what we can to prevent your kids from becoming our next casualties of war. Did DeSalle spill any clues where your kids might be?"

"He mentioned Sebastian and the Oubliette. I know all about that monster and his caretaking of the Pit of the Damned! But I've never heard of that other place."

Carmen blurted, "The Oubliette is Protectorate Command's prisoner quarters, which lies between your Pit of the Damned and the command offices. Protectorate Command's entire complex is underground within Commonwealth Cemetery, which is located in Salem, Massachusetts District. I've been fully briefed on the area."

"How do you know all that?"

"I've acquired an informant pipeline into Commissioner Quimby's operation. The first thing I wanted to know was the layout of his headquarters."

Parker exclaimed, "Fantastic, Carmen!"

Jocquin interjected, "Sounds like the setting for a hardcore rescue."

Carmen seized her holster. "Enough talk, gentlemen! I have paramilitaries stationed in Boston; say the word, Mike, and my forces will strike at your command!"

Mike rested a hand on her shoulder before answering, "I'll accompany you to Boston." He raised his hand. "No arguments, Carmen, they're my kids."

Parker turned toward his vice president and said, "The commissioner and I will use Triad Three to reach Salem. Jocquin, if I don't return, I want you to give the broadcast address at seven tonight. Moderate the secession televote and bow to the will of our people. But I warn you, they'll try to murder you for doing it!"

Martinez propped both hands against his sides and declared, "If our citizens secede from tyranny, it'll be worth it. Now go get your children."

Ten minutes later, Mike, Carmen, and his escort boarded Triad Three and dusted off for Salem.

Scansat Four observed Triad Three's lift off before awakening Commissioner Quimby after his solitary beer party. Licking his lips and dry swallowing, Abner replied, "Where's Parker headed?"

"Triad Three's flying northeast, possibly to New York City. President Parker, Commissioner Franklin, and his bodyguards are on board."

"Call me again when they land. Use TransTrak to observe their auto route."

"Commissioner Franklin ordered the destruction of the TransTrak Central Uplink and all fifty ground relays immediately after President Parker rescinded its use."

"Then use our scansats to monitor their progress."

The monitor replied, "Without TransTrak, our scansats only monitor their communications. Right now, they're maintaining radio silence."

"Then how did a scansat catch Parker boarding Triad Three?"

"We have camera hookups in the White House that Parker's people haven't detected yet."

Quimby ordered, "Then track them by radar. When they dive below your grid, call me immediately."

"Yes, sir. There shouldn't be any trouble locating the plane's destination when we monitor whatever control tower guides them down."

Abner barked, "Blast it, man, use your head! All Presidential aircraft are Mantis vertical transports; they don't need a runway!"

"Surely the President of North America wouldn't land in some obscure, unprotected area."

"I want every surveillance squad between Washington, D.C., and

Portland, Maine District, keeping a vigil on that plane's progress! If it dives below the line, then every unit within twenty miles of its last radar position will move in to locate!"

"Yes, sir."

Abner decided to go directly to Salem; he could sleep en route while his chauffeur drove. He was certain that Tau Singh would be surprised to see him take personal command over the three young prisoners trapped behind the Oubliette's stone walls. When their sedatives wore off, they'd be in a nightmarish new world. Sebastian would personally see to that.

CHAPTER THIRTY-THREE

Incursion

Triad Three entered Massachusetts air space as Carmen told the President, "Mike, I've got to go this mission without you. You're too valuable to risk."

"Who the hell's running this show?"

"You are, Mr. President. But if you come along, you'll hamper our chances."

"How the hell do you figure that?"

Minister Franklin explained, "My team requires surprise; we'll lose that if we're busy protecting our President."

Parker concurred grudgingly, "All right, you win! Is there *anything* that I can do?"

"We have to assume Commissioner Quimby knows we're airborne. But if you act as a decoy, we may calm his nerves a bit."

"How?"

"Make up some story about why you came to Boston. Alert the press. The more attention you draw, the less chance Quimby will deduce our real objective."

"It sounds reasonable, but how are you getting to Salem?"

Carmen walked to a metal cabinet, grabbed a glider parachute, and said, "I'll jump. Have Triad Three stray over my designated target."

"But your men aren't expecting you by parachute."

"I briefed my soldiers before we left; they're aware of this tactic."

President Parker exclaimed, "Why you shrewd little minx! Why didn't you inform me about this back at the White House? Why didn't you make me stay home?"

"I needed your decoy to help pull this off."

Parker shook his head, entered the cockpit, and informed his pilot of Carmen's rendezvous site. She bailed out over Salem, Massachusetts District.

Logan Control Tower eagerly anticipated the President's surprise visit and announced the event to local media professionals. President Parker descended Triad Three with his bodyguards at 4:30 A.M. into the waiting cameras of the Boston press. A welcoming committee had been arranged within fifteen minutes.

Parker arrived near the ramp gate before announcing, "Relax folks, there's nothing unusual about an early morning joyride when you've got access to a Mantis. So I decided to visit Boston for a bowl of clam chowder and some cream pie to kill a craving." The press laughed. "My bodyguards are a little nervous about landing without security clearance. But rank has its privileges. No one knew I was coming, so I judged a surprise visit would afford me better security anyway. Now, ladies and gentlemen, who's going to volunteer my staff and me a ride into town for that little binge?"

Carmen came down a quarter-mile from one of her blockades cordoning off the main road between Commonwealth Cemetery and Swampscott, Massachusetts District. Five minutes by car had her assuming command of the rescue force. Shortly thereafter, seventy- three soldiers probed the northern quadrant of the Protectorate Command before encroaching on the domed roof and windows to the Pit of the Damned. Carmen didn't like the lack of sentries as her team reconnoitered. She took point with a four-man squad and descended through the underground, rectangular, six-foot-wide entrance hole.

They stepped along a slick, moldy stairway as another squad followed a dozen feet behind and another until all eighteen groups gained access. Carmen's scouts moved down a second flight before focusing on a faint, sulfurous, orange luster illuminating the end of the passageway. Her unit scattered after entering an enormous chamber. The orange haze emanated from eight burning torches perched upon wrought iron sconces in equal distances around the inner walls.

Shimmering light animated demonic figures painted along the walls and every inverted cross mounted around the perimeter of a central, serpentine floor slab. Sulfur and incense assailed Carmen's nose as she spotted twelve unoccupied wall balconies approximately twenty feet above them. Directly above the center of the ritual fire pit, Sebastian's balcony control box loomed higher than the rest.

One of the point men blurted, "Mother of God! Where are we, the throat of hell?"

Carmen cautioned, "Keep it down, soldier. I know it's a nightmare; that's why we're here to pull three children out of its jaws."

Her scouts fanned out between the inner walls and back rows of medieval styled stone benches before the bulk of her troops entered the torch lit chamber. Minister Franklin ordered a double check on all balconies; they were all vacant.

Seven sentries remained within the amphitheater while the rest penetrated through a wall opening sixty feet opposite the stairway entrance. Naked electric lights were suspended along a stone ceiling in a straight row while sixty-six rescuers walked beneath them. The company passed through intersections leading to numerous other corridors, but Carmen maintained a path down what appeared to be the main passage. Fifty yards further without encountering a single enemy, the vanguard tensed at the faint, pitiful cries of a terrified child.

Carmen followed the sounds around the left junction of an intersection directly ahead. Six more soldiers faded into the shadows along the intersection as sentries while the commissioner's sixty comrades continued. Twenty yards farther, a high-pitched scream bounced off every wall ahead of the vanguard now mingling with the harsh, cruel laughter of a deep voiced adult. Carmen ordered her men to wait before crawling the final ten yards to the source of the noise. A twelve-foot-square, stone cell displayed an open doorway of iron bars rising ten feet from floor to ceiling. Carmen peered inside. Nathan and John Parker were huddling terror stricken upon a single bed lining one wall.

A monstrously large man stood next to them facing the door. The brutish hulk had greasy, matted black hair spiked in a dozen different directions. His ragged blue jeans were torn out at both knees and frayed at the bottoms of both calves. Course, black hair covered his shoulders and arms, but his shirtless torso betrayed a bald chest and abdomen. Both feet were bare while black patches of hair covered the knuckles of every toe. His clean-shaven face brandished a solid, bushy band of raven black hair along his brow line running uninterrupted from both temples to the bridge of his nose.

The monster's dark brown eyes glare above blood red lips that he bit repeatedly with joy. Eight-year-old Melissa Parker was hanging two feet above the stone floor by her braid of shoulder-length hair, which was attached to a leather cord and an iron ceiling spike. Her face washed a rivulet of tears while she struggled to pull up and take her weight off the strands. The moment she succeeded, Sebastian split a cruel, hideous smile with brownish-yellow teeth and embedded the red-hot embers of a cigarette into the bottom arches of her naked feet.

Carmen sprang up and furiously flung her knife into the sadist's throat. Sebastian dropped his cigarette and yanked the blade out as fresh blood trickled down his chest. She kicked the cell door behind her and sidestepped just as the monster's momentum slammed him face first into iron bars. Carmen wedged Sebastian's left arm behind his back until his knife dropped to the floor. The monster shook off his stun as Carmen kicked the knife into the corridor while reaching for her pistol. Sebastian swept the minister's feet out from under her as the pistol was launched out through the cell bars.

She nimbly regained footing as Sebastian twirled around with a snarl. Carmen waved off her soldiers as they aimed weapons through the locked bars and warned, "The cell's too small! The walls are stone! A stray bullet might hit the kids!"

The cannibal lunged forward with outstretched arms. Carmen sidestepped sending the monster's mass crashing into a corner. Sebastian roared furiously before charging again. Franklin dove low before she swept both his legs; Sebastian slammed onto the floor again. She sprang to her feet just as Sebastian lunged ahead while balancing on both palms.

Carmen jumped but Sebastian's upended left leg toppled her to the floor. She shoulder rolled onto a single knee while catching her breath. The cannibal pushed off the ground with both hands to land on his feet. He charged again.

Carmen leaped before wrapping both her legs around the brute's bloody neck, shifted her weight, and pile-drove his head into the stone floor. Sebastian recovered quickly and grasped Carmen's right leg before she could release. She kicked with her free foot and shattered the cartilage in his nose. The brute released her before clutching his blood gushing face. Carmen rolled laterally to escape, but Sebastian seized her left arm. Pulling her close to him and anticipating the pleasure of tasting soft, raw flesh, the monster aimed gaping jaws for his enemy's throat.

Minister Franklin shoved the base of her right hand under Sebastian's shattered nose with full leverage; his flesh buckled under both eyes while dislodged cartilage impaled his brain. The twitching cannibal died with the dropped cigarette extinguishing in a smear of his own foul blood.

Carmen stood up before lifting Melissa onto her shoulders as her subordinates entered the cell to release the girl. Melissa sobbed and squeezed her savior's neck until Carmen grew short of breath, but she happily endured it. Two other point men picked up both petrified boys and hustled them out of the cell. Carmen finally gave the whimpering girl to another soldier and stooped to examine the loathsome beast she'd just killed in self-defense. Sebastian's frozen, hateful stare remained as she crosses herself silently asking forgiveness to Almighty God for relishing her satisfaction after exterminating the prostrate fiend.

The rescue team was soon back to strength when they regained the amphitheater carrying three children still in shock. Carmen ordered a full retreat back onto open ground as her peripheral soldiers moved within twenty yards of the virgin forest. Suddenly five of them fell dead. Several others spread out toward the forest but were simultaneously shot to death. Carmen kept the children together while three groups of five soldiers made for the forest cover with overlapping patterns of evasive action. All fifteen were systematically killed.

Carmen radioed her executive officer. "Roberts! What the hell's going down? I left you behind to cover our ass! We're pinned down out here!"

"Correct, I have boxed you in. Commissioner Quimby says you have until daybreak to surrender the children. Otherwise, we will sniper every one of you between the eyes. He also says anyone trying to reach the forest will die immediately."

"You get these kids over my dead body."

"Sorry it had to come to this, Minister. I enjoy serving the paramilitary. Given time, I might have enjoyed serving you. But Commissioner Quimby's a bigger fish than President Parker. We paramilitaries are loyal to the Protectorate always."

"Captain Roberts, you're following the commands of a power lusting hive of global gangsters!"

"Surrender the children or die when the sun rises."

Carmen tried her Media Palm for an outside line but the device failed. Her team was on its own.

CHAPTER THIRTY-FOUR

Evasion

Tau Singh stood up when Abner entered his office. Quimby shook his hand. "Hi, Tau, how's our little ambush doing?"

"Excellent, sir. Minister Franklin's forces are pinned near the Pit's entrance; Parker's urchins should be back with their babysitter soon."

Singh suddenly answered a call from his Media Palm. "What is it? Has that been confirmed? That's most unfortunate. Yes, I will inform Commissioner Quimby at once." Tau cursed in Chinese while pocketing the device.

Quimby blurted, "What's wrong?"

"Franklin has retreated her team back inside, choosing to fight in closed quarters."

"Damn that Cuban bitch. I underestimated her! I didn't think she'd try that option with those kids in tow! Flood the Pit and Oubliette with all our troops! We must overwhelm her forces before they split up into troublesome little units!"

Tau advised, "If our soldiers charge the Pit entrance, those rebels will mow them down in a confined space."

"Captain Roberts would incur heavy casualties, but he has to try!"

Tau Singh grinned mischievously. "We could fill all passageways with poison gas."

Quimby countered, "Paramilitaries are issued gas masks as standard equipment."

"Those children aren't."

Abner nearly gasped with surprise. "Chairman DeSalle wants those brats alive."

"I shall relay your orders to Colonel Roberts."

Carmen led her soldiers into the bowels of the Oubliette thirty minutes before their outside absence was fully detected. Then the rescuers abruptly stopped at a dead end with water trickling out a sidewall.

Franklin ordered five soldiers to pry out rotten mortar before uncovering a two-foot-diameter hole. The trickle suddenly gushed to a shallow stream while exposing a natural tunnel roughly five feet across with icy water now flowing two feet deep. Three volunteers waded into the tunnel, probing the passage with collective flashlights. They disappeared for five full minutes before returning with news of a subterranean cavern looming less than one hundred feet from the ruptured wall. The rescuers and their charges marched through a narrow cleft in the cavern's side and follow an eroded passageway guided by a steady rush of fresh air. Thirty minutes later, the team discovered the welcome embrace of a railroad tunnel.

Tau and Abner chatted over tea before Singh answered another Palm call. "This is Singh. What? I want blood! But I want that Cuban bitch captured alive!" The security chief panted before calming his voice. "Kill the soldiers, but recover those brats!"

Quimby raised both eyebrows. "Tau, you look mad enough to gnaw live rats!"

"Part of our garrison discovered Sebastian stabbed in the throat with his nose jammed between both eyes! That Cuban dominatrix killed my son!"

Commissioner Quimby roared, "That tears it! We're going to exterminate those subhuman slimes one-by-one!"

Carmen's troops marched along deserted rails for three miles when she heard a faint train whistle. Within seconds, six of her troops occupied nearby trees with grapples and swinging ropes. Within minutes, her raiders successfully commandeered a ten-car passenger train while backing it up to retrieve all remaining rescuers plus three young VIPs.

Franklin herded the civilian passengers into cars three through eight while quartering her troops in the first, second, and tenth cars. Carmen stayed in car nine while keeping the children by her side along with ten other subordinates. As the train approached Boston, Nathan, Melissa, and John were fast asleep as while Minister Franklin risked scansat exposure to alert the local police with a civilian's Media Palm. Boston's finest responded with an armed escort of twelve patrol cars awaiting her at an unscheduled train stop.

Carmen evenly divided her forces among the patrol vehicles while retaining local policemen as drivers all the way back to Washington, D.C. Then she split all twelve units into four sets of three with each separate group taking alternate routes back to the triumviral capitol. Carmen kept the kids in her car as their triangular formation sped away with flashing lights and howling sirens to open their path.

CHAPTER THIRTY-FIVE

Exposure

President Parker boarded Triad Three with his guardians after leaving the Boston press. The Mantis touched down on the White House roof by nine A.M. Despite deep concern for his children, Mike was finally exhausted enough to sleep. Jocquin had been briefing Masai and Virgil for hours about the Crimson Cupola, the URC, Eric Wilford's revelation, and the Parkers' desperate situation regarding their children.

Mike awakened at one P.M. before informing Margaret of their family crisis. They vainly sought comfort in each other's arms through a mutual flood of tears. At two, Margaret released her embrace before saying forcefully, "Darling, don't let that bastard DeSalle beat you! We'll trust in Almighty God and in Minister Carmen Valdez-Franklin! Now, go do your duty for our people!"

Mike kissed her hard on the mouth and replied, "Maybe *you* should be president, Princess; right now, you've got more courage than I do!" She smiled weakly before pushing him out of bed with a leg thrust.

President Parker later joined Jocquin, Masai, and Virgil in the Triad Office for his scheduled 2:30 appointment. He dropped hard into his chair before announcing, "Gentlemen, I apologize for not hosting your visit, but I'm sure Vice President Martinez was more than adequate to replace me. I've been comforting my wife regarding a grave situation regarding our children."

Masai interrupted, "There's no need to inform us about DeSalle's despicable attack on your family, Mr. President, or about his ransom demands; Jocquin already informed us. We also know about the Crimson Cupola, Eric Wilford's claim, and the URC's treachery. No matter what you decide regarding tonight's broadcast, you have our sympathies and support."

Prime Minister Tasman nodded in agreement.

"Thank you, my friends, but I assure you I'll do my duty without buckling to CC terrorism. Now, let's proceed with the signing and validation of our agreements about Greater African grain and Australian military bases…"

Parker had just finished signing treaties when Jocquin asked, "Mike, are you positive you can go through with your speech tonight? There's been no word from Minister Franklin."

The President declared, "We're not going to weaken! Besides, you know as well as I that the Crimson Cupola will probably murder my kids anyway out of some warped sense of justice! People who kill for pleasure are only half a step above mad dogs!"

Masai put his hand on Mike's shoulder and asked, "My friend, does making a speech *always* help you to feel better? You've told us that you're not an effective speaker; you are wrong. Honest emotions yield the most persuasive words of all. I salute your resolve to defend this continent of yours and our mutual ways of life."

Virgil affirmed, "The URC be damned! If it's a fight they want, then Australia will oblige!"

Jocquin added, "Courage, my friend. Even if she did rescue them from that Protectorate throwback to the Druids, Carmen would not risk exposure attempting to contact you."

Mike wiped both eyes and said, "It lightens my burden to know that South America, the Greater African Confederacy, and the continent of Australia are now our allies. God knows that we'll need each other before this upcoming war's over. That is, assuming my people vote us out of the URC. But enough self-pity! Jocquin, how soon will our sub-orbiters be engaged?"

"*Bifrost* and *Da Vinci* are already up from Edwards and Vandenberg Air Force Bases. *Tesla* should be lifting off from White Sands ten minutes from now and *Firmament's* set to go from Nevada at the same time; all four hypercraft should rendezvous over the Bering Sea just above the Arctic Circle in less than half an hour."

Masai wrinkled his brow. "What hypercraft, Mr. President?"

Parker smirked with sudden pride toward his visitors. "Why our ultra-high altitude fighters, gentlemen. Each one is sheathed with a nearly friction-free ceramic, which offers maneuverability that no other aircraft in history was capable of. They can move at Mach Ten speeds or better and also accomplish sudden, mega-tight-arced, nearly right angle turns in any direction."

Virgil interjected, "Like a literal flying saucer?"

Masai instructed, "More like the twin, flexible, eggbeater style, propulsive rudders beneath a tractor tugboat; only except for the air instead of the water."

Jocquin blurted, "What kind of tugboat?"

Mike advised, "Look it up on the Web, Mr. Vice President. At any rate, I suspect it's the same principle, Masai. Our hypercraft are oval-shaped, armed with chlorine lasers, particle beam pulse cannons and are capable of sustained 250,000-foot altitudes. Their current mission is to zero in on all of the Central Scansat relays and destroy as many as possible before New Polaris can stop them."

Masai asked, "What's New Polaris?"

"It's a north polar base the Crimson Cupola's been operating for years. They patrol and maintain all Scansat relays in sub-earth orbit at the forty-five-mile-altitude."

"Does New Polaris fly ovals too?"

"Unfortunately yes, Masai."

Tasman added, "Then your oval crews are going to battle as we speak?"

Parker confirmed, "Yes, Virgil, our only advantage is the element of surprise. The files from my White House scansat station provided our hypercraft with all the data our crews need to locate and destroy both solar transmission boosters orbiting the North Pole and the Antarctica Circumference. Otherwise, the Cupola will jam our broadcast tonight after I expose them.

"Once I announce North America's secession, if our voting majority authorizes it, then the Cupola will sanction us with URC police actions. So it's now or never for a surprise scansat attack. I also wish to God we can take out those damned metabolic signature monitors! I hate the thought of my vice president dropping dead at the ripe old age of forty!"

The brawny Aztec assured, "That wasn't your fault, Mike. Forget about it. Maybe taking out some key scansats will screw it up."

Mike's Media Palm signaled. Mike answered, "Yes, Myrtle?'

"Mr. President, Chairman Zadock's asking for admittance into the Triad Office."

"Show him in, Myrtle. My door's always open to the GRA chairman."

Rudy ambled in before asking, "Thumbs up or down, Mike?"

"Thumbs up. What's on your mind?"

"We've found Eric Wilford."

"*Fantastic!* Where is he?"

"He's at my GRA headquarters in Denver. The inventor drove his prototype all the way from Vermont to reach us and got shot for his trouble, but he's all right. My technicians have spent the last two days examining his Bipolar Drive engine. It's not a hoax, Mike. That miraculous machine literally draws and channels electromagnetic energy out of thin air. My team claims it's the closest thing to perpetual motion they've ever seen. Internal combustion engines will soon be obsolete."

Mike Parker cheered. "Thank God! When are you leaving?"

"Immediately. Although my staff is staying here to assist you in any way they can. I've got to see Wilford's prototype firsthand. He's been in Denver since Sunday night."

Jocquin asked, "Where was he shot?"

"At the front gate of my GRA headquarters. One of our security guards must have been a Protectorate agent; he fled the scene after his act of mayhem. It is miraculous Eric escaped."

Parker commanded, "Okay, you're going home on a fully armed Triad Three with twenty of my elite bodyguards."

Rudy added, "Jennifer Scott's coming along; she insists on getting her exclusive."

"Didn't you try to talk her out of it?"

"Ever tried to extinguish a house fire with a squirt gun?"

"I'll take your word for it." Parker activated his Palm. "Good luck to us all."

Myrtle answered, "Yes, Mr. President?"

"Have Colonel Bushnell come in."

"At once, sir."

In minutes, Mike briefed Bushnell about Denver; then the colonel escorted Dr. Zadock out of the room. The President sighed, "Now, my friends, any other impending business before I broadcast tonight?"

The Triad Office was packed with cameramen, televote monitors, and his three companions. The President of North America began at precisely seven P.M. "Fellow citizens, thank you for taking the time to sanction another televote. Vice President Martinez and I appreciate your participation..."

Chairman DeSalle clenched both jaws watching from his New Corsica study as Parker continued on his Holotel.

"Allow me to introduce my two guests. The first is President Masai Gampu of the Greater African Confederacy. I have just formalized an agreement to sell surplus North American grain in exchange for African gold bullion and flawless blue diamonds. I believe our people will not begrudge this stockpile of food to our African allies, particularly since they're offering hard value commodities in exchange. My other guest is Prime Minister Virgil Tasman of Australia. He's here to authorize an agreement to lease our Districts of Guam and the Northern Marianas Islands for military installations.

"Now please give me your undivided attention. Last night, after our citizens' televote victory, I was covertly ordered to supersede our citizens by reinstating NACAM, NACEO, and TransTrak back into triumviral law tonight. I was also told that if I refused, my children would be sent back to me in pieces. I know the identity of the kidnappers; they are field agents of the Martial Protectorate, which is the enforcement arm of the Universal Regions Council.

"However, NACAM, NACEO, and TransTrak will *not* be reinstated! Now, previously this week in New York City, the URC secretly adopted the NACAM directives into their Planetary Pandect. They've changed the name to PANCAM, which stands for the Pandect Clean Air Mandate. Any triumvirate that's under URC authority must automatically comply with it. In essence, if we remain a triumvirate, our people must comply with the NACAM directive, which also mandates the resuscitation of TransTrak. If we refuse, then the Martial Protectorate will launch military reprisals to force North America back into compliance.

"The irony is that if North America votes to secede from the URC, then the Protectorate will attack us anyway; Planetary Pandect bylaws mandate no triumvirate may secede once they're annexed. The only way to escape bloodshed and conflict is for me to officially rescind your televote last night. Of course, that will put our people back under the yoke of NACAM, NACEO, TransTrak, PANCAM, and the Universal Regions Council again. The chairman of The Crimson Cupola assures me that Protectorate police actions will not take place *if* we capitulate to URC demands. Now I'll explain to you what The Crimson Cupola is…"

CHAPTER THIRTY-SIX

Enlightenment

DeSalle's jaw dropped at President Parker's candor in front of the North American masses. The chairman called North American Central Scansat Command. Hearing a familiar voice, he yelled, "Reese? Have you been monitoring Parker's betrayal?"

"Yes, sir, I was expecting your call. Why didn't the President transmit from the Rostrum?"

"Never mind that! Block his broadcast before that turncoat spills any more information! Kill Martinez right now; I want him to die at his president's feet!"

"Impossible, sir. The north polar transmission booster has suddenly gone offline. We can neither operate any metabolic signature weapons nor jam any communication signals within the Northern Hemisphere. All we can do is receive."

"Can't you bypass the defective equipment using one of the three Antarctica Circumference Boosters?"

"Negative, sir. Those units are out of range; they only operate south of the equator.

"Is anyone from New Polaris close enough to effect booster repairs?"

"They have already dispatched three hypercraft for the job while the other ovals are still on routine patrol."

"Have our Scansats detected any enemy ovals that took off from

North America?"

"We had a lock on them when they rendezvoused over the Bering Sea moments before our north polar scansat booster went offline. Without it we can't get a lock on their current positions. We could only find them now by limited radar or visually."

"Moloch's Mud Whore, Reese! *There's* the reason for your blackout! Those bastards probably disabled our polar booster and are likely gunning for our Antarctica Circumference Boosters next! Didn't you inform Commissioner Quimby of the blackout?"

"Yes, sir. But he ordered me to stand by because he was currently engaged in a woman hunt and would get back to me. That was about ten minutes ago."

"You mean Commissioner Quimby allowed our hostages and their rescuers to slip through his fingers at Protectorate Command?"

"He wasn't specific."

DeSalle nearly screamed. "I authorize you to order all New Polaris ovals to attack and destroy our four enemies before they disable our entire Scansat Network. I'll handle Commissioner Quimby!"

"Yes, sir. I'm in contact with New Polaris now. Colonel Harris acknowledges your orders and will personally scramble and command all eight new ovals to reinforce the three brother hypercraft already patrolling at the forty-five-mile-level."

"Good. Give no quarter."

Mike resumed, "...the chairman of The Crimson Cupola is Victor DeSalle. He's the grandfather of the late President Garth Brady.

Reginald Masterson, the Monitor of the Cohesion Cluster, is one of DeSalle's cousins. His sister-in-law is Telia Zendar, the Senior Magistrate of The URC's Planetary Court. All of DeSalle's blood relatives are members of First Level Dynastic Families. Abner Quimby, the Commissioner of the Martial Protectorate and Second Level Dynasty member, is also one of DeSalle's ex-bodyguards. Presidents

Barry Claude Xavier and Chu Ahn Singh of Atlanterra and Indoasia respectively belong to Second Level Dynastic Families.

"However, all triumviral vice presidents were outsiders chosen by their running mates just as Garth Brady initially chose me. All members of these dynastic families are agents and subordinates of the Crimson Cupola, which was responsible for Garth Brady's murder after he authorized our abnormal global warming debate.

"I also suspect the CC might now be preparing an attack on the Global Reaction Alliance headquartered in Denver, Colorado District, for two reasons: One may be in retaliation for them winning last Monday's debate. Two is that the complex is harboring an inventor named Eric Wilford, who has perfected an engine that converts electromagnetic energy out of the atmosphere into motive power. That's why I have dispatched military support with the GRA chairman en route to Denver. They're flying in Triads Three and Seven because those Mantis Aircraft have vertical landing capability.

"I know that I have thrown a lot of information your way, but you have the right to know these facts. Tonight, you all must vote directly on the question of triumviral secession from the URC.

"Please understand this: If we vote to secede, the URC will attack us with all the triumviral forces at their disposal. It may mean the death of millions. I don't even know if we can win. But if we remain as the Third Triumvirate, our people will once again be under the Cupola's tyrannical yoke.

"Search your conscience and vote. Time is of the essence and if our people demand freedom, then we must move swiftly against the collective enemies of individual rights, the right of common travel, and our sovereign right to govern our own land. It's now 7:30 P.M., Eastern Time; the polls will close at 9:30 P.M. , Eastern Time. Computer televote capability can easily tabulate the 350 million-vote minimum mandated to achieve a lawful quorum.

"If we vote for secession, then I'll disband the North American Triumvirate immediately and declare the North American Confederacy as a free and independent Constitutional Republic. If the vote is no, then I will bow to the will of the majority while immediately reinstating NACAM, NACEO, and TransTrak into law, thereby maintaining fidelity with the Universal Regions Council and the Crimson Cupola. As it should be, the destiny of North America is now in the hands of its citizens. Thank you."

The CRA vigilantes around GRA headquarters swelled from twenty to one hundred armed guerrillas in less than an hour. Mickey and Carl were double-checking their weapons while moving with Titus McCoy as he led ten scouts from the surrounding woods. They kept together cutting open an eight-foot tall, chain link fence and clambered uphill to stand at eye level with the GRA playing field. McCoy asked for volunteers to directly contact the GRA.

Mickey and Carl glanced at each other, stepped forward, and began stripping off gear and weapons while still retaining their flashlights and mobile radios. Then the two of them scampered up another angled lawn beyond the ball field and crouched at the top to peer at the main complex one hundred yards ahead of them.

Thirty seconds passed before Logan radioed, "Commander, Mickey and I have passed the halfway point; we're both within one hundred feet of the main building. Hold it. There's an armed guard stepping out of the shadows. We're dropping off with our hands up; out."

Two more guards emerged from the shadows as the initial one barked, "Hands over both your heads, lace your fingers, and walk ahead of me, or I'll blow moonlight through your backs! Now move!" The sentry picked up both downed radios and lights before herding his captives forward.

Broderick and Logan endured strip searches inside the main security office before being escorted into an open room with multiple tables pushed together. Ten people quietly sat on wooden and metal chairs scattered in various positions around the makeshift boardroom. The contact guard handed both his seized radios to an elderly, gray-haired man sitting at the end of the table before returning to his post. The other two sentries remained.

The gray-haired man asked, "Who are you men?"

"My name's Carl Logan. This is my partner Mickey Broderick. We're members of the Citizens Reaction Alliance."

Dr. Felix Morgan raised both eyebrows before continuing, "Citizens Reaction Alliance, eh? That's a nice play off of our organization."

"We're dedicated to protecting your group in any way we can. There are ninety-eight more of us scattered along the perimeter of your ball field. We're ready to reinforce the presidential elite now, bringing Chairman Zadock back aboard Triad Three."

"Why do you think we need reinforcements?"

"Our commander believes the Crimson Cupola will launch an attack on your facility to annihilate Eric Wilford and his prototype within these walls."

Morgan brandished one of their radios. "What's *this* for?"

"It's my commander's gesture of good faith; that battery-powered unit's tied into his command radio at the playing field. He sent the two of us unarmed as emissaries to establish contact. My commander needs to speak with you before those planes land."

"Why?"

"We have no way of communicating with your chairman. We don't want the President's men mistaking our people for Cupola agents and blowing us away!"

Dr. Morgan paused before admitting, "I believe you, Carl. What does your commander want us to do?"

Eric Wilford got up from his chair bellowing, "Felix! How can you trust this bozo? We don't know him from Adam!"

"Calm down, Eric. It is obvious Carl's telling the truth. Otherwise, he would never have betrayed his unit's position; he also wouldn't have brought us a pair of radios. And he certainly wouldn't have alerted us to potential hostility."

"I disagree. I believe the last thing in the world that the URC wants is public access to my Bipolar Drive! You're too trusting, Felix! I think the Cupola has to attack us tonight, even if such an attack puts teeth in the President's address. They can't afford the mass marketing of my engine. Their multi-trillion-dollar infrastructure's bulwarked by the petroleum industry! For all we know, these gift radios may be packing explosives!"

Morgan tossed the radio saying, "Check it out, Eric. In the meantime, I'm going to inform Rudy about our new allies at the landing zone. Then I'll chat with their CRA commander." The gray-haired old man pulled out Media Palm while announcing, "By the way, gentlemen, my name's Felix Morgan; that nervous fellow with a bandaged hand's Eric Wilford."

The inventor placed the open-backed radio on the table before admitting, "I guess we'll have to start trusting someone. But I still think the CC will try to blow us away tonight."

Felix sighed. "You may be right, but at least we have some reinforcements. I think I'll contact the CRA commander first and then talk to Rudy; he can relay paramilitary instructions to your leader through me. Eric, why don't you show these gentlemen the Bipolar Drive? They must be straining their tethers to see it."

CHAPTER THIRTY-SEVEN

Confederacy

The 9:30 deadline for the secession vote was approaching fast. During the last hour, Mike Parker, Jocquin Martinez, Masai Gampu, and Virgil Tasman had been conversing openly in front of the cameras. Each executive had taken turns giving a detailed story of their various backgrounds, some of their native land's political history, and their personal aspirations for the future; all of them were talking like common people without any political jargon.

North Americans watched while developing fresh insight into these leaders, which was a very constructive way to utilize political airtime. Most viewers never left their seats during the discourse; political honesty was too refreshing to ignore. For two full hours, the concentration of citizen political activity on the North American Continent resembled an anthill during an emergency. Only twenty-first century communication could make such a torrent of simultaneous, electronic correspondence both possible and accurate.

The final tally was calculated at precisely 9:30 P.M., Eastern Time. The tabulation monitor handed President Parker the returns. Mike read it before holding the document for the center camera to zoom in on. He announced with gooseflesh, "North American citizens have made their decision: The vote to continue triumviral status totaled at 96,792,081. The vote to secede totaled 395,024,130. Secession is carried by a three-to-one margin!"

After the close up, Mike faced a camera declaring, "By a validation of over seventy-five percent of North American voters, this triumvirate's hereby dissolved! Our continent and other affiliated landmasses are now bound together as an independent Constitutional Republic. All former districts within the defunct Third Triumvirate are recognized as sovereign nations including all fifty-one former United States. The North American Confederacy is now a reality.

"The former United States Bill of Rights is now in effect until a constitutional convention can be organized to ratify and finalize all formal laws by majority vote. The North American Confederal Government shall exercise authority in only four areas: First, this Republic establishes Confederal Supreme Courts of Appeals for all sovereign nations to use voluntarily involving disputes between each other.

"Secondly, this republic converts all monies into silver-and gold-backed currency that applies equally among all sovereign nations regardless of cultural denomination.

"Thirdly, this Republic will collect a flat, one percent North American import and export tariff on all trade goods to finance our confederal government. All other taxation will be reserved among North American Sovereign Nations to regulate within their domestic borders.

"Finally, this Republic will provide for the common defense of all North American Sovereign Nations by establishing the North American Confederal Armed Forces, or NACAF, through equal nation participation according to population.

"The election of future senators and representatives will be accomplished in November as per previous plans. Until that time, as your president, I may declare executive orders regarding any attacks against our confederacy or allies. However, executive orders can only be within the jurisdiction of Appeal Courts, currency, tariff issues, and the common defense. Because of our triumviral secession and from this moment on, a State of War exists between the URC and North America. Therefore, all Sovereign North American Nations have the collective right to keep and bear arms to defend life and property.

"Thank you, my North American brothers and sisters. Now, we have the means to safeguard not only our freedom but also to help Greater Africa, South America, and Australia as well.

"For the sake of simplicity, our four regions will now be referred to as The Quadrant Alliance. Therefore, I hereby order all Confederal Army, Navy, Air Force, Coast Guard, and Paramilitary Units to their prearranged invasion stations. Good night, fellow sovereign citizens."

CHAPTER THIRTY-EIGHT

Dismemberment

The North American hypercraft force had eliminated the north polar booster with combined laser fire enabling President Parker's secession broadcast to continue. Their raid also destroyed any metabolic murder capability north of the equator.

Colonel Oscar Becket of the *Tesla* dispatched two ovals to destroy the Antarctica Circumference trio of boosters. Due to prearranged courses, both the northern and southern equatorial squads would operate independently while each maintained the sub-orbital altitude of 200,000 feet. Major Anthony Darwin's *Bifrost* currently reinforced *Tesla's* Arctic Circle position; both hypercraft were set in ambush for any approaching vanguard of New Polaris fighters.

Meanwhile the ovals *DaVinci* and *Firmament* piloted by Captains Colin Wingate and Winston Rogers respectively maintained course for Antarctica. Captain Rogers commanded the southern team.

Tesla remained in geosynchronous sub-orbit over the Bering Sea while *Bifrost* patrolled between the Greenland and Spitzbergen landmasses.

Becket accelerated north while straddling the International Date Line. The *Tesla* suddenly burst upon a New Polaris enemy fighter trio while firing its bow and belly lasers. Becket incinerated the lead ship. A secondary fighter returned fire with emerald lasers only to miss as *Tesla* sped past its port side.

Polaris Three pursued *Tesla* towards the northern tip of Greenland but was suddenly blasted apart by *Bifrost*, whose ambushing lasers launched the enemy crew into atmospheric oblivion.

Polaris Two rocketed away in the opposite direction as both confederate ovals accelerated south toward Hudson's Bay.

Bifrost's first primary target was the central scansat above New York City. *Tesla* would home in on the central scansat over Denver.

Before both confederal ovals separated, Polaris Two barreled toward them. Becket glimpsed an impact flare out his starboard window as the enemy disabled the *Bifrost's* starboard engine. Then Becket pulled straight up and dove from its initial climb. As his enemy slowed for *Bifrost's* kill, Becket exploded the fighter with two direct laser hits.

Darwin contacted Becket. "Look, Oscar, my ship may only have half speed now, but our weapons are still 100 percent. And you can't destroy all of the centrals north of the equator by yourself; you need us."

Becket replied, "You won't do me any good if you're dead. You should guide that wounded oval down safely, then you *and* the *Bifrost* will survive to fight again."

"You know it's now or never for our surprise attack! I'm staying! Get moving, *Tesla*, you're wasting valuable time!"

"I could order you down."

"Oscar, don't make this an act of mutiny! Wouldn't you stay if you were me?"

"Very well, Major Darwin, but I can't complete my mission and cover your ass at the same time."

"Understood, Colonel. *Bifrost* out."

Ten minutes later, *Bifrost* destroyed the central scansat over New York City; Cupola surveillance died from Newfoundland to Florida and from Bermuda to the banks of the Mississippi and Missouri rivers.

Tesla's particle beams over Denver shredded scansat surveillance from Uranium City, Northern Saskatchewan, to Acapulco, Mexico. Quimby's three hundred agents converging on the GRA were suddenly reduced to hand radios.

After eliminating all three Antarctica circumference boosters, shuttles *Firmament* and *DaVinci* went on the hunt. Captain Rogers' *Firmament* lasered a central over the Amazon Basin, CC surveillance died from Rio de Janeiro, Brazil, to the Yucatan Peninsula.

Captain Wingate's *DaVinci* hovered over the Chilean Capitol of Santiago before shot-gunning another central with steel particle beam pellets; surveillance coverage died from Lima, Peru, to Tierra del Fuego, Argentina, and as far west as Easter Island.

Tesla destroyed the central over San Francisco. Scansat surveillance was removed from Juneau, Alaska, to the equator and westward to the Hawaiian Islands.

Bifrost moved at half throttle while taking twenty minutes to target a central above the Bering Strait, but Major Darwin never pulled his trigger. Two Polaris fighters intercepted and lasered the crippled confederate oval into a flaming projectile streaking downward toward a nearby mountain range.

Firmament fried the central over Tahiti while *DaVinci* shot-gunned another sub-orbiting central above New Zealand; scansat surveillance died from Australia all the way across the South Pacific.

As *DaVinci* continued southwest, Captain Wingate spotted the parallel ovals of twin Polaris fighters at his visual horizon. He overtook and blasted both from behind with laser fire. The Antarctica circumference sentries had been obliterated.

Captain Rogers maneuvered the *Firmament* into range and lasered the central scansat fixed over Sumatra; surveillance capability blacked out all through Indonesia and the southeast quadrant of the Indian Ocean. Then his navigator spotted a Polaris fighter at the extreme end of their visual horizon. Rogers accelerated hard before his copilot cut a laser swath along the enemy's port side igniting the target into a cloud of metallic fragments belching glass, rubber and human remains.

Firmament banked a 180 degree turn just as a particle beam blast shot-gunned its port side engine, stern laser, and two of its thrusters, forcing the damaged hypercraft to change its weapons from long range lasers to short range particle beams. The Polaris fighter had been surprised by *Firmament*'s sudden change of direction as they sped past their disabled quarry. Captain Rogers expected to face the enemy oval on its return pass. He aimed all his weapons ahead, but five minutes passed without sighting the enemy. Then Rogers resumed course pushing the *Firmament* at 50 percent thrust.

The *Tesla* ambushed two more Polaris fighters from behind exploding them into fireballs of shrapnel and flesh. Becket altered course before destroying the Bering Strait Central; scansat surveillance over Northern Canada, Alaska, Siberia, and the Arctic Circle perished with it. In the span of thirty minutes, the hyper-fast *Tesla* took out centrals over Midway Island, Japan, and Manila in the Philippines. Then Becket throttled hard before shot-gunning the central over Afghanistan apart.

Becket continued towards Moscow before another New Polaris fighter suddenly appeared and fired lasers through *Tesla*'s fuselage amidships. As Polaris came in for the kill, his target transmitted, "New Polaris ship, this is Colonel Oscar Becket of the *Tesla*. We request permission to board your ship as prisoners."

Polaris' captain replied, "Then depart your oval through the cockpit emergency hatch. If anyone's wearing more than a hover pack, we'll blast you into a sub-orbital shit hole!"

"We'll evacuate at once."

Soon all four confederate crewmen emerged from *Tesla* while gripping their thruster controls.

Polaris' captain waited for his hovering prisoners to advance within one hundred yards before firing his bow particle beam. The first blast shredded the *Tesla*'s navigator in half coating his visor with freezing, crimson pulp. The second shattered Colonel Becket's right arm, leg, partial rib cage, and helmet. The projector's third belch tore off the co-pilot's legs and bisected his torso into chunks of crystalizing flesh. The fourth shot vaporized the last crewman at point blank range.

The *DaVinci* continued northwest before destroying the Madagascar Central; scansat coverage from McDonald Island in the Indian Ocean to Lake Victoria died.

Captain Wingate continued due west before incinerating his final assigned target over Ascension Island in the South Atlantic Ocean. He altered course while crossing over the North Atlantic unaware that the crippled *Firmament* was now over the Congo with its power diminishing. Soon *DaVinci* was in sight of the Azores with its central still intact. Captain Wingate and his crew paused a moment in honor from the obvious demise of both *Tesla* and *Bifrost* before shot-gunning their initial target to shreds; scansat control of the Atlantic Ocean evaporated from Africa to the Caribbean Rim.

DaVinci reversed course eastward before reaching Lake Chad along the northern boundary of Greater Africa and the North African districts of Atlanterra. Wingate switched to auxiliary power while shot-gunning the Central Atlanterran Scansat; Cupola surveillance was erased from Morocco to Ethiopia and from Gibraltar to Turkey.

One New Polaris fighter suddenly peppered the languishing *Firmament* with particle bursts buffeting its port side. The confederal oval craft drifted as its lights died. Polaris came closer. *Firmament's* scuttled particle projectors suddenly exploded while destroying its killer with it.

The *DaVinci* co-pilot spotted another New Polaris fighter off the starboard bow dropping below their sight horizon. Full throttle speed for several seconds enabled the confederal hypercraft to catch Polaris from the stern as *DaVinci* fired every weapon and incinerated the Cupola enemy into burning fragments.

Soon *DaVinci* shredded the Moscow Central; Atlanterra's surveillance nerve center blew apart as its debris scattered through the upper atmosphere.

Captain Wingate traversed the rest of the northern equatorial route in his lone confederal oval but never encountered another enemy; meanwhile the sole surviving Polaris fighter returned to its north polar base.

After landing safely at Edwards Air Force Base, Captain Wingate and his crew frowned while stepping away from their parked *DaVinci*. They were congratulated by a throng of military comrades but felt as if they'd betrayed their dead brothers by surviving the first worldwide, sub-orbital, hypercraft conflict.

CHAPTER THIRTY-NINE

Siege

Commissioner Franklin's police convoy slowed to 80 mph while cruising across the Delaware/Maryland Sovereign National Line. She passed through Baltimore with less than forty miles to reach Washington, D.C.

Marshall Protectorate Forces were now reinforcing Chairman DeSalle's escort to a private airport where twelve enormous *Leviathan* cargo carriers were reserved to transport all high-ranking Cupola personnel and their assets from the North American Confederacy. The old man prepared to leave the now-sovereign continent with Cousin Reggie and sister-in-law Telia. He personally ordered both Abner Quimby and Tau Singh to be on hand before departure; both had reluctantly abandoned Carmen's pursuit to comply.

The police cars stopped in front of the White House Security Gate at 9:40 P.M., Eastern Time. Upon contact, Mike and Margaret raced to the North Wing main entrance accompanied by six sentries. Both parents clasped hands and held their breath while Carmen's motorcade parked alongside them. Soldiers fanned out of every car and coordinated guard positions among the President's contingent; the police chauffeurs smiled. Carmen stepped aside and joyfully watched three ecstatic youngsters stampede into the outstretched arms of their mom and dad. Mutual hugs erupted with torrents of happy tears. Then Margaret led her children inside under armed escort.

Mike controlled his sobs while hugging his Cuban warrior. "Carmen! Maggie and I can *never* repay you or your soldiers for this miracle! Praise God for His mercy!"

Carmen rubbed away tears of her own before replying, "There were casualties, but we were successful."

At the stateroom entrance, Mike rejoined Jocquin, Masai, and Virgil while the trio surrounded Carmen with hearty handshakes. She nodded with appreciation, loaded a plate at the buffet, and then sat alongside the White House's visiting dignitaries.

President Parker asked, "Carmen, is Commissioner Quimby at Protectorate Command tonight?"

"I don't know, but I do know Colonel Gordon Roberts is a Cupola mole. We only escaped by way of a concealed subterranean passage."

"I was curious if Quimby would be there when I bombed the place."

"You're taking out Commonwealth Cemetery?"

Parker scowled. "Hopefully that blasphemous place will fall around his wretched ears!"

"Has North America seceded?"

"Yes! We've shed our triumviral snakeskin and our hypercraft ovals destroyed the all of the Cupola's central scansat arrays!"

Carmen finished another bite. "How bad were we hurt?"

"*DaVinci* was the sole surviving sub-orbiter; it landed at Edwards ninety minutes ago. But now the Quadrant Alliance won't be scrutinized from orbit."

"Quadrant Alliance?"

"It's an official alliance between South America, Greater Africa,

Australia, and the North American Confederacy. Our nations have pledged mutual protection against any Universal Regions police actions."

The commissioner resumed, "What rights have North American Citizens regained?"

"Every sovereign, individual right that the original United States Bill of Rights ever mandated including firearms, Commissioner Franklin."

Carmen cheered. "Fantastic! If the Protectorate tries anything, we'll make them pay in blood! By the way, where do I stand in our new Confederacy?"

Mike smiled. "You're still the top-ranking military officer of North America, but there's something else you need to know right away. Before Rudy Zadock left the White House tonight, he told me his Denver staff's now hosting Eric Wilford and his miraculous invention."

"Then GRA headquarters is in grave danger; I presume you sent soldiers with Chairman Zadock?"

"Twenty of my bodyguards are escorting him to Denver; they took Triads Three and Seven. I put Colonel Bushnell in military command."

"He's a good man, but that's why I placed him here in command of your safety, Mr. President."

President Parker replied, "I'm expendable, but Eric and his Bipolar Drive are not!

Carmen stood erect. "I should join your forces in Denver right away! GRA headquarters is going to be hit hard if they haven't been already! I wish I could see Richard, but my husband's at home, in New London, Connecticut Distri…I mean Connecticut!"

"Richard shipped out with his command earlier this evening. The *Toroid's* on its way to a rendezvous in the North Atlantic. But you're staying here!"

"Why?"

"You just came out of a meat grinder. And you just said that Colonel Bushnell's a good man."

Moses Richmond's sixty-man scouting force surrounded the two vacant Mantis aircraft. They'd watched both transports for over an hour. Now with no enemies in sight and leading a small squad, Moses and his executive entered Triads Three and Seven respectively. Richmond cautiously opened the cockpit door. Suddenly he noticed a digital chronometer illuminating a countdown in red: seven, six, five... Moses sprinted away but his foot speed proved futile. Both Mantises exploded. Richmond's nearby squad incinerated in a baptism of fire. The landing area strewed debris and charred human remains beneath billows of fire and smoke.

Protectorate Captain Phillip Lemke watched the holocaust from the GRA's main gate; he scanned futilely for survivors. Then Lemke ordered his remaining 250 soldiers into a GRA ground assault. The northern force fanned out before arriving at the lab building. The eastern flank moved eighty yards before reaching a large weather station adjacent to the main structure. Both forces entered the two buildings while Lemke sent a forty-man group into the main building computer complex.

GRA personnel were scrutinizing all protectorate activity with a strategic network of closed circuit television cameras. Rudy Zadock, Eric Wilford, Jennifer Scott, Felix Morgan, and the others were comfortably buried twenty feet beneath their eastern field within a five thousand-square-foot, self-sufficient central control bunker. Eric continued smiling while Jennifer conducted their exclusive interview.

As previously briefed, all military and CRA allies were poised to strike. Rudy signaled Colonel Bushnell by encryption. Then multiple C-4 explosives destroyed the weather station and lab building taking out over one hundred of Captain Lemke's troops. His remaining protectorates surrounded the surviving computer building.

The invaders launched tear gas through every opening before securing the ground floor while leaving twenty sentries to cover their rear flank. The captain divided his troops into twin sets of fifty with his group reconnoitering the basement while the other checked out the second story. His remaining paramilitaries secured a central stairway.

Downstairs, Lemke kicked open the computer room door as his soldiers reconnoitered inside to the back wall with their commander covering the rear. Twenty gas-masked CRA allies watched from the slits of preset ceiling panels waiting for their trespassers to move into optimum range. Suddenly they collectively launched a storm of machine gun fire down on the marauders. Lemke and six others fell onto their backs while firing indiscriminately up into the ceiling. Seven ambushers dropped dead onto their slaughtered enemies like downed birds. In moments, twenty allies had annihilated every trapped protectorate agent before Mickey Broderick dropped to the blood-smeared floor. He knelt with sorrow to examine Carl Logan's bullet-ridden corpse.

The basement gunfire propelled every stair sentry along the main hall toward the building's center. Colonel Bushnell and two other second floor ceiling snipers mowed the rear five Cupola agents down as the surviving group scattered deeper into the computer building. Lionel and his team now had their enemies cornered.

GRA ally Captain Blake began phase two and deployed all thirteen pairs of his troops around the computer building's ground floor perimeter. He threw a live grenade inside; the explosion confused his Cupola enemies while the allies attacked them through separate windows. In seconds, Captain Blake's squad annihilated twenty more enemies. The remaining Cupola sentries retreated to the central stair shaft after abandoning the main level. Blake's team peppered the stairwell with random gunfire as every retreating protectorate scrambled toward the basement only to be slaughtered by Mickey Broderick's ambushing contingent.

Colonel Bushnell's ceiling snipers killed another thirty-five protectorates before the surviving nine scrambled into random offices adjacent to the main hallway. Bushnell converted his helmet radio into a bullhorn before announcing, "To all surviving protectorate soldiers, this is the commander of the GRA Alliance. If you want quarter, come out with fingers laced on top of your heads, without helmets, weapon belts, and shirts, before advancing toward the second story stairway. Rejection of any demand will get you shot on sight! You have three minutes to comply! Then we'll bring this building down around your ears!"

Every captive answered with gunfire. Then Bushnell's team activated preset fuses before evacuating the building. Three minutes later, the building exploded into alternating billows of fire and smoke while killing every concealed protectorate within it. The surface allies spent the next hour putting out fires and reconnoitering for stragglers. The Denver siege was over.

Bushnell's contingent descended down a vertical, cement passageway and then marched along a concrete tunnel before reaching a massive steel door. Lionel bounced a pry bar off its surface with a single knock, five more, and then ending with a pair of hits. Then more GRA subordinates granted them access.

Three hours after Colonel Bushnell reported via Media Palm to President Parker, all the Denver survivors boarded five Mantis Transports along with Eric Wilford's detached Bipolar Drive while ten *Sun Chariot* Fighter Jets circled the GRA field as escorts all the way back to Washington, D.C.

Eric sighed while sitting to the rear of Triad One and watched the City of Denver shrink below his sight. Jennifer Scott sat beside him and asked, "Eric, are you in pain?"

"Just relieved. It's been a hell of a week. At least my Bipolar Drive's safe. Mike Parker and Rudy Zadock are good, honest men; they can take over from here."

"Are you donating your future bipolar engine royalties?"

"Hell no!"

"Then what do you mean by take over?"

"I mean our new confederacy should spawn a pristine rebirth of the free enterprise system. If it was good enough in the past for the sovereign United States, then it should be good enough for all sovereign North Americans!"

Jennifer chuckled. "You sound like a politician running for office."

"People often forget that the best public servants are always average citizens and not professional politicians stealing wealth through legalized plunder."

"But Mike Parker's a politician; he's the President."

"Parker's no politician; he's a genuine public servant. Who else would lay his own children on the line for the sake of sovereign justice? He's been without peer in the White House since I can remember."

Jennifer giggled.

Eric blushed before admitting, "Sorry, Jenny, I didn't mean to preach. I forgot you've been entrenched in this business for fifteen years. Forgive me."

"What for? It's refreshing to hear somebody shoot ideas from the hip. There's far too much bullshit about political correctness and conformity as it is."

Eric closed both eyes while answering, "Political correctness may just have been crushed under confederal heels. I only wish Pappy could have lived to see it."

"Who's Pappy?"

"My father. He was abducted and murdered right out of our own home."

"Maybe he's not dead, Eric."

"I *know* he is! He'd have died before cooperating with his captors! But our new confederacy may avenge his and maybe a lot of other people's murder by defeating the Cupola tyrants!"

Jennifer replied, "The North American Confederacy's already gotten under your skin hasn't it, Eric?"

Wilford took Jennifer's right hand and stared straight into her eyes before whispering, "Not just the confederacy, Jenny. You're the first woman I've ever met who speaks her mind while letting the chips fall where they may. You also listen to people."

Jennifer's heart raced while she confessed, "Eric, this is getting complicated."

"What is?"

"I'm having an awful time trying to stay objective around you, and that look isn't helping."

"You see? Even when a man's making honorable advances, you still speak your mind."

"I can't finish this interview under the present circumstances."

"What a shame," whispered Eric before briefly kissing her mouth and backing away.

Then she drew him hungrily toward her while dropping a Media Palm onto Triad One's floor. Their second kiss surged into a powerful embrace.

CHAPTER FORTY

Reckoning

While the GRA entourage flew to Washington, Victor DeSalle, Reginald Masterson, Telia Zendar, Abner Quimby, Tau Singh, and Milton the Mountain were already safely within the Octavius Taj Mansion of President Barry Claude Xavier. Necessity now mandated a temporary U.R.C. seat of power, and where better than the First Triumviral Capitol of Rome, Italy District?

Milton stood erect while Victor cursed the newborn Quadrant Alliance. The chairman's audience lounged on sofas and recliners around the perimeter of an indoor, hexagonal, swimming pool. President Xavier listened intently, Tau Singh sat forward while concentrating on every word, and Reginald and Telia shivered while Abner Quimby inwardly boiled with rage from having Carmen and her troops escape him. Milton observed the protectorate commissioner while slowly moving between him and the master.

DeSalle's voice cracked, "I don't give a damn *what* it takes! I want that confederacy destroyed! Barry, coordinate yours and Chu's forces right away! And as of this moment, Tau Singh is now commissioner of the Martial Protectorate."

Victor turned to Tau and commanded, "You're authorized to take steps necessary to force the Quadrant Alliance to their knees, but only with conventional weapons! No WMDs!"

Reginald whispered to Telia, "WMDs?"

She responded quietly, "Weapons of Mass Destruction."

Singh bowed his head before replying, "Yes, My Chairman. Any other orders?"

"Just get started right away!"

Tau and Barry disappeared into the president's private office.

The old man looked at Reginald and Telia while lamenting, "Well, family, every Neanderthal serf within the Quadrant Alliance who carries a weapon now knows about the Crimson Cupola!"

Furious over his sudden demotion, Abner lunged toward the startled threesome. Milton grabbed a shock of Quimby's hair while tearing a softball-sized patch out by the roots.

Abner fell backward violently before slamming his head off the ceramic tiles. Milton bent down on one knee, lifted the madman's stunned body off the floor, wedged Quimby's back against his upraised thigh, and brutally pushed downward. Abner's vertebrae splintered as he vomited gore with widened eyes. Then Milton viciously twisted Abner's head around 180 degrees atop a shattered spine.

Masterson and Zendar huddled with horror.

Victor approved. "Well done, Milton! I was beginning to wonder how much more of Quimby we would endure before you were given sufficient incentive to exterminate him! Dispose of that vermin!"

Milton flung Quimby's body over his right shoulder, passed through a sliding glass doorway, and disappeared into some backyard acreage. Soon Barry and Tau rejoined the group before noticing a heavy splotch of blood oozing among the floor tile and grout.

Xavier asked as if his home had been violated, "What happened, Victor?"

"Abner's dead. He tried to attack me, but Milton slaughtered the pig." The old man pointed toward the doorway. "The former commissioner's being disposed of."

Tau blurted, "I *love* disposals. I'll go help." The silver-haired man ambled eagerly through the doorway without a dismissal.

Xavier stared at his floor with a smirk before commenting, "Abner must have died most unpleasantly."

DeSalle snarled, "He got off lightly. Milton broke him within five seconds. Now, did you and Tau powwow with Chu?"

"We've unanimously agreed to concentrate on North America."

"Splendid! What's the first strike?"

Captain Richard Franklin guided his Perception Class, prototype submarine *Toroid* to its rendezvous point five hundred miles northwest of Bermuda. It had arrived first to reconnoiter the submerged area while employing the ship's electrolytic, saltwater power source; targeting laser; spherical detection array; and an encrypted communication station before the balance of his confederal fleet arrived to join him.

Franklin maintained a five-hundred-foot depth while sending out electromagnetic image pulses for instant reconnaissance in every direction. The captain viewed his three-by-four-foot bridge monitor and marveled at the hyper-accurate, full color images of squid, sharks, rays, cod, coral, and hundreds of other species.

Every moving and stationary object was scanned, computed, and updated on the monitor at one thousand pulses per second. Manual control was available at the touch of the sonar man's button, whose duties included electro-pulse monitoring.

"This new monitor seems more like science fiction than fact, eh, Skipper?" commented First Officer Clark Patterson.

Franklin answered, "I never tire of watching it. It's hard to believe our prototype can see in the dark ocean depths without projecting any visible light ahead. I don't pretend to understand how this gadget alters and controls every waveband in the electromagnetic spectrum, but it obviously works."

"Nearly as well as the *Toroid*'s totally electric, saltwater power source. How can this submarine generate inexhaustible electric power without its components corroding?"

The captain replied, "I don't pretend to understand *that* either, but I'm glad that the old style subs will soon become obsolete. We've already had enough trouble with ancient payloads of volatile ordinance contaminating our oceans from sunken derelicts. Our Atlantic's *especially* dirty."

Patterson interjected, "From decades of sunken military hulks, I know. I remember when you and Senator Garth Brady petitioned the URC to salvage those subs. It's a pity you were turned down. At last count, how many corroding time bombs are lying on the sea bottom?"

Richard lamented, "I know of two Americans and four Russians, but they only represent the ones that couldn't be covered up. They're the worst."

"Where are they, Skipper?"

"The U.S.S. *Thresher* sank to a depth of over eight thousand feet in 1963, approximately one hundred miles east of Cape Cod, Massachusetts. The U.S.S. *Scorpion* sank to a depth of over eleven thousand feet in 1968, approximately four hundred miles southwest of the Azores. The Russian sub *K-8* sank to over fifteen thousand feet on the bottom of the Bay of Biscay in 1970. The *K-219* sank north of Bermuda, in 1986—"

"Whoa! You mean one of the worst radioactive wrecks in history's less than a thousand miles away from our current position with another just off Cape Cod?"

"It makes one leery about deep sea diving, doesn't it?"

Patterson said, "Please continue, Skipper."

"The *Komsomolets* sank to over five thousand feet in 1989, approximately one hundred miles south of Bear Island in the Norwegian Sea. A fourth and final Russian sub was scuttled to the bottom of the Kara Sea; I don't recall what year that was, but what difference does it make?"

Patterson shook his head. "All that contamination at the ocean bottom."

"Thousands of tons of ancient military ordinance is corroding and leaching into saltwater from submarine wrecks, and that isn't even counting all the industrial wastes dumped into our marine environment for decades."

Sonar man Young interrupted, "Captain, we have a trio of ally Cetacean Class submarines penetrating our visual sphere; their ranges are eight thousand yards directly ahead; identity confirmed."

"Very well, maintain alert status. Communications, send a greeting encryption to the submarines joining up with us."

Captain Tom Buzby's point submarine *Cachalot* responded first and was followed by Major Matt Powers' *Rorqual,* cruising three hundred feet from *Cachalot's* port side along with Colonel Howard Doyle's *Narwhal* supporting an identical position to starboard.

Suddenly the *Rorqual* exploded with a double torpedo strike from behind. The *Cachalot* turned 45 degrees right and leveled at six hundred feet under flank speed. Then *Narwhal* fired twin lamprey torpedoes from astern and veered to port from a five-hundred-foot depth, now leaving *Toroid* in the path of the unknown enemy.

Captain Franklin identified his enemies quickly as four Atlanterra Mantle Class submarines moved into visual range after their lethal sneak attack on the *Rorqual* from its stern. The enemy markings were unmistakable: the *Chiton* and *Radula* were paired in front followed later by the *Teredo* and *Siphon.* Then both of *Narwhal's* stern torpedoes suddenly blasted *Chiton* into boiling scrap.

Franklin quickly ordered all electro-pulses aimed upward in a half-sphere pattern as the *Toroid* dove to the nine-hundred-foot sea bottom. His monitor now visually tracked all three remaining enemies until they're cruising four hundred feet above them. *Toroid* locked its periscope targeting laser onto *Radula's* bow keel and launched two vertical torpedoes. *Radula* blew in half. *Teredo* failed to detect *Toroid* against the rocky bottom as *Siphon* veered 90 degrees to port.

The confederal *Cachalot* and *Narwhal* completed 360-degree turns before trailing *Teredo* and *Siphon* at two thousand yards. *Cachalot* fired twin torpedoes; the first one missed *Teredo* before impacting a submerged mountain, but the second blasted *Teredo's* twin propellers and rudder. *Teredo's* expelled ballast surged up to the deserted Atlantic surface.

Meanwhile, *Siphon* killed its sonar, took on full ballast, and dropped to the sea bottom two hundred yards in front of *Toroid's* bow. Then the *Toroid* locked on the wounded *Teredo* right before the Atlanterran submarine had blindly dropped six depth charges under its keel.

Cachalot unwittingly moved into the cluster as three explosions ripped it open amidships. The dead submarine sank into blackness.

Colonel Doyle steered his *Narwhal* hard left before ascending to periscope depth; he locked on *Teredo* and launched a single torpedo. Then *Teredo* died in a concussion of fire before its debris dropped to the sea bottom.

Siphon rose five hundred feet before firing stern torpedoes into *Narwhal's* left flank; the confederal vessel was obliterated.

Within the sole surviving *Toroid*, Captain Franklin and his crew remained silent and watched their bridge screen. Machine debris eventually settled to the ocean floor beside them on every side. But the monitor also revealed full color images of frenzied sharks feeding on the fresh human remains of both allies and enemies. Franklin hard swallowed a lump in his throat while still watching the sharks cruise among scarlet billows of watery blood.

Patterson barely spoke above a whisper, "My God, Skipper. We certainly lost a bunch of chips on this gamble."

Franklin took both eyes off the monitor and faced his executive, "All battles are fought by scared men who'd rather be someplace else. We're going to mourn a lot of comrades because of this initial skirmish.

But at least they died taking more of the enemy with them."

"But was it worth it, Skipper?"

The captain paused before replying, "How can anyone ever answer that question, Clark? We've destroyed four Mantle Class Submarines to our knowledge, the best our enemy has. But we've lost three brave crews of comrade submariners and expelled the guts of seven submarines into the bowels of the Atlantic. Your guess is as good as mine on what the cost is."

The captain looked at his radioman and said, "Ensign Meyers."

Meyers faced his captain. "Yes, sir?"

"Inform our president that we've won our first naval encounter with the enemy. Then maybe *you* can explain to him what it cost us."

"I'll try, sir."

CHAPTER FORTY-ONE

Anticipation

Mike awakened answering his bedside Media Palm. "This is Parker."

"Its Myrtle, sir. Colonel Bushnell's group will be landing at the White House in forty minutes."

"Tell him to touch Eric Wilford's plane down on the helipad; the others can land on the lawn. And wake up Vice President Martinez; he'll need time to prepare for our visitors."

"At once, Mr. President."

Parker joined Jocquin on the roof with an escort of bodyguards as the first rays of sunshine brimmed over the Atlantic horizon.

"How appropriate," muttered Martinez while looking toward the east.

Mike asked, "What is?"

Jocquin pointed toward the sliver of solar beams. "The two of us are literally watching the dawning of a new era."

"Yes, the North American Confederacy should create a free and united continent."

"I was referring to the impending death of King Oil, Mr. President. But you're also right. Our confederacy's a logical extension of the original United States of America. We've just expanded the right of sovereign citizens on a continental scale; I think your colonial forefathers would approve."

"I believe that our forefathers knew that people were either individualists or collectivists. Individualists want the freedom to be responsible for their own actions. They covet the right to prosper by their own efforts. Collectivists lust for some imaginary freedom *from* responsibility by demanding the privilege to do whatever they please without paying for the consequences. They want all of the rewards without exerting any of the labor that produced it.

"There is no such thing as irresponsible freedom. Without bearing the consequences for their actions, a person has no choices. They may grab a few unearned dollars or escape a few penalties through a collectivist system, but they never have any sense of accomplishment. I pity them; they have no identity. They only respond to common levels of greed and envy or to whatever politically correct mouthpiece happens to be screaming loudest at the time."

Jocquin smirked before saying, "You've a charming habit of digressing from specific subjects, Mike, but somehow your tangents all seem to tie back together."

"Margaret says I frighten some people when they hear me wear my opinions on my sleeve."

"It's just because those people don't have the guts to say what they believe whether they agree with you or not."

Parker replied, "Perhaps, but do you personally believe we've done the right thing inviting war from the Martial Protectorate?"

"Isn't it a little late to be questioning that?"

"I'm not questioning the morality of our decision. I didn't choose secession; the North American people did. I just wanted your thoughts about the storm looming on our horizon. Let's not kid ourselves; URC triumviral power's a potent force."

Jocquin countered, "So are we, as our first victories above and underwater have proven. And I doubt the protectorate will launch WMPs on us; they'd gain nothing by conquering a charred and smoldering ruin. URC police actions will be global because our Quadrant Alliance now spans the earth. The coming storm will be severe, but we shall prevail."

Parker rubbed the chill out of both shoulders before answering, "You're a good man, Jocquin. You have the courage to fight for North American Freedom even if something happens to me."

"If our enemies had metabolic access to either of us, we'd already be dead."

Mike heard the distant sound of aircraft approaching. Soon four Mantis Transports were descending all around the White House grounds and onto its roof. Parker glanced at Martinez while confessing, "The battle's just beginning. May the Lord God Almighty help us as we spawn World War III."

"Amen to that, Mike, but freedom's always earned at the cost of human life. Technology can't eliminate warfare because it can't change human nature." Jocquin wrinkled his brow. "If technology can't advance the human spirit, then what can?"

President Parker replied with a squint-eyed grimace against the wind, "God only knows."